THE WRONG DOYLE

THE WRONG DOYLE

Robert Girardi

Justin, Charles & Co., Publishers

BOSTON

FIRST U.S. EDITION 2004

Originally published in 2002 in Great Britain by Hodder and Stoughton

This is a work of fiction. All characters and events portrayed
in this work are either fictitious or are used fictitiously.

ISBN: 1-932112-18-9
Library of Congress Cataloging-in-Publication Data is available.

Published in the United States
Justin, Charles & Co., Publishers,
20 Park Plaza, Boston, Massachusetts 02116
www.justincharlesbook.com

Book design by Boskydell Studio

Distributed by National Book Network, Lanham, Maryland
www.nbnbooks.com

10 9 8 7 6 5 4 3 2 1

Printed in the United States of America

This one is for Little B

Let us raise a standard to which the wise and honest can repair.

—*Washington*

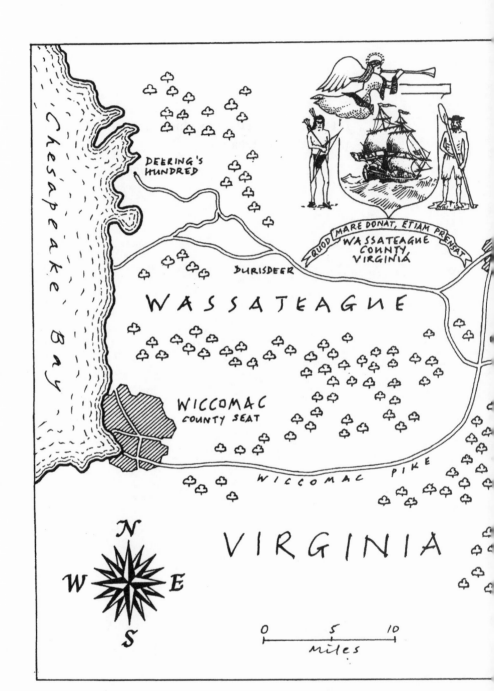

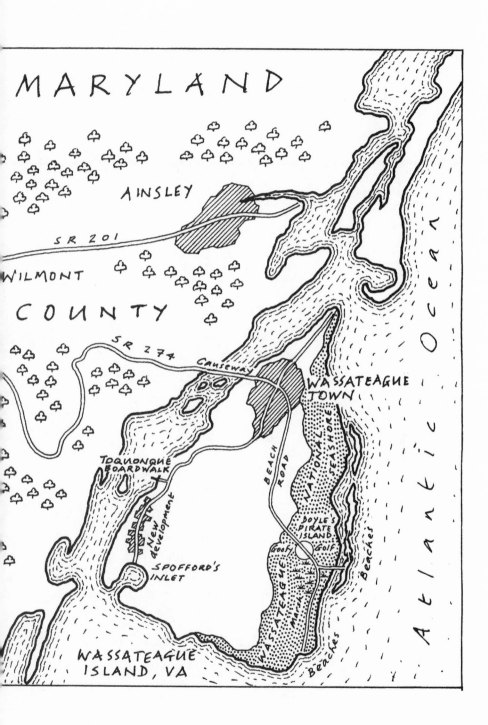

IN THE SUMMER OF 1672, *three ships sailed up the Virginia coast from the Carolinas under the command of Finster Doyle, the notorious Irish buccaneer, called Turkish Doyle by the English for the fact that he kept seven wives, and by the Spaniards El Diablo Doyle for his role in the sack of Maracaibo and the burning of Panama. For reasons he couldn't say, Finster felt some guilt over these bloody assaults, during which every last inhabitant had been put to the sword or taken for slaves. Though not a heavy burden, the guilt was nonetheless general, like darkness on water or a persistent fever, and it drove him at last to forsake the society of his fellow buccaneers at Port Royal, Jamaica, gather his wives and crew, and strike out on his own.*

Finster Doyle's small fleet consisted of the Poet's Grave, *a frigate of thirty guns captured from the Spanish Navy, the* Monstrance, *an armed East Indiaman bearing seventeen guns, and a two-gun shallop built to his specifications at Port Royal and rather grandly christened* Royal Venture. *All three ships lumbered through heavy seas along the uninhabited barrier islands that extend in a ragged line from Cape Charles to the Delaware Bay, looking for a safe anchorage in which to put up for repairs. They were crab-sided and wallowing from months under sail, and crammed to the waterline with the spoils of recent prizes: off the Matagorda Keys, Finster had taken and fired a Spanish plate ship loaded with silver ingots from the mines of Peru; in the mouth of the Chesapeake, three fat merchantmen of the Virginia tobacco fleet bound for London had been plundered and sent to the bottom with all hands chained to the gunwales.*

Finally, Finster's little navy came to a desolate region of the coast, and searching among the small, unknown bays and inlets, found a deeply forested teardrop-shaped island inhabited only by seabirds, mosquitoes, and a curious sort of albino possum. The island's windward shore stood protected from the Atlantic by a long sandy peninsula; the deep leeward channel seemed to offer shelter from any sort of weather. Finster anchored in the channel and sent his men ashore to take on fresh water and slaughter as many possums as they could get their hands on to smoke for jerky. Then he retired to the captain's cabin with all seven of his wives.

It was a curiously still afternoon, not the slightest bit of wind. Finster undressed his wives one by one and had worked his way through three of them when the sky above the mainmast went bottle green and the wind began to howl. The ships were inadequately manned, most of the crew still on the island chasing the possums, which proved very difficult to catch, and there was no time to make for open sea. The Monstrance, driven against a submerged mountain of live oysters and jagged rocks, gashed a hole in her side and went under in less than five minutes. The Poet's Grave, carrying Finster and his seven wives, ran straight up on to the beach and cracked her keel on the dunes with a sound that was like a massive human bone breaking in two.

The hurricane blew all night and into the next day. When it had blown itself out, Finster emerged from the wreck of the Poet's Grave and found himself in possession of only six of his seven wives — one had been swept overboard during the night — and in command of a mere eight of the 107 men under his command just the day before: the hurricane had inundated half the island; the men gone ashore had been washed out to sea.

Finster was considering his predicament when he sighted the sail of the Royal Venture, which had ridden out the hurricane on the bosom of the Atlantic. This seaworthy little vessel quickly made for the island, and the five sailors aboard waded ashore to embrace a relieved Finster who stood in salty tatters in the surf, arms outstretched in a gesture reminiscent of the crucified Christ. His six remaining wives, bedraggled and half-naked, huddled together, shivering, a little way up the beach.

It was at this moment that Walem, chief of the Oknontocokes, leading a war party of forty-two Indian braves, burst out from the dripping shadow of the trees. The Oknontocokes were an obscure, misanthropic tribe, who owed their allegiance to the Grand Sachem of the Nanticokes. But the Nanticokes had gone to war with the Oknontocokes the year before and driven them off the mainland and onto the barrier islands, where they lived off possum, shellfish, and the flesh of the occasional shipwrecked mariner.

The men from the Royal Venture, armed with pistols and musketoons, tried to defend themselves but found their powder wet and ruined by the storm. It would not flash, so they took up whatever lay at hand — broken spars from the wreck, boathooks, knives, stones — but were soon overwhelmed and murdered. Meanwhile, Finster herded his wives into a defensive position against the barnacle-covered hull of the Poet's Grave. The Indians encircled them, war clubs raised. They would take the women for slaves and breeding, as was their custom, and slaughter the man for dinner.

Finster stood his ground, defiant, cutlass in his hand. At that moment, grip tightening on the haft of his weapon, the imperilled buccaneer couldn't help remembering certain pleasant incidents of his distant youth. His whole life did not flash before his eyes, he was too hard a man for that, but despite himself he now recalled the happy time when he had been an innocent priest's boy at Drogheda in Ireland, loved and cosseted by his mother and sisters and destined for the priesthood himself — this before the siege and massacre, before Cromwell and his Ironsides came and laid waste to the town. In those days, Finster had believed in the Acts of the Apostles and Saints, in the Holy Roman Catholic Church, in just punishment for sins, in goodness returned for goodness, in a benevolent, all-knowing God, whose stern judgement of fallible humanity was tempered by an infinite mercy. But he had lived too long to maintain these youthful illusions and had come to believe only in sensual pleasure and the inevitable finality of death and power wielded like a scythe against the powerless.

As the Indians closed in, some of Finster's wives wept softly and prayed for a speedy end to their sufferings, others seized driftwood from the beach, determined to go down fighting. Then, one of the wives, a Guinea-born Negress named Nancy, cried out to the Indians in their own language. She had been carried off from Africa as a young girl and taken to a plantation on the James where she toiled in the tobacco fields beside enslaved Nanti-coke squaws captured during the terrible uprising of '44. Now she begged the chief to spare her husband. "Kill this man," she said, "and you will make widows of us all and fatherless the children we carry in our wombs! For this crime the mighty spirits of the earth will curse you and your people through the generations!"

Walem stopped short, lowered his club, amazed. He made a sign and his braves withdrew, and the squaws came out from the trees and began to perpetrate the usual outrages upon the genitals of the fallen. Walem settled Indian-fashion in the sand, and made another sign at Finster that meant peace. Finster stepped forward warily, still grasping his cutlass.

Through Nancy, the Indian asked a single question: "Are all these women your wives?"

Finster nodded, baffled.

A broad smile cracked the Indian's face. He leaped up, removed a necklace of shells, put it around Doyle's neck and embraced him. Any man, red or white, who can handle six women at once, he told Finster, must be a great chief and very strong and fearless. Walem considered himself a great chief and strong and fearless, so this meant the two of them were brothers and members of the same tribe in the eyes of the Great Manitou of the Oknontocokes. Finster was startled by this assertion, but he was well used to the strangeness of the world so he bowed low and accepted the honor with as much grace as possible, considering the circumstances. That night, the Oknontocokes began a ceremony that lasted ten days and ten nights and made Finster an Oknontocoke chief, second only to Walem, with a war party of twenty-five braves at his command.

For a while, Finster secretly planned to escape aboard the Royal Venture with his wives and sail back to Jamaica. There, he would find another ship, go buccaneering again. Then he changed his mind. It was better to be a king among savages, he decided, than a pirate among civilized men. Anyway, the life he led with the Oknontocokes wasn't so different from his life before. The same killing, the same celebrating afterwards, the same stars above, the same wives. He married one of Walem's daughters to cement his bond with the tribe and joined the braves in their raids against the Nanticokes. They in turn were taught to crew the Royal Venture — now renamed the Chief Walem — which Doyle sailed down the coast and around Cape Charles to prey on English shipping in the Chesapeake Bay.

A year passed happily. Finster Doyle and his Indian buccaneers captured, looted, and sank four small Chesapeake merchantmen; meanwhile, five healthy babies were born to his wives on the island. Then an English warship was seen nosing up the coast. A party of grim-faced English sailors landed at Pamunkey Bay, some days to the south, with a Nanticoke turncoat as translator. They were looking for an Irish pirate with three ships and seven wives, they told the startled Indians there, and promised much wampum for information leading to his capture.

Up to this time, Finster and his wives had been living in the hulk of the Poet's Grave, like insects in a rotting log. The riches he had captured during the course of his last buccaneering venture still lay secure in the hold. All of it had to be hidden from the English when they came this way — as Finster knew they would come, for the English could not abide pirates or Irishmen and would keep coming on until they had him strung up on the gallows. With Walem's help, Finster gathered together every available Oknontocoke, both men and women, for the work party. Digging in shifts over a period of three days, they opened a giant pit on the other side of the dunes in the soft soil that was not sand but a sort of dense, blackish marl. Meanwhile, Finster sawed down the masts and cut the ship's rigging, which he fashioned into heavy drag lines. When the pit was ready, he harnessed the entire Oknontocoke tribe to the lines and they dragged the Poet's Grave into its own grave in the earth. The pit was covered over; no trace of the ship remained.

Not long after this, the Chief Walem ran into the sloop-of-war Peacock at the mouth of the Wiccomac inlet in the Chesapeake Bay. It wasn't much of a battle — the Peacock, commanded by the redoubtable Indian fighter Colonel Brodie Deering, ran twenty guns — and Finster and his crew of five braves were quickly captured and taken to Jamestown to be hanged. The braves, being heathens and savages, were hanged without benefit of trial, but Finster was dragged through the subtler torture of legal proceedings. Before sentence was pronounced, Sir William Berkeley, chief magistrate and governor of the Virginia Colony, asked Finster for his last words. Without hesitation, Finster dropped his trousers and urinated on the bailiff standing below the dock, as the spectators in the galleries roared with laughter. Berkeley was not amused and added forty lashes with the iron-tipped cat to Finster's sentence.

A few days later, Colonel Deering and a company of militiamen escorted Finster Doyle in a slow-moving ox-cart down the dirt highway to the sea, hanging rope already knotted around his neck and coiled around his feet like a snake. Overseers and slaves watched silently from the tobacco fields as he glided above the hedgerows, stately as a figurehead on a passing ship. In the navy yard at Hampton Roads, a boatswain off the Peacock stripped Finster of his clothes and put the cat to his back till the flesh lay in bloody shreds. Then they hanged him until he was dead and left his body to rot on the gibbet in an iron cage as a warning to all against piracy.

But for years afterwards, women wrapped in buckskin and trade blankets like Indian squaws — though most were white beneath the grime and at least one a Negress — would bring dirty-faced children over the long trails out of the woods to stand in silent contemplation of Finster Doyle's blackened bones swaying there in the wind.

part one
DOYLE COMES HOME

1

TIM DOYLE paused on the dusty landing, key in the lock of the garret flat he shared with his lover, a young French woman named Brigitte Poussin. Heartbreaking amber light shone into the narrow stairwell from the bull's-eye window cut high in the opposite wall and made a target complete with crosshairs on the dark wood of the door, on the crumbling garland of dried roses Brigitte had hung there when they moved in together three months ago. Doyle watched the amber target dim to twilight and fade out — not more than a few seconds and another day gone. Through the door now came the unmistakable sound of a man and a woman making love.

The incessant mutter of city traffic floated up from the rue de la Mire; the shrill warning of a truck in reverse gear echoed from the courtyard below, almost reaching the pitch of the passionate cries within. Doyle stood immobile, listening. Of course, he thought grimly, this had to happen, this was perfect; more — this was justice. In the next moment, the cries reached their frantic crescendo, every note familiar to him. She certainly knew how to have an orgasm: she let it pour through her, let it possess her completely, and lay there afterwards utterly still, clammy as a suicide just pulled from the Seine.

Then Doyle heard the guttural male urgings of whoever it was in there giving it to her and he turned the deadbolt with a decisive slap and pushed the door open and in the moment before he crossed over, glanced out the bullseye window and caught a dim flash of the façade of Sacre Coeur, coral pink in the last sun, Paris spread beneath it to the horizons, a city already gone for him, wiped off the map. He took the last few steps to the bedroom at a run, past the winter coats bunched on the pegs in the hall, through the absurdly small kitchenette, and tore back the flimsy accordion partition and caught the two of them in the final throes on the futon: Brigitte facing backwards, impaled, oblivious, straddling a pair of dark, hairy legs — an Arab, Doyle thought, the bitch is fucking an Arab — her slim body shining with sweat, her blue eyes closed. In the next second, she opened her eyes and saw Doyle looming in the doorway like doom itself and let out a tight little scream and tried to pull herself off, but the Arab's dark hands pressed into the skin of her thighs and forced her down on him again, one more time, again, then came the explosion. Brigitte couldn't help herself. Her eyes rolled back in her head and she groaned and was seized with another long, terrible shudder and at last she gasped and fell sideways, grappling for the sheets.

The Arab gave a shout of surprise as Doyle stepped into view. He pushed himself up quickly but Brigitte put a hand on his chest to hold him back.

"Du calme, chérie," she said, in a low voice, and she looked up at Doyle without the least trace of shame in her face.

Doyle and the Arab glowered at each other for a long beat pregnant with ugly possibilities. The Arab was slim, about twenty, a little less than half Doyle's age, with pretty girlish features and thick, moist lips. Doyle knew he had seen him somewhere before, then he remembered. This Arab was a Moroccan named Hanouk Ajij, one of the waiters at the Café Ney down the street, always so solicitous when he and Brigitte came in together for an *apéritif* at the polished zinc counter. The little bastard. Hanouk Ajij hadn't bothered to cover himself with the sheet and Doyle assessed the man's deflating equipment and, for a quick second, felt a bit better about himself.

"*Le dice* get the fuck out of here," Doyle said to Brigitte, between his teeth. *"Vamos. Immediamente."* Doyle couldn't speak French. He and Brigitte had always communicated in a strange, muddled mixture of Spanish and English.

"Mas, el hombre dress his clothes," Brigitte said, sounding reasonable. *"Hace frio dehor."*

"Tough shit," Doyle said.

"Fuck you, asshole," Hanouk Ajij blurted, his black eyes narrowing.

Doyle clenched his fists, his blood surging with the animal urge to murder. He was about to tear the Moroccan son of a bitch limb from limb — but at the last possible moment, Doyle's good angel intervened and instead he reached down, picked up the man's shoes, and flung them down the hall out the open door on to the landing. One of them bounced through the railing and dropped to the dirty tiles of the *rez de chaussée* six flights below.

Hanouk Ajij looked over at Brigitte, then back at Doyle, his defiance withering all at once.

"Vite," Brigitte said to Hanouk Ajij, impatiently. *"Va t'en. Je n'aime pas te voir tuer!"* But she added in a softer voice, *"S'il te plaît. On peut discuter de tout cela plus tard."*

Hanouk Ajij jumped up, gathered his clothes, and scurried after his shoes. Doyle stepped into the hall, kicked the door shut, and turned back to confront Brigitte. In the second his back was turned, she had flung off the sheet and arranged herself across the bed. The flush of lovemaking still clung to her pale skin. Doyle stared down at her small breasts, her narrow, boyish hips. She'd have trouble if she ever decided to have kids, he found himself thinking, then stopped himself. No, women like that didn't have kids, they had orgasms instead.

Now, Brigitte parted her legs slightly and Doyle could see wetness glistening on her thighs, on the swollen tangle of her sex. A sly smile spread across her face. She waggled her finger in the direction of the growing lump in Doyle's jeans. "Ah, you are tumescent," she said in a throaty voice. It was a word she had found in the French-English Larousse.

Doyle grunted. The fact was undeniable and, in the circumstances, an embarrassment. "Unfortunately," he said.

Brigitte pushed her bottom lip out. *"Non, jamais,* never unfortunate," she said. "I think you want me, *sí?"*

Doyle didn't say anything. It was the hour when the long blue cars of the RER at La Chapelle crowd with fragrant, commuting humanity; when the boulevard cafés fill with sleek young couples murmuring over expensive glasses of wine. Brigitte slowly lifted her ass on to a pillow and put her fingers on herself down there. "He was not so good, *le Maroc,"* she whispered. "A bit small, you know?"

"Pute," Doyle said, but he didn't take his eyes away.

"Por favor," she said, her breathing going shallow. *"Baise moi."*

Doyle took a step closer to the futon, then another step and he leaned down and caught a fistful of Brigitte's thick, black hair. She gave a sharp little cry. He pulled harder and she took her hand away from herself and reached up to undo the buckle of his belt.

2

The garbage stank of rotting vegetables and coffee grounds from the kitchenette; Brigitte's underarms reeked — or perhaps Hanouk Ajij's sweat still clung to her skin, to the dirty sheets. Doyle lay beside her on the futon in the dark, smelling the unwashed sheets and feeling disgusted with himself. This was the bottom. He was not a religious man but he thought, I have never been so far from God. Years ago, Buck had sent him for seventh grade to a Catholic boarding school up in Maryland and he still remembered all the words of the major prayers, none of which seemed appropriate in the current situation.

Brigitte slept for a while, then she was awake and crying softly. She took his hand in the darkness and held it to her cheek. *"Chérie,"* she said, her voice cracking. *"Je suis désolée."*

"It won't work," Doyle said, "not any more," and he took his hand away.

When she heard the hardness in his voice, she stopped crying and he felt her body stiffen.

"Tell me something," Doyle continued with some bitterness. "Do you make it a habit? Getting caught, I mean. It's the drama. That's how you get off, right?" He was remembering the terrible afternoon they'd been caught in the act by his wife, Flor. Thursdays, back in Málaga, barely four months ago but in another life, Flor did the big shop for the restaurant, was usually out all day, and Doyle looked after the baby. But for some reason Pablo fell asleep early, one of those sweaty, mouth-open, dead-to-the world naps of toddlerhood — then Brigitte stopped by on some pretext. The thought of doing it in the house, in his wife's bed excited her, she wouldn't keep her dress on; Doyle tried to stop the whole thing from happening but . . . Flor came home unexpectedly ten minutes later to get something she'd forgotten, and there he was on the bed with his pants off and Brigitte's lips wrapped around something hard. Flor didn't say a single word. She closed the door quietly, woke Pablo, got him dressed, and took him to her parents' country house in Ecija. That he would betray his wife with his son asleep in the next room was despicable — this judgement rendered by Flor's lawyer, who also happened to be her brother. Weren't there brothels for such activities? Doyle hadn't spoken to his wife without an intermediary present since the incident.

Brigitte was silent for a while, then she said, sullenly, "I think perhaps you should not have left your wife."

"I didn't leave," Doyle said. "She kicked me out, remember? I'd go back in a second if she'd have me. I still love her." The moment he said these words, he knew they were true.

Brigitte made a hurt sound, and got up and locked herself in the little closet of the bathroom and she stayed in there for a long while, washing the semen of two men from between her legs.

Doyle put on his clothes as quickly as possible, went out of the apartment and down the stairs into the city. He wandered around for a couple of hours, smoking harsh French cigarettes and feeling sorry for himself, and around midnight found a cold bench in the place Vauban, across from the Invalides. He sat and stared up absently at the golden dome lit by white floods beneath which Napoleon's bones lay petrifying in a red porphyry coffin the size of a two-car garage. His time with Brigitte was over, his wife wouldn't have him back. Now what? He couldn't blame Brigitte for his current predicament, not really. No, he had done it all by himself. Thrown everything away on an affair not meant to last longer than a few weeks: his wife, his two-year-old son, Pablo, the restaurant, El Rey Alfonso, last year awarded its first Michelin star, his comfortable life in a beautiful city, Málaga.

Brigitte, in her own jaded way, was an innocent — twenty-three, impetuous, a student, a girl on her way to becoming a woman, her life's adventure just beginning. There would be many more men. Doyle knew this and knowing it hurt a little. Some like him, some not, some cruel, some soft, some younger, some older. And she would end well, the mistress of a cabinet minister or a minor film director, still attractive at fifty like Catherine Deneuve, with a younger lover on the side, a new Citroën at her disposal and a villa on the Côte d'Azur.

That's the kind of woman she was; there were many others in France like her, she was a national type — intelligent, beautiful, amoral as a cat. Of course, Doyle knew in his heart that he was no better than Brigitte. Some men made it their life's work to find just one woman, and finding one were satisfied; not so with Doyle. Doyle liked women, especially beautiful women, and they liked him, generally, unless he was very drunk. It was said by some, his wife included, that he resembled the actor Robert Mitchum. Not the later, bloated Mitchum, but Mitchum world-weary and glamorous in his Hollywood glory days of the forties and fifties. Doyle had Mitchum's broad shoulders, thick black hair, sleepy blue bedroom eyes, a nose that had been broken once, and being broken acquired the character it otherwise lacked.

After a while, the temperature dropped and it began to rain and Doyle rose from the bench with an effort and caught the last Métro at Invalides and transferred to the Porte d'Ivry line and got off at Barbes. There, in the dingy Algerian quarter, he found a relatively clean no-star hotel up a flight of stairs and spent a troubled night in a narrow bed, listening to the steam pipes clanking like distant, demonic music. The next morning, he got up late and exhausted and washed his face in the sink and went back to the flat in the rue de la Mire to get his things.

Brigitte had already headed off to her Spanish classes at the Sorbonne, which was how he had planned it. But she had left a note propped against a tin of CosmoLuxe on the counter in the kitchenette:

Mon cher Timy. You are so good. I do not know why I do this bad games I do. I am sorry. So forgive your poor Brigitte. You will wait for me when I get home from school. We will make love many times again while I will be whatever you want for your pleasure. Your lover, your bad girl. Je t'aime. Brigitte.

Doyle imagined the scenario implied by these clumsy words and felt a tug at his loins, and it was with some regret that he crumpled the note and tossed it on top of the coffee grounds in the garbage in plain sight. Then he packed his clothes and a few other odds and ends — he hadn't brought much with him from Spain, everything he owned now fit into two suitcases — and he carried the suitcases to the door. There he stopped and lowered them to the worn little square of Persian carpet that Brigitte had found at the Clignancourt fleamarket and the space inside his head echoed with a single basic question: where the hell was he going? He took ten seconds to puzzle this out and, for no reason at all, decided on London. It might be nice to hear English spoken in the streets, even with the wrong accent.

So, bound for London, Doyle undid the deadbolt, opened the door, and hefted up his suitcases. Then he spotted the thin stack of mail forwarded from Spain wrapped in a rubber band sitting on the mail shelf by the door, put the suitcases down again, broke the rubber band, and quickly went through the flimsy envelopes: a bill from EuroSport Cable he'd forgotten to pay, three subscription notices from the Iberian edition of the *International Herald Tribune,* an enquiry from his lawyer in Málaga regarding a tax certificate for Spanish revenue pertaining to the divorce, nothing at all from his wife, and a curious-looking letter from the States, bearing around its edges the old-fashioned black borders that announced a death.

Doyle turned this one over in his hands, disaster tolling with the distant bells of Notre-Dame de Lorette. The cancellation showed that it had been mailed from the post office at Wassateague Town, Virginia, two and a half months before. He split it open with his thumb and unfolded the single page:

I am writing to inform you of the sad passing of your uncle Buck Doyle Wednesday night from medical complications brought on by his various conditions. Maggie is too distraught now to write, as you can imagine, so the task falls to me. You knew about the emphysema, you didn't know about the cancer because no one knew. At the end, though in much pain, Buck checked himself out of the hospital in Salisbury and drove himself back down here in the Cadillac to die in his own bed in his own room above the Parrot Cage. He missed you sorely at the end. I could say more here but I won't. You will want to come home now as there is much to do with the golf course, which he has let go all to hell these last few years, and damned lawyers to see over in Wiccomac with many papers to sign, etc. Condolences, etc., Pete Piatt.

P.S. Old Buck was a good old bastard and lived a damned good life with plenty of good-looking broads and good booze and plenty of fine blue-water fishing, so other than the fact we'll miss him, there's no reason to feel too bad. He's moved on to new fishing grounds, that's all. Pete Piatt.

Doyle let the letter drop to the carpet, brought his hands to his face and found it wet with tears. Uncle Buck dead. It seemed impossible, but there it was. When Doyle's father was lost at sea aboard the *Laughing Debedeavon* during Hurricane Ava back in '63, Buck had stepped in and raised Doyle like his own son. Doyle's mother, wrapped away in her martini haze out west, hadn't cared to get involved.

Good old Buck, Doyle thought. The man was a prince. Thinking this cracked his last reserve and he stumbled back into the bedroom, threw himself down on the bed and wept as he hadn't wept for a very long time, perhaps since childhood. It was physically painful for a man like Doyle to weep, and he buried his head in the hard French bolster and let the painful catharsis rack through his body. Though whether the tears he shed were for Buck's passing or for his own miserable predicament was impossible to say.

3

A foul breath exhaled from the gaping mouth of the pirate's head straddling the fourteenth hole of Doyle's Pirate Island Goofy Golf. The stench was driven on by a fishy wind blowing across Egg Point Marsh from the Atlantic, its night-black waters just now touched at the horizon with the earliest sun. Soon, the wind found bare patches of chicken wire in the crumbling plaster and the pirate's head began to moan faintly, a low, melancholy sound in tune with the sad music of cattails bending in the marsh. The plywood arms of the windmill at the Port Royal hole, number seven, creaked to life and the waxed canvas palms of the palm-grove desert island at number three clattered against each other and the threadbare parachute sails of the pirate galleon anchored in the painted blue lagoon at thirteen billowed and the tattered Jolly Roger went flapping from its yardarm to the brightening sky.

By seven thirty a.m., the stench from the pirate's head reached through the rusty screen of the room above the Parrot Cage Bar where

Doyle lay asleep. He tossed uneasily in the sheets, pulled from vivid dreams of Málaga — Flor stepping out of her clothes in the cool white room in their first apartment on the Calle Mercado on some languid, rainy afternoon years ago, naked, her tawny skin blemishless, her bottom swaying above him like a pear about to fall into his outstretched hands — then he awoke with a gasp, bile rising in his throat, flung himself out of bed, stumbling over the wadded heap of clothes on the floor, and just barely made it to the bathroom down the hall to vomit in the sink with a throaty roar.

He leaned his head against the cold ceramic for a long minute afterwards, gulping air, his mouth tasting like that last double shot of bourbon at four a.m. Then the door scraped open from the bar downstairs and the sound of slippered feet shuffled to the landing.

"Hey, Timmy, you OK up there?" It was Maggie.

Doyle managed a weak affirmative. "Don't call me Timmy," he said. "Name's Tim."

"I mean, it sounded like you was strangling something," she said, with an audible smirk. There was no mistaking the tone of derision he'd come to know too well over these last weeks since his return from Europe to claim his patrimony. He'd been drinking till lights out in the bar every night, insulting the regulars, paying himself an allowance from the till, adrift, sinking in a sea of booze under Maggie's jaundiced eye. "Call it a sort of extended wake," he tried to explain, in a sober moment. The man had cared for him like a son, surely he was allowed one long, sorrowful drunk. But Maggie hadn't seen it that way. She was a practical person, hardened by life, grief as much a luxury to her soul as love.

Doyle pushed himself off the sink and took a step out into the hall; one look at the stained orange plaid carpet brought on the nausea all over again. Maggie stood on the scuffed linoleum of the landing, arms crossed, dirty blonde hair wrapped in plastic curlers the size of beer cans, an absurd pair of fuzzy hound-dog slippers on her feet. A blue robe with penguins all over it, loose across the pale skin of her breasts, fell just above her fleshy, dimpled knees. Not a bad-looking woman, Doyle found himself thinking, if you liked them thirty-five, big-boned, bleached-blonde, and uneducated. She had been Uncle Buck's mistress for something like sixteen years, the old goat.

"There was a really terrible smell," Doyle managed, in a hoarse whisper. "Like something rotten."

"Right," Maggie said. "Blood all over down here, you better come on out and see for yourself."

"Blood?" Suddenly Doyle didn't want to know. "First I need to a shower," he said, stepping back.

Maggie shook her head. "No time for bubble baths, buddy, there's a carcass in the pirate's mouth."

4

The stench rose out of the pirate's head, so thick you could almost see it shimmering in the air. Blood streaked the plaster grooves of his beard, blood splattered in a violent swirl on the yellow plaster flank of the plaster monkey on his shoulder. A dark bloody something was stuffed into the round oval of the pirate's mouth. During normal play, the golfer would stand at the bottom of the pink ramp, painted to resemble a tongue, and putt upward from the tee at the tip. A smart hit would knock the ball into the mouth, down through the monkey's belly, and out to the long finger-shaped green of Plastigrass molded into a tricky series of bumps and gullies. At that point you were still twenty-five feet from the hole. This was a tough one, Doyle remembered. Par four.

Now, hunched in Buck's old World War Two infantry coat, thick as a horse blanket, Doyle stood with Maggie at the tee, staring at the oozing thing stuffed up there — the paws eerily like human hands, the yellowish white fur dark and sticky with blood, the bare, ugly rat tail. A possum. A Delmarva Albino Fox Possum, to be exact, this one a large sucker, about twenty-five pounds. These ungainly animals had been trapped to near extinction for their fur — which resembled ermine when bleached with certain noxious chemicals — and were still officially endangered. But they had always been efficient breeders, and in the last decades their numbers had rebounded to the point where they infested the woods by the thousands just the other side of the twelve-foot storm fence separating the course from the Wassateague National Seashore Wildlife Preserve. Still, every last dead one had to be reported to the local police, who reported to the Fish and Wildlife people in Washington.

"OK, soldier," Maggie said, squinting at Buck's old coat. "This is what I'd call man's work."

Doyle's eyes watered. He tried to inhale a lungful of fresh air and got only stench. "I don't feel so good this morning," he said, a wave of nausea sweeping over him. "Something I ate last night."

"More like something you drank." Maggie scowled, turned around, and stomped back towards the kitchen door of the closed restaurant.

When she had gone, Doyle slumped down against the plaster flank of the hammerhead shark at the fifteenth hole, par four, and put his head in his hands. Here he was, back on Pirate Island, hung-over, forty-two years old, waiting for his life to begin again and just now suffering from a strange sort of memory loss. He could remember clearly the fatherless child, the rebellious adolescent he'd once been; it was the man he'd become since he couldn't recall. Every summer as a kid he used to hand out putters and balls to tourists right there in the buttressed guardhouse fronting the Beach Road. He could almost see the tourists of summers past lined up at dusk along the sidewalk, smelling of suntan oil and Pall Malls as June bugs zapped against the floodlights and hurtled earthward like small, charred meteorites. And he could hear the comforting plastic thwack of club against ball, and the soft murmuring of the girls in their halter tops, and the jukebox playing lonesome country music from the bar, and Uncle Buck's booming laughter echoing out across the busy greens.

A few minutes later, Maggie returned with a bucket of soap and water, a scrub brush, a thick plastic lawn-and-garden bag, and a pair of rubber gloves. She dropped the bucket at Doyle's feet. Doyle looked up at her, a dazed expression in his eyes.

"I can't," was all he said.

"Asshole," Maggie said. "Why is it I'm always cleaning up Doyle shit?"

But she pulled on the rubber gloves and climbed up the ramp as if she'd been expecting to all along. "I hope it's completely dead," she said. "Damned things can have rabies." And she seized the possum carcass by its hind legs and pulled hard. There followed a thick, wet, sucking sound that made Doyle turn away.

"Oh, God," Maggie said. "Oh, my Lord!"

A tone in her voice made him turn back. Maggie came down the ramp cradling a misshapen mess of blood and fur and despite his nervous stomach, Doyle stepped over to get a better look. The sorry creature had been cut in half very neatly, as if with an electric saw, and the festering body of a seasquab rammed headfirst into the gory end.

"Cut-in-half possum and a seasquab," Maggie said, through gritted teeth. "Marriage made in hell, if you ask me. Someone went through a lot of trouble for this voodoo bullshit — wait, hold on a minute," she interrupted herself. "Here's something else."

Duct-taped around the possum's stomach was a bloody piece of butcher's paper, words scrawled across it in black blocky letters, deliberately childish. Doyle leaned over, pinched his nostrils closed and read what was written there:

DOYLE LEAVE WASSATEAGUE NOW OR DIE SOON.

"Looks like somebody ain't too happy you're back," Maggie said in a flat voice. "And risked severe penalties to tell you so. Killing one of these critters is a fucking serious federal crime."

Doyle nodded dumbly. It wasn't the first death threat he'd received in his life, but it was a little unexpected. Who knew he was back and knowing wanted him gone again?

"Everyone knows by now," Maggie said. She dropped the dripping possum carcass into the lawn-and-garden bag and tied it tight. "This is a small town, remember?"

"Yeah," Doyle said. "I remember."

5

From Wassateague Town on the Atlantic Coast, to Wiccomac, the county seat of Wassateague County on the Chesapeake Bay, is a mere twenty-two miles as the crow flies. But there is no direct route except for a half-effaced Indian trail that exists only as a track through the deep woods and runs across acres of private property fenced off with split logs and barbed wire and marked with bullet-pocked no-trespassing signs.

By car, the journey covers a mere thirty miles over State Road 301 — the Wiccomac Pike — but takes nearly an hour driving the speed-limit. The one lane highway winds endlessly past ramshackle plantation houses, uninhabited for generations, now muffled in creepers and overhung by the branches of oak and maples, bisects dark fields of tobacco, the thick sinister leaves hanging low over sandy black soil, crosses fields of tomatoes neatly staked and dressed with grey plastic sheeting. It is lonely country back here away from the maternal presence of the waves — ancient, overgrown and poor, so different from the narrow strip of beach towns along the shore it might as well be buried somewhere in the heart of Kentucky.

There are children born in this part of the county, so the story goes, who would grow up, get old and die without ever seeing the ocean, not fifteen miles from their doorstep. Sad tarpaper shacks alternate with rust-flecked trailers and the slave cabins — now windowless and abandoned — of former days. Dusty chickens peck at gravel along the roadbed. Occasionally, a satellite dish or a line hung with fresh laundry announces the occupant is employed and industrious, but these signs are rare.

Despite the January chill, Doyle put the top down on Uncle Buck's rusty 1969 Cadillac El Dorado, cranked up the heat, passed over the causeway to the mainland and followed 301 along its erratic path across the peninsula towards Wiccomac.

He stopped halfway at Caper's, a decrepit general store at the crossing of the Wiccomac Pike and SR 274. Here three Mexican migrant workers, each wearing several layers of cheap plaid workshirts against the cold and lopsided acrylic-mesh baseball caps, sat idling on the edge of the porch, their dangling legs too short to touch the ground. They were compact, dark men, with wide Indian faces. Two sported scraggly mustaches, one was clean-shaven and probably no older than fifteen. They shared a single cigarette, passed carefully back and forth between work-hardened hands.

"*Hola, caballeros,*" Doyle said coming up the front steps. He tried, but it was not possible to suppress the cultured Castillian lisp absorbed from his wife and all those years in Málaga.

The Mexicans looked up, instantly suspicious.

"Hay trabajo hoy?"

They exchanged glances, uneasily. One of them shrugged.

"No se preocupan," Doyle said with a sad smile. *"No soy de imigración. Buena suerte."* And he walked across the porch and into the store.

Illegal Mexican labor had been a part of life in Wassateague County since the sixties, when the indigenous black population at last deemed it beneath their dignity to work the fields their people had worked so long in chains of one sort or another, and left for a life of indigence, public assistance and crime in the cities. A severe labor shortage followed for a season or two — unpicked tomatoes rotted on the vines, tobacco lay unharvested, untended corn tasseled, grew vile — then the Mexicans began to come, three or four at a time in rattling pick-up trucks, in dented old sedans, up the long unimaginable roads from the south, over mountains and deserts, across half a continent, looking for the one thing men cannot do without. The system was mysterious, Doyle had never quite understood how it worked. There seemed to be no rules, no concrete arrangements. The Mexicans appeared, they lingered in out-of-the-way places like this — or on the grassy slopes beside certain gas stations, or in the far corners of certain public parking lots, or behind the communal Dumpster in certain towns — and someone eventually drove up in a nondescript van and they got in the back without a word and went away.

The old store was a ramshackle place with uneven floors and canned goods stacked on shelves built up to the pressed-tin ceiling. Beneath the display counter's dark hand-bevelled glass, hard little donuts on a tray looked like they hadn't been touched since Reconstruction. The proprietor, a bent old man with a hatchet face and one milky eye, squinted suspiciously as Doyle stepped up to the register.

"Lucky Strikes, filterless, make it two packs," Doyle said, and the old man pulled the cigarettes off the rack and set them on the counter as Doyle fumbled to separate the big, suspiciously colorful French bills still mixing with the plain greenbacks in his wallet.

"Guess this county just can't get by without a Doyle around," the old man said suddenly.

Doyle gave a start. "Do I know you?"

"Hell, I can spot a Doyle from a mile away." The old man waved his hand. "You're the spitting image of your father." Then he paused. "That was one pisser of a storm, '63. Worst I ever saw."

"Yes," Doyle said.

"Sorry to hear about old Buck. He'd stop in every now and then for a cold one, always had something funny to say."

"He was a funny guy," Doyle said, but he didn't want to talk about Buck just now. His eye fell on a new lavender freezer chest with a cartoon crown and the words Royal Blue Delicious stencilled on the side in bold white script. "Hey, is that RB Cola? I thought they stopped making the stuff years ago."

"They did." The old man frowned. "Then along come some rich sonsabitches from out of state and buy the old RB plant in Ainsley. But this here new RB Cola don't taste nothing like I remember, completely undrinkable. Ask me, it's because they don't hire no locals. The plant is run by a bunch of Chinamen — that's what my nephew says. He tried to get a job there and they said flat out not unless you work for peanuts, no benefits, no nothing, 'cause that's what Chinamen work for, peanuts. Can you beat that?"

"No," Doyle said, uninterested, and he slid open the frosted lid, reached into the darkness and removed a can covered with a thin white layer of freezer furze that looked like it had been there for some time. He used to drink gallons of the stuff, riding his old Raleigh three-speed to the Royal Blue stand at the intersection of Paradise and Main in Wassateague Town, he and Ed Toby sitting at the picnic bench beneath the thick, forgiving shade of the magnolia tree, puberty aching like a half-healed wound and watching the roller-skating car-hop girls in their skimpy lavender and white uniforms sailing out with trays of burgers and fries and chilidogs and frosty mugs of Royal Blue Cola like young goddesses bearing cornucopia.

Now the old man leaned across the counter and winked his milky eye. "Don't you listen to anyone," he said, in a hushed, conspiratorial tone.

Doyle didn't say anything.

"We need Doyles around here, OK?"

"OK," Doyle whispered back, baffled.

"Your uncle Buck, he used to give them slick boys up at the county seat some real hell. We need someone around to give them hell."

"Thanks," Doyle said. "I'm on my way over to Wiccomac now with a couple sticks of dynamite. I'll see what I can do."

The old man looked alarmed at this, but Doyle didn't give him a chance to respond. He handed over ten dollars, got his change and went out on to the porch. The Mexicans were still sitting there, empty-handed now, staring dolefully at the ground, last cigarette gone.

"Hola, hermanos, tengan cigaros todos!"

Doyle tossed the spare pack of Luckys at the closest Mexican, got back into the Cadillac, popped the can of RB, took a sip and almost gagged. RB probably wasn't as good as he remembered it, but surely wasn't as bad as this. He poured it out in the parking lot, put the car in gear and drove the rest of the way to Wiccomac, down the winding road, through black, silent fields, in and out of bare stands of pine and oak and poplar that held the frozen mulch smell of winter in the underbrush between the trees.

6

The old Wiccomac Tavern, where Washington had once slept on his way from somewhere to somewhere else, now stood under busy scaffolding. According to a sign out front, the restoration of this structure was sponsored by some heating and air-conditioning company and would reopen in a year as office space and a brew-pub called the Wig and Gavel. Most of the colonial buildings further down Main Street wore garish coats of new paint that lent the two-hundred-year-old clapboard a hard vinyl sheen. They were giving the ramshackle town the Williamsburg treatment.

Doyle could almost smell the new money floating in the air as he followed the brick path past the former debtors' prison — recently converted into a welcome center for tourists — and around the green to the alley of small, neatly kept colonial offices called Lawyer's Row. The third office down stood out for its air of genteel decay: paint peeling off the gutters, slates missing from the dormer. A creaking shingle advertised Whitcomb, Kettle & Slough, Attorneys at Law. Doyle went in the front door and found Whitcomb and Slough waiting for him in Slough's office. Kettle was physically absent but present posthumously: his portrait frowned down at the surviving partners from its place over the mantel.

Whitcomb pulled himself with some effort out of the wing chair in which he was sitting and took Doyle's hand in a palsied grip. "Tim, allow me to offer my condolences," he said, in a thin, raspy voice little better than a whisper. "Buck was one of the last grand old fellows."

"Thanks," Doyle said, struggling to conceal his shock. He remembered Whitcomb at sixty, lean, vigorous, famed for his youthful stamina, a man who never appeared any older than the proverbial thirty-nine. In the last twenty years, Whitcomb had aged more than half a century. Now he was shrunken and waxy-looking, his old-fashioned dark suit hanging off his shoulders like a rag. Strands of wispy white hair stood off his head as if attracted to something in the ceiling.

Slough hurried out from behind the big desk, pumped Doyle's hand and pulled out a chair from against the wall. He seemed to have absorbed Whitcomb's substance like a spider feeding off its prey: he was in his early fifties, round and pink all over, with a thick head of black hair, and rather resembled pictures Doyle had seen of opera divas in the days before dieting and cholesterol.

Doyle sat down and the lawyers resumed their places, and a moment of uncomfortable silence ensued. A grandfather clock ticked loudly from the front hall. The office was lined with the thick, blue-spined volumes of the Virginia Code. The bust of some forgotten jurist showed a thin layer of dust in the eye sockets, on the plaster shoulders.

"Well, back from Spain," Slough said at last.

"Yes," Doyle said.

"For good?" Slough said, and something about the way he said it put Doyle on his guard.

"More or less," Doyle said.

"My wife and I went to Spain on our honeymoon." Whitcomb's whisper now rose to the level of a croak. "That was right before the war. We sailed on the old *Normandy* to Le Havre and took the train down through France —"

"I don't think Mr. Doyle's interested in your reminiscences, Foy," Slough interrupted.

"No, go ahead, please," Doyle said. "How is your wife?"

"Dead," Whitcomb said sadly, and he meant to say more but broke off suddenly and began to cough. The cough started off as a wheeze, grew increasingly animated and became a great hacking convulsion that enveloped his entire frame.

Doyle waited patiently for a minute, then grew alarmed. "Can I get you a glass of water?" he asked.

Still coughing, Whitcomb managed a strangled negative. Slough watched, hands folded, impassive, as his partner went red in the face, gasped for breath. Whitcomb let up suddenly and emitted a long dry rattle, but this was followed by another burst of coughing, louder than the first.

"Foy, I can handle this with Mr. Doyle," Slough said to Whitcomb, in a loud voice. "Why don't you go get something for that?"

Whitcomb nodded dumbly, still coughing, rose from his chair and coughed over to the door. Before he exited, he turned towards Doyle and held up a skeletal finger. The gesture had something urgent about it, a warning perhaps, but Doyle could read nothing coherent in the old lawyer's red-rimmed eyes before the man turned and disappeared down the hall. Doyle listened as the coughs proceeded out the front door and down the path towards the courthouse green, then grew faint in the distance.

Slough leaned forward. "It's his lungs," he said, tapping his chest.

"I gathered that," Doyle said.

"He's in what you could call semi-retirement," Slough said. "I handle most of the clients now. But he insisted on coming in today to see you."

"I certainly appreciate the effort," Doyle said. "The man was my uncle's lawyer for something like fifty years. And his friend."

Slough frowned. "Well, shall we move on to the matter at hand?" he said.

"Absolutely," Doyle said.

Slough went over to a cluttered credenza against the wall and began sorting through a pile of papers; his big womanly ass waggled a bit as he worked. He was as nearly round as it was possible for someone to be; no opera diva, Doyle decided, rather Humpty-Dumpty. But he knew the man's plush, rotund exterior hid an iron resolve.

Slough was that rare animal, a self-educated lawyer. Parents unknown, he had been raised in an orphanage and put himself through Chesapeake State by working the night shift gutting chickens on the line at Robertson Chicken in Coalville. Then he had gotten himself a clerking job working for Kettle, in his spare time reading every law book he could lay his hands on. After five years of that, he had passed the Virginia Bar on his first attempt without ever going to law school. Virginia was one of the last states in the Union that allowed this approach to the law — a tradition harkening back to the days of Jefferson and Thomas Paine when all the law there was stood contained within the pages of *Blackstone* and a few leatherbound volumes of precedent.

At last, Slough produced a manilla envelope, withdrew a single sheet of white notebook paper and handed it over to Doyle. "An unorthodox document," Slough said, "but completely legal. Would you like me to give you some privacy?"

"That's not necessary," Doyle said, and he took the piece of notebook paper and began to read:

Dear Tim,

I won't call this a Last Will and Testament because I am a superstitious old bastard, but unfortunately that's what it is. You're in Spain now, living the high life with that beautiful Spanish wife of yours and a cute little kid and that's just the way it should be. If you can help it, don't come back to this God-forsaken country, it's gone to hell in a handbasket ever since they shot Kennedy. I am writing this now because I am sick and the Docs say it's the big C and tell me I don't have much longer, so here goes:

You get everything I have — the whole kit and kaboodle of Doyle's Pirate Island which means all the land and everything under it or on it to do with as you see fit. Except the Cadillac, that I promised to my girl Maggie Peach. She's a good girl, and still young. I hope it's not too late for her to find somebody else who appreciates her considerable talents. I want you to take care of her as best you can.

I tried to do right by you in the absence of your father and mother and I'm real proud of the way you turned out after a somewhat wild and at times criminal youth. I think of you as my own boy and love you that way. Always have. Kiss your wife and kid for me in Spain. Love and God Bless You, Uncle Buck

Doyle finished reading Uncle Buck's will, suppressed the lump in his throat, folded it carefully and put it on the desk. "So what happens now?"

Slough handed over a stack of legal papers fixed with brightly colored tabs. "What happens now is you sign and initial these documents where I've put in tabs. Then we get ourselves a date in Probate Court. But the way the docket looks we're talking two, maybe three months."

"Probate Court." Doyle frowned. "Is that necessary?"

"In Wassateague County, yes." Slough nodded sadly. "An appearance before the judge is mandated by statute."

Doyle took the documents and looked them over for a few minutes, just for show. They might as well have been written in Chinese. Then he signed and initialed at all the tabs and handed them back.

"But what happens after probate is up to you." Slough leaned back in his chair and, for a bare instant, Doyle thought he saw something malicious and cold gleaming in the depths of the man's steady gaze, but couldn't be sure and the moment was gone. "Your uncle's will stipulates only that you are to take care of Ms. Peach as best you can. I believe those are his exact words. Needless to say, this is not legal terminology and could be interpreted in a variety of ways by the courts. You are the sole executor, therefore you possess the right to liquidate all assets immediately and divide the proceeds as you see fit. And there are other matters to consider — by which I mean estate taxes, a number of outstanding debts . . ." Slough drummed his fingers on the desk, and Doyle could hear the man's mind working, clicking like an adding machine. "Listen, if you don't mind, let's cut through the bullshit."

"Cut away," Doyle said.

"We have a very reasonable offer on the table right now to buy the Pirate Island property."

This was unexpected news, given the strict zoning regulations imposed back when Buck had been forced to sell the balance of the neck to the National Park Service. Doyle opened his mouth to speak, but Slough waved one fat, pink paw, and launched into a lengthy summation of Buck's dealings with the Park Service — much of it already known to Doyle.

In 1954, when the Park Service set about assembling the collection of pine barrens, salt marshes and barrier islands that eventually became the Wassateague National Seashore Wildlife Preserve — the sixth most visited national park on the east coast — the Doyles owned an inconvenient eight-hundred-acre wedge from town to shore, including the marlish eminence on the near side of the dunes where Buck Doyle had built the Pirate Island Goofy Golf Course and Marina just six years earlier. The land had come to the descendants of Finster Doyle directly from the Oknontocoke Indians, upon the extermination of that unfortunate tribe by a coalition of English and Nanticokes in the early years of the eighteenth century. Deeds bearing the great red wax seal of the kings of England and lesser seals denoting the colonial governor and his factor, preserved in massive bound volumes in the courthouse at Wiccomac, confirmed this ownership. But the Park Service had no feeling for history and claimed the Doyle holdings by right of Eminent Domain. Buck contested that right: in a sense — as Foy Whitcomb ingeniously put it in court — the Doyles were themselves as much an indigenous species as the possums, birds, squirrels and other wildlife the Park Service sought to preserve by creating a sanctuary. The case went from decision to appeal, from appeal to reversal, from injunction to injunction, from circuit court to superior court to the state supreme court in Richmond. Eventually a compromise was reached. Buck was allowed to keep the twenty-five acres immediately surrounding the goofy-golf course and marina under certain very specific restrictions. . . .

". . . thus, according to the terms of the agreement no new structures may be built on the Pirate Island site, ever," Slough concluded. "Existing structures may be razed or remodeled and only after a world of red tape and the prior approval of a committee of Park Service architects. Tim, that means you are now the owner of a dilapidated miniature golf course, a run-down bar, a defunct restaurant, a half-dozen termite-ridden, moldy tourist cabins no one's rented in thirty-five years, and a completely unuseable twenty-slip marina with rotted pilings and the channel silted up to the bay. That's all there is now, that's all there will ever be — no new condos, no new house, no new marina, no hotel or motel, no nothing. So don't get any big ideas. And any subsequent ownership is also bound by the terms of the original Park Service agreement with the decedent. Do you understand?"

"Yes," Doyle said, warily.

Slough pressed his fingers together and closed his eyes. His lids were pale and showed faint purple veins. Through the window, Doyle saw a row of chained prisoners in orange jumpsuits being led by a state trooper with a shotgun down the brick path towards the courthouse.

"No, I don't think you understand, not really," Slough said, his eyes popping open like a wide-awake doll. "That clause makes your property the biggest white elephant on the shore. A financial liability that could bankrupt even the most pecunious owner. As it stands, Pirate Island does not quite manage to pay its own taxes."

A small pink tongue darted out to moisten his lips. "And yet, despite all this, a local entrepreneur has contacted this office with an offer of two hundred and ten thousand dollars for your property. He is prepared to expend a great deal of money — certainly over a million dollars — to refurbish the restaurant and bar in close cooperation with the Park Service."

"What about the golf course?"

"The golf course will be razed to accommodate additional parking — that is my understanding."

"Raze the golf course?" This prospect brought an unbidden pang to Doyle's gut. He couldn't imagine Wassateague without Doyle's Pirate Island Goofy Golf.

Slough nodded.

"Tell me something," Doyle said, "why is this entrepreneur willing to take on — what did you call it? — the biggest white elephant on the shore?"

Slough thought hard, wheels grinding away. "He's a bit of a romantic," he said. "Also, he can afford to lose money foolishly, should it come to that."

"Does this foolish romantic entrepreneur have a name?"

"Actually, he wishes to remain anonymous."

The back of Doyle's neck tingled with warning. He almost mentioned the cut-in-half possum and the threatening note, but he held back. Instead, he studied the faded kilim carpet on the floor, the plaster bust of the unknown jurist, as Slough squirmed nervously in his seat. A long minute passed, then Doyle pushed himself up abruptly and took a step towards the door. "Hey, I've got to get going."

Slough followed down the hall past the grandfather clock to the front door. "At least give me an idea as to your inclinations in this matter," the lawyer pleaded.

Doyle paused, hand on the brass latch that had released generations of clients, a little lighter of pocket, back into the world. Pirate Island wasn't much more than subsistence living, a broken-down third-rate tourist attraction, but there had been Doyles on the land since the beginning and it had never actually occurred to him to sell the place. Where would home be if home belonged to somebody else?

"No sale," he said. "I've decided to get the restaurant up and running again." This last thought had just occurred to him. "I ran a restaurant, you know. In Spain."

Then he pressed down on the latch and the door swung open and he stepped out into the hazy sunlight of the courthouse green as Slough receded into the dimness of his office, like a man sinking back into murky water. Cold wind rustled the bare branches of the oaks in the little park behind the debtors' prison. Two pieces of military ordnance, planted on either side of the Confederate War Memorial — a field gun dating from the Spanish-American War and a stout howitzer of uncertain vintage — both agleam with shiny black rust-proofing paint, cast lengthening shadows on the grass.

7

In the end it was all about the game.

Call it miniature golf, goofy golf, putt-putt, kiddie golf, minigolf, minilinks, pony golf, monkey golf, pee-wee golf, Tom Thumb. Think of all the courses in all the resort towns from Puget Sound to Mobile Bay — all the wonderlands, the prehistoric-caveman courses, the flying-saucer courses, the raging-volcano courses, the Voodoo Island courses, the mermaid courses, the Civil War courses, the spectacular waterfall courses, the Wild West courses, the Japanese pagoda courses, the Chinese pagoda courses, the Spanish Mission courses, the Liberty Bell courses, the Eskimo village courses, the Tahiti Tiki courses, the

Hawaiian Hula courses, the dinosaur courses, the fighting-ace courses, the moonwalk courses, the undersea-adventure courses, the bikini-girl courses, the rock 'n' roll courses, the multitudinous pirate courses, the courses with no theme at all that were just a collection of plain Plasti-grass greens pierced by slotted tin cups. A game for plaintive summer nights at Myrtle Beach and the great black ocean heaving in darkness beyond the boardwalk; a game for suburban evenings outside some dusty prairie town, the click and thwack of ball and cup making faint, delicious music beneath the purple flickering arc lights; a game for warm evenings on the Santa Monica Pier where it's never truly dark, far-flung, palm-fringed islands floating off somewhere beyond the green edge of the horizon.

Buck's mistress at seventeen, Maggie had lived half her life in the game's shadow; Doyle had learned to crawl, walk, talk, drink, fuck and fight not fifty yards from tiny turning windmills, pirate galleons, giant squids, hammerheads and other monsters. The game was as much a part of his blood as corpuscles and T-cells. His first memory: the pirate's head and yellow monkey at fourteen hole, big as the Empire State Building, on some lost sunny morning impossibly bright, a white ball sluicing up the pink-tongue ramp into the huge darkened maw of the pirate's mouth.

Like most things American, Doyle's Pirate Island Goofy Golf had its roots in war: two days after Pearl Harbor, Buck and his brother Jack had ridden up to Baltimore on the train with a thousand other volunteers. Jack enlisted in the Marines and served through some of the worst battles of the Pacific theater. Buck went Infantry and saw action at the Casserine Pass, at Anzio, at Monte Cassino. After VE Day, he transferred to the Quartermaster Corps and was eventually sent to Japan with MacArthur's Army of Occupation. In Tokyo, just a few days before his enlistment expired, Buck was taken by the ranking sergeant of his outfit to an expensive whorehouse called Kinichi Michiko, or Golden Light Playland, down an alley lit with swaying paper lanterns in Tokyo's Bunraku red-light district.

This whorehouse was not like other whorehouses that Buck had seen in his years as a soldier; nothing like the grim, shuttered warrens of Europe stocked with half-starved sluts who would fuck unenthusiastically for a couple of potatoes and a chocolate bar. Golden Light

Playland was a small, self-contained world. A sort of erotic amuse-ment park set up in a former ball-bearing factory with — of all things — an indoor miniature golf course installed on its ground floor. The course was one of the most exquisite things Buck had ever seen. It ran across a beautiful tiny landscape of placid two-foot-wide streams, lily-pad seas, bedspread meadows of brilliant green moss and calf-high forests of bonsai trees to an exquisite paper village of tiny houses whose open windows revealed tiny wax couples making love in a variety of interesting positions. White-powdered, black-toothed geishas, naked except for Scotch plaid tam-o'-shanters on their heads acted as caddies for the lusty GI golfers. After completing nine holes, the men would retire with one of these tam-o'-shantered courtesans to a paper-walled cubicle upstairs for half an hour of sordid sexual activ-ity that never equalled the odd elegance of the game below. What Buck remembered in the end was not the giggling, naked, powdered women with their black-painted teeth and disinfectant smell, but the minia-ture golf course itself, as precious and comforting as a crèche under a Christmas tree.

Golden Light Playland entered Buck's soul that night and took root in fertile soil. Two years later — July 4, 1948 — in civvies again, flush with GI Bill loans, to a fanfare of fireworks and bottle rockets and the music of a hillbilly band playing "The Cowboy Yodel" Buck opened Doyle's Pirate Island Goofy Golf, an exotic black flower transplanted from darkest Tokyo to the mundane possum-infested environs of home.

8

Just enough light now to make out the course ahead. Doyle selected a nicked orange ball and battered old rawhide-handled putter, both dat-ing from the heady days after World War Two and before Korea when Uncle Buck was flying high and the course was new and it seemed the whole world awaited a brilliant atomic-powered future. He gave the ball a jaunty toss high in the air back over his shoulder with one hand, caught it just as jauntily in the other and set it on the deep gouge in the Plastigrass that marked the tee, then he whacked it down the slight grade and through the teeth of the gaping death's head of the first hole. The ball bounced off the cement rim of the circular green — and by the angle of the hit and the spin of the ball rolling out of sight, Doyle knew it was good: he didn't need to hear the tight little clunk to know he'd scored a hole in one. First time in twenty-plus years, he had a hole in one.

He shook the putter at the dark, possum-infested pines of the Wassateague National Seashore Wildlife Preserve beyond the storm fence and hopped up and down on one foot around the tee, a little Indian dance from his youth. Then he crossed the coquina path to examine a few troubling structural cracks where the skull connected to the open jaws. Directly behind the death's-head hole, the path made an S through a stand of overgrown bamboo and turned left to confront a large wooden sign suspended between two six-foot plaster duelling pistols. Doyle still knew the text on the sign by heart and was able to fill in the words in spots where the fancy script had ghosted to nothing:

Welcome, Me Hearties! Follow the REAL adventures of dastardly, dashing, notorious Pirate Doyle! Yes, the ancestor of the present owner was a REAL Pirate who sailed with the famous buccaneer Henry Morgan on the Spanish Main almost three hundred years ago in the Golden Age of Piracy! Step lively, maties, and keep a sharp lookout! For legends say Pirate Doyle left a fortune in treasure buried right here on PIRATE ISLAND!

Doyle chuckled at this bit of nonsense and stepped over to the Port Royal hole, par three, a plaster and plywood metropolis about the size of a large doghouse, surmounted by a working windmill — all now in a sad state of disrepair. Chicken wire and rusted steel-rod reinforcements showed through the gabled houses; the Plastigrass green was pulling up around the half-dozen conch-shell obstacles surrounding the cup. He putted through the tunnel beneath Port Royal, around the conch shells and made par.

Then he made par at the palm-grove desert island, where most of the fronds were hanging loose from their wires, and he made par through the crossed sabers at number four, despite some random debris and an unknown tarry substance splattered across the green, and made par again at the treasure chest, number five, which seemed more or less intact, but certainly needed a new coat of paint. At hole six, the Caribbean sugar mill, Doyle managed to avoid the sand trap — which was now all mud and punctuated with the chimney-like burrows of mud-dauber wasps. But he lost a stroke when his ball bounced off one of the slaves — Uncle Buck had adapted them from conventional plaster lawn jockies — and hit the ball all over the pitted green before it landed in the tin cup with a disgusted plop. He'd always had trouble, he remembered, with those slaves.

The plank at seven was an easy hole in one, and was fine except for the paint again, then came Porto Bello — essentially a replica of the Port Royal hole, and suffering from the same structural neglect — but which for some reason he bogied at two over par. From here, the coquina trail led across a rotting rope suspension bridge, directly to Maracaibo's plaster battlements, its hollow log cannons commanding the approach. Doyle climbed the steps to the ramparts and was saddened by what he saw. Rusted cans of paint stood along the inside wall between the cannons. Patches of the floor had rotted through, revealing the secret workings below. Maracaibo concealed one of Uncle Buck's fine original touches — a device the old man used to call his Patented Trap-O-Matic although it was patented only in his imagination.

Rubber rollers laid in a special cavity beneath the floor and operated by a lever connected to the third cannon were designed to change the configuration of the green after each shot. When the lever was notched up, the green heaved and shuddered as if subject to earthquakes. Balls knocked within an inch of the cup rolled all the way back to the tee or bounced down the stairs; gullies appeared where bumps had been a second before; the cup itself shifted and changed position. Thirty-two concealed rollers meant uncounted permutations on the green; even the most expert putters damned the hole as impossible. Maracaibo was the great leveller, the balance point between luck and skill. It could never be played the same way twice.

Now, Doyle set his ball on the tee and putted. The ball rolled through the opening in the barrier that divided the fixed half of the green from the movable half and stopped ten feet shy of the hole. He put aside his putter, found the lever on the cannon and pulled hard. The lever wouldn't budge. He pulled harder. It cracked and broke off in his hand and he let out an exclamation and fell back.

"Goddamned thing hasn't worked in years." It was Maggie's voice.

Startled, Doyle jumped up to see Maggie perched like an angel on the head of the giant squid at the eleventh hole, just the other side of the coquina path. "Jesus," he said, "you scared the piss out of me."

"No, you scared the piss out of me," Maggie said. "I could hear you crashing around out here all the way over at the cabin." And she reached down and pulled up an ancient lever-action Winchester from the fork between two tentacles and laid it across her lap. The heavy old rifle made an odd complement to her penguin robe and fuzzy hound-dog slippers. She grinned and stroked the long barrel. "Old faithful," she said. "Nobody better fuck with me."

Doyle was startled by the sight of this weapon. During his years in Europe, he had come to embrace European notions of a gunless nation. "What you're going to do is shoot yourself in the ass one of these days."

"Bullshit," Maggie's lip curled into a sneer. "Got me a badge in marksmanship when I was in Campfire Girls. And, in case you don't know it, some weird shit's been going on around here lately — our friend Mr. Cut-in-half-possum's just the last thing."

"Like what?" Doyle said, skeptical.

"Like couple months back, asshole or assholes unknown came along and fucked with Cap'n Pete's electric lines at the road. Plus down at the Bight, charter boats owned by locals keep turning up, seacocks wide open, deliberately sunk in the muck at the bottom of the channel. So someone tries to mess with me, piece of lead does the talking."

"You're crazy," Doyle said.

"Hey, I'm not the one out here five a.m. shooting a round of goofy golf in my PJs."

"Couldn't sleep," Doyle grinned, "with all the work needs to be done."

Maggie offered a rare smile and her face lit up and for a moment, she was almost as beautiful as a girl in a magazine. "Listen to you!" she said, beaming. "Old Tim puts away the bottle, gets off his shitter and gets to work! I think this calls for something."

"OK," Doyle said. "How about breakfast?"

*　　*　　*

After breakfast Doyle played out the back nine. He putted through the giant squid and the shark and the pirate's head stained with possum blood, through the sinking merchantman, around the waterfall and the too-blue lagoon, dry and heaped with leaves and crud; putted through the pirate galleon, beneath the gallows, swaying with a molting papier-mâché and shellack representation of the unfortunate Finster, and on to the pirate's grave at last. Doyle shot right into the coffin in one and watched the ball disappear between the skull's grinning jaws. The mouth sprang shut with a satisfying snapping sound, its rusty mechanical action still good after all these years.

But when he pulled open the grate below to retrieve the ball, he found the reservoir clogged with what looked like a possum nest made of sand and pine needles. The ball was lost, trapped somewhere in the blocked drain. Then he retraced his steps over the coquina path, this time making careful notes regarding necessary repairs for each hole and surrounding real-estate.

That afternoon, in the faltering hour when the sun slips towards the marsh, Doyle came into the bar and showed Maggie his carefully annotated list of necessary repairs.

Maggie took out a pair of reading glasses with half-moon lenses and fixed them on the bridge of her nose, prim as a spinster, and read the list very slowly, her lips forming the words as she read. Doyle waited, his attention wandering. He hadn't been down in the bar sober and in daylight since his return and now he contemplated all the little touches instituted since Buck's day: the cracked old Formica bar counter had been replaced with one made out of real wood and nicely polished; the broken-fronted legal bookcases that had once served to store bottles had given way to a real back bar with staggered shelves, mirrors, and lights. The fishing trophies hanging from every available inch of wall space looked surprisingly clean and free of dust. A new jukebox and a cigarette machine awaited the evening's customers like boxers in their respective corners. Only the 3-D portrait photograph of JFK remained in its usual place over the bar.

"I never knew you wore glasses," Doyle said, when Maggie had finished reading.

"You never seen me read before, now, have you?" Maggie said.

"I guess not," Doyle said.

"Can you do it all yourself?" she said.

"No," Doyle said. "I'm going to have to hire some help."

"Tell you what, county's got this new program. They give you a juvenile delinquent out of the system long as you pay minimum wage and work him like hell. What do you think?"

"Sounds like slave labor," Doyle said.

"Call it what you want," Maggie said. "At least you don't got to pay the health insurance." She reached over, suddenly, snatched away Doyle's bourbon, and poured it down the sink. "No more drinking in this bar, son. Not for a while. Better get sober if you want to open that course anytime soon."

Outside the big plate-glass window, evening was coming on fast. Doyle felt bereft, defenseless. For the first time in a long time, he would have to face Happy Hour without a drink in his hand.

9

Big flowerpots bearing withered tufts of begonias stood just as Doyle remembered them on either side of the wooden gate that separated Pete Piatt's pier from the rest of the world. A yellow light-bulb assailed by moths shone down from its cage on a rusty sign that read PRIVATE PROPERTY — PROTECTED BY SMITH & WESSON. The yellow light was answered by another yellow light marking the front door to Cap'n Pete's tiny white clapboard house, suspended over the brackish water of the Wassateague Inlet. Half-way down, the pier branched off, descended a short flight of mildewed wooden steps, and there, beneath the glare of a powerful flood, Cap'n Pete's classic Chris Craft sport-fishing boat, the *Chief Powhatan,* sat low in the water, moored to stout, tarry pilings.

Doyle pushed open the gate and headed down the pier. The slap of water against wood and the deep croak of bullfrogs from the marsh brought back a whole host of memories. He hadn't heard the croaking of a bullfrog in all the years away. He went around the side of the house to the screened-in porch and was about to knock on the screen door when an unmistakable ratcheting sound froze him in mid-gesture.

"State your business." A muffled voice came out of the darkness behind the screen.

"That you, Pete?" Doyle said, squinting towards the voice.

A thick shadow detached itself from the other shadows and came forward and Doyle was able to make out a beer-bellied, shirtless old man, despite the cold wearing only an oversized pair of canvas pants pulled tight beneath his gut with a square-buckled belt. A few wiry white hairs stuck out of his bare chest; a too-small captain's hat pinned all over with Catholic religious medals perched like a skull-cap on the back of his large bald head. Doyle looked down at the antique double-barrelled shotgun the old man held steadied against his thigh and laughed.

"What the hell's so funny?" the old man said.

"You, Cap'n Pete," Doyle said. "Still collecting those old cannons. Expecting Indians?"

"You never know," Cap'n Pete said, but he lowered the shotgun, grinning.

"It's Tim," Doyle said. "I've been meaning to come over here . . ." His voice trailed off.

Cap'n Pete set the shotgun aside, unlatched the screen door, pushed it open, and Doyle found himself caught in the old man's spidery embrace.

"Old Buck's gone," Cap'n Pete said, into Doyle's shoulder. "We'll never see his like again."

"No, we won't," Doyle said, a thickness rising in his throat. Once again, he fought to keep back the tears. "Listen, got a drink for a thirsty man? Maggie cut me off."

"Beer," Cap'n Pete said.

"Beer it is," Doyle said.

Cap'n Pete opened the screen door, led Doyle on to the darkened porch, and pushed him down on an aluminum glider that Doyle felt but couldn't see.

"Hold on," Cap'n Pete said, "I'll get the Coleman." And he went inside the house and Doyle heard him banging around in the darkness and cursing. A few minutes later, he emerged in a cocoon of white light, carrying a lit storm lantern, which he set on a table beside the glider; then he went back into the darkness again and dragged out an old steel cooler that proved to contain a chunk of dry ice and brown bottles of home-brewed beer. Cap'n Pete opened two beers, handed one to Doyle, took one for himself, and squatted on a camp stool across from the glider. The beer was green-tasting and over-proof and packed a punch.

"That shotgun really necessary?" Doyle said, when he was comfortably settled.

"Still got my electric down in case you didn't notice," Cap'n Pete said, anger in his voice. "Them sonsabitches did what they did to my line ain't going to get away with some other bullshit! Electric Co-op still hasn't told me when I'm going to get my lights back."

Doyle was surprised by the old man's vehemence. "What's going on here?" he said. "You got enemies?"

"Every man if he's a man's got *personal* enemies," Cap'n Pete said. "That's life. This ain't personal. This is different."

"How different?" Doyle said.

"You been into Wassateague Town lately?"

"Not in twenty years," Doyle said.

"Let me put it this way . . ." Cap'n Pete paused. The *Chief Powhatan* bumped against its mooring in the moonlight, moths fluttered at the screen and fluttered off. "These days there's some real serious money floating around this mosquito-ridden shithole and money brings the bastards out of the woodwork. Remember your old buddy Roach?"

Doyle drained his bottle and tasted the bitter sediment at the bottom and called to mind a whiny, acne-pocked stoner who wore Grateful Dead tie-dye as a sort of uniform and who had all the right connections for the wrong drugs on the Eastern Shore. They had been uneasy partners for a while in high school, retailing weed and pills to the local heads, though Roach somehow came away with all the money.

"Roach Pompton was a pissant little bastard," he said at last. "I wouldn't call him my buddy."

"Well, that little bastard's a real big bastard now, practically a tycoon," Cap'n Pete said. "They love him over in Wiccomac. You should see the condos he's got going up all over Southside."

In Doyle's day the south end of the island was an uninhabitable salt marsh where every fall for years his uncle Buck sat out in a mud and wattle duck blind drinking whiskey and taking the occasional haphazard potshot at feathery clouds of migrating waterfowl. "If I remember rightly," Doyle said, "there's nothing but swamp down there."

"Not any more," Cap'n Pete said. "Go down yourself, have a look. They drained most of the swamp and what swamp was left they call wetlands, protected by the Federal Government. After that, they dredged a channel into Spofford's Lagoon so it's an inlet now and they got fancy sailboats going in and out like on a postcard." He made a disgusted sound and sucked some air through the gaps in his teeth. "Then I guess what happened is someone up and decided old charterboat captains like yours truly just don't fit in around here no more."

"Wait a minute," Doyle said. "Someone? Who's someone?"

"Someone's everyone, son," Cap'n Pete said. "The politicians over in Wiccomac putting up new safety regulations faster'n you can spit, the developers, you name it. Throw in some dirty money from up north and you're starting to get the picture."

"You mean what — organized crime?" Doyle said, incredulous.

"You'll figure things out yourself soon enough." Cap'n Pete made a dismissive gesture. "So let's move on. Tell me, how goes it with you? How's your boy — Pablo, is that right?"

Doyle nodded sadly and told Pete about the divorce.

Cap'n Pete reached up to his hat and touched one of the religious medals, a gesture that Doyle remembered now as one of the man's nervous tics. "Well, that's a pity," Cap'n Pete said. "You want to tell me more or do I got to guess?"

"Guess," Doyle said.

"Was it another woman?"

Doyle didn't answer. He didn't have to. Every family has their curse. Booze in one, cruelty in a second, or stupidity or just plain bad luck, or having no curse at all, which in its own way is also a curse.

10

Just drunk enough on more bottles of Cap'n Pete's potent homebrew to make the drive back to Pirate Island a questionable undertaking, Doyle lay wrapped in his coat in a hammock strung on the porch, listening to the small sounds of fish surfacing for insects in the brackish water of the inlet and the rustlings of night critters through the reeds, and thinking again of Flor.

He was a man who hated to look back, for whom introspection was painful — he'd based his whole life on the present moment, on what was happening right now — but he had been thinking about his wife with increasing frequency in these last few weeks. They had been together on and off for almost twenty years. They had met at a penthouse party in Manhattan, not long after Doyle's final break-up with his college girlfriend, a debauched, half-crazy Virginia blue-blood named Bracken Deering. This was back in the early eighties when he lived in Chinatown and tended bar at a series of illegal clubs in Alphabet City, then the hip edge of nowhere.

Doyle couldn't remember whose party it was or how he'd got there. But he remembered feeling out of his element in the beautiful expensive rooms in the penthouse of a building overlooking the Park, everyone very drunk or high and the music so loud you couldn't think, and then he saw Flor sitting quietly in a corner in a high-backed chair, the party swirling around her, a glass of red wine in her hand, her long black hair shimmering in the pier glass across the room. She was like a visitor from a calm, distant planet where no one was ever drunk, only pleasantly intoxicated, and people had long, meaningful conversations in the shade of lime trees as romantic guitar music floated on the wind. Not far wrong, as it turned out. Flor was from Málaga, in Spain, on the part of the Spanish coast that faces Morocco across the Mediterranean's dark blue waters. She was over on a two-year work–study visa, working an apprenticeship with Garcia-Guadix, the famous chef at La Coruña in Manhattan, then one of the best Spanish restaurants in the world.

That first night, they drank more red wine and a bottle of Portuguese arak and ended up making love in her tiny Upper East Side apartment at five a.m.; then she woke him at eight insisting they go to the nine o'clock mass at St. Patrick's. Doyle remembered his amusement at the suggestion and her utter seriousness.

"Doyle. This is Irish, *sí?*" she said, leaning over him, her thick black Spanish hair brushing his face. He was drunk and hungover at the same time, exhausted, tangled in her sheets.

"Actually, I'm from Virginia."

"Yes, but Irish," she insisted.

"OK, Irish," Doyle said. "Once upon a time."

"Then you must be a Roman Catholic."

"I could be an Orangeman," Doyle said. "They're Irish Protestants."

She frowned. "I do not understand this," she said.

"I was born Catholic," Doyle said, "if that's what you mean. Actually did a stint as an altar boy once."

She smiled. *"Bueno.* We go to mass."

"We'll go next Sunday," Doyle said, reaching for her breast.

"We go *immediamente,*" she said, slapping his hand away.

"Sorry," Doyle said. "No mass for this sinner today."

She nodded thoughtfully. "If I let you fuck with me again," she said, "will you go to mass?"

They made it to the noon mass at St. Patrick's. And Doyle remembered the sweet smell of the incense and the sunlight coming through the stained glass, and afterwards the walk all the way downtown to a quiet restaurant she knew, his arm around her waist for sixty blocks, and the pigeons splashing happily in puddles on the rutted cobbles of SoHo and the clear blue shadows of the buildings and the brightness on the river and the bridges arcing straight into the clouds, and every church bell in the city, it seemed, ringing, ringing.

11

Constable Smoot made a show of reading a thick beige file folder at his desk as Doyle came in and sat down in the visitor's chair. The office was large and plush and new, one wall made up entirely of glass bricks. The Stars and Stripes and the blue banner of Virginia hung limply from poles in opposite corners. On the other wall, a series of framed photographs of a far younger Smoot in battle fatigues in Danang, Vietnam. Underneath these, an honorable discharge from the Marines and a citation for the Purple Heart.

"Where were you wounded?" Doyle said.

Smoot closed the file and looked up. He was a big-boned man but not obese, about fifty-five, with square-cut grey hair and hard grey eyes. His small ears stood close to his head like the ears of an animal; he wore a crisp khaki uniform, totally devoid of insignia, and a pair of gaudy Nike sneaker boots. He ignored Doyle's question.

"Doyle." He said the name like an accusation. "You're the last SOB I want to see."

Doyle was surprised by the man's instantly hostile demeanor, then he wasn't surprised. It brought back Friday nights spent in the lock-up for some minor infraction, the humorless small-mindedness of small town law enforcement. He met this attitude with one of his own, conjured from that era of his life like a spirit from beyond the grave — a sort of hostile levity one might call it; jail-house cool.

"Welcome home, Mr. Doyle. Is that what you're trying to say, constable?"

"Guess what," Smoot said, tapping the file folder. "Seems like you had a pretty good time back in the day. A lot of under-age drunk and disorderly, couple of reefer charges, some nice fights, vandalism."

"That's not the half of it," Doyle said, with a barely perceptible smirk, "but juvenile offenses don't count, remember? They vanish in a puff of smoke when you hit eighteen. I won't ask how you got your hands on that file, but I'm sure the District Attorney would like to know."

Smoot leaned back and clasped his hands behind his square head. "We heard you blew into town a couple of weeks ago," he said, "so I took the precaution of having your file sent down from records in Wiccomac. Sorry to disappoint you, new state law allows us to examine the juvenile records of any person whose actions we suspect might be deleterious to the well-being of the community."

"Deleterious?" Doyle said.

"You got it, buddy." Smoot smiled in an unpleasant way.

"That's rich," Doyle said, and he laughed. "Then I guess you must have a big fat file on my old partner in crime. I'm talking about Roach Pompton. Once upon a time he was just about the biggest dealer on the Eastern Shore."

Smoot unclasped his hands and leaned forward, an ugly expression on his face. "You've been gone a long time, Doyle," he said. "These days Mr. Pompton's a respected member of the Council of Burgesses."

"You're kidding." Doyle gaped. Wassateague was the last jurisdiction in Virginia run by a committee of non-elected prominent citizens called burgesses, harkening back to the days when all officialdom owed their positions to the royal governors. The Council's membership, restricted to landowners of a certain fixed minimum acreage, still determined local taxation rates and property values, oversaw public services and appointed the constable who — like his English counterpart — was not permitted to carry any weapon more deadly than a nightstick.

"And it's not Roach anymore," Constable Smoot added, in a stiff monotone. "He goes by James now."

"Right," Doyle said. "Jesse James."

"I'm warning you," Constable Smoot said, "Mr. Pompton has no place in this conversation."

"Now that we've got all the friendly chit-chat out of the way," Doyle said, "why don't we talk about what I came to talk about?" And he told the constable about the possum carcass in the pirate's mouth. This absurd police report hadn't been Doyle's idea: Maggie was a stickler for the letter of the law. "If it were entirely up to me, I'd just let it go," Doyle concluded. "One possum more or less is no big deal — those damned overgrown rats are about as endangered as flies on shit."

Smoot took up a ballpoint pen and began to click it up and down in an annoying manner.

"You're absolutely sure we're talking about the carcass of a Delmarva albino fox possum?"

"Unfortunately," Doyle said. "If you want to check it out for yourself, Maggie wrapped it up and put it in the old meat locker in the restaurant. Though I believe she threw away the seasquab."

"Is this mutilated possum the only unpleasantness so far?"

"I've only been back a couple weeks. Give me time."

"And you have evidence the alleged possum carcass was directed as a kind of threat at you personally?"

Doyle reached into his pocket and pulled out a Zip-loc bag containing the bloody piece of butcher's paper that had been wrapped around the possum carcass. He opened the bag and unfolded the paper and the dead possum-fish stench immediately filled the room.

"Sweet Jesus," Smoot said.

Doyle folded it back into the bag, zipped up and tossed the bag across the desk. "See what I mean?"

"All right," Smoot said. "I'll take that to the county evidence clerk over in Wiccomac and we'll dust for prints and make a few other tests. But I've got to warn you — you're making a formal report here so I'm obliged to call the Fish and Wildlife boys. It'll be their game from here on out and they get pretty riled when somebody messes with one of their possums. They'll probably want to inspect the remains, so you tell Maggie just keep that possum ass in the freezer nice and frozen. Don't know what else I can do, unless there's something you're not telling me."

Doyle thought for a moment. Then he told Constable Smoot about Slough and the anonymous offer.

"I suppose I could look into that one," Smoot said, without enthusiasm, and leaned back in his chair. Doyle heard the big man's joints crack. "You want my advice?"

"No," Doyle said.

"You watch your back, report any unusual incidents to this office or . . ." Smoot paused. ". . . you take the offer, sell up and get the hell out of town."

Doyle stood up and flashed his most disarming smile, the one he'd reserved for the predictably difficult customers at El Rey Alfonso — the rich, cranky matrons, the local politicians angling for a free bottle of wine, the ranking officers of the Guardia Civil with their oily, truncheon mannerisms. Then he stepped forward in a smart, courtly fashion, hand extended. Surprised, the constable took Doyle's hand and shook it.

"Fat chance, Smoot," Doyle said, still smiling. "I'm home to stay." And all at once the smile was gone, and he dropped the constable's hand as he would a piece of rotten meat and walked out of the room without another word.

12

After his hostile interview with the law, Doyle drove around for a while to clear his head and found himself amazed at the changes wrought in his absence upon Wassateague Town. It wasn't just Wiccomac, he realized now. They were doing over the whole goddamned country like Disneyland.

He remembered a friendly southern backwater, Fourth of July parades, buxom majorettes working their flaming batons down Paradise Street. The word "condo" had yet to enter the language. Clapboard houses, weedy yards full of chicken plants, sandy thoroughfares little more than alleys. Thrift stores, bait-and-tackle-shops, a row of middle-class motels, a few rough taverns — where no one much cared if you passed out on the table after a schooner of whiskey — accounted for the rest of the townscape. Now, town center resembled a Club Med in the Virgin Islands, everything slathered in muted tropical colors. Two uncomfortable-looking palms wilted dolefully in stucco urns out front of the old post office painted the color of an unripe mango. Designer beach-wear shops alternated with too-expensive-for-the-mediocre-fare fish restaurants and frozen yogurt parlors that sold Haägen-Dazs and Ben and Jerry's like every other frozen yogurt parlor in America — all closed till the first wave of tourists, Memorial Day weekend. The only bar Doyle saw was the franchise of a global chain called Margarita Johnny's — he'd walked into one of them in Berlin a few years ago and walked right out again. They all looked exactly the same, had fake-plastic flamingos stuck on the walls, played bad music at top volume and offered various candy flavored Margaritas endlessly mixing in clear plastic mixing machines. Could anyone get drunk in such a place?

Presently, Doyle swung a left and made a slow pass down Edgewater Street. He was looking for Futterman Bros. Hardware, one of his favorite places from the old days, a cozy, narrow-aisled emporium full of shiny steel buckets and shovels and American flags, wooden cabinets stacked with puzzling electrical switches, drawers piled with nuts and bolts and screws, everything permeated with the smell of sawdust and chewing tobacco. Instead, he found an empty lot surrounded by a high plywood fence posted with a sign that said, COMING SOON — WACKY WORLD.

He drove on, disconsolate, until he saw an old woman coming down the street leaning on a cane, so hunched over she was nearly staring at the ground. He pulled over to the curb and buzzed down the window.

"Excuse me, ma'am?"

The old woman paused and looked up at him with some difficulty.

"I see the old hardware store is gone," Doyle said.

She nodded. "About ten years now," she said. "After Futterman died, you know."

"Oh," Doyle said. "Is there another hardware store?"

The woman narrowed her eyes. "Are you a Doyle?" she said.

"That's right," Doyle said, smiling. "Tim Doyle."

The woman scowled and moved on.

Doyle crossed the causeway to the mainland and a half-hour later out on 13 came to a Home Fix-It Warehouse — a megastore with all the atmosphere of a Zeppelin hangar. He wandered the endless aisles of this place, past walls of paint cans and green poor-quality lumber, without a clerk in sight. Birds fluttered around the steel rafters of the ceiling. At last a young pimply kid in an orange apron wandered up to him. "Looking for something?" he said.

"Yeah." Doyle handed him a long list of supplies.

The kid squinted down at the list for a half a second. "Can't help you," he said. "This stuff is not in my department."

"All of it?" Doyle said.

"That's right," the kid said, and he turned and wandered off.

It took Doyle an hour to assemble just half of what he needed. He pushed two handcarts full of lumber, chicken wire, plaster mix, paint, thinner, paintbrushes and other stuff up to the register. The check-out cashier, a thin woman with a yellowish complexion, was complaining about her boyfriend to another cashier. Doyle stood there for a while and the woman kept talking.

"That's the thing about the service economy," he said, in a loud voice. "The service sucks."

The woman broke off her conversation and turned towards him. "What's that?" she said.

"You want to check me out here?" Doyle said.

The woman scowled, seemed like she would refuse, then she took a price scanner and scanned the barcodes into her register with an attitude that could only be described as murderous insolence. Doyle was angry, but he summoned the energy to imagine the woman's life and wasn't angry anymore. It was probably worse than his. And he watched the birds hop around in the rafters and wondered if they had been hatched in some nest up there made of cobwebs and packing peanuts and so did not know Home Fix-It Warehouse wasn't the whole world.

13

A soft shape filled the darkness in the doorway to the hall. "I thought you might need this," Maggie said, her Farrah Fawcett hair gleaming like tinsel in the yellow light. The peopled murmur of Happy Hour reached up from the bar below.

Wearing only a pair of Spanish silk boxers printed all over with tiny pink hearts, Doyle lay stiff and sore propped up on pillows atop the bedspread in his room. Earlier that afternoon he'd gone for a hard run down the beach as far as Loomis Point and back again — at least ten miles — the first serious exercise in months.

Now he struggled to sit, gave up, and fell back against his pillows with a gasp.

"You stay right there," Maggie said, stepping into the room. She wore a black halter top with a Japanese cartoon character on the front and white jeans so tight they made camel toes between her thighs. She held out a wrinkled tube of BENGAY in a manner that seemed somehow langorous. "Want me to slather you up?"

Doyle found himself thinking she had beautiful arms, supple and nicely muscled. He considered her offer for a long moment — Maggie's strong hands kneading his flesh — and felt an embarrassing twitch in his loins. "No, thanks," he managed. "I'll do it myself."

"OK," Maggie shrugged, and she dropped the tube of ointment on the bed, turned with a wag of hip, and padded out of the room. Doyle watched her go. He almost called her back, but didn't. After a while, he got the tube, squirted out a blob of BENGAY and rubbed the ointment into the sore muscles in his shoulders, back, and legs. It felt cold at first then hot, and he lay back gingerly, glistening like a peeled onion, and let the medicinal warmth seep into his strained flesh. In a few minutes he was asleep and taken with a version of the recurring dream that had haunted him since early youth: in the dream it was always Hurricane Ava and the *Laughing Debedearon* foundering in heavy seas off Plummet Point, the waves rising black and terrible above the prow. Doyle's father, Jack, smiling, with a huge kingfish mackerel in his hand, was trying to fight the storm at the wheel, but it was no use now, only a question of seconds. Doyle himself hovered somewhere above his father's shoulder, encased in a giant waterproof see-through egg.

"The thing to do is ride it out," his father shouted over the roar of the maelstrom. "It's your only chance in a blow like this!"

Doyle was afraid but his father seemed happy, laughing as the final mountainous wave smashed down over him, and the deck split apart and he sunk with the wreckage. Safe in his egg-bubble, Doyle followed, down into the darkness of the oyster beds, his father's face shining like the moon.

"Remember," his father burbled, "whatever happens, you've got to ride it all the way to the bottom," and he vanished, leaving Doyle alone in eel-infested depths.

A moment later, Doyle's egg-bubble cracked open and the black water came pouring in, choking him, but instead of water it was the long, tangled strands of a woman's hair. Then this was gone, replaced by red flashes and crashing sounds and quite suddenly Doyle was awake, his heart beating wildly, and the orange glow of fire came in through his window and the room was full of black smoke and he heard the loud report of a heavy-caliber rifle being fired: *crak, crak, crak.* He threw himself to the floor and crawled out of the room and down the hall in the tight layer of air just beneath the smoke. He found the top of the stairs with his hands, lost his balance and slid down to the landing, head-first. From there, he scrambled up and threw his shoulder into the door. It sprang open and he fell into the bar, empty and eerily calm and aglow with electric lights, Melvin Teeter singing from the jukebox:

"Hello, walls, how are you today . . ."

Burning, Doyle thought absurdly. He scrambled around the tables and leaped through the screen door across the porch to the crushed shells of the parking lot, lungs bursting. There he collapsed against the rusty flank of Buck's Cadillac and had a good long cough. When he could breathe freely again, he pushed himself up and followed the red glow around to the goofy-golf-course side of the restaurant. The fire rose out of a trash barrel that had been pushed against the outside wall just below his window; flames were curling up the shingles towards the roof. The thin whine of sirens could be heard now in the distance, growing louder, speeding down the Beach Road from town.

Four or five of the regulars stood watching the fire without apparent concern from the sandy strip along the road, beers in hand. Doyle recognized one of them from Buck's day — a wizened old man known only as Woon — and ran over to him.

"Where's Maggie?" he shouted. "Is she all right?"

Woon studied him calmly from beneath the peaked bill of his fisherman's cap and said nothing. Then he looked down at Doyle's pink-heart Spanish silk boxers.

"Some fancy pants you got there," he said. They might have been standing outside on any normal evening, without the flames, drinking beer.

Just then another loud shot crashed out over the goofy-golf course, and Doyle turned in the direction of the sound and caught sight of Maggie's white shoulders looming above the battlements of Maracaibo. She had the Winchester and was firing into the darkness in the direction of the storm fence and the trees.

"She got some bastard pinned down out there," Woon said.

"Bastard that set the fire," another regular said. This was an old drunk called, for obvious reasons, Fisheye by the other regulars. Fisheye had been malingering at the bar since the days of Eisenhower's first administration.

"Damn tough girl, that Maggie," Woon said.

"Good shot, too," Fisheye said.

Doyle didn't wait to hear more. He dashed through the skull-mouth gate into the golf course towards Maggie's redoubt, trying not to feel the rough surface of the coquina path cutting into his bare feet. He took a short-cut across the lagoon, ducked under the bowsprit of the pirate galleon, grabbed on to the barrel of one of the log cannons, and pulled himself up behind her. Maggie swung round and brought the rifle to bear, levering a shell into the chamber with a quick, practiced motion.

"Whoa," Doyle said, stepping back. "It's me."

She scowled and swung back just as a dark figure leaped up from behind the sinking merchantman and began to scale the chain-link fence.

"Got the fucker," she yelled and flipped up the sharp-shooter's sight and took careful aim down the long barrel. Doyle hit her arm just as she squeezed the trigger. The shot went wild and the dark figure vaulted over the top of the fence and was gone into the blackness of the woods.

Maggie let out an angry exclamation, dropped the rifle, and lunged at Doyle, her hands balled into fists, but he caught her by the wrists and pushed her back against the plaster battlements. She struggled against him, cursing, anger in her eyes; Doyle bore down hard. For a few seconds they stood like that, breathing heavily, nose to nose. Doyle could smell the beer and cigarettes on her breath, could feel her muscles tensed against his own.

"I just saved you a world of shit," he said. "Do you realize that? You might have killed somebody." Then he let her go and stood back.

"Fuck you," Maggie said. "That son-of-a-bitch tried to burn us out. He —" Her words were lost as the fire truck roared into the parking lot, siren blaring, and disgorged volunteer firemen in hats, boots, and long rubber coats. Doyle and Maggie turned towards the noisy spectacle unfolding below.

"I just thought of something," Maggie said, in a loud voice. "We don't got a hydrant."

"You sure about that?" Doyle said, heart sinking.

"This is National Seashore, buddy," she said. "No hydrant out here."

"If that's the case," Doyle said. "There goes everything."

The blaze had reached the roof. The mesh screen over Doyle's window melted all at once and a landward breeze swept the flames inside. But the firemen seemed to know exactly what to do. They unrolled a long canvas hose, secured one end to a chrome fitting in the side of the truck, and a spray of white foam that looked like soap suds emerged from the nozzle and began to smother the flames.

"Look at them boys go," Maggie said, relieved.

A few moments later, a hook-and-ladder truck pulled up beside the pumping engine. The ladder went up and the fireman with the hose climbed to the level of Doyle's window. He rested the nozzle on the sill and let out a long burst of foam. From the battlements of Maracaibo, Doyle could see the white mass growing inside his room, like a monster in a science-fiction movie, and suddenly he remembered his clothes in heaps on the floor and his open suitcases.

"I don't think I'll have anything to wear tomorrow," he said.

Maggie looked over at the window then back at him, and her face wrinkled from the chin up and she began to laugh. "Better get used to wearing those pretty silk drawers," she managed, and sagged back against the parapet, weak with laughter, tears in her eyes.

"Yeah, very funny," Doyle said, in a grim voice, but he couldn't suppress a smile at the ridiculousness of the situation.

A cold moon rose over the dark wood as they descended from the fortress a few minutes later and picked their way up the path towards the extinguished blaze. It had been a bad year. Over the course of the last twelve months, Doyle had lost everything: wife, child, livelihood, last living relative, and now the shirt off his back.

Later, huddled in a sleeping bag in one of the leaky, termite-ridden old tourist cabins, Doyle couldn't sleep. The briny odor of the night, the moist pressure of the atmosphere, the certainty of water near, the plaintive kwok-kwok cry of the herons on the marsh, all this was comforting, familiar — and yet only served to remind him how much things had changed. The Wassateague he had known was gone, vanished in an instant like a city of ghosts that appeared for one eerie hour every century. Then the realization came to him — as in a fairy tale, this magic instant was much longer than it seemed. Like Odysseus from Ithaca, he had been gone from the odd little island he called home for twenty years.

part two

GUNSLINGER DOYLE

INIGO DOYLE *knew the brackish waters, sandbars, and oyster beds of the Chesapeake as well as he knew anything in the world; he knew the hidden shoals and inlets and still lagoons where the largest and most succulent varieties were to be found, some nearly as long and thick around as an ear of Indian corn. In the tense decade immediately preceding the Revolution, the Chesapeake Bay was worked by a motley oyster fleet of some four hundred vessels manned by hard-scrabble watermen much like Inigo Doyle, and the struggle to tong up the biggest and tastiest oysters often resembled a war. Claims were staked by one waterman, only to be worked in secret in the dark of night by another; piracy and murder were the accepted methods to settle these disputes. Inigo Doyle, who had inherited some of the toughness of his great-great-grandfather — the notorious pirate Finster Doyle — was the victor in many hard fights. He was a great oyster captain but he was not a good businessman. Lesser watermen often beat Inigo to the wholesale markets at Port Tobacco, Taylor's Landing, and Oxford, where they sold inferior oysters at inflated prices.*

And there was something else: Inigo's religion stood against him in all these places. The wholesalers, men of influence and strong opinions, were mostly high-church Anglicans or strict Presbyterians. They held the fierce prejudices of their caste against Quakers and free-thinkers on one hand, and Roman Catholics like Inigo on the other. Buying oysters from a Catholic waterman was held by some as mere heresy, by others as tantamount to taking part in a popish conspiracy to bring the colonies under the onerous yoke of Rome.

Inigo had heard these bigotries expressed many times in taverns and in other public gathering places and never suffered them lightly. Once, he attacked a Presbyterian minister preaching a sermon heavily alloyed with fervid anti-Catholic rhetoric from atop a barrel of salted cod on the oyster wharf at Onancock. Inigo knocked the obstreperous cleric off the barrel with a well-aimed blow from a boathook, fought back the angry crowd with the same weapon; at the last possible moment he jumped aboard a grain wherry just leaving the wharf, and a following wind propelled him out to safety. But incidents like this only served to make Inigo Doyle and his oysters unwelcome at the little ports along the Virginia shore and he was at last forced into far and unfamiliar waters to find wholesalers who would consent to deal with him.

One blustery February afternoon, a printed broadside fell into Inigo's hands: a certain Virginia squire was offering a very reasonable three shillings per bushel for "excellent table oysters" at the wharves adjacent to his residence some leagues up the Powtomack River. There, the squire maintained a modest facility where the bivalves were cured in salt and Indian herbs, packed with ice in oaken barrels and shipped across the Atlantic to England. Inigo Doyle abhorred this particular breed of men — these damnable haughty Virginia country gentlemen, living like lords off the backs of a thousand enslaved Negroes — but he had no choice. Another week or so and his current catch, one of the best ever, would begin to grow fetid in the tubs.

He packed up his wares, assembled his usual crew of Pamunkey Indians, leavened with one or two escaped plantation slaves, readied his forty-foot oyster shallop called Defiant, and made the rough bay crossing as the light waned over the storm-tossed water. He spent the evening fighting strong currents up the Powtomack and reached the squire's landing in the forenoon. A grand white house, with a square-columned gallery and a cupola topped by a burnished copper weathercock, stood on a ridge overlooking the wide brown river. Inigo Doyle caught the unseasonal fragrance of roses and orange trees floating down on the wind, mixed with the mundane sulphur stink of coke fires and horse manure.

Below the house along the embankment, a series of sturdily built wooden wharves served for the prosecution of several busy industries: in one low shed, tobacco hung curing from the eaves; hemp dried on racks in another. Slaves loaded huge hogsheads of green winter wheat into covered wagons for the long journey to the Pennsylvania country; more slaves unloaded molasses and rum in tenpenny kegs off a scow whose barnacled sides told of a long ocean passage.

Inigo moored his shallop at the nearest wharf, jumped up and approached a self-important-looking factor wearing a scarlet frock coat and powdered wig, and carrying a brass-headed staff. He handed the man the printed broadside and gestured to his vessel piled high with mounds of glistening, horny-shelled oysters. "We are come to sell oysters," Inigo said, "three shillings per bushel. Just like it says on this sheet here."

The factor walked over to the edge of the wharf, poked his staff at Inigo's beautiful oysters, sniffed at them and sniffed again. Then he gestured to a slave, who seized one up and cracked it open for him. He screwed up a piggy eye, inspected the meat as if he knew what he was looking at, and shook his head. "Halfpenny a bushel," he said, "and lucky to get it. These confounded mollusks are about to turn."

"You're a damnable liar," Inigo said, through his teeth, "as well as a cheat. I'll sell my soul to hell before I'll sell my oysters to a blackguard for ha'penny a bushel."

At these words the factor went red in the face and he raised his brass-headed staff to strike Inigo across the shoulders, but the tough waterman was faster. Inigo knocked the staff aside and smashed his fist into the factor's face. The man went down hard. Slaves came out of the tobacco sheds to watch the altercation, amused smiles on their dark faces.

"Bring me your master," Inigo shouted, standing over the prostrate factor, "and I'll knock him down too!"

The factor scrambled off on hands and knees and bleeding from the nose and ran up the hill towards the big house.

"Master's not going to like what you done," one of the slaves said to Inigo. "No, Master's not going to like it one bit." He rolled his eyes gleefully. "You in some trouble now, mister."

"We'll see about that," Inigo said and sat down on the piling and waited. A few minutes later, the factor returned in the van of a column of indentured servants bearing muskets primed and loaded and led by the squire of the place, a tall, wigless, muscular man with a pock-marked face, his long greying hair tied back with a simple black ribbon. The squire wore a fine gold-embroidered waistcoat, a spotless white linen shirt, white lace ruffles cascading down the front, and a pair of polished black officer's boots that shone like glass in the winter sun when he walked. The armed servants and the factor halted at the head of the wharf; the squire advanced alone to confront Inigo Doyle.

"I am master here," he said, in a stern voice; his manner showed that he was used to command. "You struck my factor, you did him bodily injury, and now you shall answer for it."

"Go to the devil," Inigo said calmly, for he knew these Virginia country squires, despite their bristling demeanor, to be soft, weakish fellows. The wigless squire stepped back, removed his fancy waistcoat and his ruffled shirt, and stood bare-chested in the cold wind and Inigo had sudden doubts. The squire was an ugly creature on account of a certain sagging about the mouth and the heavy tread the pox had left on his face, but his eyes were a sharp and penetrating blue, and the muscles in his arms were of formidable size. Inigo almost backed down, but it was too late for that now. He rose off the piling and clenched his fists.

"Your factor is a blackguard and a cheat," he said, waving the broadside, "and so are you, I'll warrant! This printing says three shillings per bushel and your man says half a penny, and I say again go to the devil! My oysters are the best oysters in the whole damned Chesapeake!"

The squire hesitated and glanced over at the pile of oysters in Inigo's boat. "Very well, let me taste one," he said.

Inigo nodded, and his mate, a Pamunkey Indian named Amoki, threw the biggest oyster he could find right at the squire's head. The squire reached up, snatched it out of the air, and cracked open the hard shell between his thumbs. He lifted the oyster to his nostrils, inhaled the aroma, then swallowed the pulsing muscle all at once. He wiped his mouth on a scented handkerchief withdrawn from a concealed pocket in his trousers and nodded. "A tasty bivalve indeed," he said. "We may do business yet, but first you must answer for your affront," and he swung out one long arm and a heavy blow crashed against Inigo's jaw and knocked him flat against the wooden planking of the wharf.

In the time it took Inigo to shake the stars out of his head and rise again, the squire had assumed a fighting stance, fists up, legs apart. Inigo had a second try at the man, but got knocked down again, then got knocked down a third time. As he pushed himself off the wood, bloody and battered, he could feel the scrutiny of his Indian crew upon him, the disappointment in their eyes more painful than any of the blows he had yet received. He tried again, for their sake, but this time the squire lifted him in the air and threw him into the muddy, cold waters of the Powtomack. Inigo came up sputtering, treading water. "I'll dump my oysters in the channel," he screamed, "before you have them, you cheating bastard!" and he issued a quick order to that effect in the Pamunkey dialect, but the squire counter-manded it with a quick order of his own in the same, and the Indians raised their paddles but did nothing. Then, the squire leaned back and laughed, a big booming sound that echoed along the river, and the slaves caught up his laughter and the air was filled for a long moment with the sound of merriment.

"Is it a cheating bastard that pays five shillings a bushel for a goodly pile of oysters?" the squire said.

Inigo blinked up from the cold water, incredulous. "F-five shillings?" he managed, through chattering teeth.

"Aye, and worth every shilling," the squire said. "Tastiest bivalve I ever et, bar none. That drubbing, my man, was just to teach you not to lay a hand on my factor again."

Then he reached down and pulled Inigo Doyle out of the water and caused an Indian trade blanket to be wrapped around him and led him up the trail to the big white house. They went along the portico, through a side door and into a room the squire reserved for his business affairs. It was a plain, square chamber, far plainer than Inigo had expected in such a grand house, but full of more books than he had ever seen in one place in his life. A standing desk piled with papers and pots of ink occupied one corner. Charts that showed heavy use along the creases hung from pegs on the walls. The squire went over to the desk and quickly wrote out a short docu-ment and affixed a seal in red wax that showed a shield with three stars and three stripes, and he signed his name large and with a flourish.

"This contract makes me the sole purveyor of your oysters in the colonies and in England," he said. "I agree to pay four or five shillings a bushel, de-pending on size, and you agree to supply them to me and only to me. Is that arrangement in confluence with your desires?"

Doyle peered down at the document with some difficulty through an eye swollen closed where the squire had hit him. Then he looked up and met the squire's gaze with his good eye and something about the man stirred his soul. Here is a fellow who has never told a lie, Doyle thought, and hon-esty must be met with honesty, else the world be given over whole to falsifiers and knaves.

"You'll like to tear that paper up, and send me to the devil yourself," he said, in a quiet voice, "after I tell you what it is I'm going to tell."

The squire said nothing.

Inigo took a deep breath and tried to stand up straight, despite his bruised and aching limbs. "I'm a Roman Catholic man," he announced. "You've been decent enough about my oysters and you're the first man that ever bested Inigo Doyle in a fight, so I'm telling you now."

The squire nodded thoughtfully. He toyed with a reading glass cut so as to make letters on a page appear bigger than they were. "If you were the Vicar of Rome himself I'd still purchase your oysters," he said. "Catholic or Protestant, the oysters don't care to know the difference — and neither does the great God Jehovah, if you ask me. So I'll have your hand on it."

Inigo Doyle shook the squire's hand and took the contract and folded it into his pouch and walked out of the house and down the trail to the brown river, the leather purse full of gold pieces jangling with a pleasant sort of music from his belt.

A few years later, when the colonies resolved to split from England and the terrible wars came, most of the watermen of the Chesapeake remained loyal to the Crown and King George. Inigo Doyle himself had nothing against the King and didn't care much for the rebels, led as they were by a passel of slave-owning Virginia aristocrats and self-righteous Boston merchants interested only in lining their own pockets — but he soon heard that the leader of the rebels was the pock-marked squire who had given him the paper for his oysters.

"They will win, you have my word on that," he said, to some loitering watermen in a bayside tavern one day waiting out a storm. And this at a time when it didn't seem the rebels would win at all, when they had lost New York and Boston and Charleston to the red-coated British soldiers.

The other watermen were skeptical, but willing to enter into a debate on the matter. "How do you know that so certain?" said one of them.

"Because I am well acquainted with their leader, this General Washington," Inigo said. "He's a man knows a good oyster when he swallows one, and he's the only one ever bested Inigo Doyle in a fair fight. If he can best a Doyle, then he can best the King himself."

The watermen laughed at this, and listed all the reasons why the rebels were already as good as beaten, but Inigo Doyle would have none of it. And the next night he sailed his shallop through the blockade at Cape Charles and up the Delaware to enlist with the rebel army encamped near Philadelphia.

1

T HE WASSATEAGUE COUNTY fire investigator drove down from Wiccomac in a red Hyundai with a blue siren flashing without sound to show he was on official business but in no particular hurry. He pulled the Hyundai around back and stood in fire-resistant thick-soled shoes for an hour on the border of scorched shells below Doyle's window and contemplated the burnt-out trash barrel and the inverted triangle of fire damage scrawled up the side of the old restaurant. The shingles were charred and had burned through in several places, revealing blackened joists and exposed pipes. The fire had marked an oval of black around the frame of Doyle's window. The fire investigator wore a J. C. Penney suit and was a broad-chested man with black hair and a neat grey moustache. He carried a small tape-recorder into which he mumbled unintelligible comments from time to time.

Doyle looked on impatiently, hands stuffed into the pockets of a pair of ancient, paint-encrusted army-issue overalls he'd found hanging in the utility closet behind the bar, which now, along with Buck's old combat boots and one pair of yellow silk Spanish boxers, represented his entire wardrobe. At last, the fire investigator turned to Doyle and gestured to the trash barrel with his tape-recorder. "That's where your fire started," he said.

"Did you have to go to school to figure that one out?" Doyle said. He was in a bitter mood this morning, for obvious reasons.

The fire investigator frowned and mumbled a few more words into his recorder. "Tell me something, Mr. Doyle," he said, "is there an insurance policy on this building?"

"I guess so," Doyle said.

"This was set deliberately, that's obvious. Some people are crazy, they just get a kick out of seeing things burn. And some people," the fire investigator looked pointedly at Doyle, "have been known to set fire to their own property to collect the insurance money."

"No kidding," Doyle said, in the same tone that he might say, "Fuck you."

For the next few minutes, as the fire investigator poked around in the ashes, Doyle tried to put himself in a more reasonable frame of mind but could not. The Doyles had nurtured a contempt for official-dom ever since the days Finster sailed around the Spanish Main hanging royal functionaries from the yardarm of the *Poet's Grave*. It was part of their genetic heritage, like black hair and sleepy blue eyes, and inseparable from such grander wellsprings of the soul as love, honor, courage.

"Now, how about telling me what happened in a calm, civil fash-ion?" the fire investigator said at last.

Doyle gritted his teeth and told him. There had been two arsonists. Maggie caught them in the act, grabbed her rifle and started shooting: one ran out to the road, jumped into a pickup and took off; the other hid in the golf course for a few minutes, then made for the woods. They'd come with cans of gasoline, kerosene-soaked rags; another minute, the whole place would have gone up.

The fire investigator nodded gravely at this account, his eyes half closed. "Did anyone get a good look at these miscreants?"

"No," Doyle said, "but I've got a suspect." And he told the investiga-tor about Slough and the anonymous offer to buy the property. "You might start by grilling that fat bastard. His office is over in Wiccomac."

The fire investigator shut off his tape-recorder with an irritated snap. "Out of the question," he said. "Mr. Slough is an esteemed member of the Bar. If I go around making spurious accusations on nothing more than a hunch, it could mean my job."

Doyle was astounded at this response. "Screw your job," he said. "Someone just tried to burn me out!"

"I think my business is finished here," the fire investigator said curtly and he turned on his thick heels and headed back to his red Hyundai.

"Hey, asshole," Doyle called after him, "next time my house goes up in flames I'll try to be in a better mood!"

The investigator slammed the door and headed back to Wiccomac.

2

Later that afternoon, Doyle drove into town to Dollar Mel's to get new underwear and socks and other personal items to replace the stuff ruined by the anti-incendiary foam. He parked the Cadillac out front against a yellow curb and when he came out of the store not ten minutes later, bags in hand, the car was gone, towed, and this meant only one thing: it was way out at Toby's Marine Salvage in the barbed-wire compound reserved for offending vehicles on the far side of the island.

Doyle left the bags with the clerk at Mel's and slogged out along the Pamunkey Channel Road, hunched against a soaking rain, his paint-splattered overalls heavy and cold and stuck to his skin. When he came through the fence into the junkyard at last, a large, filthy mechanic was in the process of unhooking Uncle Buck's Cadillac from the dolly of a tow truck. The mechanic wore a stained denim jacket with the sleeves cut off, showing what looked like a faded verse inscription tattooed on one bare ham-hock shoulder. He grunted aloud as he knelt in the mud to remove the steel chocks from the Caddy's front wheels.

"Hey, asshole!" Doyle called, coming down towards the truck. "Get your fat greasy paws off my Cadillac!"

Startled, the mechanic jumped up and spun around. "It's fucking interdicted back here!" he shouted, angry, waving his big bare arms. "Begone, maleficent fuckhead!"

"Didn't bring my dictionary." Doyle perched himself atop a fifty-gallon drum marked with a skull and the word DANGER. "All I got was the fuckhead part."

The mechanic advanced towards Doyle, fists clenched. Then, all at once, he stopped, and something like amazement creased the thick stubble on his face. "Well, I'll be a monkey's shit!" He grinned. "Old brother Doyle. The man gives up a castle in Spain to walk among us again. How the hell are you?"

"Just fine, Toby," Doyle said. "Except for the fact that you've got my car there."

Toby glanced over his shoulder at the Cadillac. "Thought that was Buck's mobile," he said. "Come on inside."

Doyle followed the big man's denim-covered posterior across the yard, picking around piles of unnameable, dismantled machinery and the great rusting cast-iron blocks of marine engines, pistons the size of coffee cans rust-frozen in mid-stroke.

Years ago, Ed Toby and Doyle had played varsity football together for the Wassateague High Fighting Possums. Even then, in the first flush of youth, Toby had been an odd bird, freshly tattooed with the first verse of the *Aeneid* in Latin on his shoulder, spouting Virgil, Seneca, Homer, and obscenities in equal measure in the huddle. "Sing, O muse," he would bellow, before the ball was snapped into play, "of arms and the man — fuck you hike!" He belonged to that rare type still found occasionally in out-of-the way pockets of the South — the Redneck Savant: by inclination a thinker of abstract thoughts; by upbringing a countrified good-old-boy whose ambitions extended no further than a good drunk Saturday night, followed by a nice long hung-over Sunday afternoon fishing from the back of a beat-up aluminum skiff. But a great-great-grandfather had been a famous translator of Tacitus in the nineteenth-century and somehow Toby had inherited this gone scholar's facility with dead languages. Following high school he had wrangled a classics scholarship to Dartmouth. They kicked him out sophomore year for breaking the nose of a roommate who had objected to the Confederate battle flag flying from the dorm room window.

The machine shop's cement floors were so black and slick with grease that Doyle had trouble staying upright; he slid across the workbay and into the tiny, stifling office. Here, buxom pin-up girls cradling power tools against their breasts smirked out of flyspecked out-of-date calendars hanging on the walls. A long, sagging shelf supported by two cinderblocks showed an incomplete set of the Loeb Classical Library, out of order and grease-smeared: Doyle saw Xenophon, Epictetus, Marcus Aurelius, and stopped looking.

Toby opened the top drawer of a grey metal filing cabinet and took out a bottle of Old Overholt.

"No, thanks," Doyle said, squatting on a pile of Chilton's manuals. "That stuff's rotgut."

"You been in Europe too long," Toby said. He pulled the cork with his teeth, took a long swig, and handed the bottle to Doyle. "Pretty soon you'll be taking a piss sitting down."

Doyle gargled down a mouthful of the rye and handed the bottle back. "Disgusting," he said.

"But before we get all misty-eyed reminiscing," Toby cracked his knuckles, "let's get down to the haggling — that's sixty-five for the hook-up, twenty-five for my time. In case you forgot, you were parked illegally at the yellow curb in front of Dollar Mel's, thus impeding that worthy merchant from receiving critical deliveries of plastic sandals, colorful nylon beach towels, and genuine Wassateague mother-of-pearl knickknacks made out of polyurethane paste in Sri Lanka. In short," he drew himself up and sucked in his gut, "you haven't changed one bit since your bad old drug-running days and are the very pinnacle of what we call in the trade a motherfucking scofflaw!" Then he let out his gut and sagged back against the desk. "Now, I'm the first to admit that without scofflaws such as yourself, I would starve — which puts me in an interesting situation, ethically speaking. But, as that old scalawag Epictetus says, 'the perfect man will not be angry with the wrongdoer' — in this case you — 'and will only pity his erring brother, as anger would only betray that he thought the wrongdoer gained a substantial blessing by his wrongful act, instead of being, as he is, utterly ruined.' In short, brother Doyle, throw me a fast fifty and we'll call it fair and square."

"Twenty-five," Doyle said grinning. "It's all I've got."

"Done," Toby said, gravely.

The money changed hands and the men settled down to some serious drinking. Over the next two hours, as the Overholt dwindled, they talked about the past, friends they had known and who were dead, married, or incarcerated, high school days, old loves, drunken escapades down country roads and the law on their tail. Doyle told Toby about his divorce, Toby told Doyle about the series of devious redneck sluts that had culminated in his current state of bittersweet bachelor solitude, more or less permanent, among hulks of rusted metal and the tattered remnants of the Loeb Classics Library. "I haven't given up hope," Toby said. "What I need is a woman who can cook me up a nice batch of grits and pork chops, fuck me good, then read Catullus out loud in Latin when it's all over."

"Then you're doomed," Doyle said, swallowing the dregs of the bottle.

"So are you, old son."

"I know," Doyle said. "I still love my wife."

"That's a problem," Toby said, "since you done fucked your way from one end of Europe to the other."

They stumbled out into the waning light in the yard and Doyle got into the Cadillac and turned the key and the old car stuttered to life. Then he switched it off. During their nostalgic exchange of memories, romantic failures, old jokes, he had neglected to tell Toby about the bungled arson attempt, the bisected possum. He told him now.

"That's some deadly bullshit." Toby shook his head grimly when Doyle was finished. "But it doesn't surprise me at all."

"What the hell happened to this town?" Doyle said.

"Big question," Toby answered.

"Try me," Doyle said.

Toby squinted up at the grey drizzle. "Well, you could blame it on old bastard Roach, your former companion in lawlessness," he said. "That weevil has become the veritable Donald Trump of Wassateague. Or you could blame it on a whole host of zombie-hearted real-estate men who live in high-security high-rise complexes in places like Washington or Boston, or fucking Hong Kong for all I know, and speculate in shore property hereabouts and who can smell the tourist dollars like sharks smell blood. But if you ask me, there's more than just tourism and real-estate sharks at work here, old brother. To put words in your mouth, you're really interested in a much larger question. You really want to know what happened to America itself."

"OK," Doyle said. "I'll bite. What happened to America itself?"

"Shit." Toby rolled his eyes. "That's easy. Progress."

Buck's room at the far end of the L-shaped hall upstairs, at the opposite end of the building, was untouched by the arson, a tightly closed door saving the interior from smoke damage. Maggie spent two days in there cleaning — discarding unopened bills, outdated subscription renewals, empty pill bottles, old copies of *Fish & Game,* the green funeral oxygen tanks, the bed where the man had endured his final agonies, where he had given up the spirit at last — as the aluminum casement windows stood open on the marsh and the dunes to admit a fresh briny ocean breeze, disturbing the dust that lay across every surface like a shroud.

Doyle balked at first. Moving into Buck's room, wearing Buck's clothes seemed like cracking a tomb and rifling its contents — but necessity convinced him in the end: where else would he sleep and what would he wear when he woke up? Maggie's cabin, refurbished years ago for her use, was the only one suitable for permanent habitation and there wasn't room for two; the others had holes in the roof, were as good as gutted, infested with frogs, snakes, termites.

Maggie helped Doyle sort through Buck's old clothes — a veritable mountain — over the course of a long, melancholy afternoon, aided by two six-packs of Wassateague lager and a pint bottle of Jim Beam. The man had been a pack rat, never threw a thing away; an entire lifetime's worth of clothes hung dusty and untenanted in the double closet stuffed to capacity. Maggie emptied the closet slowly, took each item off its hanger with gentle solicitude, running her hands across the threadbare shirts, the old jeans worn at the cuff, tucking in pockets, brushing off lint, a tear in her eye all the while as if she were burying the man a second time. When everything was laid out across the bed in even mounds, the quantity of clothing seemed sufficient to fill the racks of an average-sized thrift store.

After some fumbling with tape measure and thread, they found that the clothes of an earlier, slimmer Buck fit Doyle almost exactly and he came away in the end with a complete wardrobe spanning the Cold War years from Stalin to Sputnik: square-bottomed rayon sports shirts and high-waisted gabardine pants, striped long-sleeve flannel pajamas, no-nonsense blue boxers, socks with clocks on the ankles, yellowed-armpit pocket Ts, Argyle golf cardigans, a complete sharkskin suit that had somehow escaped the depredations of moths for nearly fifty years, a genuine Mackintosh raincoat, several pairs of two-tone wingtips, a pork-pie Stetson hat still in its original box, and lastly, a stained, Gothic-looking tuxedo circa 1944. A man never knows when he might need a tuxedo and thus they hang forgotten, gathering dust on the shoulders, in the very weave, from one decade to the next.

When the clothes were assembled, Doyle took off the paint-splattered overalls and dressed in a pair of yellow gabardine slacks and a yellow and black rayon bowling shirt, with Buck's name stitched on the pocket and on the back an embroidered dragon and the inscription USAMP BOWLING — TOKYO, JAPAN — LEAGUE CHAMPS — 1946, and slipped his feet into a pair of black and white two-tone penny loafers, and stood in front of the mirror tilted over the dresser.

"This get-up is truly ridiculous," he said, in response to Maggie's amused scrutiny. "I'm ready for a bit on *I Love Lucy*."

"I saw in *Vogue* that vintage clothes are real popular," Maggie said. "People pay a goddamned fortune for stuff like that, especially over there in Japan where that shirt come from."

"You read *Vogue*?" Doyle said, archly.

"I read a lot of things, Mr. Smartass," she said. Then she turned towards the tangled heaps left on the bed and wiped a last tear from her eye. "You got everything you want out of this stuff, right?"

"Right," Doyle said.

"Then you bag up the rest and get it over to the Salvation Army in town before I bust out in tears."

Driving to the Salvation Army in Buck's Cadillac an hour later, wearing Buck's clothes and shoes with half of Buck's wardrobe flapping in the back seat and the other half stuffed into the trunk, Doyle felt the old man's presence lingering in the car like a miasma, the cigar and whiskey wheeze of his laughter mixing with the grinding of the tires on the rough surface of the road.

Despite the bitter legal struggle with the U.S. Park Service, the eventual confiscation of eight hundred acres of ancestral Doyle demesne, and a generally negative attitude towards the politicians in Washington, Buck nonetheless maintained to the end, like Gatsby, an unswerving faith in the romantic promise of America. He believed that in America any man with a decent education and a willingness to work hard could get just about anything he wanted out of life. He had wanted a goofy-golf course, he had gotten a goofy-golf course. What was to prevent anyone else possessed of similar gumption and respect for civilization doing the same?

Now Doyle recalled a sudden journey he and Buck had taken together back when Doyle was a kid, the summer he turned nine. This was at the end of May, the golf course getting ready to open for the season and no time left at all — but Buck came up to Doyle's room one morning with an old cardboard suitcase in hand and told him to get up, get dressed, brush his teeth, pack his things: they were going on a little trip.

"When?" Doyle asked, surprised.

"Right now," Uncle Buck said.

Doyle did as he was told and they got into the battered old Ford Woody that Buck drove in those days and headed south to Cape Charles and across the new bridge to Norfolk. At Norfolk-Hampton Airport that afternoon, they boarded a large, modern, four-engined jet that seemed about as marvelous as a magic carpet to young Doyle. He had never flown before, was busy watching the ground pass far below at five hundred miles an hour out the window, so it was not until they were most of the way across the continent that he thought to ask his uncle where they were going.

"California," Uncle Buck said.

"Why are we going to California?"

Buck thought about this. "You were born there," he said. "I guess you don't remember that, do you? Your old dad and you lived there for a little while before you and he came back east."

This was a surprise. Doyle only knew the golf course, the beach, the marsh, the little town of Wassateague where he went to public school. The rest of the country existed for him only as pictures in the books at the local library or colored maps in the *National Geographic* atlas his teacher kept in the classroom.

"The world's a big place, Timmy," Uncle Buck said expansively. "Except for the war, I've barely been off the island my whole life. You want to get off the island, you've got to have education. With a good education you can go anywhere you want, do anything you want. We're going to see someone about that. OK?"

"OK," Doyle agreed, even though he had no desire to get off the island, as his uncle put it. He knew he wanted to spend *his* whole life comfortably ensconced between the breakers and the bay, pedalling down to the beach, into town for an RB Cola, chasing possums through the woods with a slingshot.

When they landed in Los Angeles, it was earlier than it had been when they left Norfolk — or so it seemed from the light in the sky. Uncle Buck rented a new Chrysler and, with the air conditioning blowing ice cold, they drove in and out of heavy traffic and along wide streets lined with squat, ugly buildings and palm trees and up into the yellow-brown hills surrounding the city. The light shining through the haze on everything was hard and blinding, not like the soft light on the marshes back home. There was something familiar about all of this, but Doyle could not say what.

At last, they came along a quiet street to a neighborhood of big beautiful homes, some set behind brick walls, others with deep green lawns that rolled under shade trees all the way down to the sidewalk. Brown-skinned men in green uniforms tended the lawns and the beds of bright flowers. Uncle Buck rolled down the windows and the sharp whirr of push-mowers, the hush-hush of sprinklers, and the faint chirping of songbirds filled the car. Then he took a left on to a long drive that led up to the largest house Doyle had ever seen.

Two white towers loomed against the bright sky at either end of the house; the wide porch in between was crowded with men and women in fancy clothes, talking and drinking and laughing. Beneath a big white tent set up in the yard, a full orchestra played very slow dance music; a few couples danced there close together on a wooden floor laid down over the grass. Buck pulled the Chrysler to the end of the drive and parked in the middle of a row of big, glossy limousines. He told Doyle to wait, then he got out and walked up to the porch, through the crowd. The back of his shirt, Doyle noticed, was dark with sweat despite the cool inside the car.

Doyle waited and played with the knobs on the radio and watched the people dance. A few minutes later, a woman in a long white dress carrying a bouquet of flowers came down off the porch and hurried across the lawn to the car. She leaned down close and looked in the window at Doyle for a long time but didn't say anything. Doyle felt funny beneath this scrutiny, but he thought she was pretty and looked real nice in her white dress. She had eyes that were green, almost yellow, and reminded him of the eyes of a cat and she smelled like perfume and like the bottles of booze that Uncle Buck kept behind the bar.

"So you're Timmy," the woman said, when she was done looking at him.

Doyle nodded.

"You look like a good boy, are you a good boy?"

"I guess so," Doyle said.

"I'd like to spend some time with you today," the woman brushed a strand of blonde hair from her eyes, "I really would, but I just can't. You see, I just got married again an hour ago, and I've neglected to discuss the fact of your existence with Jim, my new husband. I mean, he doesn't even know I was married before — it's not a dark secret, it's just that the subject never came up, I suppose because I never brought it up. One likes to start with a clean slate, you know, even if the slate has been — shall we say? — already written on. Do you understand, Timmy?"

The woman talked in a rush that came to a stop all at once, like a telegram. Doyle had no idea what she was talking about but he said he did.

The woman frowned. "Your uncle Buck tells me you'll want to go to school some day, is that right?" she said.

"I'm in school right now," Doyle said, puzzled. "I'm going into the fourth grade next year."

"I mean to college, silly." She waved her hand. "You see, he wants me to put money in the bank for your college expenses and it's rather a lot of money. So I said, 'What's the use of putting money away for college if the boy doesn't want to go?' So Buck got all angry like he does and said, 'Why don't you ask him?' and here I am, asking. Well, do you want to go or not?"

Doyle didn't know what to say. He didn't have a clear idea of college.

The woman waited for him to speak, then she grew exasperated.

"Oh, you're no help," she said, and she turned and hurried back up the lawn past the people dancing in the tent and through the crowd on the porch and into the house. More time passed. Uncle Buck appeared, smiling to himself and wiping sweat from his forehead with his red handkerchief.

"Timing is everything, son," he said to Doyle, when he got into the car. "Looks like you're going to college," and he winked.

"Now?" Doyle said, surprised.

"No, one of these days," Uncle Buck said, laughing. "When you're older. Don't worry about it."

He started up the car and they drove away from the house and down the brown hills and across the city to the beach. There they parked at a parking meter, took off their shoes, and walked on the sand for a while, then Uncle Buck stopped and made a dismissive gesture towards the blue-grey expanse of the Pacific, the limitless distance. "Trouble is, the whole thing's on the wrong side," he said.

That night, they stayed in a motel with a color television set in the room and a bed that vibrated like a dozen possums were running around inside the mattress when you put quarters in a little machine on the headboard. Buck pumped it full of quarters and fell asleep with his clothes on, mouth open, snoring, the television fading from jets flying over the Statue of Liberty and the flag waving to grey static.

The next morning they got up early and flew back to Virginia.

5

A lone blue heron followed the *Chief Powhatan* down the Wassateague Channel and around the bare sandy shoreline of Pinuxent Hook; then, as they passed the narrows, the elegant bird veered off on its big wings to alight somewhere in a low sawgrass meadow dotted here and there with the tentative red specks of cardinal flowers. It was a beautiful winter morning, February 15, Washington's birthday, but so warm it felt like April or early May.

"Want to know something?" Cap'n Pete shouted, over the steady

burble of the twin diesels. "President's Day don't mean shit to me!"
The old man stood at the big mahogany wheel, bottle of homebrew in
one hand, cheap cigar smoldering in the other, steering the big boat
by the dexterous use of his elbows. "I celebrate the General's birthday
on the General's birthday. Luther King's got his own personal holiday,
how come they took Washington's away and lumped him in with old
Abe like that? Man was the father of our country, am I right?"

"You're right," Doyle said, from his place in the bow, but he wasn't
listening.

"You ought to have a strong opinion on this matter, son," Cap'n
Pete persisted. "The General was a special friend of the Doyles, and I
mean way back, before the war with England. He used to say Doyle-
drudged oysters were the best he ever tasted."

Doyle smiled absently. He took the fresh salty air deep into his
lungs, filled his eyes with the broad horizon, and wondered why he'd
stayed away so long. The *Chief*'s polished brightwork gleamed like
white gold; beneath the bows, the water changed from green to grey-
blue as they passed out of the channel and the shore receded off the
port bow like a bad memory. He came aft and took a beer out of the
cooler in the cockpit.

"You do any serious fishing in Spain?" Cap'n Pete huffed a cloud of
cigar smoke in Doyle's direction like a question mark, but it floated
off over the stern.

Doyle adjusted his sunglasses. "Only for the kind that wears skirts,"
he said.

Cap'n Pete laughed at this.

"What are we going after today?" Doyle said.

Cap'n Pete thought for a moment, scratching his beard. "Too early
for blue or tuna," he said. "Makos feed on them so they're out. Let's
call it kingfish at the twenty-fathom line."

He pushed down on the hand throttle and the *Chief Powhatan* lifted
her bow into the waves and the cold salty wind blew through Doyle's
hair. They crossed the Porpoise Banks and churned over the Wrecks —
anonymous patches of open sea distinguishable one from the other
only by a fisherman raised on these waters. Flat green shreds of sea-
weed floated on the surface of the waves; the atmosphere smelled
heavily of fish. In the hidden currents of the deep, the multitudinous

schools were already warming, growing hungry, turning as one towards coastal waters to feed and spawn.

Cap'n Pete killed the engine, came out from beneath the cowling, and settled himself into one of the fighting chairs to watch Doyle work. The religious medals in his hat flashed brightly in the sun. "Think you can remember what you got to do?" he said.

"Don't you worry about me," Doyle said, and he squatted down on his haunches at the equipment locker and tried to recall all the things he had forgotten. Summers out of college he'd spent on the *Chief*, working parties of anglers out to the banks twice a day; he'd been good at it, known the deep holes and all the fish and just what they liked, what lures were best with cobia and dolphin fish, what bait tautog was likely to take, how to drop the chum upwind of the big schools.

"Are we deep trolling?" He squinted up at Cap'n Pete.

The old man didn't say anything; he readjusted the cigar between his teeth. This was a kind of a test.

Doyle scanned the gunwales. "Where's your downrigger?" he said.

"I made the mistake of trading in the good old hand-crank job for an electric rig a couple of years back," Cap'n Pete said. "Came in a box said, 'Made in Indonesia.' Damn thing lasted three months before it quit on me, so I heaved it overboard. What do you think they know about going after kingfish in these waters all the way over in Indonesia?"

Doyle thought hard. No downrigger. What next? "OK," he said, "then we go it the old-fashioned way. Diving plugs, wire lines. We throw down some chum and drift along with the lines deep and see what comes up."

"You ain't so dumb after all." Cap'n Pete nodded.

Doyle picked two sturdy-looking deep sea boatrods from the locker and attached the ceramic-spooled trolling reels wound with wire filament. He tied the diving plugs to the line, then got the bait out of the bait freezer. The ballyhoo were already rigged and three-hooked, their frozen eyes reflecting nothing. The trouble came when he tried to attach the leader to the wire line. He tried a blood knot, but his fingers had forgotten the moves. He tried twice more but couldn't get it right. Meanwhile, the hooked ballyhoo were melting into the deck, releasing a stale, frozen-fish smell.

Cap'n Pete watched with a critical eye; then he took up the rods and leader and pushed Doyle aside with a grunt. Doyle got up, feeling like a dumb kid, went back to the bait freezer, and removed the raw bait-fish from its plastic container.

"How do you want it, Cap'n?" Doyle called.

"Snowballs," Cap'n Pete said. "Think you can manage that?"

Doyle packed the half-frozen fish into eight tight balls with fine white sand kept wet in a bucket for this purpose, brought the balls aft, and stacked them in a neat pile on the deck. Cap'n Pete handed him his rod tied with leader and fixed with the ballyhoo.

"Have a seat, son." Cap'n Pete grinned, and pointed to the fighting chair.

"Not me," Doyle said, and braced himself against the gunwale. Cap'n Pete strapped himself into the chair and, at a signal, both men dropped their line overboard. Doyle watched the coppery filament disappear into the water, and tried to judge when he had let off sixty feet of line. In the end, he braked his reel at the captain's signal. They waited. The *Chief Powhatan* rode the swells. Doyle watched the sunlight play along the chrome frame of the lookout tower. Cap'n Pete got the first strike. His line waggled a bit, went taut, and spun off with a fast mechanical whirring that sounded to Doyle like the forgotten music of his youth.

"Listen to it sing!" Cap'n Pete called, and Doyle leaned down, scooped the first chum-ball off the pile, and tossed it into the water, then a second, which broke apart as it hit the surface. He didn't have to wait long for his own line to strike. He felt the first hesitant pressure, his spool unwound, and a thrill went through him and he was happy, in the moment, and everything else — his failed marriage, his current predicament, his uncertain future, was forgotten. He waited three short seconds and tightened the drag on the spinner and the fight was on.

"I think we've got a nice deep hole here," Cap'n Pete said. "Yes, I do. A nice deep hole full of kingfish mackerel."

Doyle fought the first fish for ten minutes, felt the rod pull and buck in his hands; the living force caught on his hook telegraphed vehemently up the wire from the depths. But he fought back too hard, the leader snapped, and in a second there was nothing at all and he realized suddenly that he was covered with sweat, the muscles in his shoulders coiled painfully tight. He remembered now why they called it *sportfishing*.

Cap'n Pete looked up from his fish, calm and easy as a man sitting out on his porch glider on Sunday night. "I tied you a beautiful line and you done lost it," he said.

Doyle wiped the sweat from his forehead and was angry with himself.

"But don't fret the ones that get away." Cap'n Pete grinned. "Just move on — it ain't life, it's only fishing." Doyle knew the old man was right and his anger broke immediately and he spooled up the broken line and started all over again.

6

Later that night Doyle lay in bed in the darkness in Uncle Buck's room visited with remorse and thinking of Spain. He closed his eyes and saw his wife in the spotless white kitchen of their apartment in Málaga some bleary Sunday morning, gourd of *maté* cupped in her hands, *bombilla* clenched between her teeth, tousled, wearing one of his old shirts; then came another image, unbidden, of her shirtless and spent in his arms after sex. But nostalgia was no better than poison to a man like Doyle. At last, with an ache in his gut, he forced himself up and switched on the light. Then he switched on Buck's small, ancient television set — it warmed up slowly and the picture twisted into view, color all blurry and exaggerated — and he flipped through the channels, finding only static except for the NBC affiliate from Pokamoke City: the hard, perfect face of Carolyn Morita on a late-night investigative news show, less like news and more like entertainment, gave way to a long, loud series of commercials.

Doyle hadn't seen American TV in years and he watched the commercials with perverse fascination: they were fast, loud, more numerous and less overtly manipulative than he remembered and seemed the product of an unfamiliar culture. The token black in commercials

of the 1970s had been joined by the token brown of uncertain ethnicity, the token Asian, the token whatever, until they weren't tokens at
all but smiling ironic representations of a new uni-ethnic America
that might be anywhere. The slick, waggish references were lost on
him; what product a few of the commercials were pushing he absolutely couldn't say. One commercial, which the station seemed to
air every few minutes, kept him guessing: a small, evil-looking man
in a green leprechaun suit shivered alone in a snowy rear-screen-
projection fake landscape until a leggy blonde woman in a bikini
placed a crown on his head; then the scene changed and the same leprechaun, crownless again, was seen sweating miserably into his green
suit in a rear-screen-projection blazing desert, camels lurking around
in the background. The bikini-clad blonde appeared again and set the
crown on his head and the scene faded to black as a disembodied
voice crowed, "Hot or cold the king can help!" But who was this king
and what was he selling? Was this humor or pathos?

Doyle switched off the television and lay back and thought of the
old men at the cafés in Málaga at that moment on the other side of the
world, their afternoon brandies in tiny finger-thin glasses nursed for
hours, copies of *El País* or *La Voz de Málaga* unfolded carefully across
a table in the sun; the humming sound like music the electric trollies
made along the wires as they passed.

7

The car was a glossy black Mercedes with tinted windows, one of the
swoopy new models with exaggerated oval headlights like cartoon
eyes and a small black Delaware tag set in a chrome link license plate
surround. Slough sat in the driver's seat looking fat and pink and uneasy. His red paisley lawyer tie flapped absurdly in a breeze from the
sea. Classical music wafted from the interior along with the bright
smell of new leather.

"As I say, I'll be happy to take you down there right now," the lawyer
said. "I'll wait and drive you back. It's no problem."

Doyle didn't say anything for a long minute. They'd towed his car again, this time from a yellow curb on Mermaid Avenue behind the high school where he'd gone to inquire about getting help for the golf course from the work–study program for juvenile offenders, and the bastards hadn't taken him to Toby's but out across the causeway to County Impound on the mainland.

"OK, why the rush?" Doyle said at last. "Why not next week?"

Slough let out a sigh. "I was contacted by Constable Smoot with what are, frankly, malicious and unfounded suspicions regarding certain vandalisms occurring on your property. My client absolutely wishes to allay any concerns you might have as soon as possible!"

"Forget the arson for a minute," Doyle said. "That sliced-up possum was a real work of genius."

"Possum?" Slough seemed confused

"Possum ass and a seasquab," Doyle said, grimly. "Ugliest thing you'd ever want to see."

Slough shook his head. "Honestly, I don't know what you're talking about."

"Neither do I," Doyle said. "Not yet."

Slough drove down the south side of the island on the Mosquito Bight Road, past Klingford's Rods, Reels, Bait, and Supply and past the Mosquito Bight Marina, the fishing tackle of the charter boats waving at the greying sky like so many insect antennae. After this, Doyle recognized nothing. Everything was new, built up from swampland in the last few years. A strip mall called Oknontocoke Center Plaza boasted among other attractions a Belgrano's Brick Oven Pizza, a Gap, a Thai restaurant called My Thai, a Blockbuster Video, and an unfinished Mega Food Warehouse. Past this eyesore, one new residential development gave way to the next: Spindrift Estates, Atlantic Terrace, Oyster Flats. The two dozen units of an unnamed gated condo had been cleverly fashioned to look hastily thrown together from driftwood. A yellow stucco apartment block, its three towers capped with onion domes, reminded Doyle of something out of *The Arabian Nights*.

"That's an assisted living complex," Slough said. "Mostly retirees from Baltimore and Philly. I'd hate to tell you what an apartment there costs per month."

"Then don't," Doyle said.

Slough pressed his lips together and pushed a button on the Blaupunkt to change the disc on the CD. It went from classical to sad Irish ballad in an instant; a gloomy-voiced Irish tenor rang out from six concealed speakers. Slough's thick features were taken with a faint shudder as he leaned forward and switched off the CD player.

"Listen to me, Doyle," he said. He dropped his unctuous manner and his words had an unpleasant edge to them. "Don't go fucking things up for yourself. Because you could really fuck things up here if you're not careful."

"Meaning?" Doyle said.

"Meaning listen to the man's offer with an open mind. He's sweetening the pot. He doesn't have to."

"Tell me something," Doyle said. "What are you getting out of all this?"

"I'm your legal counselor." Slough mugged an expression of professional concern. "Pirate Island is a serious liability to you, especially in light of recent fire damage. As it turns out, I'm also *his* legal counselor. My position in this matter is very straightforward — I arrange the sale, I collect commission and fees from him. I arrange the buy, I collect commission and fees from you. I win coming and going, really. For me, it's a no-brainer."

"And what does Whitcomb have to say about the obvious conflict of interest?"

Slough squirmed in the leather seat, adjusted his grip on the steering wheel. Doyle thought he saw a faint, self-satisfied smile ghost across the lawyer's heavy lips.

"Foy has been in the hospital since the day you came to our office in Wiccomac," Slough said. "He's not expected to pull through this time, I'm afraid."

"I'm real sorry to hear that," Doyle said, and he was.

"Yes, I'm absolutely crushed myself," Slough said, but his lip twitched at the words. He touched another button on the Blaupunkt, a CD slotted into the changer, and in the next second, the high sorrowful plaint of Verdi's *Requiem* filled the compartment.

8

The iguana stalked around the plate of chopped kale and watermelon, blinked a fathomless, ancient black eye, blinked again, then slowly cracked its mouth to reveal a tongue glistening with self-secreted adhesive. The tongue unrolled, stuck to a bit of watermelon, rolled back again, and the creature began to chew. Very slowly. Its scales showed an iridescent green at the moment, the color of jungle leaves in a rain storm, but that could change.

"You should see when the little guy gets pissed," Roach said, and reached into the terrarium to stroke the lizard's spines with his finger. "Fucking thing goes black as soot then starts whipping you with his tail. Beautiful, though, don't you think? *Iguanidae chalarodon*. Comes from Madagascar."

"I don't have all day, Roach," Doyle said. He stood sweating in the doorway to Roach Pompton's reptile room, a glass-walled terrarium that occupied one whole wedge of Roach's gaudy pink eight-sided mansion built on a private pier in an exclusive new development called Spofford's Landing at the southern tip of the island. Purple heat lamps in the reptile room burned purple light; a humidifier sent out a mist of warm steam. Huge glass tanks filled with a variety of lizards and snakes lined the walls.

"You're all business, dude." Roach flashed an idiotic smile. "Wham bam, thank you, ma'am, that's old killer Doyle for you. Well, shit, it's been twenty fucking years, right? Just give me another minute here. I've got to feed the little guys, OK?"

Doyle didn't say anything. He recognized this reptile-feeding as a kind of performance, pure Roach. I'm important, Roach was saying, I'm a big man now and I can make you wait — but actually he looked uncannily the same, as if he possessed a portrait somewhere that aged and grew corrupt in the place of his own blotchy flesh. He was still lean and uncomfortable as a teenager, all sinews and elbows with a scruffy goatee that looked glued to his chin and a head of greasy blond hair pulled back in a ponytail and the same guileless expression that Doyle knew concealed a special brand of malice. Even Roach's outfit was the same — a tie-dyed long-sleeve Grateful Dead T-shirt, a pair of ragged, patched jeans, and no shoes or socks. Roach's long bony feet reminded Doyle of the feet of tortured saints in paintings by El Greco he'd seen at the Prado in Madrid, but there, with his grimy toes, the saintliness began and ended.

Roach made a slow tour of the tanks, dispensing lizard chow, chopped vegetables, chatting nonsensically all the way around. When he reached the large terrarium that contained the boa constrictor, he took a cage of live white mice out of a perforated metal cabinet.

"I hate this part," Roach said, but he didn't look like he hated it at all. He reached into the cage, extracted one of the mice by the tail and dropped the terrified animal into the terrarium. The huge snake lifted its head, opened one lazy red eye. The mouse scurried nervously over the wood chips, pawed at the slick glass. The boa watched and would keep watching until the mouse tired of running — then, at the moment of least resistance, the reptile's big jaws would snap open and mouse would disappear into throaty pink oblivion.

Doyle couldn't abide this spectacle and stepped out into the hall away from the heat and the ugly creatures inside and forced himself to recall all the things about Roach he had purposely forgotten. This took him back to Wassateague High, 1976, the era of bong hits, Thai-stick, Columbian Red, when America went to hell in a handbasket, as Uncle Buck used to say, when the last traditions fell off into the dust and an entire generation of American youth dulled their passions in clouds of pot smoke, in heavy metal, pills, disco, all the rest of the squalor.

Roach was a freak in those days, a small-time dealer of mail-order speed and home-grown reefer cut with oregano — for this petty treachery and for his odd, chirpy demeanor, he was a greatly perse-cuted figure at Wassateague High. The football jocks who ruled the school — Ed Toby among them — hated Roach with a passion. They hounded him relentlessly in the halls between classes, in the parking lot before school and after, at the bus stop, in the bathrooms, every-where they could get their hands on him and get away with it. Hound-ing in this context meant beatings, humiliations, more beatings. Roach did not acquire his nickname as might be surmised from the grade-Z skunkweed he sold in nickel bags in furtive transactions in the breeze-way smoking zone during free period, but from the way he scurried down the halls like a cockroach in a desperate attempt to outrun his brutal schoolmates.

The unlikely partnership with Doyle stemmed from an episode in the cafeteria during lunch one afternoon junior year when, for no rea-son at all, Doyle had defended Roach against two football meatheads who had decided to knock the little bastard's lunch to the floor and wipe his face in it. The student body settled back to watch this crucifixion with apparent satisfaction: the spectacle of someone else's misfortune temporarily took their minds off the bad cafeteria food, the common miseries of adolescent life in a public high school, and no one lifted a finger to save Roach from his usual torment. All were disappointed when Doyle brought down the meatheads with two well-aimed blows and Roach scurried off to safety.

Afterwards, Doyle couldn't quite explain why he had come to vol-unteer himself for Roach's defense. Maybe he didn't like to see one skinny guy, no matter how obnoxious, get beaten up by a couple of big assholes. Or maybe he had something to prove to his former team-mates: he had just been kicked off varsity football for insubordina-tion — his crime, calling coach a creepy fucking prick — the man had a habit of malingering around the showers as the young athletes in his charge soaped up after games. Roach, of course, preferred the first explanation. Their friendship, one-sided at the beginning — hero worship on Roach's part answered by a sort of tolerant amusement from Doyle — changed over the course of the year as Roach's for-tunes suddenly improved. More by accident than design, Roach de-veloped a serious hashish connection in Delaware. From this single connection came others, and his network of drug contacts blossomed like an evil flower that he couldn't cultivate alone. He needed help, someone to ride shotgun, and was willing to pay a hundred dollars a run — a decent piece of change in those days. Doyle wouldn't have to deal with any rough characters or play bodyguard, Roach promised; it was just better to have someone along. The hundred dollars was for the whole illegality thing, they were running *contraband*, right?

The word "contraband" was sure to inspire any Doyle, from Finster to the current representative of the species; even honest old Buck had at one time run cigarettes out of North Carolina in defiance of the Revenue men. So Doyle plunged without hesitation into a criminal existence that now, years later, he could barely recall — a blur of dark country highways, palms sticky with dread; tense meetings with outlaw biker types in grim roadside taps halfway to Dover; then rolling home at three a.m., Roach's jacked-up Camaro billowing pot smoke from the Philly-sized spliff burning in the ashtray, empty beer cans clattering in back, Quaaludes stuffed in baggies behind the eight-track in the glove compartment, bricks of hash in a hole cut under the seat.

Doyle's life of drug-running lasted ten months. At the height of it, he and Roach ran three trips a week and once went as far as Vineland, New Jersey for two kees of blond Albanian hash. Roach made a lot of money, tens of thousands perhaps, but never gave Doyle more than his hundred dollars a run. Doyle being Doyle somehow never thought of asking for a salary increase. Meanwhile, his grades plummeted; he slept through his classes, flunked calculus and American history and none of it mattered. The thrills after dark more than made up for academic failure, speeding down the obscure back roads of the Eastern Shore, eight-track blasting the Grateful Dead, Bob Marley, Blue Oyster Cult, Bad Company, Foghat.

Then, a few months before graduation, Roach arranged his biggest deal yet for a quarter kee of cocaine; the score was supposed to go down in a dilapidated little farmer bar way out in the country somewhere up in Delaware. This cocaine was a first for Roach, an escalation; he was nervous from the beginning. Doyle remembered the rank fertilizer smell of the beet fields around the bar — called Lusso's Roadhouse — the faint, ominous lights of Christiana on the horizon.

They waited for two hours, a green glowing neon clock grinding from the wall over their heads and the place emptying out slowly and with each minute, Roach's anxiety worse and worse until it made a stink in the air stronger than the stink of the fertilizer outside. Finally a couple of hardcases showed up: a squat man with one pop eye and a .45 sticking out of his belt, and a jittery Irishman who carried a sawed-off shotgun beneath his raincoat. Popeye guarded the door while the Irishman pulled out his sawed-off and cleared the last remaining drunks from the bar.

"Just a precaution, darlin'." The Irishman winked at Roach. "His lordship's coming with the swag any minute now and the man don't like no innocent bystanders." Then he went behind the counter, poured himself a shot of whiskey and smiled in a horrible way through broken, brown teeth. Roach had never seen either of these men before. He tried to stay cool, pumping coins into the jukebox for courage. Doyle could still hear the ominous bassline of "House of the Rising Sun" — an unfortunate choice — crackling out of the old speakers, filling the place with its dire warning: ". . . Mama, tell your children, not to do the things I've done . . ."

This admonition had an unfortunate effect on Roach's nerves. He went white, stumbled off to the bathroom to vomit and didn't come out again. Ten minutes later, the Irishman kicked the door down and found Roach gone, the window jimmied open and the Camaro missing from the parking lot. After that things didn't go well for Doyle. They beat him up a bit, emptied his pockets, and drove him out past the beet fields to a wooded area where they tied him to a tree with a pair of greasy jumper cables.

"The long and short of it is we're coming back when we get our hands on your friend, boyo," the Irishman said. "Meantime, you think on how you'll be wantin' to die — like a man or like a dog."

Doyle tried not to think at all. After an hour of desperate wiggling, he managed to work the cables free and found his way out to the highway. He put up his thumb and got a ride, and another ride, and after ten hours of hitching and walking and hitching some more, with nothing at all to eat or drink and no money, found his way back home to Wassateague. His life of crime was over, his grades improved. He went off to Hampden-Sydney on his mother's money in the fall and had never spoken to Roach again. Until today.

9

Bulbous African masks and blunt, deadly-looking tribal weapons hung on the walls of the stark white living room. Roach muttered a few words into the intercom and after a while a black woman wrapped in kinte cloth from head to foot appeared from somewhere, pushing a drinks cart laden with bottles, mixers, and ice. She was beautiful and had smooth chocolate-brown skin and the aloof, vulnerable demeanor of a princess held hostage. She mixed Roach a vodka martini without being asked and Roach took it and sprawled back on a green leather easy chair.

Doyle asked for a bourbon on the rocks. The woman poured it for him disdainfully without once looking his way. Doyle squatted on an Ashanti stool, whose curved seat had once received the rumps of savage chieftains. The ceiling soared up fifty feet to the reinforced-glass floor of the fake widow's walk.

"Nomi, baby, this is my old pal Timmy Doyle," Roach said, just as the woman was about to turn away.

"Hello," Doyle said. "Name's Tim."

Nomi, eyes averted, made no acknowledgement. Roach patted the green leather at his left side and she came over and lowered herself gracefully to the wide cushion. Doyle sipped his bourbon and admired her sharp profile. Then Roach lifted one of his narrow bare feet, the soles calloused and nearly black.

"I think you forgot something, baby," he said, a familiar idiotic smile fixed to his face.

Without a word, Nomi went over to the drinks cart and unfolded a steaming white towel from a heated tray. She sat back down on the green leather chair, leaned forward, and began wiping the bottoms of Roach's dirty feet. He sighed contentedly and squirmed back into the leather as she drew the towel carefully between his toes. She performed this humbling service with an admirable dignity, eyes lowered, long eyelashes grazing her cheek. Doyle felt embarrassed on her behalf. Another one of Roach's goddamned performances.

"Go on, baby," Roach said gently. "Be nice now. Go ahead and say hello to good old Timmy Doyle."

Nomi paused, looked up, her black eyes expressionless. "Hello, Mr. Doyle," she said, in an accent that sounded like Jamaica; then she went back to washing Roach's feet.

"You should have seen Doyle here in the old days," Roach said, smiling again. "He was tough, let me tell you. Took on the whole football team once just to save my ass. Just like Mannix. Remember Mannix?"

The woman didn't say anything.

"Mannix was this tough-guy detective on TV way back when, used to beat the shit out of five or six bad guys at once. Old Doyle here could handle eight or ten, isn't that right, Doyle?"

"Why don't we cut the bullshit, Roach?" Doyle said, sharply. He had reached the end of his patience. "We're here to talk about the sale of Pirate Island, right?"

Roach rolled his eyes. "Aren't you even going to ask how I'm doing? We used to be friends, remember?"

"I see how you're doing," Doyle said. "You're living like a fucking maharajah. You hire chicks just to wash your feet. You mention the friend thing one more time, I'll be happy to ram my friendly foot up your ass."

Roach colored at this, but before he could speak, Nomi dropped the cloth, pushed herself off the leather chair, and went straight for Doyle. The woman's nails were painted bright red and sharp-looking. Doyle jumped aside, knocking the Ashanti stool to the floor. His bourbon went splashing across the white carpet. Laughing, Roach caught Nomi by the kinte cloth of her skirt and pulled her down on to his lap.

"Hey, calm down, baby," he said. "Breathe deep. That's right, breathe."

Nomi took a few deep breaths, and appeared to grow calmer. Roach gave her a consoling little pat. "Why don't you go get the fixings, OK?" he said.

Doyle stood watching from a safe distance beneath an owlish African mask large as a garbage can lid. Nomi flashed him a gesture he had never seen before, whose meaning nonetheless was clear, stalked across the room, and was gone. Doyle righted the Ashanti stool and sat back down.

"Sorry about that," Roach said, chuckling. "Nomi has some very fierce loyalties. But I don't flatter myself. Like most women, she's attracted to power. Lose the power, lose the woman. That's love for you."

"Yeah," Doyle said. "I hear you're on the Council of Burgesses these days."

Roach grinned. "Hard to believe, isn't it?"

"Very hard."

"Want to hear how I got on the Council of Burgesses?"

"No," Doyle said.

"Money," Roach whispered. "Lots of money."

"No kidding," Doyle said.

"And since we're old buddies in crime, I'll tell you straight out how I raised all the cash to begin with. You could say I made a couple of very astute business decisions — I got in on the ground floor of the crack thing in the eighties and got out just in time, about ten years later with almost three million stashed under my mattress."

"Crack?" Doyle said, incredulous.

"Don't believe everything you see on TV." Roach waved a yellow hand. "Crack's just like anything else. Pot, cocaine, booze, smack — they're all dopamine inhibitors, right? They all do the same thing, make you feel good when you want to feel good. Now, some people would have taken that kind of dough and put it right back up their nose. You know what I did?"

Doyle said he didn't want to know.

"I invested." Roach ignored him. "Real estate. Now I'm completely legit. You should have stuck with me, Doyle."

"I bet you would have found me a nice little cage right next to the boa constrictor," Doyle said. He was going to say more, but at that moment, Nomi returned, carrying a long ebony pipe inlaid with silver like an Indian peace pipe and a small square object wrapped like a candy bar in tinfoil.

"Ah," Roach said. "Miller time."

Nomi sat down on the arm of Roach's chair again without a glance in Doyle's direction and unwrapped the tinfoil to reveal a sticky black brick of Burmese tar heroin. Doyle smelled the sweet medicinal reek and turned away. He had never liked smoking dope of any kind, not even in the old dope-smoking days when he smoked just because everyone else did, because the rest of America was stoned and not being stoned made it difficult to seduce women of the era who insisted on the intercession of a joint before they would let you in their pants. Still, the stuff had always made him stupid in a way he didn't enjoy. But this was something else, another level, the sleek black reptile of the opium family. Nomi scraped a small pile of shavings off the brick with the sharp end of her fingernail, packed the pipe loosely, and handed it to Roach. He lit the bowl, took a deep breath, held the smoke in his lungs, and held the pipe out to Doyle.

Doyle shook his head.

"Of course not." Roach coughed, exhaling a cloud of thin white smoke like steam. "Not Mannix." He handed the pipe to Nomi, his face went slack, and he leaned his head back against the green leather. Nomi took a long, deep-lunged hit, exhaled in Doyle's direction and stared at him sullenly through the cloud.

"I don't like you, mon," she said, in an accent that sounded like Jamaican, her eyes already gone glassy. "You're a right miserable wanker."

"Fuck you too, sister," Doyle said.

"And these fucking clothes," she said, indicating Uncle Buck's gabardine pants and checked rayon shirt-jac that now, activated by Doyle's sweat, released the faint musty smell of a hot afternoon in 1955. "Who the fuck your tailor? Fucking Laverne and Shirley?"

"Guess what," Doyle said. "I hear all the street whores in Kingston wear kinte cloth outfits, just like the one you have on now."

"Fucking wanker!" she hissed, but the heroin had taken the punch out of her expletives.

"Kids, kids," Roach said, grinning lazily. Then he said, "So let's talk about Pirate Island. Doyle, you held out for a nice little while and that kind of perseverance ought to be worth something. I'll up the offer to two hundred and fifty thousand for that miserable pile of shit out there in the woods, OK?"

"Tell me one thing," Doyle said, trying to sound casual. "What do you want with the place, really?"

"What the hell," Roach said. "You'll find out eventually, right? They're making Royal Blue Cola again, did you know that?"

"Yes," Doyle said. "I had some. Awful pisswater."

Roach made an impatient gesture. "It's all about marketing — when are you going to learn that? We're going to turn your place into a Royal Blue Cola stand just like that old drive-in they used to have downtown. Remember that place? Ah, those big-titted roller-skating carhops in their tight uniforms!"

"Who's we?" Doyle said.

"We is yours truly and a group of investors behind Royal Blue Cola," Roach said. "It's that simple."

"OK," Doyle said. "So why all the subterfuge?"

"I figured if you knew I was involved . . ." Roach took a hit off the pipe and exhaled, ". . . you'd be a hardass about the sale. And I was right. Here you are, being a hardass."

"And the possum?" Doyle said, anger rising in his voice. "The arson attempt? I know it was you, Roach. Just the sort of stupid shenanigans you'd get up to. Did you really think I'd cave to that bullshit?"

Roach blinked through the thin, poisonous smoke. His eyes looked heavy-lidded and vacant, dopamine molecules diving into the abyss in his brain like a thousand suicides off a bridge into murky water. He stuttered out a denial, which was only half intelligible.

"You won't remember this," Doyle cut him off. "You're already too goddamned stoned for that. But listen anyway. You send anyone else out to Pirate Island to burn me out or trash the place or whatever — this time, I'll kill them. Then I'll come after you right here in your fucking palace and I'll break your fucking neck and feed you in pieces to your goddamned creepy snakes. Do you hear what I'm saying?"

Roach gave him a blank astonished look. "You came all the way out here just to lay on that bullshit?"

"You got it, old buddy," Doyle said, grinning. "No sale."

Baffled, Roach glanced over at Nomi, who no longer seemed to know what was going on. Then he waved his long yellow hand. "You're fucking nuts, Doyle," he said, pulling a cell phone out of his pocket. "I've got work to do, get the fuck out of my house."

Doyle turned and went through the front door, which he left standing wide open. Slough's Mercedes was gone from where it had been idling at the curb. He waited a while: no Mercedes. The bastard had left him high and dry with a long trek on foot back to Pirate Island.

10

Saturday. A bright afternoon, stiff wind kicking up white caps in the channel. The battered no-name development of rusty Airstream trailers and peeling two-room tourist cabins built in the 1930s sprawled in muted sun amid a thicket of weeds, scrub pines, and discarded appliances at the ass-end of town hard by the ramp to the causeway. Immune to the upscale transmutations afflicting the rest of the island, this neglected neighborhood had long ago become a little piece of Redneck America, part of the shadow country of poverty, prejudice, and low-down toughness that exists in every state in the Union but is marked on no maps.

Doyle parked the Cadillac in front of a flame-pink cabin which had sprouted a CozyLand mobile home like a monstrous appendage where the back porch used to be. A shredded old couch in the yard looked like it had become a nest for possums. The rusty tank and coils of an unidentifiable machine grew weeds of its own in the weeds. He stepped up to the front porch through the tall, uncut grass and rang an old electric bell that somehow still worked and kept ringing, and presently a huge woman in a voluminous yellow housecoat came to the screen door, floorboards creaking beneath her heavy tread. Like Maggie, she was tall, broad-shouldered and bleached blonde, but she beat Maggie's weight by at least a hundred pounds. Her sagging jowls spoke of too much ham and potatoes, scrapple fried in butter and drenched in molasses, rhubarb pie, beer; her knowing jade eyes hinted at other indulgences.

"Who are you, the fucking Good Humor man?" she said in a loud, angry voice, then she smiled to show it was a joke.

"Hello, Traci," Doyle said. "How you been?"

"I been good," Traci said. "Only there's a lot more of me lately, as you can see."

"More to love," Doyle said, catching a flash of a lost Saturday night after a football game the last year Nixon's dark spirit haunted the White House, this same woman in the passenger seat of Uncle Buck's old Ford Woody 125 pounds leaner but so hungry even then, twisting down below the big Bakelite steering wheel to take his erection into her mouth.

"You might see it that way," Traci said, "but other folks don't. I'm starting at Weight Watchers in the fall, I swear it."

"Fuck 'em," Doyle shrugged.

"That's just it," Traci said, "I'd like to," and she laughed, a deep rumbling sound that came up like a volcanic eruption from beneath her massive breasts. Then she stopped laughing and looked Doyle in the eyes. "Hear you been running into trouble lately," she said.

"Nothing I can't handle," Doyle said, frowning. He didn't feel like talking about it. "Is he in?"

Traci rolled her eyes. "More or less," she said.

"Didn't his parole officer call to say I was coming?"

Traci shrugged her big shoulders, sending off a ripple effect that ended at her toes. "No one tells old Mom anything," she said. "You better ask him yourself."

Doyle followed her inside. The place was a shambles of dirty dishes, unwashed clothes, back issues of women's magazines full of advice about how to be financially independent and have multiple orgasms. But a side table tangled with out-of-control plants in pretty majolica pots and a framed Norman Rockwell print gave Doyle the impression that once she had tried to make a home out of the place.

"I guess I stopped cleaning after Beau up and left," Traci said, following Doyle's gaze. "He took off with some shiny little bitch from Louisiana." She led Doyle through the living room and squalid kitchen — more dishes piled in the sink and garbage overflowing — and into the CozyLand trailer, which seemed to have been affixed to the back with soggy cardboard and duct tape. Doyle heard sounds of electronic explosions coming from down the narrow hall.

"That's his room," Traci said, waving towards a door at the back of the trailer. "Be careful, he bites."

Doyle found a teenager squatting in his underwear an inch away from a new, wide-screen color TV on which a violent cartoon video game blasted away. Monsters kept climbing over a mound of dead bodies and a muscular Marine in torn fatigues kept blowing them to bloody pieces with an out-of-proportion assault rifle. On the veneered plywood wall over the kid's bed hung a poster for a rock-and-roll band Doyle had never heard of called Mop the Moose and a centerfold from one of the more graphic skin magazines showing two naked, big-haired young women fiddling with each other, the pink flesh of their pudenda spread open with eager fingers. Metal shelving lining the opposite wall was full of CDs and expensive electronic equipment.

"Hey, Harold!" Doyle called from the doorway, but Harold didn't respond. He was a wiry kid, about sixteen, with a shock of black hair like a Mohawk rising off the top of his head; his bare arms showed ropy muscles; his pale, narrow face was taken with a vengeful, determined look in the pulsing video light. Doyle called again; the kid still didn't respond. A monster exploded in a puddle of bloody organs on the screen. This time, Doyle stepped into the room, reached down, and yanked a cluster of black electrical cords from a power strip along the wall. The TV screen went blank in mid-blast.

"What the fuck?" Harold jumped up, swinging. Doyle dodged the trajectory of the kid's bony fists, managed to grab a wrist, spun him around, and got him in a wrestling hold with an elbow crooked around the kid's throat. He squeezed just a little. The kid hung there, gasping, toes dangling an inch off the ground.

"Motherfucker! Put me down!" he squeaked.

"By authority of your parole officer, I am your new employer," Doyle said into his ear. "So that's 'Mr. Doyle, please put me down.' I get respect or you get your neck broken."

Harold struggled, clawing at Doyle's arm; Doyle squeezed harder and the kid went limp.

"Put me down, Mr. Doyle-motherfucker," he squeaked out, still defiant.

Doyle threw the kid down on the bed; the kid bounced right up, fists cocked again, but Doyle held up a hand. "Try it again, and I'll really knock your lights out."

Harold saw Doyle was serious; he moved back against the wall, rubbing his throat. "Almost choked me, motherfuck —"

"Ah-ah!" Doyle shook his head. "Remember — Mr. Doyle."

The kid said nothing, pipe bombs in his eyes.

"You know Pirate Island?" Doyle said after a beat.

Harold hesitated. "The goofy-golf course?"

"That's the one."

"I seen it," Harold said, sullenly.

"Don't you play goofy golf?" Doyle said hopefully. "In the summer?"

Harold shook his head. "That's for fags and tourists."

"You don't know what you're missing." Doyle attempted a smile. "Nothing like a good game of goofy golf on a summer night."

"You're really weird," Harold said.

Doyle sighed. "You're working for me now, kid," he said. "We're going to fix the place up. Together. You'll need —"

"No fucking way!" Harold interrupted, hotly. "I got a summer job already."

"A criminal enterprise is not a job," Doyle said. "You can't sell beer on the beach anymore. First, it's illegal for a minor to possess beer.

Second, it's against the law to sell beer on the beach, period. They arrested you twice already. One more time, you're going up to the juvenile hall in Ainsley where the inmates will rape your tender white ass with broom handles and whatever else they can get their hands on and enjoy every minute of it. Got that?"

Harold's eyes went slightly out of focus contemplating this painful violation.

"You start just as soon as the paperwork goes through," Doyle said. "I'm already running out of time to open for June. After school and we work until it's too dark to see. Maggie will feed you dinner. When school's out in May, you come to work at eight, knock off at six. When we're done fixing up the place, you work in the guardhouse handing out clubs, dealing with the customers with a smile on your face. Every evening except Monday. Understood?"

Harold didn't seem to be listening; Doyle couldn't resist one small jab.

"And by the way," he said, with a malicious grin, "you're on the payroll at minimum wage." Then he stepped out and shut the door firmly.

The kid's outraged curses penetrated the thin plywood like invisible projectiles from the pixel Marine's video-game assault rifle, followed Doyle down the hall through the filthy kitchen and living room, back out the open door, across the porch, into the Cadillac, and down the street.

11

Doyle and Toby slouched on wobbly chrome stools at the bar at Cap'n Pete's Oyster Shack in the ramshackle bit of old amusement park at Toquonque Beach called by locals the Toquonque Boardwalk. Rain and cold had blown in from the South Atlantic and the pair huddled in their coats, collars turned up, as behind the bar Cap'n Pete pulled out a bottle of Old Overholt and three lowball glasses and poured out three double shots.

The oyster shack, open to the elements on all sides, was little more than a tin roof raised over an ancient, weathered bar, fantastically carved, that had once been the pride of the gentleman's lounge at the old Atlantic Beach Hotel, before it blew down in Hurricane Hattie back in '26. Cap'n Pete shared the boardwalk with several other concessions, all on the seedy side — a tattoo parlor patronized by bikers, a storefront fortune-telling scam set up by a Melungeon woman from North Carolina who pretended to be a gypsy; a small, rattling ferris wheel, recently condemned by the county as unsafe. And at the landward end, complete with its own parking lot, a fried-fish place that had gone Mexican and changed its name from the Fisherman's Catch to El Bodega del Mar. Tonight only the Mexican restaurant and Cap'n Pete's showed their lights to the cold drizzle. The decommissioned ferris wheel creaked restlessly in the wind; the cry of an unnamed animal echoed eerily across the still water.

"Nothing like a good shot of rye for what ails you." Toby shivered and heaved his big elbows up and brought the Old Overholt to his lips. "Warms you good on a night like this."

"Rye is not my drink," Doyle insisted, but no one was listening. "Here's to the oysters, Cap'n Pete."

"And the men that drudge 'em," Toby said.

"*Olé,*" Doyle said, and all three emptied their glasses in one long swallow.

"Now for the main course." Cap'n Pete went behind the plywood partition at the back of the bar. Toby took up the bottle of rye, filled his own glass again, then filled Doyle's glass without asking.

"No, thanks," Doyle said, pushing the glass away. "Getting ready to do a piece of work on the golf course. Up at six tomorrow. Up at six every morning till June."

Toby wagged his big head disdainfully. "If Alexander — so Arrian tells us — conquered the kingdom of the Medes whilst drunk, a campaign that lasted some months, surely you can do an itty-bit of painting and scraping on an itty-bitty goofy-golf course slightly hungover?"

"Hard to argue with a classical education." Doyle grinned. And he took the glass and drank, and was feeling numb around the edges when Cap'n Pete came out of the back with a big tray of six-dozen shucked large Wassateague oysters resting on a bed of shaved ice. On the side was a basket of oyster crackers, a half-dozen lemon wedges, a bowl of fresh hot horseradish, a tin of Old Bay seasoning, and a bottle of ketchup. "Eat up, gents," he said. "These are some of the nicest oysters we've seen in a long while."

Cap'n Pete mixed the horseradish and ketchup, squeezed a lemon wedge into the mixture, and added a dash of Old Bay, and the men ate hungrily and washed the oysters down with bottles of cold homebrew and were sated and pleasantly drunk, and Toby let out a loud, obnoxious belch. "That says about all I got to say," he grunted. "Now, if you please, old man, let's get on with the business of the hour."

"I thought the business of the hour was eating oysters and drinking beer," Doyle said.

"That's the food-and-drink portion of the evening's entertainment," Toby said. "This here's the firearms part." Then, to Cap'n Pete: "Go ahead."

Cap'n Pete nodded and pulled a flat wooden case from under the bar and tapped its glossy lid. The case was made of beautifully polished cherrywood and fitted with shiny brass hinges and a lock that gleamed like gold. He unlocked the box with a small key and opened the lid, revealing a massive nineteenth-century revolver nestled inside, all blued gleaming steel, its grip of polished horn, its octagonal barrel at least ten inches long. The firing accessories sat snugged into separate velvet-lined compartments: a brass powder flask embossed with an American eagle, a round carton labeled Ely's Caps, a dozen lead balls, a neat pile of white cotton revolver wadding, a bullet mold like a pair of pliers.

"Booze and guns." Doyle shook his head.

"Don't worry, old brother," Toby said. "This isn't just any Saturday night special here." Eyes gleaming, he hefted the revolver out of the case and sighted along the barrel at the smoky darkness in the peeling mirror over the bar. "You're looking at the famous 1847 Whitneyville-Walker Colt Dragoon, issued to the Texas Rangers during the Mexican War by Samuel Colt himself."

"Or at least a reasonable facsimile thereof," Cap'n Pete added. "Got a real one in the collection. Damn thing's worth more than the *Chief Powhatan*. This one here's just for fun. It's a firing replica, made in Italy by Italians."

"Try it on for size." Toby handed the big revolver to Doyle, who almost dropped it on the bar.

"How much does this damn thing weigh?" Doyle said.

"Four and a half pounds." Toby grinned. "Heaviest revolver ever made .44 caliber hand cannon. Go boom, make big hole."

Cap'n Pete took the gun from Doyle, pointed the muzzle at the floor and cocked the hammer and the chamber aligned itself to the bore with a precise, oily click. He held the cylinder to his ear and repeated the action. "Sounds good," he said.

"What kind of powder you using?" Toby said.

"FFV 6," Cap'n Pete said. "Just like it says in the book. Only smokeless."

"Smokeless?" Toby frowned.

"That's right," Cap'n Pete said. "I'm getting old. Smoke makes me cough. Anyway, even smokeless makes plenty smoke."

Toby nodded. "What charge?"

"Sixteen grains."

From here, the conversation deteriorated into the arcane jargon of black-powder-gun collectors. Doyle heard terms like rifling, trajectory, crossfire, and stopped listening. The wind picked up and rustled through the cattails; the rain had abated to a thin drizzle. The sky was utterly black without a trace of stars or moon. Beyond the marsh and the dunes, the Atlantic, lightless at this hour, whispered its secrets to the night. Down at the other end of the boardwalk, the double doors of the Bodega del Mar pushed open suddenly and two men dressed in dark clothing stepped out into the drizzle.

Now, Cap'n Pete was loading the revolver on the bar. He took the copper percussion caps out of their carton and pressed them against the nipples on the cylinder. He took the powder flask and measured out powder into the chambers, inserted the revolver wads, pressed the lead balls home firmly with the loading lever. Then he laid the revolver, capped and loaded and ready to fire, carefully on the bar.

"First, one last little taste of rye," he said. "Second, we step out back and shoot at some fish." And he leaned down to retrieve a second fifth of Old Overholt from the Royal Blue Cola cooler.

"Count me out . . ." Doyle began, but he stopped himself. In the phantom reflections at the back of old mirror, he saw the two men from the Bodega coming fast towards the oyster shack. They quickened their pace to a trot, then stopped abruptly a few feet away in the darkness, just beyond the awning. One of them pulled something black and shiny from the inside pocket of his jacket.

"Freeze, ya fucking clowns," he said, in a heavy accent that sounded to Doyle like Irish — but low-class, hardass Irish.

Doyle froze.

"All right, gents, hands on the bar where we can see them," the other one said, his voice soft, almost weary. "Hurry up, please." Also Irish, but a touch more middle class.

Cap'n Pete put his gnarled hands on the bar, and Doyle saw they were trembling against the dark wood. The old man's face showed no expression at all. Toby looked green; his breath came in quick unsteady rasps. "I think I'm going to be sick," he whispered.

"Stow it, ya fat shyte," the hardass Irishman said. "Now, which one of you miserable fucks is Doyle?"

Doyle watched the two men in the mirror; the hardass Irishman had a narrow, pointed chin, circles under his eyes, pale, unhealthy skin. The gun in his hand a 9mm, probably a Glock, square and deadly-looking.

"Come, gentlemen, be reasonable now," the soft Irishman said. "We don't want to have to whack all of you. It's just Doyle we want."

Cap'n Pete stiffened and tiny beads of sweat broke out on his forehead. Toby let out a little moan of fear. Oddly, Doyle felt nothing. And the rye he had drunk was gone from his bloodstream, replaced by adrenalin. He glanced down and saw the Walker Colt lying capped and loaded, its butt less than three inches from the ends of his fingers. Then, somehow, the big gun was in one hand and he spun around and fanned back on the hammer with the other, just as if he'd been doing it that way all his life. The Colt jumped and spit fire, the explosion came loud as a cannon.

The hardass Irishman went down hard on the wet boards and skidded on the seat of his pants a few feet and slumped over. A cloud of blue sulphurous smoke billowed into the drizzle. Doyle quickly cocked the hammer again and levelled the long barrel at the man's accomplice.

"Do you want it too?" he said, in a steely voice that didn't sound like his own.

The soft Irishman stood there wide-eyed, speechless.

"What?" Doyle said. "I didn't hear you."

"No," he croaked. "I'll be off now, yer honor, if yer honor pleases."

"Excellent," Doyle said, "Then get your hands in the air and be off the fuck out of here."

The man raised his hands, backing away slowly. When he had gotten far enough, he turned around and ran. As the last of his footsteps died away down the pier, the tension broke. Cap'n Pete sagged against the Royal Blue Cola cooler, muttering a prayer to himself. Toby slammed the bar with his fist. "Goddamned!" he shouted. "I'll be goddamned!"

Doyle carefully released the hammer and set the Colt on the bar. His hands were shaking; his stomach unclenched and began to churn wildly. "Is the guy . . . I mean . . ." he whispered. "Go and see."

Toby leaped up and went over to where the Irishman lay crumpled and bleeding. He prodded the man's leg with the end of his boot, knelt down. "You got him good, all right," he said, jumping back quickly. "You're fucking Wild Bill Hickock! I think the motherfucker's dead!"

12

Later, after the interrogation under the lights in the constable's office, after witnesses' statements and the waiting, Doyle's gut twisting with the thought he might have killed another human being, he was too shaky and bilious to drive home. How had he done what he had done? How had he taken a gun in his hand and . . . He couldn't finish the thought. He didn't believe in guns, he believed in a world without the staccato report of gunfire, sincerely wished guns were outlawed everywhere. Especially tonight, especially here in Wassateague. The shooting was clearly self-defense — even the constable agreed — but knowing this didn't stop the horror, didn't expunge the image of the man lying there, still and white and his life's blood draining into the dark wood of the boardwalk.

For a while longer, until just before dawn, Doyle sat shivering and unable to move in the driver's seat of the Cadillac pulled over in deep shadows beneath the magnolia tree in the lot behind the public library. Then, radio tuned to a redneck religious station — *Are you saved, brothers? Amen! Have you taken Jesus into your soul? I say*

Amen! — he closed his eyes and willed himself to forget the terrible gunfight, and with an act of will conjured happier days:

Now, in his mind's eye, he steps out from behind the bar and on to the terrace of El Rey Alfonso on some glittering, balmy evening during the summer high season in Málaga. There he goes, mixing with the well-heeled Málaguenos; they are drinking, laughing, eating, as he wends his way from table to table, practiced smile fixed to his face like a comfortable mask. He sees the gleam of heavy gold jewelry against tanned skin; a gold watch worth six-months' salary ticking inaudibly from a woman's supple wrist; a silk scarf tied over a smooth shoulder just so. The sleek black hair of both sexes reflects the colored lights hanging in rows from the grape trellis overhead. He is on stage, playing the part of the solicitous restaurateur — a role learned gesture for gesture beneath Flor's patient tutelage. He offers tapas suggestions at one table, insists on a cocktail on the house at another, tells a political joke currently making the rounds, ventures an opinion on the prospects for a Basque ceasefire — all rendered in his charmingly accented Castillian.

Meanwhile, behind the steamy window of the display kitchen, Flor stands regal and beautifully calm in ordinary chef's whites in the midst of the hectic action. The frantic sous-chef, the trembling pastry chef, the waiters, the wine steward are like children lost in the woods compared to her; they seem about to burst into tears. Then, quite by accident, Flor's eyes meet Doyle's through the glass and she smiles as if at a secret they both share. Folding napkins later at four a.m., they will murmur softly of the evening behind them, of inconsequential matters; hip to hip at the cash register, the last waiter gone, they will add up the receipts. And they will stroll at dawn down the deserted *paseo,* leaning into each other, back to the apartment and bed where, too exhausted for sex, they will fall asleep in each other's arms.

part three

DOYLE AND CIRCE

AUGUSTUS DOYLE, *a lazy, haphazard fellow who at this time had no other occupation in life than to squander his substance in barrooms drinking sourmash juleps and playing poker and narrating formidable lies concerning his exploits on the famous march from Vera Cruz to the Halls of Montezuma with General Scott's Army — actually, he had been a buck private cook in the Quartermaster Corps, ambling along at the rear of the advance in a jangling mule-drawn wagon full of cast-iron pots and sacks of beans and barrels of flour, and had only fired at the Mexicans once or twice and from a safe distance — found himself in the gentlemen's lounge of the old St. Hubert Hotel on Chartres Street in New Orleans on the hot night of 2 August 1851 in very slick company and down to his last silver dollar.*

Augustus wagered this sacred coin on a pair of aces and eights and was beaten out by a smooth-talking Creole planter with a mouthful of gold teeth and a straight flush. The smooth-talking Creole planter added Augustus's last dollar to his growing hoard of paper dixies and silver and gold coins on the other side of the felt-covered table, and did it in such an unctuous manner that Augustus determined to persevere against the man, no matter the cost. On subsequent hands, he wagered his six shirt studs, and the cufflinks made from rather pretty freshwater pearls, and the small ebony-handled pistol he kept in his boot and then his boots themselves and lost them all.

The management of the St. Hubert Hotel lost no time in turning Augustus out into the street in his stockinged feet, cuffs dangling, shirt hanging open, because it was their policy not to allow indecently dressed gentlemen to linger in the gentlemen's lounge, and he wandered around the Vieux Carré in a blue funk, impotently ogling the octoroon women in their yellow flounces and feathers talking and smoking cigarillos and looking down on him pitilessly from the upstairs galleries of the fancy French sporting houses.

Ten years before this unfortunate turn of events, upon taking leave of his mother, brothers, and sisters in Wassateague Island, Virginia — his father even at that distant date long dead of scurvy and drink — Augustus had conceived in his heart the youthful ambition that a sunny temperament held as the certain result of his wanderings: the acquisition of a Roman Catholic wife. Such a woman was not to be found on Wassateague Island where there were no Roman Catholics to speak of, except for the Doyles, and so Augustus had gone into the world in search of a female co-religionist as generations of Doyles had done before him. Alas, the acquisition of a wife of any denomination, as has been observed by many ill-starred young men, first requires an adequate fortune, and Augustus had never been able to keep money in his pocket for long — but this was the absolute bottom: for the first time since commencing upon his life of diversion and adventure, he was completely destitute, without a single penny; had nothing to eat for dinner, no place to sleep that night, and in the morning no prospects for breakfast or employment of any kind.

Consumed by a bitter sort of nostalgia, Augustus considered returning to the miserable island of his birth, a hopeless bachelor, to join his brothers in the oyster-drudging trade, which he dearly hated — indeed, had he the price of a fourth-class berth on the Baltimore Packet, history might have heard no more of him — but as a pauper he continued his destitute and aimless ramble, and around midnight came to a place very much like despair, which happened to be the corner of Decatur and Ursuline hard by the levee. There, by the light of a dozen flickering torches, the sidewheeler Pampero was loading men and supplies for the secret invasion of Cuba in the morning.

Being an intimate of most of the barrooms in New Orleans, Augustus had heard all about the proposed secret invasion, for men love nothing better than to talk of wars past and present while imbibing their favorite potations, and he knew that the Cuban rebel, General Narcisco Lopez, had been recruiting volunteers for a small army of filibusters with the intention of wresting Cuba from the Spanish Crown. General Lopez had proposed to land his filibusters somewhere in the thickly foliated and remote western quadrant of the island, there win a couple of swift victories against unprepared provincial troops and, subsequent to these actions, with the support of the oppressed Cuban people who would flock to his victorious banner, lead a much-expanded army of liberation on to Havana. This strategy, all the drinkers of New Orleans agreed, however noble, audacious, and secret, had little likelihood of actual success.

Augustus stood brooding in the shadows of a cotton warehouse for a good half-hour, listening to the scratching of the rats within and watching the brawny riverfront Negroes rolling barrels and hefting military supplies up the gangplank into the hold of the sidewheeler, his thoughts in turmoil. Then he saw General Narcisco Lopez himself emerge on deck in the company of several of his senior officers, all of them puffing on fat Cuban cigars. The general descended alone to the levee to direct the efforts of the Negroes — or, at least, to appear to be doing so, for the Negroes were paying no mind to his exhortations. Still, he cut a splendid figure in his spotless white uniform, a bright red sash wrapped around his middle. A single gold star woven into the collar of his tunic was the sole apparent indicator of rank, his only side-arm a telescope in a red leather case slung over his shoulder. The man's hair showed salt-and-pepper grey — he was of an indeterminate age on the far side of sixty; nonetheless he appeared robust and healthy, full of youthful vigor and reasonably worthy of a man's loyalty.

It was at this point, as the general issued ignored orders in all his martial dignity, that Augustus Doyle hit upon a bold course of action. He rolled his undone sleeves halfway up his arms to strike the appearance of a man who had just torn himself away from some important task, tucked in his studless shirtfront as best he could, pulled up his socks, and stepped out of the shadows and made straight for the general on the levee. An eager young officer — an American with long yellow hair, wearing a fashionably tailored blue uniform — drew a Colt repeater and hurried down the gangplank to intercept Augustus's approach, but the latter stopped a few paces away and bowed respectfully and General Lopez held up a restraining hand.

"General Lopez, if I may have the honor of a moment of your time," Augustus Doyle said.

The general smiled politely and nodded.

"Sir, it has come to my understanding that you are seeking veterans of the late hostilities with Mexico to fill out the ranks of your valiant force. I am one such veteran and ardently desire the freedom of Cuba from her oppressors, though undoubtedly not as ardently as you who are a native of the place and have experienced the damnable oppression of the Spanish firsthand. However, I would willingly serve beneath your standard and give you the benefit of my experience in the victorious army of General Scott for the *inconsequential consideration of a pair of shoes and one or two meals a day, even if those meals should consist of nothing more than hardtack and navy beans."*

Puffing on his cigar, General Lopez clasped his hands behind his back in an authoritative manner and looked Augustus Doyle up and down, pausing on his stockinged feet and studless shirt front. "What rank you during the Santa Anna war?" the general asked, though the cigar in his mouth and his thick accent made him difficult to understand.

"I was a cook, sir, I will not tell a lie," Augustus said, after a puzzled second. "But I saw not a little action."

The general smiled broadly at this, showing a set of healthy horse-teeth. He took the cheroot out of his mouth, pushed it between Augustus's lips, and put a fatherly arm around his shoulder. "You know thees Napoleon, l'Empereur, eh?"

"Not personally, sir," Augustus said, happily discovering that the general's cigar was very good indeed.

"L'Empereur, he say an army travel on his belly. You know what this mean?"

Augustus wasn't sure, but he said he did.

"El liberation de Cuba," the general said, fierce suddenly, "thees also need the cooks!" And he drew himself up and saluted. Augustus put his stockinged feet together and saluted back, and the young officer with the drawn Colt — a certain Colonel Crittenden of Kentucky, as it turned out — holstered his weapon, stepped forward, shook Augustus's hand warmly, and led him aboard, where he was issued an old squirrel rifle, a blue blouse of cheap, scratchy wool, a pair of stiff marching boots, and four thousand dollars in newly printed script, redeemable for land or cash on the day Havana was taken. And this is how Augustus Doyle enlisted for the invasion of Cuba with Lopez and his filibusters.

The next morning, sailors aboard the Pampero *cast the tarry mooring lines to an enthusiastic crowd on the levee, in which Augustus thought he saw several of the beautiful octoroon women who had frowned down upon him from their unassailable galleries during his gloomy wanderings the night before. Now the women threw flowers to the deck and high-hatted sporting gentlemen shouted bellicose slogans and a band played the "Cuban Polka," recently composed by the famous Gottschalk for the occasion, and* the ship's boilers built up the requisite head of steam and the Pampero heaved itself out into mid-channel.

At the stern rail in his scratchy blue shirt and uncomfortable boots, Augustus watched the busy crescent of the city disappear around the bend and heard the music growing faint on the wind. Suddenly, he felt a sharp pang of remorse over his precipitous decision to join this mad attempt on Cuba, and he knew in his heart that this time his adventures would take him far beyond the reach of any decision to return to the happy, carefree life he had known. He had never desired to see the foreign parts of the globe, the United States was world enough for him, but now it was too late. Refusing for melancholy's sake to mingle with his new comrades, Augustus stayed at the rail for some hours, watching the rich bottom land slide by and the dark backs of slaves laboring in the cotton fields and the great white-columned plantation houses shining in the sun like distant palaces, until at dusk, the Pampero slipped into the Gulf of Mexico, its great wheels churning brown water to brackish to salt blue.

After a few days of this pleasant paddling, the filibusters reached Key West, where a few more men came aboard. Then, at dawn, the Pampero was towed across the bar and turned south towards Cuba, almost visible not a hundred miles distant just the other side of the horizon. Broken out of his initial gloom by the bracing sea air, Augustus had come to know the men of General Lopez's motley little invasion force: 450 volunteers had crammed themselves into the ship — 125 of them experienced Indian fighters of the Kentucky Battalion of Volunteers led by Colonel Crittenden, the remainder evenly divided between the disappointed and somewhat malnourished refugees from various failed European revolutions and the good-for-nothing flatboat ruffians who had wandered down the Mississippi to New Orleans from unsettled regions of the Plains with nothing better than destruction in mind. All of these were under the immediate command of a general staff of Hungarian officers, who had fought with the doomed hero Kossuth against the Austrians and the Russians. The Hungarians made impressive and disciplined soldiers — never drunken or insubordinate, colorful uniforms always neatly arranged — their chief drawback being that they spoke only Hungarian so could not issue a simple order and have it understood.

Augustus, quick with a humorous tale and quicker to join in any game of chance presented to him, soon made a number of friends — among them, the young, yellow-haired, pistol-ready Colonel Crittenden. Crittenden was a graduate of the military academy at West Point and a nephew of the former governor of Kentucky, an aristocratic young man who proved most unaristocratic in his manners, playing cards with the men for the Cuban script they had been issued, chewing plug tobacco, and swearing as good as any one of his rough-hewn Kentucky volunteers. Then there were Hiram Prescott and Jeremiah Bingley, both backwoodsmen who had cut their teeth fighting bears and Choctaw Indians in the unforgiving mountains of Tennessee, and a willowy, unintelligible Hungarian gentleman, Captain Szatzky, who seemed to possess the only pair of dice aboard.

As the Pampero paddled its way towards the lush Cuban shore, General Lopez, sequestered in his stateroom for the better part of the voyage, came out in his splendid white uniform to circulate on deck. He was a personage of considerable accomplishments, and to buoy the fighting spirit of the men during these last tedious hours, he went about practicing upon them the latest European science of phrenology — which is to say he examined, with a womanish delicacy of touch, the nodes and gullies of their skulls in an effort to determine what sort of men they were. By this mysterious process, he claimed to be able to reveal those secret details of character and personal history which their physiognomies otherwise obscured. To most, he spoke very prettily of bravery and fortitude and honor; others he warned against certain tendencies towards drink or obesity, and to a few he maintained that their skulls were in some way clairvoyant. The uneven landscape that revealed itself to his touch proclaimed, he said, their inevitable fate.

When Augustus's turn came, the general spent no little time with his pale fingers buried in the former's greasy hair, an examination that Augustus found curiously relaxing.

"Interesting head you have today," the general said. "Very thick."

"Thank you, General," Augustus said.

"You enjoy playing of cards and the women too much," the general said, clucking through his teeth.

Augustus allowed that this might be true.

"For a cook, you are very bad."

Augustus allowed that this also might be true. Beans stewed with blackstrap molassas and pork fat was just about the only dish he knew how to make.

"Your people, they find the living on the sea. Correct?"

Augustus looked up, amazed. "Oysters," he said. "My brothers and my father and grandfather and his father too, all the way back before the first war with the English they drudge oysters."

"Ah," the general said, unsurprised, and pushed Augustus's head down again. Then, his fingers stopped their rovings and stiffened and he lifted them all at once from Augustus's scalp and stepped back. "I am sorry, my poor cook," he said.

"What is it, General?" Augustus said, a chill going up his spine.

The general put a paternal hand upon his shoulder and leaned close. "No one must have knowing the hour of death," he said, in a sad whisper. "And so I will no say more except to say you must try to meet it like a soldier and not a cook." Then he turned away and examined the next man, a shaggy-headed Pole who had maintained an impenetrable silence since the beginning of the expedition on account of the fact that he spoke none of the languages of anyone aboard.

Augustus Doyle was cast into an immediate gloom by the general's phrenological examination, which seemed to him a sentence of death, and might have thrown himself into the blue Caribbean waters churning beneath the wheels to hasten its inevitable arrival, had not a series of absurd misfortunes immediately overtaken the filibusters and rendered suicide superfluous.

The island of Cuba appearing on the horizon off the port bow did not look like anyone aboard the Pampero *expected it to look. The men cheered, then they stopped cheering all at once when they realized their predicament. This was not in fact the desolate region of coast General Lopez had selected for his invasion, but the white tower of Moro Castle and the spires and crenelations of San Cristobal de la Habana itself. The* Pampero *wheeled into the wind at this disturbing sight, too late — three heavily armed frigates gave immediate chase from Havana Harbor, and only the contrary winds and absence of steam-powered vessels in the Cuban navy allowed the filibusters to escape capture. Still, the damage had been done; the whole island was now alerted to the imminent invasion.*

The Pampero *paddled east along the coast; undaunted, the general was determined to reach his chosen beachhead. The sun sank red over the green island, silver fish leaped in and out of the waves. The men sang patriotic songs to keep their courage up. Then, around ten thirty that night, the vessel's portside wheel struck a coral reef just east of Bahia Honda and*

General Lopez was forced to establish his beachhead on this unknown shore. Scouts were sent inland and managed to locate the muddy village of Las Posas ten miles distant, which, situated atop a slight eminence, seemed to offer an easily defensible position.

But while landing supplies on the beach, the men were harried by the musket fire of Cuban irregulars from the covering thicket of palms. The general sent his Hungarians with fixed bayonets after these scoundrels, much dismayed at his reception by the very people he had set out to liberate, and the irregulars faded off into the night. Augustus Doyle had never been this close to any sort of shooting before and felt an uncomfortable tightness in his bowels, followed by an equally uncomfortable looseness. The men huddled on the beach that night behind the barrels and crates. Strange birds with bright sleepless eyes made gaaking noises from the trees.

In the morning, General Lopez assembled the full regiment in parade order and separated out Colonel Crittenden and his Kentucky Volunteers. The Kentuckians, with Augustus attached as chief cook, were ordered to stay behind and guard the beachhead. The Hungarians and others, led by General Lopez, would liberate the village of Las Posas then send back ox carts for the men and supplies. The general marched off at noon at the head of his Hungarians, colors fluttering in the sea breeze, someone playing the fife, another playing a small drum, others singing a strident Hungarian patriotic song. Augustus watched as this bold, musical contingent disappeared into the green shade of the jungle.

Colonel Crittenden ordered the Kentuckians to arrange the supplies as a sort of breastwork halfway up the beach and there dig a shallow trench in the sand. When these tasks were accomplished, they settled down to nap and play cards. Augustus, Colonel Crittenden, and Prescott played three-card Lonesome Jack with a barrel of molasses as a table into the still, unbearably hot hours of the afternoon. Some of the men, tired of napping, stripped off their blue woolen shirts and ragged trousers and jumped about in the waves. Augustus tried not to think about Cuba at all. He tried to pretend that he and his friends were instead encamped on the broad, sandy beach at Cockle Bay back home, on Wassateague Island, Virginia. At dusk, as the parrots began their evening chatter in the shadows, the Cubans attacked.

The battle that followed was full of confusion, explosions, and screaming. The yellow smoke of gunpowder billowed through the air like fog. Augustus hid behind a large tin of candle tallow for a while, fingers in his ears, then he was persuaded by Colonel Crittenden, at saber point, to load his squirrel rifle and return fire. It appeared the Cubans had fielded somewhere around eight hundred men, a veritable army versus the bare brigade of 120 Kentuckians. Every shot counted. Trembling, Augustus took up a position beside Bingley and Prescott, who seemed utterly calm under the attack, joking one to the other between reloads. With these brave men as an example, Augustus tried to steady his aim, but couldn't keep his hands from shaking and each time shot high into the trees.

Just before dawn, the Cubans brought up from somewhere a small field piece of antique vintage and blasted a round of grapeshot into the breastwork. Augustus heard the high-pitched whistling of the shot slashing through the humid air right for his position and threw himself into the sand; Bingley and Prescott disdained any such precaution as cowardly. Following the hard, reverberating thump-thump of the grape hitting all around, Augustus raised his head to see that these two brave woodsmen had been blown to pulp, their various limbs scattered here and there across the bloody terrain. He felt himself frozen in the face of this explicit example of man's ultimate insubstantiality and watched in horror, unable to move, as the Cubans primed again and touched off another round. This time, apparently overloaded, the field piece itself exploded with a muffled bang, the gun crew fell dead, and Augustus was saved for the moment. An exhausted cheer went up from the Kentuckians, but within the hour the Cubans brought two more field pieces of a more modern design down the track through the jungle and the Kentuckians' makeshift fortification was soon raked with murderous crossing fire. Twenty men died, blown to bits in the next fifteen minutes. Augustus could hear the gentle lapping of the water on the smooth sand in the silent moments before the surrender.

The Cubans, sullen-faced, swarthy little men whom Augustus could not distinguish from the Mexicans he'd cooked against on the glorious march from Vera Cruz to the Halls of Montezuma, came down the beach with bayonets fixed to their muskets and, despite the white flag, dispatched the wounded right away with brutal thrusts to the head and torso. The bloody remnants of the Kentucky Volunteers were relieved of their weapons, stripped of their shoes and valuables, tied each to each slave-style by a thick rope around their necks, and set barefoot on the rough trail to Havana, some two hundred miles distant.

Many good men perished on this long death march; they were simply cut out of the line and left to rot by the side of the jungle path. Augustus,

Colonel Crittenden, and forty-two others arrived at the Cuban capital almost two weeks later, exhausted and starving, and were paraded through
the streets before the jeering multitudes. Even in this depleted state, Augustus could not help noticing that the women of Havana were every bit
as lustrous, dark, and beautiful as the ones he'd left behind in New Orleans — the chief difference between these two examples of femininity being that the women of New Orleans had tossed flowers and packets of
tobacco tidily wrapped with ribbon to the men when the Pampero pulled
away from the levee, and the Cuban beauties were now throwing rotten
vegetables, worn-out shoes, rancid eggs, the excrement of dogs and horses.

The Kentuckians marched on display beneath the sting of this humilia-
tion back and forth through the city for the next few hours. Then they were
imprisoned in the Atares citadel in a tiny cell no more than eight feet long
by six wide. Forty-four men confined in a space originally intended for one,
so tightly packed there was no room to lie down or sit.

One of the men, a tough old Texan who had fought with General Sam
Houston at the battle of San Jacinto, understood a fair degree of Spanish
and overheard the guards at the door talking about the fate of General
Lopez and his Hungarians. There had been a pitched battle at Las Posas.
The general had successfully defended the place against a vastly superior
force of Cubans but, failing to seize the advantage of his victory, had then
retreated into the thickly forested and rainy mountains of the interior. His
men had scattered and were now being hunted down one by one with
mastiffs like runaway slaves.

Augustus and Colonel Crittenden had managed to secure a fortunate
spot directly beneath the barred window and the occasional sweet scent of
oranges and papayas reached them in their fetid bondage, blown by a fresh
sea breeze from a fruit market in the square beyond the prison walls.

"I wonder if you can die just from standing up," Augustus said. His knees
hurt.

"You could," Colonel Crittenden said, "if you stood up for long enough
without food and water."

"Looks like old Lopez was right," Augustus said, and he told Colonel Crittenden about the dire fate the general had discovered written on his scalp.

"Don't believe a word of that fiddle-faddle," Colonel Crittenden said. "In
two weeks we'll be eating turkey pie and drinking rum punch on the balcony of Gifford's Hotel in Mobile. My uncle will see to that."

But two weeks later the Kentucky Volunteers remained incarcerated in the same cell, rendered more spacious by the death of another dozen men. It was now possible to lie down in shifts of two at a time on the offal-covered flagstones. Then, one morning, the door swung open and the Kentuckians were chained together by the waist and prodded at bayonet point through the streets to a central square where a large crowd had gathered before a curious-looking scaffold. On the scaffold a heavy wooden chair was affixed to a post with a neck-sized iron ring and hand screw attached just above the chair-back. A large, muscular Negro, his face obscured by a black hood, stood behind the chair, waiting grimly, thick arms crossed, like a murderous servant at a banquet where all the guests were to be killed following coffee and sweets.

"The garrotte," Colonel Crittenden whispered, in a parched voice. "God help us!"

The Kentuckians waited in the hot sun for another hour while Cuban officials gave long-winded speeches. Then, a dirty, skeletal little man, his tattered white uniform hanging in rags from his emaciated limbs, mounted the steps to the scaffold. It was Narcisco Lopez, captured after a month of roaming the inhospitable mountains of the interior.

"It looks like the general read his own fate in my head," Augustus said.

"Don't worry," Colonel Crittenden said. "You'll be joining him soon enough to make his prognostications come true."

General Lopez, though much thinned by his wilderness ordeal, had lost none of his revolutionary fervor. His captors allowed him a short but fiery speech to which the majority of assembled Cubans listened with something like amused disinterest and which he ended with the words "Viva Cuba libre!" — a cry nonetheless echoed by a few brave souls present, who were quickly pulled out of the crowd and beaten mercilessly by the soldiers. Then, the Negro executioner stepped forward and, with a touching delicacy, motioned General Lopez towards the garrotting chair. As the general turned, reconciled apparently to his terrible fate, he caught sight of the pitiful remains of the Kentucky Volunteers, huddled in chains to the right of the scaffold.

"My poor brave boys," he called out. "Narcisco Lopez is sorry for the grief he will cause your wives and sweethearts. Forgive him!" And to their credit, in response to this plea, the Kentuckians managed a pale hurrah. A few seconds later, the rebellious general was strapped to the garrotting chair, the metal collar clamped around his neck and the Negro executioner gave a few quick, practiced twists to the screw. The general made a weak, strangling sound, his eyes bulged out of his head and he slumped forward, dead.

"Not a bad way to go, all in all," Colonel Crittenden muttered.

"I'd rather go in my own bed," Augustus responded. "In about sixty years, after a good dinner, a long jug of sourmash, and a rambunctious tussle between the sheets with a big, soft, comfortable woman."

The Kentuckians, now barely thirty in number, expected to mount the scaffold one by one presently to meet their doom, but the spectacle was over for the day. Instead, they were thrust through the crowd, which appeared subdued in the wake of General Lopez's execution, and taken to the barracks room of an arsenal a few streets away. There, they were released from their bonds, given hard cheese, loaves of black bread, water, and a little wine. After they had eaten and drunk, a sleek, mustachioed young officer entered, followed by a subaltern bearing paper, ink, pens, and blotters. "I am Captain Eugenio Manin," the officer said, in perfect English. "Who is in charge here?"

Colonel Crittenden rose unsteadily and saluted. "Colonel Crittenden of Kentucky."

Captain Manin returned the salute and arranged for Crittenden to distribute the paper, pens, and ink to the men.

"You see, we Cubans are not without mercy," Captain Manin said. "Lopez was strangled as a traitor but you are no more than honest soldiers sadly misled, and for such as these, the garrotte is not a just punishment. Rather, you will be shot in the morning by firing squads of picked men, according to long established military custom. But before that regrettable necessity comes to pass, His Excellency the Captain General of Cuba in a fit of magnanimity has decided to allow you to write one last letter to bid farewell to your kith and kin in the United States. Be warned, however, please limit yourself to personal sentiments. Do not insult or calumnize this island or the Spanish Crown, which you have so unjustly wronged by your ill-considered aggression. The letters will be read by myself in the morning before being sent out on the New Orleans packet and any not conforming to the stated parameters will be immediately discarded."

These letters were perhaps the cruellest punishment the Cubans had devised thus far. The men, who had borne so much suffering with equanimity, were, over the course of the following night of composition and painstaking drafts, reduced to tears in remembrance of the dear faces back home they would not see again. Augustus withdrew to a dim corner of the room, his mind filled with a ghastly blankness at the coming certainty of his death. His father and mother were dead, his sister was dead, only his brothers remained alive. These unsympathetic siblings had long since ceased to concern themselves with his fate; undoubtedly they already thought him perished in some foolhardy contest with the hostile Indians of the western frontier. Nor had he any sweetheart to speak of — his most poignant memories in this arena involved an ardent little raven-haired whore named Lucy, with whom he had spent a few pleasantly carnal afternoons at Madame Jenny's sporting house in St. Louis a year ago, but he didn't flatter himself that she would much remember him. Indeed, no one would miss him when he had been dispatched by Cuban bullets into the next world; his name and face would be utterly forgotten.

The deepest gloom imaginable seized poor Augustus Doyle upon these painful considerations, and he felt his limbs invaded by that sad lassitude reserved for condemned men awaiting their appointed hour. After a while, Colonel Crittenden came over and squatted down beside Augustus. He had finished his letter, he said, addressed to his father in Kentucky, and had also included lesser epistles to be passed on to his mother and sisters.

"I'll leave it to my poor pa to disseminate the unfortunate news of my demise," he said. "And I must say, it will break the old man's heart." His hands were now trembling so badly he had to fold them in his lap like a schoolboy to keep them still. "What about your letter?"

"I'm not writing one," Augustus said. "I don't have anyone to write to."

"No one at all?"

Augustus indicated by his demeanor that he wished to be left alone and Colonel Crittenden crept off to comfort another weeping comrade. Some men paced the room, jittery, nervous; others prayed to the Almighty in quavering voices. These letters, the sharp instrument of the Cubans, had reduced the brave Kentucky Volunteers to terrified shadows of their former selves. Now, out of the high window of the barracks room, the sky pinkened towards dawn, a single star still glittering in the pink. Through the thick door came the fateful clinking of jailers' keys and the scrape of boots across flagstones and the muffled sound of laughter. A guard appeared and announced in Spanish that the military escort was coming in a few minutes. Augustus pressed himself into his corner and closed his eyes tight, and some-

how, in this self-imposed darkness, an idea occurred to him, shining like that single star in the pinkening firmament, and he knew it was the best idea that had occurred to him yet in his life.

He rose out of the corner, seized a sheet of paper and a pen, and scribbled furiously for the next several minutes. He had just sanded the ink and affixed the address to the obverse when the guard came to collect the letters. Then, the sun rose in malevolent heat over the harbor and the Kentucky Volunteers, surrounded by an entire regiment of soldiers led by Captain Manin, were marched back to the square where the execution of General Lopez had taken place on the preceding day. But that place had changed, been cleared of impediments like the floor of an abattoir. The scaffold had been removed in the night; the Kentuckians were now faced with a bare wall, much pitted and gouged by musket fire, and the crowd that had gathered to feed its spite on their deaths was in an ugly mood indeed. Scuffles broke out here and there among the spectators and Augustus heard the sound of a glass breaking and the high-pitched wailing of a woman coming from a nearby street.

The Kentuckians were then unchained and the first group of four was taken from the ranks and made to kneel facing the stone wall. Then, squads of Cuban soldiers formed up and fired off volley after volley, each so clumsy in aim that two among the Kentuckians were not dead but left writhing and moaning in pain on the bloody cobbles. These wretched survivors Captain Manin ordered dispatched by the cruel expedient of having their brains beaten out with the butts of the soldiers' muskets. The crowd roared at this savage display, at the thick, wet sound of skulls opening with a crack, spilling the grey matter within upon the ground.

Colonel Crittenden and Augustus were reserved for some reason for the very last group to face this inept butchery. The bodies of their comrades lay, some still twitching, in bloody heaps on either side of the killing ground. Colonel Crittenden turned and shook Augustus's hand. "I don't know much about you," he said, "nor you about me. But you're the last friend I'll have in this world. My given name is Joseph."

Augustus squinted at the sun to keep the tears from his eyes. "Friend Joseph," he said, "I'll most assuredly look for you when I get to where you're going and we'll raise a celestial jug to the bad old days on the earth, but it may be some years before I show up, so this is probably goodbye for a while."

Joseph Crittenden's brow clouded. "You're going to die at my side," he said gently. "You must face it now and accept death like a brave Kentuckian."

"Remember, I'm from Virginia," Augustus said, "and it's harder to kill us than some others. Was there anything you didn't say in your letter that you'd like me to convey to your pa?"

Crittenden didn't get the chance to respond to this absurd question as, at that moment, a squad of Cuban soldiers came over and took him and the two remaining Kentuckians to face the wall of death. But Augustus was not taken. He averted his eyes as the first volley exploded from the muzzles of the muskets so he did not see his friend Crittenden, bleeding from the mouth and breast, stumble to his feet and turn to shake his fist at the crowd.

"A Kentuckian kneels to no one except his God and always dies facing the enemy!" he shouted, before a second volley cut him down.

As the Cuban regiment fell into marching formation around Augustus Doyle, now sole survivor of the brave Kentucky Volunteers, the spectators suddenly transformed themselves into a mob. A bloodthirsty howl echoed into the hot, merciless Cuban sky and the mob raced towards the heap of Kentucky dead, and the bodies of Augustus's former comrades were dragged around the square and torn to bits as if set upon by a pack of ravenous animals.

Later that afternoon, Augustus Doyle was allowed to bathe and shave, and a clean, serviceable suit of clothes was brought to him. He dressed and ate a meal of grilled meat, beans, and beer, and in this fed and comforted state was taken to see Captain Manin in the latter's chambers in the palace of the Captain General of Cuba.

Captain Manin shook Augustus's hand, apologized for the unfortunate nature of recent events, settled him in a plush armchair, and offered a cigar and a glass of sweet rum slightly adulterated with lime juice. Augustus lit up and puffed smoke rings at the ceiling, waiting for the Cuban to speak. Presently, Captain Manin withdrew Augustus's letter from a pile of papers on his desk and handed it courteously back to him. "We will not need to send this now, I'm sure," he said.

"No, I guess not," Doyle said, and folded the letter into the pocket of his shirt.

"Naturally, passage has been booked in your name on the New Orleans packet," Captain Manin said. "Is there anything else that I or my subordinates can do to make your remaining hours in Cuba more pleasant?"

Augustus thought about this. He let his gaze roam the tastefully appointed chamber. He took in the fine old pictures on the wall, the dark, heavy furniture, the pearl-faced clock, and came to rest finally on a pretty little knife, its ivory handle carved in the shape of a naked woman, hanging on a gold embroidered strap from the Captain's belt.

"There's something, Cap," Doyle said, pointing at the knife. "How about that knife as a souvenir?"

"Certainly," Captain Manin said, without a moment's hesitation. He detached the knife from his belt and handed it to Augustus. "Anything else?"

"Yes," Augustus said. "See that eight hundred dollars in Spanish gold is placed in a locked trunk in my stateroom aboard the packet. Call it compensation for suffering incurred."

"Quite a reasonable sum," Captain Manin nodded pleasantly, "considering the circumstances." He stamped the heel of his boot on the polished tile floor, bringing a subaltern scurrying in from the adjoining office, and was about to translate this request when Augustus raised a hand.

"Not so fast, Cap," he said. "I'm Roman Catholic, you know, like you people."

"Ah?" Captain Manin seemed puzzled by this.

"So I've got one more small request."

A suitably Roman Catholic wife was found for Augustus Doyle from among the whores who stocked Madame Gavrotti's brothel, a reputable establishment patronized by army officers, planters, government ministers, and high officials of the church. She was a pale, small young woman of nineteen, known to her fellow whores as La Santa Maria for the fact that she often recited the rosary to herself while submitting to the sexual ardors of her clients. She did not seem surprised when told she would be marrying a Yankee and leaving with him for the United States, but when she passed through the iron filigree gates of the brothel into the world she wept copious tears: that carnal establishment had been her only home for the preceding ten years and she held her fellow whores as dear as sisters. But there was no trace of this melancholy a few hours later as she recited the rosary and Augustus pounded away above her in the wide bed in his first-class stateroom aboard the Catawba Belle steaming out of Havana Harbor for New Orleans.

Augustus kept on his person the letter he had written when he lay under sentence of death in the barracks in Havana for the rest of his life. In later *years, on the occasion of a national holiday, or when he was drunk enough to wax nostalgic for the foolish and unsettled wanderings of his youth, he would take out the letter and read it aloud to whomever would listen — his disgruntled brothers, his fellow captains of the Wassateague oyster fleet, his wife Maria, his seven sons. The letter, addressed in a large hasty hand to PRESIDENT MILLARD fiLLMORE, WHITE HOUSE, WASHINGTON CITY, USA, went as follows:*

Dear Friend Millard

Greetings, you old coot you! It is with heavy heart that I write to tell you that I will most likely not survive to look upon another day. These Cubans are threatening to shoot me dead at first light, along with a good couple dozen of my fighting comrades from Kentucky. Not that I blame them much, the Cubans, I mean. We joined up with this flashy fellow Lopez, who met with his death yesterday in a most unpleasant manner, and were trying to invade them down here when they caught us at it red-handed and shot us to pieces on the beach. In the old days when we knew each other so well in Washington City, you often warned me against such ill-considered adventuring but, no, I would not heed a word of your sound advice!! I was too full of piss and vinegar and now my own recklessness would seem to have brought about my end. So, in the interests of peace and amity among the nations of our hemisphere, I plead with you to forgive the poor Cubans and do not order my old comrade-in-arms General Scott to lay siege to Havana at the head of the same glorious and invincible army that took the City of Mexico a couple of years back, like you said you was going to do should the least hair on my head be harmed. But if you do invade this place, do not make good your threat to raze every last building to the ground, as Havana seems a pleasant enough little town with plenty of good-looking women besides. So, in closing, my best to your wife and kids and also send my regards to our mutual friend the King of Spain, and please send along to His Majesty the case of good Virginia sipping whiskey which I promised when last we met in his castle in Madrid. That royal fellow sure can drink!

Yours, etc., Augustus DOYLE

1

A BATTERED, unmistakeable Aston Martin convertible leaned top down on worn springs at a rakish angle to the crushed shells of the parking lot in front of the Parrot Cage. It was a classic old model from the sixties, faded blue and rust, with one fender smashed in — as Doyle remembered — from a rash encounter with a parking meter on 79th Street. An incredible feminine rat's nest of trash — wadded stockings, crumpled packs of Kool Menthols, a Manolo Blahnik pump with the heel blown out, melted tubes of expensive French lipstick, unread letters marked URGENT!, sun-faded copies of the *New York Observer,* half-eaten apples showing the impression of nicely even teeth like orthodontist's wax — lay strewn across the ancient rump-worn maroon leather of the seats.

Doyle had just come up from his morning run along the beach. He walked around the car; smelling the familiar burned-oil-mildewed-carpet-English-old-car smell and experienced an odd sensation: his life had become a decomposing canvas, peeling off in layers, each layer revealing the portrait of another woman beneath the faded pigment. Now, in the presence of this vintage machine he was taken back twenty-five years to a deliciously hurried fuck in the cramped front seat, in the rainy green mountain fall on a road-trip weekend during college. They'd gone up to Charlottesville for a party; rain drummed hard on the mohair top as she clambered over the gear-shifter, straddled his thighs, and pulled up her skirt and settled herself down on him with an erotic little grunt, some old R&B standard thumping through the rain from the shattered living room of a nearby frat neatly in synch with her lewd gyrations. But this pleasant episode called to mind other episodes, not so pleasant — screaming fights on the Brooklyn-bound F with the sour morning commuters watching, irrational black moods, casual betrayals.

Thus distracted by the past, Doyle had barely registered the presence of a suspiciously nondescript beige van parked two spaces away, but coming around it up to the porch, he noticed the official U.S. Government tags and groaned aloud — this could only mean one thing, another encounter with petty officialdom! And he glanced from the Aston's supple flank to his own dull reflection in the plain slab side of the van and he knew his life was about to get very complicated indeed.

2

They were waiting at the bar. At one end, Bracken Deering teetered on a stool in a billowing cloud of cigarette smoke, second martini of the morning in hand; at the other end two government types, a man and a woman wearing sober dark undertaker suits frowned into empty cups of coffee. Maggie stood behind the bar in the dead air between these two parties, looking worried.

"I can't believe it!" Bracken shrieked, when she caught sight of Doyle, her eyes gleaming with the feverish animation that a couple of martinis would inevitably ignite in any Deering. Then she launched herself off the stool and into his arms. Doyle stumbled backwards, almost fell over as she kissed him hard, smearing his face with scarlet lipstick.

"My God, Circe . . ." he managed.

She pulled away giggling. "No one's called me that in I don't know how long!" It was a nickname from college, after the sorceress in Homer who turned men into pigs.

"Yeah, wow, how long has . . . I mean it's been . . ." Doyle stumbled over his words. For a moment, the years stood between them, a lost regiment, bedraggled remnants of the army of the past. She still looked great — long and thin with that aristocratic Deering swan neck and the pale, elongated, oval face of a Pontormo madonna. If anything, time had added luster, a sophisticated weariness that came from life in New York City, from midnights in bed with another woman's husband, traffic barreling down Park Avenue thirty stories below. Today she wore her glossy brown hair caught up in an elegant silver clasp, a tight black stretchy top that revealed every bump and button of her long torso, comfortably faded jeans, and carefully scuffed black cowboy boots chased with silver, and she smelled wonderfully of some very subtle, very expensive perfume. Doyle's reaction to her presence in his deprived state was immediate. He wanted to drag her back into the kitchen, pull off her jeans, and do her right there on the steel counter. Ten thousand years of civilization intervened to suppress this urge.

"Aw, Tim, honey," Bracken smiled and patted his cheek, "I know, where do we start? Well, let's not start, let's pretend we just saw each other yesterday and now we're having a nice little drink, OK?" And she took his arm and led him gently over to the bar. "Set this man up with a martini," she said to Maggie. "We're celebrating just being us!"

Maggie ignored her. "I wouldn't go getting all drunked-up right this second," she said to Doyle, under her breath, and slid her eyes towards the government types waiting patient as death and taxes down the bar.

Doyle refused to follow the direction of her gaze. Let them come to him, whoever they were. "Bourbon," he said.

Maggie sighed, and, relaxing her prohibition, poured out the drink. Then she took an emery board from behind the cash register, leaned back, and went to work on her chipped nails, feigning disinterest but watching all the while from beneath her lashes. Doyle noticed she was standing exactly opposite where the Winchester hung on wooden pegs beneath the register.

"Well, we've got to drink to something," Bracken said, taking up her martini again.

Doyle thought for a moment. "Let's drink to mantel diving."

Bracken grinned and they touched glasses and Doyle finished his bourbon in one quick swallow. Mantel diving referred to the night they met with a bang at a Sigma Nu frat party at Hampton-Sydney years ago: Beautifully drunk and just as naked — having stripped off her clothes on a dare — Bracken clambered up on the baroque carved mantel in the ballroom of the frat house, closed her eyes, and, announcing "Somebody catch me!", threw herself off into the crowd. Fate had positioned Doyle just below; he reached out, caught her in his arms, and carried her off into the warm spring night where they fucked in the fragrant mulch beneath a rose bush without exchanging a single word. Ah, innocent times!

"Hang on, honey, before I forget," Bracken said presently. She rummaged around in a large shapeless leather purse, pulled out a sheet of newsprint, and unfolded it on the counter. It was the front page of a three-week-old copy of the *Wassateague Breeze* with a picture of Doyle sliding into Constable Smoot's departmental Hyundai, baseball cap obscuring his face; and in a separate shot, the Whitneyville-Walker Colt black and deadly-looking. The headline read, WILD WEST STYLE GUN BATTLE LEAVES ONE DOWN, ONE STANDING. She uncapped a red Sharpie and pushed it at him. "Go ahead, sign it for me," she said. "I'm a Doyle groupie. So how about that, back from NYC couple of days ago, going through my old newspapers and there you are, on the goddamned front page! I thought you were over in Spain. Hell, I thought you were gone for good."

"So did I," Doyle said. He took the Sharpie, capped it, and tossed it into the open maw of Bracken's purse.

"Come on, Tim, honey," she pushed out her lower lip in a mock pout, "just one little old signature. It's not going to kill you. Pun intended."

"No," he said quietly. "I'm not proud of what happened. You might say the gun took over. I didn't —" He interrupted himself. At that moment he felt the purposeful gaze of the law like a cold hand on the back of his neck and turned to see the two government types standing close behind.

"Do I know you people?" he said, irritated. He was going to play this out to the end.

"Mr. Doyle, I'm Agent Detweiler." The woman stepped forward and extended her hand. Doyle shoved his hands in the pockets of his coat. Agent Detweiler frowned. She was a short, muscular woman, built like a bulldog. Her partner introduced himself as Agent Keane. He was slack-looking, cadaverish fellow, tall as a basketball player.

"We drove down from DC," Agent Keane said, "and we'd like a word with you if you don't mind."

"I mind," Doyle said. "I'm busy. Make an appointment."

"We can call this official, if you like," Agent Detweiler snapped. "Which means we come back with a warrant this afternoon and turn the place upside down."

"Don't get yourself busted on my account," Bracken said to Doyle. "I'm out of here." She finished her martini in one hasty swallow and gathered up her purse. "Just dropped in to tell you I'm having a party out at the Hundred on Saturday. You've got to come — we do need to have a nice long talk, don't we?"

"We do," Doyle said, feeling a disquieting lump in his pants.

She patted his cheek again and glanced down at his unorthodox running attire — Uncle Buck's infantry coat tossed over a pair of Uncle Buck's striped flannel pajamas. "And, honey, it's black tie."

Doyle nodded dumbly. Bracken kissed him again and was gone. A few seconds later, the Aston burbled to life. Doyle listened to its worn suspension creaking over the shells out to the Beach Road and the engine working through the gears, until it faded in the distance like hope departing.

"Old girlfriend," Doyle said to Agent Keane. "Haven't been laid in months and you two come along."

"Are you willing to cooperate, Mr. Doyle?" Agent Detweiler said, coloring at the last comment.

Doyle threw open Uncle Buck's coat. "I need to put on some clothes before we do anything."

Agent Detweiler raised an eyebrow. "Do you often go out in your pajamas, Mr. Doyle?" she said.

"More and more these days," Doyle said.

"Fix yourself up," Agent Keane said, with a thumbscrew grin that made Doyle shudder. "We can wait till you're presentable to have a look at the remains."

"Remains?" For a long beat, Doyle had no idea what they were talking about.

Maggie brought the possum carcass out of the deep freeze still wrapped in the lawn-and-garden bag now frozen and brittle. She dropped the bag to the floor with a clunk, went over and got the front page of the *Wassateague Breeze* Bracken had left on the bar, and spread it across the table by the window. "No one's getting dead possum shit all over my clean table," she said. Then she opened the bag and shook hard and the possum rolled out on to the newspaper, seasquab still at home in its entrails.

"I thought you got rid of that damned seasquab," Doyle said to Maggie.

"I didn't," Maggie said.

"Not a pretty sight," Agent Detweiler said, peering down.

"No, indeed," Agent Keane said, whistling through his teeth.

Doyle couldn't keep a smirk off his face. "So, how are things over at Fish and Wildlife, guys?" he said.

Agent Detweiler shot him an angry look. "I get the feeling there's something here you find amusing," she said. Then she paused and wiped a blush of freezer frost from the sheet of newsprint covering the table. "Is this you, Mr. Doyle?" She pointed to his picture.

"Not a good likeness," Doyle admitted. "Mostly you get the hat."

"Allow me to be frank," Agent Keane said. "You appear to be a fairly unsavory character."

"I didn't come all the way down from DC to stare at a possum's ass," Doyle said.

"We do not appreciate rough language, Mr. Doyle," Agent Detweiler said. "You may consider that admonition official."

She unbuttoned her dark suit jacket and took a pair of white surgical gloves out of the inside pocket. Doyle caught sight of a pearl-handled .38 Special nestled in a black leather holster in the humid dimness just below her armpit before she buttoned up again. She snapped the surgical gloves on her wrists; Agent Keane followed suit and the two of them bent over the carcass. Doyle and Maggie retreated to the bar as the agents worked. Maggie poured another shot of bourbon for Doyle and mixed a Bloody Mary for herself.

Ten minutes later, the agents carefully replaced the frozen possum carcass in the lawn-and-garden bag, closed it tightly with twisty-ties, snapped off their surgical gloves.

"Definitely the remains of a Delmarva Peninsula Albino Fox Possum," Agent Keane said grimly.

Agent Detweiler offered a stiff, assenting nod.

"Don't forget the seasquab," Doyle said, grinning. He felt giddy from the bourbons and the possibilities implied by Bracken's invitation.

"Considering the circumstances, your levity seems a little out of place," Agent Detweiler said, so angry suddenly she was shaking. "This animal has been savagely murdered!"

Agent Keane put a restraining hand on his partner's thick biceps. "Are you aware of the penalties for killing an endangered animal, Mr. Doyle?" he said.

"I've got to tell you two something," Doyle said. "Those damn possums are about as endangered as my ass. They're all over the woods. Just go on back and have a look for yourself."

Agent Detweiler went red, shook off Agent Keane's hand, and advanced a menacing step in Doyle's direction. "At Fish and Wildlife we have a special folder that contains the profiles of certain offenders," she said, in a voice so tight it hurt to listen. Flecks of spittle hit Doyle's face as she spoke; darker patches of sweat suddenly appeared on the dark suit beneath her arms. "Some very sick individuals get their rocks off torturing animals — that's how Ted Bundy started before he moved on to sorority girls, that's how they all started. But for the real hard cases, a regular animal just doesn't work anymore. No, these sick, sick individuals need an endangered animal! That's right, an animal whose numbers have been so depleted by the cruelties and excesses of *men* that the entire species is nearly extinct!" Her voice rose nearly to a shriek on the last word.

Doyle pictured the .38 gestating like a malignant tumor beneath her left armpit and thought it prudent not to respond.

Agent Detweiler drew a sharp breath, turned on her heels, and joined Agent Keane, who had gathered up the bag containing possum carcass and seasquab and made a move towards the door. She took the bag from him without a word, went out and got into the van, slamming the door. The possum had begun to thaw a bit since its removal from the deep freeze. A faint, unpleasant, rotting odor permeated the bar.

"I advise you to put that thing in the far back of your vehicle," Doyle called to Agent Keane.

"And open all the windows," Maggie said.

"You will be hearing from us." Agent Keane pointed an accusatory finger in Doyle's direction. "For the time being, Fish and Wildlife will consider any attempt on your part to leave the area as evidence of guilt and a warrant will be issued for your arrest through the proper local authorities."

"Hold on a minute," Doyle said, exasperated. "That goddamned possum was a death threat against me."

"That's what you'd like us to think, isn't it?" Agent Keane said, and he turned and followed his partner.

"By the time they hit Pokamoke that thing's really going to reek," Maggie said, watching the van pull out of the parking lot.

Doyle slumped back down at the bar and made a weak gesture for more bourbon. But Maggie refused and brought him a cup of coffee.

"You got to work today," she said. "You're cut off."

"I'm cut off *again?*" Doyle said. He felt like pounding his head against the bar.

"That's right," Maggie said, then she relented and poured a dollop into his coffee.

"I got to say you're a man with more troubles than anyone I ever met, even your uncle Buck."

"What is it about me?" Doyle managed.

Maggie thought this over for a long minute. "You really want to know?" she said.

"I do," Doyle said.

"It's your face," she said. "Some people look guilty, some people can get away with anything. You look guilty. Like a gangster in an old-time movie."

Doyle threw up his hands. "Then I suppose I must be guilty," he said. "We're all guilty of something, right?"

"Speak for yourself," Maggie said. And she went back to work with the trace of a smile on her lips.

4

Doyle spent the rest of the morning breaking up the sagging plaster jaw of the skull mouth at number one with a five-pound sledge to expose the rotted wooden substructure. It was hard going alone. The heavy joists of the scaffold, the large chunks of plaster needed two sets of hands. A few minutes after noon, a mufflerless red Subaru Brat burped up along the Beach Road and skidded to a halt. The door slammed. Doyle picked up the sledge warily as an unfamiliar figure wearing a pair of paint-splattered jeans and a plaid workshirt came down towards him. Then he saw it was Harold, the kid, reporting for his first day of work hours earlier than expected and carrying his lunch in a brown-paper bag.

"Hey, dude," Harold said, when he was close enough. He looked paler and scrawnier in the natural light than he had in the violent glow of the video screen in his mother's trailer.

Doyle wiped sweat out of his eyes and checked his watch. "Shouldn't you be in school at the moment?" he said. "I don't want to get into some shit with your truant officer. Or do they have truant officers any more?"

The kid shrugged. "You want me to work, right?" he said. Standing there, crumpling the top of the brown-paper bag with both hands, he seemed uncertain, harmless, and all at once, Doyle felt sorry for him.

"You skip class?" Doyle said. "Don't worry, you can tell me."

"Just history," Harold said. "I'm getting a D minus no matter what I do and it sucks anyway."

"You don't like history?" Doyle said.

The kid shook his head. "It's boring," he said. "Our teacher's this hippie chick. I get tired of hearing about all the bad-crap dead white guys did to the Indians and the slaves and everyone else — like no other dead guys ever did anything bad. It's bullshit. Everyone's bad, so I already know that, so why go to class?" The kid paused. "Look, do you want me to fucking work, or what?"

"Yes, I want you to fucking work," Doyle said.

"OK," the kid said. He set down his brown-paper bag and Doyle showed him around the course, explaining the repairs necessary to bring each hole up to playable condition. Halfway through, somewhere between the sugar mill and the giant squid, Harold unrolled a pack of Marlboros from his sleeve and lit up.

Doyle plucked the cigarette from the kid's mouth and stamped it out on the coquina path. "No smoking on the job, kid," he said. "Those things are real hell on the lungs."

Harold jumped back, clenching his fists. "Don't fucking do that again, fuckhead!" he spit out.

Doyle reached over and caught the kid around the shoulder in a tight grip. Harold tried to squirm away — "Lay off, homo!" — but Doyle held fast.

"I like you, Harold, I really do," Doyle said, in what he thought might be a fatherly voice. Surprised, Harold quieted all at once; Doyle didn't think anyone had ever said this to him before. "Let me tell you why I like you," Doyle went on, in the same tone. "You've got spunk — no one can deny that — you're a real entrepreneur. Hell, your mom tells me you bought all the video equipment and pornography in your room by yourself, is that right?"

Harold mumbled an assent. Doyle lifted his arm from Harold's shoulder and the kid ambled along placidly at his side.

"Let me ask you a question," Doyle said. "How much money did you make selling beer on the beach?"

The kid grinned. "A shitload," he said. "Sometimes them damn yuppies from DC were so fucking jonesing for a beer they would go six, seven bucks for a fucking skunk-tasting can of National Bohemian that you can get for three ninety-nine a *case* at Dollar Mel's."

"Excellent," Doyle said. "But that's what almost landed you in jail for the next three years. I'll tell you what I'll do — stick with me on this project, which means we get the course up and running by June, and at the end of the summer I'll cut you in for a percentage of the profits in addition to your salary."

Harold thought about this. "How much a percentage of the profits?" he said.

"Two and a half percent," Doyle said, pulling a random figure out of his head. He knew full well that the course would probably not show a profit at all this summer, or the next, or the next.

"You got to make that an even ten percent," Harold said.

"Three," Doyle said. "That's my last offer. Also, you do what I say when I say it. Now, give me those cigarettes."

Harold hesitated, muttering curses under his breath. Then, he slapped the pack of Marlboros into Doyle's open hand.

"At the end of the day, you get them back," he said, and put the pack into his pocket.

Harold acquiesced wordlessly, which seemed a victory to Doyle, and for the rest of the afternoon they worked side by side at the skull mouth. The kid proved a great help. Stronger than he looked, skinny and limber, he was able to reach hitherto unreachable areas of the wooden substructure via small apertures in the chicken wire through which Doyle could not pass. In this manner, they were able to rebuild several stress points without dismantling the remaining chicken wire plaster skin, thus saving hours of painstaking reconstruction.

At last, the sun began its descent into the darkening pines of the wildlife preserve. It was the hour when, in search of food, female possums poke long pink snouts from the mossy dens wherein their young lie blind and squealing, the hour when the gulls turn east towards their beds in the gentle swells a mile from shore, in the soft bosom of the waves. Doyle's hands were raw and blistered; the kid had scraped the right side of his face on a rough-hewn bit of lumber. Doyle secured the tools and dusted himself off. "Let's call it a day, kid," he said. Then he noticed Harold's brown-bag lunch had gone uneaten. "I guess you forgot to eat your lunch."

The kid shook his head. "No, those are for you. Cookies. Chocolate chip. My mom made them."

"Hey, that was real nice of her," Doyle said, taking the bag.

"That's what you think," the kid said. "You never know what that woman's got up her sleeve. She told me not to eat any, she told me not even to look in the bag. They were all for you, she said."

"We'll see about that," Doyle said. He opened the bag, and took out a cookie, which had been made in the shape of an erect cock and balls.

"See what I mean?" Harold said, rolling his eyes. "The woman's desperate."

Doyle was abashed. He held the obscene cookie gingerly between thumb and forefinger. "Chocolate chip is chocolate chip," he said at last. "Doesn't matter what it looks like, right?" He broke the cookie in half and ate it shorn of protuberances, then broke another and handed the pieces to Harold and the two leaned back against the low, crenelated wall fronting the beach road and munched away in the gathering twilight.

"What about your father?" Doyle said.

"What about him?" Harold said.

"Ever hear from him?"

The kid shrugged. "I get postcards sometimes. He went down to work on this oil rig 'cause he couldn't find a job around here and he and Mom hate each other." He paused, mid-munch, then he looked over at Doyle, a question in his eyes. "So, what did it feel like?"

"What?" Doyle said.

"Shooting someone."

"It happened too fast to feel anything," Doyle said. "After that, I felt sick."

"Sick," Harold repeated. "Did you puke?"

"No," Doyle said. "But the scary thing was I knew that next time, if it ever happened again, I wouldn't feel sick at all. I would feel just fine. And that's what really scared me."

"Huh?" Harold said. He didn't understand; Doyle didn't have the energy to explain. The kid ate the last phallic cookie, crumpled the brown bag, and pushed himself off the wall. "Tomorrow?" he said.

"Tomorrow," Doyle said. "But go to history first."

"Whatever," Harold said.

5

The nondescript brick building rose from the middle of its vast gravel lot like a fort on the prairie. A threadbare American flag flapped in the wind from a flagpole sprouting out of a huge, bunker-sized forsythia. Aluminum letters over the door identified the structure as VFW POST 116. Doyle stepped inside, his eyes adjusting to the eternal, dim twilight of bars in the forenoon. Only one figure huddled in the shadows, halfway down.

"Buying me a drink, Constable?" Doyle said, straddling a stool two stools removed from the policeman.

Constable Smoot shook his head. "I'm buying myself a drink. You're buying your own."

A few moments later, the bartender stepped through the curtained doorway that led to the party room. He was a middle-aged man with patchy Elvis sideburns and a gut reminiscent of the King's fluffernutter years.

"Morning, Herb," the constable said.

"Semper Fi," Herb said to the constable, then he shot Doyle a suspicious glance.

"Business," the constable grunted, by way of explanation. "Mr. Doyle here's a local authority on possums." Then he consulted his watch, a complex affair of concentric bevels and dials that looked as big as a hubcap. "Barely ten a.m.," he said. "Make it a bullshot."

"Make it two," Doyle said.

The bartender quickly assembled the vodka, raw eggs, low-ball glasses, condiments. He poured a shot into each glass, broke the egg on top. "Worcestershire or Tabasco?"

"Why not both?" Constable Smoot said.

Doyle followed suit and dashed the stuff into the bright yellow yolk staring up from his glass. "Here's to salmonella," he said.

"Something's got to get you sooner or later, in your case sooner," Constable Smoot said, and they both drank. Doyle felt the egg slide down his throat like a raw oyster and the harsh grain taste of the vodka, and a comfortable warm feeling spreading in his stomach.

"Herb was in 'Nam same time as me," the constable said, when the bartender had retreated again behind the curtain. "Served with a Marine artillery unit at Khe Sahn. Self-published a book about it called *Caissons at Khe Sahn*. Damn good book."

"Khe Sahn, I hear that was pretty rough," Doyle said.

"Wouldn't know," the constable said. "Wasn't there. But I was other places."

"How were they?" Doyle said.

The constable thought for a long moment. "Bad and not too bad," he said. "Saigon was a hoot, full of cat-eyed Vietnamese whores, good eats, good times. The jungle sucked, the usual five seconds of terror followed by weeks of boredom, the usual stinking body bags. But it enters your soul, if you'll permit me. And afterwards when you get back home, it's like a long green silence."

"OK," Doyle said, impressed. "What comes after the silence?"

"Don't know yet," the constable said. "More silence, probably." Then he pushed a thick vinyl-covered binder across the bar. "This here's a special Irish crook-book, just got it from the FBI who got it from Interpol. See if you can identify the other man, our shooter's accomplice."

Doyle struggled through the pictures, a grim collection of hardened criminals, all with the same cruel, vacant look in their eyes. These were the ones who had tortured the family cat to death with firecrackers and gasoline at eight years old, who at ten had beaten the neighbor's daughter with a two by four studded with tenpenny nails, who at twelve had stolen food money from their mother's purse to buy cigarettes, condoms, and booze. Maybe they had been poor, misunderstood, abused when helpless, maybe not; one thing was certain — here, stupidity, selfishness, and violence danced a familiar dance to the same evil tune.

"Nope." Doyle pushed the pictures aside.

"You are aware that this department is far too small to offer you any more than minimal protection," the constable said. "And I stress the word minimal, which in this context means you're already a dead man."

"Thanks for the warning," Doyle said, "but I take the long view — we're all dead men. Now, what about the shooter himself? Still unconscious?"

"You plugged him pretty good with that goddamned hand cannon." He flashed Doyle a glance that might have concealed something like admiration. "You know the Walker Colt weighs over four pounds?"

"Yes," Doyle said.

"Even if he does wake up, he's not going to tell us anything because he won't know himself. A faceless assassin hired by someone he never met for a quick hit on someone he didn't know. If he's Irish, like you say, could be he's former IRA. I've already asked the Feds about what they can come up with on that score. Meanwhile, I checked the man's license and whatnot. All phoney, but top-quality fakes. And I checked his weapon, a completely anonymous 9mm Glock, grip wrapped in electrician's tape. The serial numbers have been etched off very carefully by someone who knew exactly what they were doing. Now, the fingerprints are where it gets scary, my friend, because there are no fingerprints to speak of. The ends of his fingers were surgically altered not too long ago, also by someone who knew exactly what they were doing."

"Shit," Doyle said. The back of his neck felt cold. "This is crazy."

"Somebody really wants you off Pirate's Island," the constable smirked, "dead or alive don't matter to them."

"Brilliant deduction, Constable," Doyle said.

"You're a real smartass, Doyle. It's a wonder somebody hasn't tried to knock you off before."

"Listen, I can solve this case right now," Doyle said, peevishly. "Roach Pompton! You know the bastard's made an offer on the place, you know he's been turned down. And let me tell you how he gets when he can't have something. From an ethical standpoint, the man's a fucking two-year-old."

Constable Smoot didn't say anything for a while. In the back room, the bartender turned on the old Wurlitzer and Doyle heard the first notes of Johnny Horton's "Battle of New Orleans."

"I'll grant you Pompton's a little pissant," the constable said at last. "But he's a smart pissant and he's got a shitload to lose these days. Money, property, legitimate investors — and, hell, he's on the Council of Burgesses. I can't see him risking all that just to needle you out of a little patch of swamp worth next to nothing in the long run. Ask me, I think you've got other problems," he lowered his voice for effect, "and I mean Royal Blue problems. Now ask me who owns RB Cola."

"All right, who owns it?" Doyle said.

"That's a damned good question," Constable Smoot said. "Nobody knows exactly. Far as I can tell a holding corporation in Delaware owned by a group of investors — of which Roach Pompton is only a very little fish — owned by another holding corporation, owned by another group of investors. Who can say where that trail ends? These days, everything's global and, hell, if there ain't some funny global-type shenanigans going on up at that RB plant in Ainsley."

"Like what?" Doyle said.

"Like Chinese." Constable Smoot's voice descended to a hollow whisper: "The whole place is crawling with Chinese. No locals, not a single local employee. Just a whole bunch of Chinese. They ship 'em in and ship 'em out on buses with cages over the windows. They sleep 'em in dorms on the property. Not one of them ever utters a peep. Now, what do you think of that?"

A few minutes later, after the constable had gone on his way, Doyle got a beer and wandered through the curtain into the party room, bottle in hand, thinking dire thoughts. He had been here before: this auditorium was where they used to hold the big VFW fish-fries every

Saturday from May to August. He remembered coming out in the old days with Uncle Buck, the patriotic songs played by a legless veteran on the accordion, the big platters of sweet, batter-fried grouper, hush puppies, and coleslaw for a buck fifty, all washed down with luke-warm nickel cups of National Bohemian.

A corkboard on the far wall was stuck with curling snapshots of Wassateague men in battle fatigues in Korea and Vietnam, and a ros-ter for an upcoming seniors' darts tournament. A display case below this held stiff black and white portrait photos of sailors and airmen from the Second World War and a captured Nazi battle flag, scorched and shrapnel-torn. What if the constable was right, and the forces ranged against Pirate Island went far beyond the despicable Roach and were part of some complex corporate conspiracy? How could one man alone battle the thousand-headed Hydra of global capitalism?

More relics from America's wars gathered thick layers of dust in another case in the far corner. Doyle wandered over and peered into the dusty glass: ancient weaponry lay arranged on faded bits of burlap cloth, each piece accompanied by a description typed on a yellowing square of shirt cardboard. He saw rusty Indian hatchets from before the Revolution, short-bladed navy swords from the war of 1812, steel still gleaming, Civil War-era Springfield percussion rifles — and a cu-riously wrought dagger, its ivory handle carved in the shape of a woman's body. For this item, the card read, "Captured in Cuba with Lopez, 1851."

6

Ainsley was the color of dried blood and rust, made of red Virginia clay. Shabby red-brick streets radiated out from the red-brick town square where a red-brick clock tower showed hands stopped at half past some forgotten hour. Idle black girls with cornrowed hair threw sticks at the birds in the shabby park, a few old drunks lolled on a bench doing what old drunks do. The Ainsley bakery, once home to the best donuts and pies on the peninsula, had closed the summer Doyle left for Spain.

Once, Ainsley had been the industrial crossroads of the Eastern Shore: the railroad came right through the center of town to bear away the peninsula's shellfish and produce to the markets of Baltimore, Philadelphia, New York. In those days the town supported a shipyard on the Ainsley estuary, machine shops catering to the railroad, a dozen garment manufacturers, two good hotels, a department store, saloons and restaurants and three movie theaters along Main Street. All that had dried up so long ago as to be part of history; the last six hundred manufacturing jobs left after NAFTA in 1997 when a Virginform bra assembly plant took its facilities to Mexico. Now, like most American small towns, Ainsley was dust, a memory — except for the newly refurbished Royal Blue Cola cannery, which occupied three square blocks downtown and seemed, to Doyle's eyes, incongruously bustling, as if a new breed of wasps had colonized a worn-out old hive.

He pulled the Cadillac over at the curb on an unnamed sloping street across from the main gates just to see what he could see. White-sided trucks laden with RB Cola thudded in and out of the main gates, Chinese workers in white overalls moved about efficiently within the busy precinct of razorwire. After a while the lunch whistle blew and Chinese women in quilted jackets came out with hot noodles in tin lunch pails and sat at the benches in the small triangular park just beyond the gate and ate and laughed.

Doyle watched them for a long time, admiring their graceful gestures, their thick, shining black hair reminding him so much of his wife's — and watching them brought to mind an exhibition of ancient Chinese artifacts he had seen with Flor some years ago at the Museo Arqueología in Madrid: Han dynasty bronze bells of incredible complexity, beautiful lacquered armor, ivory and jade knickknacks so old as to be unspeakably so — but in the end the most memorable objects were a dozen or so carefully inscribed bamboo splinters, each about the size and color of a popsicle stick left out in the rain. There was something ominous, even sinister about these splinters, appropriately as it turned out: they told the story of devastating famines a thousand years ago, a terrible era when Chinese mothers had been driven to the most shameful expediency — forced to kill children deemed unlikely to survive a winter with minimal food so stronger ones might have more to eat and a better chance. On each splinter could be read a prayer addressed to a murdered child.

Doyle's Spanish was not yet fluent, Flor had translated the Spanish translation of an inscription that had been translated from the Chinese: "Oh, little Wo, with a face like the spring wind / may black earth softly take your bones / Oh, little ghost / forgive your mother this dire necessity / as we forgive black earth for not granting grain / sky for not letting fall summer rains. / Do not weep much as you enter the dim halls of your ancestors alone. / Soon shall we follow and take you by the hand."

A cry of anguish echoing down the years that on the long ride from Madrid back to Málaga had kept Flor's cheeks wet with tears. They were a resilient people, the Chinese, Doyle thought now, watching the women eating and laughing in the park; they had borne much and prevailed, and in prevailing were perhaps capable of expediencies undreamed-of in the West. But did these expediencies extend to possumicide, arson, attempted murder? And how to account for the Irishness of his assailants? Any destiny that brought the Chinese to the Irish was strange beyond contemplation.

These disquieting thoughts were interrupted a moment later by a sharp, metallic rapping noise and Doyle turned, startled to see a security guard in a rumpled uniform come around the back of the car, nightstick in hand. "Hey, you! What you doing there?" The guard was Irish. The short hairs at the back of Doyle's neck stood on end.

"Nothing," Doyle said, truthfully. He watched the guard carefully in the rearview.

"Why don't you do your bit of nothing somewheres else?" the guard said, now rapping his stick on the driver's window. Doyle looked up to see the man's sidearm, the usual nondescript semi-automatic, strapped into a leather holster worn too high, just beneath his ribs.

Doyle buzzed down the window. "Don't touch my car again," he said, trying to restrain his temper and not succeeding. "Last time I checked this was a public street, and I think it's OK to sit in your car in a public street as long as you're not masturbating or smoking pot. Yes, I'm pretty sure about that."

"Shove off, pervert," the security guard said angrily. "Now."

"Go to hell," Doyle said.

The guard's face twisted into a snarl and he reached for his gun.

Doyle took a half-second for surprise and indignation — surprised and indignant that the guard was so soon responding with deadly force — then he acted. He shoved out of the car and caught the guard across the pelvis with the heavy door. The guard went over, his gun went skittering across the bricks. The Chinese women fell silent all at once, watching open-mouthed from the park, noodles hanging off their chopsticks. Doyle lunged for the gun and kicked it down the street into the intersection, beneath the wheels of an incoming RB Cola truck. Swearing, still on the ground, the guard fumbled for his nightstick. Doyle caught the stick against the bricks with one foot and held it down.

"Don't get up!" Doyle growled. "End it!"

But the guard struggled to get up. Doyle placed a well-aimed kick at the guard's ribs, just hard enough, and he cried out and rolled over on his side.

"That's for pulling a gun on me," Doyle said. "Think twice next time."

Down the street in the compound, more guards were hurrying towards the gate. Doyle got into the Cadillac, jammed the car in gear, and drove off, rear tires squealing. His hands were shaking against the wheel, sweat rolled down his forehead. In the rearview he saw the guard rise up, clutching his ribs. Then he saw the man pull out a pad of paper and a pencil and scrawl something down — the Cadillac's plate number? And he fishtailed the big car in a hurry around the corner towards 15 back to Wassateague.

7

The phone in the bar kept ringing. At last Doyle woke from muddled dreams and stumbled downstairs, old linoleum cold on his feet. The digital clock above the bar read three a.m. Somehow, every time he turned around, he thought bitterly, it was three a.m. Nobody calls with good news at that hour.

"Yeah?"

"You know that old rifle of Maggie's?" It was Constable Smoot.

"Huh?" Doyle was still half-asleep.

"I'd get it if I was you and put it beside my bed all loaded and ready to go, because your demise is the next item on their list, brother. Because I'll tell you what, our patient the shooter is gone."

"So he's dead." Doyle felt a pit open in his stomach.

"Not as far as we know," the constable said. "Vanished, you might say. Disappeared. Gone."

Then he told Doyle about what happened two hours ago at the hospital in Drayton. An ambulance pulled up at Emergency and four men dressed as paramedics came into the triage station and showed transfer papers for the shooter. They said the shooter was to be moved for security reasons to a private hospital in Delaware. The papers appeared to be in order, the nurse had no reason to suspect their authenticity. It was only when she went back to reassign the room at the end of her shift and saw the glucose drip dangling and dripping all over the floor that she suspected something was wrong. One of the men had a funny accent, she said later, to police. Maybe Irish.

"They just yanked the tube out of the bastard's arm and wheeled him on out of there," the constable said. "Now, I want you to be real honest with me, Doyle. Is there something you want to say about yourself and the IRA? Because whatever's going on here's obviously got Irish written all over it."

"I've never even been to Ireland," Doyle said, annoyed.

"That doesn't mean shit," the constable said. "Plenty of Italians in the Mafia never been to Italy. You're Irish, aren't you? Doyle — that's Irish, right?"

Doyle sighed. "I'm from Wassateague Island," he said. "I'm an American."

The constable didn't seem to hear this. "These people obviously have some pretty formidable resources at their disposal. Professional killers, ambulances, forged paperwork, fake uniforms. Jesus, it's a major conspiracy. And now I'm thinking it's definitely got to be IRA."

"A couple days ago you thought it was RB Cola, remember?" Doyle said, ruefully.

"That's still a definite possibility," the constable said, and he hung up.

Doyle replaced the receiver and stood for a painful minute trembling behind the bar. Just now he felt weak, utterly helpless. It had come over him all at once, this feeling of helplessness, and here it was, thrashing around in his gut like a possum in heat. Chills ran up his spine, his mouth went dry from sheer panic. Doyle was just another name for a guy way out on a limb while someone sawed away at the trunk below. Timber!

8

The tuxedo was high-shouldered and double-breasted, of uncertain provenance, its silk lapels gone green and sheeny with age, the shoulders and sleeves punctuated by not a few strategically situated mothholes. Buck had worn it in seriousness only once, to a formal party given by Foy Whitcomb in Wiccomac celebrating Harry Truman's close squeak into the White House in 1948 and, except for the occasional New Year's Eve joke behind the bar, it hadn't really been worn since.

Doyle scrubbed at the worst stains with rags soaked in industrial solvent, then Maggie helped him with ironing and starch. When she was finished, the tuxedo hung stiff as a board and gave off a distinctive odor Doyle couldn't say was pleasant. He put on the accompanying dingy pleat-fronted shirt, a droopy bow-tie, and stepped into the tux gingerly, so as not to crack the old fabric along the creases.

"You look like that fellow in the theater — you know, he's got half a face," Maggie said.

"Who's that?" Doyle said.

"You know, they made one of them musical plays in New York out of it. This fellow lives in the basement of this theater and he kidnaps this woman singer who —"

"*Phantom of the Opera*," Doyle said, to shut her up.

"Yeah." Maggie grinned. "That's the one."

She accompanied Doyle down the steps and out through the bar into the parking lot. Doyle got into the Cadillac and put down the top, and Maggie leaned up against the car door and smirked down at him.

"What?" Doyle said, annoyed.

"Nothing," Maggie said. Then she looked away and a slight flush came to her cheeks. "You be careful with that one," she said to the treeline. "You're so dumb when it comes to women you just can't see it, can you? She's crazy as a loon. I seen 'em crazy and a little bit of crazy's a good thing sometimes but that one's too crazy. Hell, she knocked back three martinis before ten a.m. and was asking for more. And the way she talks, all pumped-up and fake-like."

"You don't need to warn me off Bracken," Doyle said, smiling to himself. "I know how crazy she is. I dated her in college. Hell, I lived with her for a year in New York. The whole Deering family's crazy, been crazy for two hundred years. Everyone in Wassateague County knows about the Deerings, isn't that right?"

"Yeah, but you're just stupid enough not to care," Maggie said. Then she stepped back and folded her arms over her breasts, and Doyle pulled out of the parking lot on to the Beach Road. He crossed the causeway to the mainland as the last yellow light settled over the reedy islands in the channel below, and turned south on the Wiccomac Pike, darkness thickening the trees.

9

Strange lights flickered through the underbrush, as if cast by the campfires of Indians long dead. Doyle bumped the Cadillac up the Deerings' private road, hemmed in on both sides by creepers and large, prehistoric-looking ferns, eerily illuminated in the wavering spread of the headlights.

Once, the Deerings had ranked prominently among the FFVs — the First Families of Virginia — near the top of a list that included such illustrious names as Washington, Lee, Jefferson. Colonel Brodie Deering, the first Deering to emerge from obscurity, arrived in the Virginia colony by way of Barbados, just in time to lend a hand in the capture and hanging of Finster Doyle, the polygamous buccaneer. For his role in that affair, and for his gleeful ruthlessness in the suppression of Indian uprisings along the Allegheny frontier, Colonel Deering was granted ten-thousand acres by royal decree — a swath of rich, uncleared land that cut across the heart of the peninsula from ocean to bay. The grant became known as Deering's Hundred — a sort of ironic commentary on the actual acreage. It was the cornerstone of a plantation and shipping empire that, at its height, exported cotton, tobacco, indigo, lumber, hides, and honey to the various corners of the world. Built on the back of Deering's People, as the plantation's numerous Gullah slaves were called, and served by Deering's Navy, a private fleet of merchant vessels — this vast enterprise ceased its existence abruptly in April 1863 when rampaging Union troops burned every last Deering field, barn, and outbuilding, sparing only the Big House to use as a stable for their cavalry horses. Post-bellum generations of Deerings removed to Richmond, leaving Deering's Hundred unplanted and tangled with underbrush and creepers, fallow as a widow in perpetual mourning. Each generation promised the next that the neglected fields would be cleared and planted again, that the land would once again burgeon with cash crops. The promised regeneration never materialized. And these latter-day Deerings, lesser men and women harried by drink and madness and lethargy, seemed haunted by a curse they could not articulate. Bracken was the last frail green bough on a withered tree — her father, brother, and mother dead (suicide, suicide, and cancer respectively), her sister living as a Hindu nun at an ashram in Uttar Pradesh.

Now, Doyle recalled the long, exhausting year he and Bracken lived together in New York after college. It rained a good deal that fall; the reservoirs were brimming, the Hudson flooded upstate and somehow caused sewage problems in Manhattan, which stank like rotten fish for weeks.

Bracken found a dark, low-ceilinged efficiency on Mott, a former storage attic above a twenty-four-hour Chinese restaurant, whose name translated meant "Ripen at Noon," the place chosen solely for its picturesque appeal. She liked the way the neon good-luck dragon blinked red and blue and green out the window all night long, the lowdown, gritty atmosphere of the neighborhood, the Chinese men in their undershirts smoking cigarettes in ivory holders and playing mah-jongg at card tables set up on the sidewalk, the screaming, homicidal fights in Cantonese from the kitchen just below the bedroom window.

They never slept, up on speed, caffeine, booze, youth.

Every night Doyle wasn't working behind the bar at Save the Robots or Candyland, or catering the Oak Room at the Washington Irving Club on East 59th — where octogenarians snoozed in club chairs beneath genuine Tiffany chandeliers trailing dust — they spent chasing fun from one hot new dance club to another, in bars till 5 a.m., at parties drinking, fighting, flirting with strangers. The painful, grainy mornings, waking up late, they spent fucking — and Doyle recalled with a vivid pang long hours in dirty sheets, the odd positions, sex toys, contortions, and feats of stamina he hadn't been able to perform since. But all this strenuous sexual activity had not proved sufficient for Bracken. She was the only woman Doyle had been with whose appetites exceeded his own: Bracken had affairs and Doyle had affairs to counter her affairs. The bar business has many temptations, is in fact the most oversexed profession of them all; bartenders get even more action than movie stars. Publishing — Bracken's field of endeavor in those days — also has its temptations, and Bracken was one of the least sexually exclusive women in the city.

This easy, libidinous life had to end. The blow came over a pleasant meal at Vico in the West Village, a cozy basement restaurant specializing in dishes from the Basilicata region of Italy, much patronized by big-suited Mafia wise guys of the era. Doyle ordered *linguine al fruitti di mare,* a heaping plate of pasta covered with squid, crabmeat, shrimp, lobster; Bracken the house specialty, a garlic-studded veal shank served with *tagliatelli verde* in a cream-lentil sauce, according to the menu the favorite pasta of Cicero, the great, murdered Roman orator. There was a bottle of wine — Spanish, as it happened — that they had brought in for a corking fee. Despite the gangsters who patronized the place, the proprietor hadn't been able to obtain a liquor license.

The food arrived. Doyle's seafood linguine was one of the best dishes of any kind he had ever tasted. Wise guys in big suits cracked loud, off-color jokes at nearby tables and stuffed their faces with pasta. Bracken picked at her food. Her aristocratic features, sculpted by candlelight, seemed heartbreakingly beautiful to Doyle that night. Suddenly, he couldn't say how, he knew an unpleasant revelation, the last of a long series, was at hand. At last, Bracken spoke.

"Honey, I'm going to Italy with Hermann."

Hermann was her boss, a senior editor at Athenaeum, a cynical multi-lingual German expatriate about fifty, involved in something Bracken described as an open marriage, which meant he and his wife cheated on each other whenever possible. With his close-cropped convict haircut and baggy, slightly unfashionable suits, the man reminded Doyle of pictures he had seen of Albert Speer, looking guilty and defeated, at the Nuremberg trials. Hermann had come to one of Bracken's crowded parties above the Chinese restaurant: he had sat in a corner with a beer and followed her ass around the room, punctuating her every move with his beady editor's eyes.

"When are you leaving?" Doyle said.

"Tomorrow morning."

"You're kidding!" He was shocked. "Business or pleasure?"

Bracken looked down, her eyelashes gently fluttering against her cheeks. This was a kind of answer.

"How long?" Doyle persisted.

"Six months, at least," Bracken said, still not looking up. "It's a safari, you might say. We're going to hunt for the New Italian Writer —"

"Is that why you wanted to eat Italian tonight?" Doyle interrupted, angry. "To get me ready for the bad news?"

Bracken ignored him. "The Italians are coming up with some really fantastic stuff, these days. It's very surreal and yet very real at the same time. There's Calvino, of course, but also a bunch of people you've never heard of."

"I've never heard of any of them," Doyle said. He was starting to get mad.

"And except for weird little Italian literary magazines, most of these guys have never even been published —"

"Hey, Bracken, shut the fuck up!" Doyle's voice loud enough to raise the eyebrows of the wise guys at the next table.

Bracken looked up at him, startled, her blue eyes suddenly brimming with tears.

They fucked viciously that night and again for the last time in the morning. Then Doyle did the gentlemanly thing and, while Bracken packed, went uptown on the C train and got the precious Aston Martin out of the heated garage she rented for a small fortune at 78th and

6th. She loved that car: a gift from her father two weeks before his suicide — he had thrown himself off the twenty-seventh floor of the Jefferson Hotel in Richmond for reasons best explained by the women's underwear the coroner found beneath his seersucker suit.

Doyle squeezed Bracken's bags into the small trunk and drove her out to Kennedy through a roaring downpour. The tiny English wipers squeaked inefficiently against the windshield clouded with the mute condensation of their breath, with the specter of their lost youth in the Virginia countryside, college days, all that had gone before. An accident blocked the departure lane with stalled traffic. Bracken got out of the car in the rain and got her bags out of the trunk, and came around to the passenger window and put her hand against the rain-streaked glass.

"Goodbye, Timmy," she said. "Take care of yourself." Her voice trembled, but Doyle knew her heart was full of the excitement of new adventures, a new lover, Italy. She leaned down, and kissed him awkwardly on the ear, then turned and walked off between the cars in the rain without looking back.

Doyle didn't return the Aston to the garage right away. He kept the car for six months, parked it maliciously on the wrong side of the street on street-cleaning days, gathering tickets, made love to other women in the front seat, ran into a parking meter, left it in front of the Chinese restaurant, where it got covered with pigeon shit and restaurant trash. At last, it was towed by the city to the impound lot on the West Side Highway whence, upon her return from Italy a year later, Bracken was forced to ransom it back at the cost of three thousand dollars' worth of violations, towing, and impound fees.

A cheap revenge on Doyle's part, but sometimes cheap revenge is the only kind worth taking.

10

A dozen SUVs sat parked beside Bracken's Aston on the crescent of lawn opposite a vast, rambling house of the indigenous type known on the peninsula as big-house-little-house-colonnade-kitchen, each consecutive wing larger than the last, all looming over the Colonel's original mortise and tenon-jointed log cabin, now covered with white clapboard. The Big House, dating from the Federal period, was immense yet democratically severe, with a Grecian portico added sometime in the 1840s.

Now, the front door stood open to the night. Light shone from all the windows of the house, even from the smallest panes of ancient green bottle glass. Doyle parked the Cadillac at the end of the row, got out, straightened his fragrant tuxedo, and went up the front steps. The bright, formal entrance hall was deserted, empty of furniture, but coats and scarves lay heaped at dead center like the carcass of a bear. A fine mahogany staircase with carved railings seemed to float without support up to the second floor. At the far end, another door stood open on to an English topiary garden, cast in fantastic shadows by footlights hidden in the brick walkways.

Doyle came through the hall, went into the drawing room, and found this also empty, stripped, a Persian rug the only remaining item of décor. From fresh indentations in the weave of the rug it looked like the furniture had just been moved. He crossed the drawing room into the little house wing, also empty of furniture, then through the enclosed colonnade — the bare, empty rooms telescoping down till he felt like Alice after swallowing the cake that made her grow — but he couldn't find anyone. A little uneasy, he hurried back through the expanding rooms until he came back to the formal hall. Then he stopped short: a blonde in a midnight blue velvet evening dress had appeared from somewhere and was sitting on the bottom step of the staircase, bottle of Irish whiskey sloshing between her knees. She was just then in the process of rolling a large joint, one eye closed, with all the tongue-biting concentration of a six-year-old making a sandcastle. She wasn't having much luck: flakes of the rancid weed sprinkled down over her dress. A fat baggie full of pot and a pack of rolling papers lay on the step beside her.

"Having some trouble there?" Doyle said.

The blonde looked up. "If I wasn't so drunk this would be a lot easier," she warbled. "Here, you do it." She held out the half-assembled joint. Doyle took it from her and licked the paper, slightly damp from her spittle, twisted both ends, and handed it back. The blonde put the joint in her mouth and patted her velvet haunches. "No matches," she said.

Doyle produced Uncle Buck's Zippo, the one the man had carried at Anzio and through the Italian campaign, lit the blonde's joint, and put the Zippo back in his pocket.

The blonde took a deep-lunged hit, held the smoke until her face went red.

"Much better." She coughed, handing the joint up to Doyle, who shook his head.

"Makes me stupid," he said.

At this she snapped her chin up and gave Doyle a long, hard look. She had an angular face, high cheekbones, an interesting nose with a pronounced bump in the middle, and large, slightly lopsided eyes of an intense color Doyle couldn't quite name, between green and blue. He found her attractive, but maybe it was the dress and the pearls and the Park Avenue voice — and also he thought, she would probably look good naked. Some apparently beautiful women didn't. He had the odd feeling he'd seen her someplace before, couldn't say where. She took another hit and started to hiccup. "OK, I'm high," she said at last. "Don't listen to me."

"Where is everybody?" Doyle said. "I can't seem to find the party."

"What do you want with that circus?" the blonde said, hiccuping. "It's cruelty to furniture, if you ask me." Then she patted the step. "Come sit here a minute, pumpkin. Have a drink."

Doyle moved the baggie of pot out of the way and sat down. He took the bottle of whiskey from between her legs and took a long swallow; he hadn't eaten and could almost feel the stuff rushing right into his blood like an army into the breach. The blonde took the bottle back from him and put it to her lips.

"*Slainte,*" she said, and drank, joint burning down unattended, like any ordinary cigarette, between her fingers.

"You're going at it pretty hard," Doyle said, admiring her unusual profile.

"I always go at it hard," she said. "I've got a few things to forget."

"Like everyone else," Doyle said.

"No, like me," the blonde said. Then she shot Doyle a sideways look. "You remind me of somebody."

"You too," Doyle said. "I'm sure I've seen you somewhere before."

"It's that stupid fucking commercial." The blonde snorted. "It's haunting me."

"Oh, yeah," Doyle said, though he didn't know what she was talking about.

"But listen, you, you're somebody famous." She snapped her fingers. "Mitchum, that's it. Not old fat Mitchum or even slightly aging 1960s Mitchum. I'm talking beautiful, tough, droopy, pot-smoking 1947 Mitchum from *Out of the Past,* which is, by the way, a masterpiece. Have you seen *Out of the Past?*"

"No," Doyle lied. As it happened, he knew that film. He'd seen it on TV in Málaga, in Spanish but somehow not unduly affected by the clumsy dubbing — and he could still recall a few lingering details: a beautiful, sharp-featured broad with a gun, a rumpled trench coat, shadowy woods, Mitchum's snap-brim gangster hat, the wet streets of some dangerous city at night.

The blonde put the joint to her lips again, took another deep hit, and, letting it out, began to hiccup again but kept talking rapidly through the hiccuping and the smoke.

"I must have seen *Out of the Past* a dozen times back when I was in film school at NYU before da yanked me out. God, I loved that film. But, no, the family business, the old fruit says to me, 'Who's going to take over the family business when I'm gone?' So I dropped out and went to Harvard Business School instead and learned that business is a crock of shit, just men making money with marketing plans and leveraged buy-outs instead of guns and hoodlums so if you ask me —" The blonde stopped herself suddenly, took a sharp breath and looked up at Doyle. All of a sudden, her eyes were swimming. "Actually I'm not feeling very good," she said. "I think I need to lie down." And she pitched sideways and fell directly into Doyle's lap. Her red eyelids fluttered a bit and were still.

"Hey!" Doyle called. "Are you all right?" But his words couldn't reach where she had gone. She was out, oblivious.

Doyle sighed, looked around the bare hall, and saw the pile of coats. He hefted up the blonde with some effort — she was solid and heavier than she seemed — and laid her atop the pile. He bundled a coat under her head as a pillow and laid another over her dress. A low whistling sound came through her nose and she stirred but didn't open her eyes. Then he turned and went out of the door into the garden to find Bracken's party.

11

Empty champagne bottles cluttered the grass like spent artillery shells. Candles anchored with gravel in white-paper bags illuminated a group of about twenty-five guests — the men all suitably attired in tuxedos, the women wearing spangled evening gowns glowing softly in the fluttery light. A bewildering array of antique furniture had been grouped as a sort of obstacle course down the slope of the hill in the darkness behind the garden, more paper-bag candles placed here and there to light the way. Cole Porter's line about getting no kick from cocaine sang out of a portable CD player, background music for the strange event now taking place.

"OK, here's the stopwatch." It was Bracken's voice. "Who's ready this time?"

A handsome young man with dense hair perfect as an otter's fur stepped forward. He took off his jacket, handed it to a bystander, and crouched down in a sprinter's stance. "I'm ready," he said.

"This is the slalom event, honey," Bracken called. "You weave in and out of the furniture without touching anything. Knock a single thing over, you're out of the game. Now, Jack, wait till I say one, two, three, go!"

She stepped into view now, holding up the stopwatch, wearing a skimpy silver dress that only served to accentuate that she had nothing on underneath. Doyle hung back, observing the unfolding spectacle from between the paws of a topiary lion at the edge of the garden. This scene was typical drunken Bracken craziness. Sometimes people got hurt, sometimes they didn't; inevitably there was property damage. Doyle remembered the time she'd organized a scavenger hunt in Central Park like an heiress in a screwball comedy — one of the items to scavenge was a mounted policeman's helmet. A couple of her friends assaulted a cop to get one and spent the next ten months in jail.

"One, two, three! Go!"

Otterhead dashed down the slope, slaloming between the furniture, and disappeared into the darkness. Then there came a crashing sound and a loud *"Fuck!"*

"I think he levelled your painted highboy, Bracken, darling," said a woman in a red dress.

"Is he hurt?" a man asked.

"Who the fuck cares?" somebody else shouted. "The bastard's disqualified!"

A moment later, Otterhead came scrambling back up the slope and threw himself sprawling at Bracken's feet.

"Time?" he managed, panting heavily. "Time, anyone?"

Bracken put a foot in the small of his back and held him down. "You are so fucking disqualified," she said. "You wrecked my painted highboy, you creep."

"The fucking thing fell over, I barely touched it," Otterhead's voice muffled in the grass. This statement was greeted with general hoots of derision.

"That was a rare example of Baltimore painted furniture, circa 1795," Bracken said. "Been in the family since new. I hate painted furniture, ugliest fucking piece ever, but worth at least fifty thousand."

"Fifty thousand dollars?" Otterhead sputtered. "For a fucking chest of drawers?"

"Not worth fifty thousand now," the woman in the red dress observed.

"I warned you, Bracken." A tall woman in a black dress stepped forward. She was approaching fifty but had succeeded, at least under current lighting conditions, in looking twenty years younger. "See what happens when you screw around with valuable antiques?"

"Fuck valuable antiques," Bracken said. "Let's play ball! Who's next?"

The woman in the black dress shrugged it off with one quick motion, revealing zebra-stripe underwear and a tight, brownish body showing about as much fat as a lean piece of chicken. At the signal from Bracken she dashed off down the slope.

Doyle waited for a lull in the action, then stepped across the line of paper-bag candles to where Bracken was standing. "The damnedest way to redecorate I've ever seen," he said into her ear, and she spun around and kissed him on the mouth. Doyle tasted the gin she had been drinking and a bitter something else — the blonde's pot? — on her breath.

"He came!" she shouted to everyone. "I knew he'd come!" Then she kissed him again and wiggled against him, and Doyle felt a familiar pressure between his legs.

"Careful, Bracken," he said, stepping back. "You're looking at a man that hasn't been laid in months. I just might explode."

"Beautiful, baby." Bracken lowered her voice to a throaty whisper: "You can explode all over me later."

And with this promise ringing in Doyle's ears, she took him around to meet the other guests — a collection of catty New York charity-ball types, whose names and faces vanished from his consciousness almost instantly. Bracken still lived in that city nine months out of the year in a vast, luxurious apartment on Central Park West that had once belonged to her uncle, a bankrupt financier who had somehow managed to emerge from bankruptcy with $30 million and a villa on the Côte d'Azur. Doyle recognized not a single face from the old days in this crowd and wondered how many successive lives and circles of friends Bracken had sloughed off in the years between then and now. "You've come up since Chinatown," he said, when the introductions were over.

"About sixty blocks," Bracken said. "How's your wife?"

"I don't know," Doyle said glumly, and told her about his troubles.

"D-I-V-O-R-C-E," Bracken sang. Then she waltzed away and procured a bottle of champagne from somewhere and tossed it to Doyle.

"Cheers," she said.

"By the way," Doyle said, "one of your friends passed out in the hall on top of everyone's coats."

"I don't have friends anymore," Bracken said gleefully. "Only acquaintances."

Doyle shrugged and unwrapped the foil and popped the cork and drank down half the bottle then the other half, and began to feel pretty good about himself.

The game continued. More pieces of priceless antique furniture were smashed beyond recognition — an Empire secretaire, a mother-of-pearl inlaid bombé chest, a card table once used for gentlemanly games of whist and piquet.

"Damn," Bracken said, with a pout. "I think George Washington signed something important on that table."

"What's the point in ruining all your good furniture?" Doyle said. "Is there something I'm missing here?"

Bracken waved him off. "Honey, the point is furniture just doesn't matter," she said. "Bunch of old wood, if you ask me. And no one's trying to ruin anything, we're just trying to have a little fun. It's the land that matters. That's what we're celebrating tonight."

"The land?" Doyle was confused.

Bracken turned to him with a lazy smile. "Go ahead, smell the wind, take a real deep breath." She pointed Doyle towards the southwestern darkness and he gave in and filled his lungs with night air.

"There," Bracken said. "What do you smell?"

Doyle took another breath. "Manure," he said. "Fertilizer."

Bracken clapped her hands. "Exactly!" she said. "So what does that mean to you?"

"That you got some cows shitting in the woods," Doyle said.

"No, honey! It means Deering's Hundred is a working plantation again. We're expecting the very first crop since the Civil War. And guess what it is? Go ahead, guess."

"I have no idea," Doyle said, a little surprised.

"Strawberries!" Bracken said, as if this were some sort of revelation.

"OK, strawberries," Doyle said. "But you always used to say there was a curse against planting anything at the Hundred."

"Don't talk like that," Bracken said, frowning. "I'm superstitious."

"One question — how are you managing without slaves?"

"I've got a secret weapon," Bracken smirked. Then she lifted her face to the manure-scented wind. "Enrique!" she shouted. "Enrique!"

As if conjured by magic, a stocky Mexican man in a spotless white suit appeared out of the darkness. "Finish your games, Señora Bracken?" the Mexican said. "You want I should take the furniture back inside?"

Bracken shook her head. "No, no, Enrique," she said. "I just wanted you to meet my friend Mr. Doyle. You two have so much in common."

Doyle looked at the Mexican and the Mexican looked at Doyle, each trying to figure out what he could possibly have in common with the other. Turquoise and silver rings cluttered the Mexican's thick fingers; a silver steer's skull with turquoise eyes glared out from the center of a ridiculous-looking bolo tie. From Doyle's point of view, the Mexican's sinister pock-marked face seemed to conceal many secrets. Doyle caught a sudden intimation of shallow graves, shady deals gone wrong Tijuana-style, mute melancholy stars in the black-domed Sonoran sky the only witnesses.

"OK, why don't you tell us, Bracken?" Doyle said at last, giving up. "What do we have in common?"

The Mexican nodded; he also wanted to know.

Bracken laughed, a shrill, mischievous cackle. "Your machismo, darlings!" she said. She gave Doyle a kiss on the cheek and floated off to rejoin the furniture races.

Doyle and the Mexican eyed each other warily for a few seconds longer, then the Mexican gestured towards the furniture and said, "You play the games tonight, Señor?"

"No," Doyle shook his head. "You?"

"In Mexico, tables are for eating," the Mexican said. "And the chairs, they are for sitting. But here," he made an untranslatable gesture, "Señora Bracken like to play many games. She is a great lady. It is the honor of such a lady to play such games with her beautiful furniture."

"Maybe, maybe not," Doyle said.

"Ah, you do not approve." The Mexican smiled sadly.

"Destruyendo meubles caras no es mi desportes," Doyle said, in his Castillian Spanish.

"You speak very good!" the Mexican said, alarmed, as if he had never met an American who spoke anything but English and this had proved to his advantage.

"Ay si, vivia en Málaga en España por viente años . . ." Doyle began. Just then, a loud shriek from the playing field caused him to turn away. When he turned back, the Mexican was gone.

12

The tomb of Colonel Brodie Deering stood in a grove of mournful cypress trees in the far corner of the topiary garden. Fantastic leafy animals guarded the entrance to the grove — a box-hedge hipogriffin, a chimera, the dreadful Kraken sculpted improbably from a rhododendron bush. The tomb was simplicity itself — weathered white marble, squarish, each cornice supported by plain Ionic columns, like the tomb of a Roman aristocrat on the Appian Way. There was no name. The worn, barely legible inscription seemed more of a threat than a promise: THE DEAD SHALL BE RAISED. Black-headed tulips had begun to push up from the beds around the perimeter.

As dawn paled the ridge above the house, Bracken led Doyle past the topiary monsters into the grove. They were barefoot and naked, without a stitch between them except for the pink down comforter Bracken carried bunched beneath her arm.

"I don't like this one bit," Doyle said. "My ass is cold, my feet are freezing."

"Shut up, honey," Bracken said, "you'll break the mood," and she pointed to the flat marble slab capping the tomb. "I want you to fuck me up there, right on top of that asshole's mausoleum."

Doyle hesitated, then he thought of a simple question. "Why?"

"Because it's something I've always wanted to do," Bracken said. "Ever since I was a little girl."

"You were a very strange little girl," Doyle mumbled, but somehow he began to warm to the idea.

Bracken dropped the quilt and hooked her toes around the base of the nearest column and swung herself over the pediment and on to the capstone. Doyle tossed the quilt up and scrambled after her. The marble felt icy against his skin; chilly air puckered his privates. But the capstone of Colonel Deering's tomb offered an excellent vista of house, garden, and fields. Looking down the slope of the hill, Doyle saw the wreckage of furniture strewn across the dew-wet grass, the very last guest trailing off and, in the distance, migrant workers laboring in the freshly turned fields, planting strawberries even at this early hour.

Then Bracken spread out the comforter and they rolled themselves up in it, and right there above the moldering remains of Colonel Brodie Deering, that redoubtable Indian fighter, they made love with an unexpected tenderness that recalled the fleeting sweetness of college days: Bracken waltzing gracefully at a sorority ball at Southern Sem, a rose in her hair; the two of them holding each other close on the veranda of some old house in the moonlight. What a bewildering combination of sentiment and wildness she had been — swilling bourbon and throwing shoes at bouncers one minute, the next weeping profuse tears over a baby elephant abandoned by its mother on a nature show on TV. At nineteen, for all her sophistication, even Bracken had maintained a certain innocence, her secret hollows as yet uncaressed by the rough hands of the world.

An hour later, the sun came up pale yellow over the hill and they made love again. Afterwards they rolled apart and Bracken produced a pack of Kool Menthols from somewhere and she lit up, and a stream of cigarette smoke floated into the empyreum.

"Where did you get those?" Doyle said.

"From up my ass, honey," Bracken said. Then she added, "Just kidding," but Doyle declined a smoke anyway. They were silent a while, the sun warming the garden. Now the wind assailed them with the strong smell of fertilizer from the strawberry fields.

"What made you decide to do it?" Doyle said at last.

"What?" Bracken said, blowing smoke away from him out of the corner of her mouth.

"Plant strawberries."

"It looks like I'm not going to have any children," Bracken said. "I've got to make something grow."

"You could still have a child," Doyle said. "One at least. Especially these days. Medical science —"

"Not me," Bracken interrupted. "Too many abortions. It's all scarred-up in there. I imagine it looks like —" she rapped her knuckles against the marble "— the interior of this asshole's tomb. All black with decay and rusty red."

They lapsed into silence again, perhaps by way of epitaph for children unborn. Then Bracken rolled on to her back, nipples perked at the chill morning sky. "Listen to me carefully, honey," she said, her bright tone suddenly dull, neutral. "I'm supposed to ask you something. I'm supposed to ask if you'll sell Pirate Island. To me."

Doyle didn't quite understand. He asked her to repeat herself.

"You heard me the first time," Bracken said.

"You going to tell me who asked you?" Doyle said quietly.

Bracken shook her head. "I can't," she said.

Doyle felt himself getting angry. "So that's what all this was about," he said.

"No, honey! This was about you and me, about being kids again." Bracken sat up and tried to take him in her arms but he pushed her away.

"Save it," Doyle said. "And you tell Roach to go fuck himself." He rolled over and, with a quick motion, jumped down into the soft topsoil of the tulip bed.

"Timmy, please!" Bracken peered over the edge.

Doyle turned reluctantly and looked up at her. The excesses of the evening showed as a red rim of disquietude around her eyes. She looked old, sunk in the black gloom of a post-coital funk.

"I don't know anyone named Roach," she said. Doyle met her gaze with his own. She blinked and looked away, and he thought she was probably lying.

"Who is it, then?" Doyle said. He was in no mood for riddles this morning.

Bracken shook her head. "I can't tell you," she said, in a voice that sounded scared. "Believe me, you're better off not knowing. And, listen, it's not like you won't have someplace to go. After you sell, you can move in with me here for a while, then we'll go back to New York. It'll be just like the Chinese restaurant again. You really ought to think carefully about this one, Timmy, because it's probably your last chance to sell in a peaceable manner."

"Tell me what you know, Bracken!" Doyle was yelling now, angry. "I've been burned out, threatened at gunpoint, assaulted, the Fish and Wildlife cops think I'm an animal killer, Constable Smoot thinks I'm a member of the IRA, and you're playing fucking coy? This is not a fucking game, Bracken! This is deadly stuff. Now what's going on?"

Bracken made a zipping motion across her lips with two fingers. She was capricious and resolute at once, and when she decided something, it was decided. Doyle knew she wouldn't talk. She reached out a hand. "Help me down," she said, attempting a smile, "and I'll tell you who it's not."

"Help your fucking self down," Doyle said. He turned and strode angrily across the garden towards the house, leaving Bracken perched naked and enigmatic as the sphinx atop her ancestor's marble tomb.

13

The Mexican boy jumped out from behind an oak tree, arms waving wildly, just where the Deerings' private road ran from gravel to asphalt. Doyle swerved sharply to avoid him and the front bumper of the Cadillac ploughed over a weed as large and woody as a sapling before the big car came to rest in the underbrush inches from a deep gully.

The boy scrambled around the side of the car and clawed at the window until Doyle had recovered sufficiently from the shock to buzz it down. The boy was twelve or thirteen, thin, his cheeks hollowed out by hunger, his coloring dark intermingled with the reddish tints of the deep south where Mexico bleeds into the jungles of Guatemala and the last remnants of the Mayans skulk about beneath half-extinguished volcanos in the jungle fastnesses.

"*Por favor* — help!" the boy cried, tugging at the door handle. "You quick, help! *Vamanos!*"

He was dressed in a ragged Chicago Bears T-shirt and very dirty khakis, none of which offered sufficient protection from the morning cold. He had no coat or socks. The ancient pair of wingtips on his feet were held together with duct tape.

"*Calmate, vengo!*" Doyle got out of the car and the boy clawed at Doyle's arm and dragged him off into the underbrush. Branches lashed Doyle's face and it was rough going down into the gully and over some fallen logs slippery with moss. Soon, they reached a narrow trail and the woods began to thin and they emerged into a clearing. The fecal stench of a latrine trench announced the presence of the migrant camp, a pitiful assemblage of ragged tents, lean-tos constructed from packing crates and bits of Styrofoam, old pick-up trucks with makeshift shelters precariously attached. Scraps of laundry, little more than threads, flapped on twine tied to sticks fixed in the red mud.

The boy drew Doyle towards a two-man pup tent marked with a faded Boy Scout fleur-de-lis, the canvas thin and tattered from too many camping jamborees and other, less educational uses.

15

Friday, Maggie and Doyle drove into Wiccomac for their date in Probate Court. They sat in the back of the old courtroom on creaking Windsor chairs for two hours waiting for Slough. Then Slough showed up and it was another two hours before they went up together in front of the judge. The hearing itself was little more than a dry formality, utterly anticlimactic.

Slough mumbled a few affirmatives in response to the judge's mumbled questions — the whole thing took ten minutes — then Maggie and Doyle followed Slough over to his office and signed some more papers and agreed to a fee schedule for the estate taxes and the lawyer straightened his glasses and adjusted his suspenders and, stone-faced, handed over a piece of white paper large as a diploma and embossed with various gaudy seals.

"Good luck to both of you," Slough said, unconvincingly. He didn't seem happy about the transaction.

"I guess your friend Roach must be disappointed," Doyle said.

"You know my opinion," Slough said, pursing his thick lips. "I think you're making a mistake. I'm afraid I'll see you both back in here in a couple of years filing for bankruptcy."

"Hey, why don't you just keep your goddamned opinion to yourself?" Maggie said. Slough turned his liquid gaze on her and didn't say a word. He held his eyes on her face for a few seconds and Maggie made a sound in her throat and turned around and stormed out on to the courthouse green. Doyle turned to follow, then he stopped at the door.

"I don't think it's going to surprise you any to hear I'm looking for a new lawyer," he said. "One day, I'll find out how deep you let yourself get and with whom and the legal malpractice board will have more than enough dirt to nail your fat ass to the wall."

Slough's jowly face quivered, but he sat back hard in his chair and turned his attention to some papers on the desk, and Doyle went out and joined Maggie on the green. He found her perched atop the howitzer, tears rolling down her cheeks.

"That man's got the evil eye, I swear," she said. "There's something rotten in him, way down inside."

"Maybe," Doyle agreed.

She stood up, smoothed her skirt, and wiped her eyes on her knuckles. "Well, we got our piece of paper that says what's ours is ours," she waved the deed at the blue sky, "but it's not over yet. We still need the final go-ahead."

"What do you mean?" Doyle said.

"Something you should have done a long time ago," Maggie said.

16

Inside, the church was very white with pews of blond wood, modernistic stained-glass windows and a burnished-steel cubist Christ hanging from a burnished-steel crucifix made out of recycled war materials circa 1947. Its congregation greatly diminished in recent years — along with every other Catholic church in America — St. Mary's Star of the Sea in Wilmont had a worn, half-abandoned look, the parquet flooring buckled and scuffed, the acoustic tiles brown from rain leaking through the roof.

Maggie knelt in stained-glass sunlight in the pew closest to the altar, deeply absorbed in prayer, beads wrapped twice around her knuckles, pre-Vatican II lace mantilla covering her bleached Farrah Fawcett hair. She was saying the rosary and being slow and methodical about it, taking her time over the Hail Marys. Meanwhile, Doyle loitered in the vestibule like an evil spirit barred from entering consecrated ground: churches made him nervous — the shabby condition of his own soul was something he didn't care to contemplate. Then he got up and wandered over to the literature rack and was absently leafing through the latest misalette when Father Scipio came in from outside.

"Tim Doyle," the old priest said, surprised.

Doyle spun around, guilty as a thief robbing the poor box. "Father S!" he said.

The priest offered a paternal smile and patted Doyle on the arm with a hand made knobby by arthritis. He was an old man now, over eighty, but possessed an astonishing head of white hair and bright, intelligent eyes staring out from a face that was otherwise a mask of wrinkles. He was one of the last examples of the tough, muscular World War Two generation of American Catholics: in those days every large Catholic family had fielded at least one son to the seminary and one daughter to the convent as the proper human tithe to God. Father Scipio had been an army chaplain, landed on the beach at Anzio alongside Uncle Buck, and advanced with the troops up the spiny back of Italy to Rome. At Monte Cassino, it was said, he had grabbed a machine gun from a wounded soldier and cleaned out a Nazi sniper's nest. But this was a legend from Doyle's boyhood. No martial fierceness showed now in the priest's gentle manner.

"Will you take a little anisette?" Father Scipio said.

Doyle nodded and followed the old priest into the rectory, whose oppressive low ceilings and ponderous, dark-wood furniture held more than a touch of the odious Frank Lloyd Wright. Doyle settled on a hard wooden chair and Father Scipio brought out a bottle, of the sweet-sour Italian liqueur and two glasses no larger than thimbles. The priest filled the glasses, handed one to Doyle, and raised his own in a toast. "To your uncle Buck," he said. "A good man and a good Catholic."

"A prince," Doyle said, and he drank, remembering with some embarrassment the last time alcohol had passed his lips in this rectory. He'd served a brief stint as altar boy, this during seventh grade, the year before he'd been sent up to Catholic boarding school in Maryland. But his altar-boy career had ended abruptly one morning during eleven-thirty mass: Doyle and another kid, sent to the rectory at the last minute to fetch Father Scipio's sermon notes, had somehow found the stash of communion wine. Between them, they managed to choke down an entire sour half-gallon of cheap burgundy in two minutes flat; during the gospel, up it came, red as the blood of Christ, all over their white surplices, to the scandal of the congregation.

Now, Father Scipio set his glass aside and folded his knobby hands in his lap, a gesture that suggested at once judgement and forgiveness. "All right, son," he said. "Let's hear your version of events."

Doyle looked up uneasily. He'd given his version of the wine incident thirty-five years ago. But no — this must be about the shooting on the pier.

"I don't know what you've heard, Father," Doyle said, "but the man came at me with a gun. It was self-defense."

Father Scipio shook his head. "I'm talking about your wife," he said. "Your son."

Doyle found himself sweating. He caught a flash of Pablo asleep on Flor's lap beneath a beach umbrella at Ibiza — was it last year or the year before? — a pretty seaside *pièta*, wind flapping the tassels of her robe. Now he found himself making a sort of spontaneous confession. He told the old priest about Brigitte, about all the others. There had been eight over nearly twenty years of marriage. Not that many if you looked at it a certain way — less than one betrayal per every two conjugal years.

Father Scipio frowned. "Who were these women?

Doyle shrugged, regretting that he had broached the subject with a *priest*.

"Prostitutes, harlots, *filles de passage*?" Fatha Scipio persisted.

"Just women, Father," Doyle said.

"Attractive women?" Father Scipio said.

"Most," Doyle admitted. "But not all."

"Then we might excuse you from the sin of vanity, if not the sin of lust."

"OK" Doyle said, slightly confused. A moment of silence followed in which he thought back over the list. Yes, he could remember all their names. This made him feel a little better about himself; there had been a couple of one-night stands but he had never slept with anyone he wouldn't sleep with again: Inez, an acupuncturist met on a bus from Cadiz to Madrid; Silka — her stage name — a Balinese dancer actually from Bali, an aficionado of the bullfights; Clara and Carmen — yes, both at once — two of his wife's more irresponsible friends; Paulina, a teacher of Latin whose remorse afterwards had been equal to her hunger before; Rachel, a tourist from Australia who had the finest ass he'd ever seen; Ursula, a French travelling saleswoman — bathroom fixtures — who claimed to be a lesbian but wasn't; Nieves, an actress who had done a film with Almodóvar. And lastly Brigitte, a student from Paris working as a nanny for the neighbors; the rock upon which he'd smashed everything.

"Did you love your wife while you pursued all these . . . liaisons?" Father Scipio said presently.

"Oh yes," Doyle was adamant. "Always. Still do. She's wonderful."

"Then you're a damned fool."

"Yes."

"One last question," the old priest hesitated. "Why?"

Doyle said he didn't know but he did. Yes, it was all the beautiful women in Málaga, a city famed since antiquity for the beauty of its women, but it was also something else: it was his bottomless hunger for just one more adventure, for one more new face, for someone new to laugh at his jokes, and later to show him just how and where she liked to be touched. It was unspeakable escapades in strange bedrooms, fan whirring overhead, the husband's voice plaintive on the answering machine from a lonely business trip to Switzerland and the whole night and morning ahead, Flor off with the baby to Ecija. In Spain, of course, a certain amount of cheating was expected, he explained to Father Scipio, and in that department he hadn't really been any worse than your average Spaniard.

Father Scipio's expression darkened. "Do you try to excuse your sins?"

"No, Father," Doyle said. "And now that it's too late I miss my wife more than I can say. And Pablo, I really miss the little guy. Typical buyer's remorse, I guess."

"So you acknowledge your guilt?"

"I do," Doyle said, and he hung his head in shame.

"That's the first step." Father Scipio nodded sadly. "I'll say a prayer for your reconciliation."

"Thanks," Doyle said.

"But, meanwhile, you've got to pray yourself. You've got to ask God's forgiveness. You've got to *change.*" He emphasized the last word. "'Not in rioting and drunkenness, not in chambering and wantonness, not in strife and envying,' as Paul says in the Epistle to the Romans. In other words, clean up your act, son. Give up your excesses, start leading a more Christian life. Maybe then you might be able to get your wife back."

"I think it's too late for that one, Father," Doyle said.

"Never too late, Tim," Father Scipio said gravely. "Scratch a voluptuary and you'll find a saint struggling to get out. Look at Augustine.

In his youth, the man was a member of a gang of leather-jacketed toughs, maintained several mistresses, fathered illegitimate children, the works. Then one day, walking in his garden — with a slight hangover, one would imagine — he heard God call him beneath a fig tree and he gave up everything to follow that call."

"Yeah," Doyle said. "I've heard the story before. In your catechism class."

Father Scipio grinned, showing a set of healthy teeth. "You've got a good memory, at least."

Then he got up, put away the bottle of anisette, and ushered Doyle out into the churchyard. A new cemetery extended across the bare field between church and highway. There were no tombstones or monuments of any kind, just dismal brass plaques set into the ground. A groundskeeper on a riding mower rode in wide circles across the graves.

"I'll never see the beauty in these modern cemeteries," the priest said, shading his eyes against the sun. "Sometimes I think they were a conspiracy perpetrated by the groundskeepers' union. Easier to take care of the grass, I suppose, without all those annoying tombstones getting in the way." Then he turned to Doyle and his expression was serious. "Let's talk about your other troubles, the ones that made the newspapers."

"OK." Doyle sighed.

Father Scipio's voice assumed a confidential tone: "The secrecy imposed by the confessional does not allow me to say more than this — you'll find some answers in Delaware."

"Delaware?" Doyle said, alarmed, but the priest made a gesture that meant he had already said enough and he squeezed Doyle's arm with affection and went quickly back into the rectory.

A few minutes later, prayers sent off to heaven like celestial email, Maggie exited the church carrying a pot of marigolds. She still wore her mantilla, and the addition of a pair of cat-eye sunglasses made her look like a repentant prostitute in an Italian movie. She handed Doyle the marigolds and together they made their way across the field of graves to the dry rectangle of dirt beneath which Buck Doyle lay gently decomposing in a pressboard coffin covered with imitation leather. Maggie took the marigolds from Doyle's hand, knelt and scratched out a circle of dirt to make a seat for the pot, then she looked up at Doyle looking down at her. She made a charming picture kneeling there, in her cheap tight sweater and her Italian sunglasses, and despite the priest's recent advice, Doyle could not keep himself from impious thoughts.

"Marigolds, Buck always liked them," Maggie said. "He thought they were bright and cheery. I used to put a bunch of them in a big vase in the bedroom . . ." Her voice trailed off.

"Marigolds," Doyle said awkwardly. "I had no idea."

"There's a lot you don't know," Maggie said. "A lot you'll never know. Tenderness, that's one thing you could have learned from the man. I got this picture of him carrying you around on his shoulders — you're just a tot, maybe two or three, wearing these cute little duck overalls and you're laughing way up there and he's smiling like the happiest man in the world."

Doyle didn't know such a photograph existed and he said so.

"Well, you ought to have a look at it sometime," she said. "You might learn something."

And she stood up, brushed off her knees, and headed back towards the Cadillac parked by the highway across the field of graves.

17

Scattered bunches of poverty grass, *Hudsonia Tomentosa,* some with tender yellow shoots still attached, floated on the softly flexing main. They had been washed out of the marsh by high tides the night before. The water showed a deep and complex green this morning, like the iridescent shimmer of parrot feathers; the April sun gave a warmth to the air that made Doyle think of the summer ahead — a season any full-time resident of any beach community anywhere regards with an uneasy mixture of anticipation and dread.

Cap'n Pete and Toby stood under the foul-weather cowling of the *Chief Powhatan,* beers in hand, arguing about something not worth arguing about.

". . . already feels like July," Toby was saying.

"That's my point," Cap'n Pete said. "Global warming."

"There's that word again. I hate that word," Toby said.

"What word?"

"Global."

By late afternoon, the tin-lined fishing cooler amidships was mostly filled with flounder of various sizes; a couple of snappers, dolphin fish, and an amberjack had mixed in with the gasping flatheads. Doyle balanced himself against the stern ladder and watched Harold squatting on the deck, his hands sticky with fish guts and sand. He was making chum balls with all the tongue-chewing concentration of a five year old.

Harold had showed a marked improvement in attitude lately; today he had willingly pitched in to help with the catch — icing down the fish, fetching beers, lighting cigarettes, steadying the *Chief Powhatan* through the swells that began to rise after two o'clock. In the clear ocean light, his eyes were bright and free from shadows for the first time since Doyle grabbed him from his mother's trailer and the clutches of the pixel video Marine. Harold had never been fishing before, as it turned out.

"I can't believe no one ever took you fishing," Doyle said. "You live at the ocean, for God's sakes."

The kid squinted up at him. "Nobody ever took me anywhere," he said.

"What did your parents do with their time?" Doyle said.

"Before he run off to Louisiana my Dad drove a truck," Harold said. "Hardly ever saw him. When he was home, he and mom were either fucking or fighting. Once I had to sleep out back in a tent because they had another couple over for sex. I watched some of it through the window, though."

Doyle's mouth went dry. "And what did you see?"

Harold scowled. "Why do you ask so many weird questions?"

Doyle left the kid alone with the fish guts and went to join Toby and Cap'n Pete beneath the cowling. Later, when the fishing was through, Harold came forward as Cap'n Pete turned the big wheel towards home.

"I guess you're old enough, punk," Toby said, handing over a bottle of Cap'n Pete's home brew. "Hell, I was a drunk at half your age."

Harold glanced over at Doyle for permission.

"Go ahead," Doyle said, flattered. "But two's your limit."

Harold took the bottle, cracked the cap with his teeth, and chugged the contents. He took a breath, swallowed the last drops, and tossed the bottle over the side. This display was followed by a long, evil belch.

"You'll kill yourself drinking like that," Doyle said.

Harold frowned out at the horizon lost in haze in the east, then he looked at Toby. "You were with him when it happened, weren't you, fat man?"

"What did you call me, you fucking punk!" Toby sputtered into his beer.

"When he shot the guy," Harold said, ignoring Toby's outrage.

Toby wiped the beer from his five-o'clock stubble and smiled grimly. "Yeah, I was there kid," he said, nodding at Doyle. "You're looking at the fastest draw on the Eastern Shore. This man outgunned a trained hoodlum carrying a thoroughly modern 9mm semi-automatic. And this is the amazing part — that feat was achieved with a Whitneyville-Walker Colt .44 fucking horse pistol, model 1847. A classic firearm, don't misunderstand me, but not built for speed. No telling what the Gunslinger here could do with a more appropriate weapon. The good old cap and ball 1851 Navy Colt .41, for example, which was Wild Bill Hickcock's gun of choice. Or of course, the justly famous and beautifully balanced Colt .45, called the Peacemaker."

Harold's eyes went round and credulous. Suddenly, Doyle could imagine the kid getting his hands on an old revolver, shooting up his hippie history teacher at school.

"Enough bullshit," Doyle said to Pete. "I'm trying to put the whole sorry episode behind me."

Toby shook his head. "A beautiful moment like that must not be forgotten, Tim," he said. "The people need examples beside Charles Manson and Monica Lewinski. To paraphrase Thucydides' paraphrasing of the funeral oration of the great Pericles — The world itself is the tomb of famous Doyles."

"I don't know what that means," Doyle said. "I'm just asking you to keep your mouth shut." And he stalked around the fish cooler and joined Cap'n Pete at the wheel.

The ship's radio was tuned to the Coast Guard weather station, a course of amiable static interrupted by the occasional garbled forecast which only Cap'n Pete could understand.

"Storm's coming," Cap'n Pete said presently.

"Big storm?" Doyle said.

"I think so," Cap'n Pete said.

"Will we weather it?" Doyle said.

"Maybe," Cap'n Pete said.

And as the *Chief* dieseled closer to the dark teardrop of land that was Wassateague Island, Doyle glanced over and saw Toby and Harold the kid leaning close, the big man making a pistol out of his thumb and forefinger, spinning lies into legend against a backdrop of ocean darkness.

part four

THE WRONG
DOYLE

TENCH DOYLE *ran a gaff-rigged log canoe off the wharf of a disreputable little hamlet called Bridger's Hole on the Chesapeake side of the peninsula near the mouth of Wiccomac Creek, and went after the oysters from October to April as his father had done and his grandfather and great-grandfather, but unlike these men, Tench went out alone, wielding the tongs without a culler or a hand at the tiller even in the worst weather, rudder lashed, sail furled tight against prevailing winds, because no one would sail with him because he was known as a difficult and embittered man.*

The wellsprings of character remain mysterious: the youngest two of Tench's six brothers were charming loafers, who took after their Cuban mother and didn't much like oystering and eventually ran away to San Francisco where they could be found loafing and drinking in one saloon or another, famous among the denizens of the Barbary Coast for their sharp talk and their jokes; the middle two brothers learned figures somehow and attained respectable positions in business; the twins, dead at age twelve of typhus in the epidemic of 1872, had been generally well-liked by their schoolmates before they died. But Tench was hated by everyone.

No one could say for sure why Tench had turned out that way, with a harsh word for his neighbor and a quick temper and a mean spirit spoiling for a fight, but there it was. Perhaps some inherited quirk of the damnable Doyles who, since the days of their piratical ancestor, had been a troublesome and unpredictable tribe. At the beer slops and gin palaces in every ramshackle oyster town up and down the bay, the watermen told the story of how Tench once threw a culler over the side in heavy seas for complaining about the cold and the wind on his back and the shells cutting the flesh of his palms and the poor pay and long hours — just the usual things cullers complained about as they broke apart the tough clusters on the board. When the oil lamps burned low and the last dollar had been won or lost at dice or cards and the men fell to talking about war and murder, they avowed Tench was wicked to the bone. A hard, bad man who had drowned many others, a half-dozen maybe, in fits of rage — just poor helpless Paddies fresh off the Baltimore steamer from Ireland without a soul to raise a question at their absence.

Of course, the watermen didn't have the story completely right. Yes, Tench once threw an obstreperous Paddy off his board into the bay for drunkenness on the job, but he swung round minutes later and fished the poor bastard out, still alive, just dripping wet and a little frozen around the edges and sober. If not exactly good, Tench wasn't as bad as they said he was. But the watermen, like all sailors fresh or salt, preferred tall tales to the truth and needed someone on the outside looking in to reassure themselves how comfortable it was in their miserable corner with a bucket of skunk beer and a cold plate of oyster stew on the table before them.

Any man who would go out after bivalves with Tench Doyle, they said, had to be tired of life or plain ignorant or the Devil himself.

Gradually, Tench's reputation as a murderous bastard and a dangerous man grew to the point of legend. Many black crimes were attributed to his name, impossible massacres, robberies, the kidnapping and despoliation of a dozen young virgins. When Tench came into the bar at the Broken Limb on Samuel's Island for a glass of whiskey and a plate of pickled eggs, or stopped at Honest Abe's Crab House in Bluster Creek, for crabs and a beer, the watermen quietly took their plates and glasses and moved across the room and left him to drink and dine in silence.

Tench was not the sort to question the judgement of his fellows in their opinion of his evil nature. After two or three years of the silent treatment, he became used to the solitude of his own company; after another few years it grew on his soul like barnacles on the hull of his log canoe and he lost the habit of the world. He became wild, unkempt, seedy, could be heard muttering to himself as he walked down to the wharf every morning, tongs over his shoulder like the oar carried by Odysseus to the land of the people who had never seen the ocean.

A woman might have made Tench's life bearable but he was through with women, except the kind for rent at two dollars an hour in the warren of grim, red-curtained little rooms above Molly's Tap in Pembroke. Anyway, he had abandoned a wife in Wassateague Town, who did not love him, and three children by her he hadn't seen in years and who wouldn't know his face in a crowd. Some few charitable individuals pointed to this abandoned wife as the original source of Tench's bitterness. She was a Maryland Catholic from some tough little burg west of Baltimore, a well-known harridan with a tongue sharp as a razor. They said it was her constant, merciless harangue that had driven Tench out of his own house to live in a shack in Bridger's Hole where he went after the oysters alone and drank himself to sleep on hard cider most nights and grew more sullen with each passing year.

In the brief pleasant weeks immediately following his marriage, Tench had changed the name of his log canoe from Chief Powhatan to Emily Rose, in honor of his new wife. When he left the wife behind for good, he painted out Emily Rose and sailed with the stern plate blank. Not long after this renunciation, a police schooner belonging to the Virginia Maritime Commission came alongside and insisted that his boat must be called something, if only for the purpose of record-keeping at Commission House in Norfolk. Tench thought for a long minute and said, "Fine, boys, let's call her No Name," and this became another reason for the watermen to hate him: Chesapeake tongers' log canoes were always called after a woman, or a famous American hero, like Davy Crockett or Jefferson Davis, or a long-dead Indian brave. A log canoe named after nothing at all was deemed an evil omen for everyone on the water.

Then, about the end of the decade, which is to say the winter of 1887–8, the supply of deep-water oysters suddenly gave out. These extinguished mollusks had been over-harvested for years in defiance of the law by dredge boats belonging to the big oyster-packing syndicates out of Baltimore and Norfolk. In the opening weeks of this dreadful season the deep bottoms were found scraped clean of everything except mud and weeds.

Legislation had long allotted the open waters of the bay to the syndicates, the shallow coastal waters and oyster-rich estuaries to the private tongers. A typical syndicate oyster sloop ran to ten tons, was fitted with a pair of hand-crank windlass dredges, and carried a captain, mate, cook, and six crewmen. The big iron dredges were dropped into the deep water, dragged along the oyster bars, cranked up, emptied into the hold, dropped again and so on, from dawn till night drained the last exhausted light from the sky.

Cranking a dredge was hellish, backbreaking labor, to which no local waterman would stoop, so the dredges were only worked by Paddies —

fresh-off-the-boat Irish immigrants who didn't know better brought down to the various oyster towns by train from Baltimore at the beginning of each season. Dredge captains worked their Paddy crews under the whip like slaves until the men collapsed from exhaustion. When a Paddy could no longer work, he was often just tossed over the side like so much oyster trash. Despite this harsh treatment, such men were in ready supply: to replenish his crew, a dredge captain had but to put into one of the Paddy shacks — prison-like compounds hidden on islands at the far fringes of the bay — where surplus men were kept, half-starved and desperate for work.

Hard times generally make for hard men: soon Tench Doyle had more company than he could bear. As winter closed in, the dredge-boats scraped the very last oysters out of the deep beds and moved their operations to shallower waters and the war was on.

No God-fearing Wassateague tonger — not even Tench, who didn't believe a single word of scripture — would work the oysters on Sunday. Sundays were made for home and family, for happily married men on good terms with their conscience and their neighbors; the bars and taverns were closed, wheezy organ music and communal singing rose from the arched windows of the clapboard churches and floated to heaven on the oyster-tainted wind.

This particular Sunday, Tench sprawled on the rough plank bench outside the unpainted shack in Bridger's Hole where he lived, listening to the faint, distant strains of a familiar hymn and drinking sourmash out of a stoneware jug and smoking a pipe filled with rank local tobacco and staring at the sky and thinking about nothing in particular. He was watching a sow-shaped cloud blue with rain scud across the Bay when a wild-looking young man stumbled out of the brambles bordering the piny wood behind the shack, holding his hands before him as if they were on fire.

Startled, Tench stared at the young man. The young man stared back. He was about twenty, barefoot, dressed in tatters, flushed and feverish-looking and so thin his ribs could be counted at a distance. His pale eyes held the dull glare of the permanently starved and his head was covered with the most absurd carrot-colored shag from which large pink ears protruded like the ears of a monkey. But it was his hands Tench remarked upon first: they were red and infected, swollen twice their normal size, the fingers thick and fat as sausages.

"Not meaning to trespass on your property, sir," the young man said, in *a heavy Irish brogue, "but could you be telling me which way to Baltimore City?"*

Tench put his jug aside, rose off the bench. "Let me see your hands, boy."

The young man blinked and showed his hands. Tench peered down and shuddered at what he saw there. "Oyster hand, all right," Tench said, immediately recognizing the affliction. "About the worst case I ever saw and I been tonging the damnable bivalves twenty seasons or more."

"Me hands are just fine," the young man retorted. Then his eyes fell on Tench's jug of sourmash. "Is that a bottle of whiskey ye have there?"

Tench hesitated. In one sense, solitude is freedom: the solitary goes through life blissfully unmolested by duties, entanglements. But, as it turned out, Tench was not one of these. He offered the jug and the young man took it with difficulty between his swollen fingers and indulged himself in a lengthy guzzle, whose effects were instantaneous: his blue, hunger-haunted eyes rolled back in his head and he pitched forward and fell insensate to the ground at Tench's feet.

The young man's name was Connor Malone. He was a marooned oyster Paddy set ashore without pay off the dredger Artemis B. Ward, but until the previous year he had lived with his aged father and four spinster sisters on a poor tenant farm in County Clare, Ireland. The soil of Connor's home was hard and rocky and they barely managed a subsistence crop of rye sold to the local distillery. With the proceeds they bought rye whiskey and bread, and grain for the lone, rangy milk cow and feed for the pitiful chickens who laid no eggs — these animals, along with a single broken chair and a rag of a curtain, represented the entire earthly wealth of the Malones.

Upon attaining his majority, Connor had gone off to Dublin, where he worked for shillings a week in a pestilential lamp-black factory in the grim shadow of the castle. Then, like so many others from that poor green island, he found his way aboard a ship bound for America. He landed in Baltimore, destitute and starving — "I been so poor and so starved all my life," he told Tench, "I wouldn't know what to do with a nice bit of beef liver and roast potatoes if you hit me on the head with them" — and there luckily found work as a gravedigger for the city at three dollars a month before he was let go in favor of a Bohunk who would work for half that amount. Ejected from his rooming house for non-payment of rent and wandering the streets hungry and without prospects, one day he saw the big black-lettered posters advertising positions for able-bodied men in the Ward syndicate oyster fleet. A two-dollar-and-fifty-cent enlistment bonus was promised upon signature.

Connor cheerily marched down to the syndicate offices in the harbor, signed up, and received his two dollars and fifty cents, more money than he'd seen at any one time in his life. He promptly went on a drunken tear, spent every last penny in a single night, and so arrived destitute as usual aboard the Artemis B. Ward, dredge No. 21 of the Ward syndicate. Unfortunately for Connor, this vessel was cursed with the devil as a captain — the notorious Bull Rawson, known up and down the bay as a mean, tight-fisted bastard who administered beatings with a tarred, nail-studded length of rope kept coiled around his waist like a poisonous snake. The Artemis B. Ward had one of the highest mortality rates in the fleet; each bushel out of her hold was paid for with the blood and bones of the Paddies.

Rawson maintained another notorious practice: he would take on more men than he could pay or feed, wear them down with repeated beatings and ceaseless labor until at last, unable to work, they would be paid off at the boom. Which is to say he'd set them on aft watch at dusk and when the wind was right, swing the wheel without warning and the boom would go crashing across the deck and sweep the poor Paddies unawares into the dark icy waters of the bay. Thus, the frozen bodies of Irishmen washed up like driftwood all winter long on the beaches at Cape Charles.

Comparatively speaking, Connor Malone suffered a gentler fate than most of the crew: after a long, backbreaking stretch at the windlass, Captain Rawson set him to a spell of culling at the board. Inexperienced, Connor sliced his hands again and again on the sharp edges of the shells and soon his palms were swollen and running with the green pus affliction the watermen called oyster hand. Then his fingers swelled up and he wasn't even good for the culling anymore.

After that, Rawson administered a last beating with his tarry flail, took Connor's wool jersey and his shoes, and set him ashore with nothing on a desolate spit of land twenty miles south of Oknontocoke Point, and the poor bewildered Irishman had been wandering for two days when he wandered upon Tench drinking whiskey on the log bench in front of his shack on Sunday. By this time, Connor was out of his head with fever and halfway down the road to that grey monotonous country, Death.

For reasons Tench couldn't articulate to himself, he went that evening *for the doctor in Wiccomac, who came out in his mule-drawn surrey for the princely sum of three gold dollars to examine the raving, prostrate Paddy who had risen out of the brambles behind the shack like an apparition. Pills and salves were prescribed and soakings in water treated with certain salts, and plenty of food and rest. Oyster hand this severe might take months of recuperation, the doctor said, but somehow Tench didn't care. He didn't even mind that the medications cost a fortune, which he paid without indulging in the luxury of thinking himself a fool for doing so. Then he hired an old hag from the village at two bits a day as a kind of nurse while he went back tonging aboard* No Name, *the black-hulled dredge boats lurking on the horizon like flocks of large, evil birds.*

Connor Malone's fever burned its course in a fortnight. He awoke with useless, bandaged hands, but alive. And when Tench returned from the bay the following Sunday, he found Connor waiting there on the plank bench before the shack as if he owned the place, a jug of Tench's good whiskey cradled in his lap. Tench stopped short, disconcerted by the sight of another man taking his ease on the premises. But Connor raised the bottle and offered a broad, friendly grin. "My benefactor, I presume," he said.

For a long moment, Tench didn't know what to say. He felt oddly shy. He took a drink of the whiskey and shyly handed the bottle back. Quite by accident, and for the first time in many long, lonely years, he had found a friend.

Over the course of the fall and early winter, Tench and Connor were seen together everywhere — at the tavern on Pilot Point, at Dodie's saloon playing skittles, at Murdoch's eating shad roe and fried tomatoes washed down with yeasty bock, at Molly's, taking their turn with the two-dollar girls upstairs. The other watermen wondered over this spectacle and some said old Tench had found himself a strange sort of wife, but none said it loud enough that he might hear.

When Connor had regained enough of his strength to work the tiller, he accompanied Tench on the long days oystering aboard the No Name, *Tench tonging, Connor draped over the shaft with his bandaged hands, the musical sound of his talk drifting out across the waves. As it turned out, Connor was a prodigious talker, a teller of the old Irish stories. This was the real currency by which he had earned his way through life thus far — telling stories to his father and sisters on the farm, to his mates in the lamp-black factory, to the other immigrants in the hold of the miserable coffin* ship that had brought him to America from Ireland — and by the telling earning an extra bowl of soup, a spare shilling or two, a more comfortable berth, even a bit of mercy from the black-hearted Captain Rawson. He had learned the stories from his grandmother in Ireland before she died of being old. And that old woman had learned them from her grandmother by a peat fire in a whitewashed sod hut on the banks of the Shannon in the days of Wolfe Tone, and that old woman had learned them from her grandmother, and so on — back in an unbroken chain to the days when the stories were true and giants walked the earth and the Children of the Sidh with shining faces romped through the tall, delicious grass of the Country of the Young.

Tench had never heard such fantastic stuff, the forgotten lore of his ancestors. The bitter cold winter days on the bay were warmed by tales of beautiful, cruel Deirdre of the Sorrows; of Kilhoolan, the mighty warrior, enchanted and set to fight the ceaseless waves; of Finn, whose beautiful playing on the fiddle caused the dead to wake from their graves and dance a sprightly jig; of Urusan, King of the Cats, who once showed that rogue McMannon the secret door to the treasure house of the Fairies for the price of one very nice cod; of the marvelous Ossian who crossed the Western Ocean on a magical horse in search of silver-haired Niamh, his spectral love; of Nor and Bin, the fearsome giants who supported the foundations of the world on their wide, knobby shoulders.

"And a dry, dusty piece of work it is, holding up the whole world," Connor said. "So, you see, those poor damned giants have worked up a powerful thirst over a thousand thousand years and 'tis said that the first mortal wanders into their sunless cavern with a fresh-poured pint of stout in his hand and the giants smell it, then off goes the world like a threadbare coat and down it comes crashing into the black sea of night and that's the end of us all. But for the moment the giants are so thirsty they're beyond thirst itself and it'll take a good strong whiff of a nice frothy pint to remind them what it's like again."

Tench allowed he knew how they felt, those giants — a rare comment for him. He was a man of long, habitual silences and too busy working the tongs and culling the board to speak much. Anyway, young Connor did enough talking for both of them.

Meanwhile, events on the bay put the lie to these fairy stories. Dredge-boats, now seen everywhere in the shallow oyster-rich waters, faced the violent resistance of the tongers who objected to their illegal presence with rifles and Colt revolvers and light artillery placed in mud and timber earth-works at the mouths of the estuaries.

In December, tonger cannonfire sent the dredger Marie Dombowski down in sixty feet of water off Sutter's Reach and four Paddies locked in the forecastle drowned. The syndicates responded by sinking six log canoes on a single day in January. Then the dredge Nicholson Sawyer was dismasted with a round of chainshot, which also killed the captain and the mate. The death of these two officers alarmed the cigar-chewing oyster magnates in Baltimore more than the death of a thousand Paddies. A convention was held in the Congressional Hotel at Cape May, New Jersey, at which the syndicates resolved unanimously to pursue drastic action against the tongers in an effort to combat what the newspapers they owned were call-ing Anarchy on the Bay.

By the end of February, most of the dredge-boats had been armed with Gatling guns acquired from the U.S. Army, their crews filled out with an ex-tra contingent of shotgun-wielding roughnecks recruited from the scum of the docks in cities as far north as New York. Though the law was on the side of the tongers, the government was not, and refused to enforce existing statutes. In times of scarcity, the bay belonged to everyone, said the Vir-ginia State Attorney General — which meant the bay belonged to the strongest arm. The struggle proved unequal: the tongers were being pushed off oyster beds fished by their families for generations. The public wanted oysters, they didn't care who dragged them up from the bottom. By the sec-ond week of March, dredger captains and their thugs had sunk sixty log ca-noes with twenty-seven lives lost.

Inevitably, Tench Doyle found himself drawn into this bitter struggle. In-evitably, also, his friendship with Connor Malone began to wear thin. Friendships between men after a certain age are prickly, difficult undertak-ings. Masculine pride, drink, the competitive impulse all play a part.

One foggy dawn the first week of March, Tench raised the sail on the No Name and Connor took his customary place at the tiller and they made their way out to Brown's Inlet, long a favorite oyster bed of the Doyles. Once there, an unfamiliar sight reared out of the fog — a black-hulled dredge-boat of the Ward syndicate lay dredging the bar, lanterns still burn-ing yellow from her masts against the gray light, the clatter of the windlass cable echoing loud in the stillness.

"Them bastards been here all night," Tench whispered. "Shallow waters is for tongers by law, goddamnit, not them dredge sonsabitches!" He hoisted his massive duck punt and fixed it to the bow swivel, primed the fuse and packed the breach with sharp oystershells from the pile and covered the ungainly weapon with a canvas shroud. "What are you going to do?" Fear tightened Connor's voice. "Don't be a crazy man, Doyle!"

Tench turned back towards the Irishman gone green with fear at the tiller. "Drop your head, boy," he said, grinning. "We're going to give them pirates something to remember."

The Chesapeake log canoe is low and sleek in the water and the No Name was one of the fastest on the bay and had slipped beneath the gunwales of the dredger before anyone aboard noticed. The dredger's nameplate read Savannah Kelley W17. Half-starved Paddies at the windlass paused as the No Name's sail appeared out of the fog. The captain, a burly, bearded figure dressed head to toe in canvas foul-weather gear, the very picture of the mariner, hurried to the rail. "Clear off, you varmints!" he said. "Or there's no quarter given."

"This is my shoal, oyster pirate!" Tench shouted, shaking his fist. "Back to your own waters!" Then he pulled the shroud off the duck punt, dropped to his knees and swung the long barrel towards the dredger's sails. The punt exploded with a roar and the air filled with the black flying shards of oyster shells. The captain went over, struck in the head, oath stilled on his lips; two Paddies fell away from the windlass, bleeding. The dredger's mainsail was shredded to tatters in an instant. Tench Doyle figured he had no more than a minute before the dredgers regrouped and returned a deadlier sort of fire.

"Come about, Connor!" Tench shouted. "Come about!"

But Connor dropped the tiller and threw himself down beneath the board in terror, hands over his eyes. Swearing, Tench jumped back, pushed the quavering Irishman aside and turned the No Name into the wind and the sail filled and billowed out, and the spry little vessel shot towards the horizon like an arrow. A few rounds came splashing after them harmlessly, then nothing.

Tench found rich oystering later that day at Pogget Narrows and culled several very nice bushels, but it wasn't pleasant work. A tense silence had settled over his crew of one. Connor abstained from his usual chatter and lay hanging off the tiller like a dead man, listless, mute.

"You're a damned weight today," Tench growled at last, as they turned towards home, hold brimming with glistening bivalves.

Connor said nothing, shook his head, but Tench pressed the argument.

"It was you acting the crazy, murderous fool back there," Connor whispered at last. "I'll not be party to such violence. I'm a peaceable man."

"You're a coward!" Tench shouted, angry. "Them pirates are the ones put you in the state you're in today, boy. A cripple, living off the charity of others!"

Connor looked up, last light off the water shining in his blue eyes. "You hit two innocent Paddies with your blasted cannon," he said softly. "I saw it with my own eyes. One of them I recognized, a lad from County Mayo, come over on the steamer with me from Baltimore. Decent fellow, too."

"Work for the devil," Tench said grimly, "and you pay the devil's wages."

"You talk rightly of the devil," Connor said softly, "for it's you did the devil's work today."

Tench Doyle's chief sin was the sin of anger. At this comment he lunged across the board and struck Connor hard across the face with the back of his hand. Connor fell against the gunwale, his nose spurting blood. When he tried to stand, Tench kicked him back down.

"Stay down!" he said. "Or I'll kick your teeth in."

Connor stayed down, huddled with the refuse, his useless hands across his knees. Tench immediately felt sorry for what he'd done, and he knew their brief friendship was at an end, but nothing in the world would induce him to apologize. He had never apologized to anyone in his life. He steered the No Name across the black waters to the nearest oyster town, which happened to be Cauleysville — little more than a row of saloons and an oyster-packing house — and Connor scrambled up on to the wharf.

"I'll be wishing you good fortune," Tench said.

The Irishman looked down in silence, blood staining his chin.

"Here, take this." Tench reached into the pocket of his trousers and produced a ten-dollar gold piece and held it out. "I figure you earned it."

"I'll not take your money, Doyle," Connor said.

"Damn you, then," Tench said, and he pushed off and reefed the sail for the prevailing wind. He allowed himself one backward look and saw Connor still standing there on the wharf staring out to open water, a dark form picked out in silhouette against the wavering lights of the town.

As spring approached, the oyster war intensified. The struggle for the last fragrant bushels brought more bodies bobbing like driftwood in the murky waters off Wassateague County, more frozen carcasses caught in the drags. War loomed over the bay like a black cloud. The Baltimore syndicates had men, money, and six hundred lumbering vessels armed like battleships, the tongers little more than their wits and an inborn knowledge of native waters.

Tench knew he was outgunned. After the incident with the Savannah Kelley, he did his best to avoid the oyster war altogether, haunting out-of-the-way fringes known only to a few old-time tongers, but at last even these lay under the long shadow of the dredge-boats. Two close skirmishes in which he was forced to run for the deep, fast water caused him to expand his arsenal: he acquired a second duck punt, mounted aft, two heavy-gauge shotguns kept loaded in a waterproof satchel, a brace of Colt pistols strapped to his waist at all times, a Winchester repeating rifle, for those times when delicate shooting was wanted, and a case of odd-looking, British-made phosphorus hand bombs acquired in trade for a ten-gallon jug of sourmash from a sailor off a Royal Navy dreadnought, drydocked for emergency repairs in Newport News. These bombs were no bigger than baseballs and launched in a similar manner, deadly in theory but woefully unreliable in practice. Most failed to ignite at all — or, worse, ignited when clutched in the palm of some poor sailor's hand.

Tench tried not to think of Connor. This proved impossible. He hadn't noticed the silence before, the hollow slap of waves against the hull, the creaking of the spar, the mournful cry of the terns from somewhere over the grey horizon. Now these things filled his ears louder than the roaring of a cataract. It's one thing for a man to be lonely and not realize the fact, another for his loneliness to become aware of itself all at once. Tench missed the Irishman's stories, his light touch on the tiller, his sad, bandaged hands. He began to drink more than ever. Most nights he could be found dead drunk at the Mollusk in Darnestown, a hard, seedy place frequented by some of the toughest watermen on the bay. He passed out at the bar more than once, and each time the regulars gleefully rifled his pockets, hefted him up, and tossed him out into the muddy street where half-wild pigs foraged for refuse.

It was at the Mollusk one Saturday afternoon that a bedraggled scarecrow named Bill Rose sidled up beside Tench and nudged him with a sharp elbow. "Stand me a glass of applejack and I'll tell you something you'd like to know," the man said, an obnoxious smirk pasted across his toothless mouth. Bill Rose was a well-known drunk who'd drink kerosene when no booze was to be found. He'd been shanghaied by a Ward syndicate press gang and forced to work sober on one of their dredgers for a couple of months before he managed to jump ship last week in Chrisfield. For a while, they'd kept him at a paddy-shack on Lanyard Island, he said, a flea-ridden pesthole five miles north of the Pasamquaset light.

Tench wasn't interested in the rest of the man's story. "Shove off!" he interrupted. "There's nothing I'd like to know you can tell me now."

"One stinking glass of applejack." Bill Rose's toothless smirk got broader and even more toothless. "Bet you'd like to know who I run into down there, white as a ghost and near dead but talking, talking."

Tench felt a tingling at the back of his neck. The nasty smirk on Bill Rose's face told him all he needed to know. He cracked the drunk's head against the battered brass rail for that smirk and to give himself a taste of the bloodletting to come. Then he went down to the No Name sitting low and lean and empty in the water, except for the guns and bombs, raised the red sail to the wind, and slid off into the darkening twilight.

The Paddy shack on Lanyard Island was little more than a collection of lean-tos open to the weather, surrounded by a palisade of hewn logs. The current residents — those unfortunate Paddies unlucky enough to fall into the hands of syndicate press gangs — huddled miserably beneath the bare shelters with no blankets or warm clothes, little food, and nothing to drink except rainwater drained from mosquito-ridden barrels. They were not kept in irons; hunger proved the most efficient restraint. Many were too emaciated and feeble to use the privy trench and lay in their own filth. An old-timer who had seen the prisoners at Andersonville during the War Between the States said those poor bastards were better off. Three times a week baskets of stale bread were tossed into the enclosure, along with tepid pans of chicory coffee and buckets of slightly rank oysters, which not one of the prisoners would touch, blaming the innocent mollusks for their own current misfortunes.

The dozen or so syndicate thugs charged with guarding this compound lived in sturdy canvas tents raised on a wooden platform just above the palisade, each tent nicely fixed with a stove and camp furniture. They patrolled the perimeter in four-hour watches, guarding not against the law, which didn't give a damn about the lives of a few dozen starving Irishmen, but against the rapacious vessels of other syndicates. The crisp white sails of the Virginia Maritime Police cutters had not once appeared on the horizon.

Every so often, one or another Ward syndicate dredge anchored beyond

*the breakwater and the captain and the mate would come ashore in a dory
to select replacements for their dead. The poor Paddies clamored to go —
anything was better than this starvation. Inevitably, the most recent ar-
rivals were the first selected. The longer a Paddy remained, the longer he
would remain; after a certain tenure, death became the only possible
means of escape.*

*At midnight on the second day, Tench Doyle saw a faint, reddish glow in
the darkness and the vague black lump that was Lanyard Island against
the stars. He aimed his bowsprit towards this light, trimmed his sail to the
wind, and prayed to an unknown god of wind and water to meet no rocks,
no uncharted shoals. He didn't have a fixed plan: like many Doyles before
and since, he would take what came. This philosophy prescribed the most
direct approach, strategy be damned, and he pulled the keelboard and ran
the No Name, sail flapping against the boom, over the bar and straight up
on to the beach, not two hundred yards west of the palisade. He smelled
the strong human stink of the place like despair on the wind.*

*Through his spyglass, Tench made out the sturdy tents and the silhou-
ettes of the syndicate thugs inside eating and laughing at cruel jokes and
the warm, golden glow of their pot-bellied stoves against the canvas. The
flickering lanterns of the watch did not waver in his direction; not a single
voice was raised in alarm. He had landed unobserved. As he charged and
capped the Colts and chambered rounds into his Winchester and hooked
the phosphorus bombs to his belt, he thought oddly of the black shells of
oysters, how where the pearls nestled in the viscous heart of the meat the
walls were smooth and lustrous, beautiful as a woman's hair undone. The
smell of dying men growing stronger on the wind, he advanced towards the
palisade.*

*At the log wall a few minutes later, a face suddenly appeared out of the
gloom in an oily halo of lantern light. A well-fed face, broad in the cheek
and mean, a syndicate face.*

*"Who in the bloody hell are you?" the face demanded and Tench drew
his Colt and fired, and the face fell away with a guttural cry and Tench
leaned down, seized the oil lantern and hurled it against the logs. The glass
shattered; yellow flame caught the dried, splitting wood and a yellow glare
spread up into the night. A second later, shouting came from the direction
of the tents, followed by the shriek of an alarm whistle.*

Tench hurried towards the gate and there nearly collided with another

thug, so close he could smell the whiskey on the man's breath. This one carried a sawed-off, but the man fumbled with the trigger lock and Tench fired
first and the man pitched forward and didn't move. The gate was a simple
affair, kept closed by a heavy bar of split timber lying across the front like a
barn door. Tench shouldered the bar, heaved it aside, and the gate swung
open. Inside, all was darkness, but he quickly became conscious of human
forms huddled in misery all around. He heard a cough, a low moan.

"Do you have bread?" someone said, in a reedy whisper nearby. Tench
went two steps and stumbled over a corpse stretched out cold on the
ground. Wind blew smoke from burning logs into the enclosure, bright cinders began to float down like fireflies.

"Connor!" Tench called. "Connor Malone!" But now syndicate thugs
were at the gate, at least six or seven men firing pistols and repeating rifles,
and gunfire cracked all around him. Bullets thumped into the dirt, one
spent shell struck him in the foot without doing any damage. Tench
dropped, unlimbered his Winchester, and returned fire. Men fell, he was
certain of that, but others immediately filled the ranks and now they were
firing wildly in all directions and sulphurous smoke and bullets thickened
the air.

Somehow, in this hail of fire, Tench was not hit. Presently the yellow
bloom of the flames reached the top of the palisade, and in this thin, garish light, he saw one of the worst things he had ever seen: a hundred emaciated Paddies crouched in the furthest shadows beneath the lean-tos, their
eyes wide and staring out of hunger-chiselled faces. A shadow detached itself from this spectral company, a thin hand was placed upon Tench's
shoulder and, after a startled moment, he recognized the visage, much reduced, of his friend.

"Are you able to follow me any distance?" Tench shouted over the fusillade.

"I can't walk for more than a step or two," came Connor's voice, faintly.
"I can barely breathe."

"Can you hang on?"

"I'll try."

Tench squatted down and Connor grappled himself on to the man's
back — the skeletal Irishman weighed nearly nothing, not more than a
pair of oyster tongs — and Tench unholstered his Colts and fired until the
chambers were empty. The thugs found themselves in a moment of confu-

sion and fell back to reload. One turned and ran to the tents for another case of ammunition, as if an army lurked within the darkened palisade. Tench threw aside his spent pistols, unhooked the first phosphorus bomb from his belt, turned the ignition screw, and tossed it underhand through the gate. It failed to ignite and dropped with a harmless thump to the soft earth.

Now the syndicate thugs formed up in two ranks, infantry fashion, and began to pour volley after volley into the palisade. Tench threw himself down, Connor still clinging to his back. The shots rang over Tench's head, most striking the emaciated flesh of the Paddies beneath the lean-tos. These half-dead men died the rest of the way with no sound louder than a soft, bewildered groan. Tench pulled another phosphorus bomb and rolled it through the gate but this, too, failed to ignite. He threw another over his head, hard against the palisade. Nothing. The syndicate thugs were advancing in rank now: soon it would be over. Tench felt his friend's bony arms tighten around his neck, heard the man's shallow breathing in his ear, and didn't regret this end. Better this way than twenty more years alone on the grey water, impervious to human suffering.

Then, the first phosphorus bomb ignited with a white flare and the explosion set off the second, which Tench felt like a tremor in the earth, and the third went off and something, a man's leg shod in a good leather boot, went sailing wetly through the air and there followed a moment filled by the high, awful sound of screaming.

The third explosion had opened a breach in the timber palisade and Tench struggled up and made for this, carrying his friend on his back like a bundle of old clothes. No one followed. Minutes later, he reached the No Name, laid Connor gently in the bow, and pushed her off into the rising tide. From the palisade now the shooting had commenced again; they were firing indiscriminately, killing everyone. Tench pictured the thin carcasses of the Paddies now ripped apart by bullets and figured they were better off dead, but this was just a way not to think about the murder of so many helpless men.

It was an hour out to open water; a bloody, upended moon hung low over the mast. The sound of mayhem had faded in the night. All was silence, and the wind pushing the sail and the murmuring slap of the waves. Tench moved his friend gently from the bow, laid him amidships on a heap of oyster shells and covered him with a heavy coat. The black shells shone darkly in the light of the upside-down moon.

"I knew you'd come before long," Connor managed, then he didn't say anything else and his hands fell to his sides and he drew a long breath, which was his last, and Tench heard the man's death as another silence against the grander silence of the night and the waves.

"All for a goddamned oyster," Tench said aloud, to Connor's departing spirit. "All for oyster fricassée and oyster stew and oysters fried in butter with onions or eaten raw as God made them. Lord, what a miserable trade we have been born into."

Then he, too, fell silent. He had been hit in the side with a .44 round in the last of the action in the palisade, and the pain had his guts in its claw now. The pain was spreading like an evil warmth through his insides as he set the tiller towards the farthest shore.

1

DOYLE CHECKED his watch; he had been killing time at Blueheart Antiques for almost an hour, aimlessly picking up broken, over-priced old objects and putting them down again. Blueheart was one of twenty or so antiques dealers along that stretch of SR 201 called Antiques Alley, most housed in converted barns or tumbledown creeper-covered boatsheds crammed with the debris of the past: piano rolls and collapsible top hats, carnival glass bowls and molasses fly-catchers, mute Victrolas, rusty oyster tongs, stacks of love letters writ-ten from one dead person to another and tied with faded ribbons, brass sextants, pairs of never-worn ladies' stockings from the 1920s still in their original cardboard box, emblazoned with the plump, smiling nymphs of another era.

He was leafing through the November 1933 issue of *National Geo-graphic* off a moldy stack of the same when the owner — a florid middle-aged woman named Celia Mimms — came up to him at last. "We call those the yellow plague," she said. "Can't get rid of the damned things. Every week people come in to sell their parents' valu-able collection and I say, 'No, please get those *Geographic*s out of here before they fornicate and multiply,' but it's too late. I turn around and the randy little things have already popped out a few more copies."

Celia Mimms readjusted her glasses and offered a thin smile. She was the last remnant of one of the old-time Wassateague oystering families, which somehow after generations of dozens of stout offspring had come down to one wry spinster in a nubbly, lime green housedress.

Doyle put aside the magazine with a slight twinge of embarrass-ment: the issue he'd been looking at featured large, hand-tinted photos of naked native women with huge brown-nippled breasts; some wore

THE WRONG DOYLE / 194

shiny copper rings distorting their necks till they resembled a cross between human and giraffe.

Celia Mimms dusted the cover with a fingertip and pursed her lips. "Those poor African girls," she said.

Doyle affected a blank look.

Then: "They're ready for you in the back now."

The chilly cement-floored granary had been turned into a sort of high-tech command center: translucent phone cables snaked into the dim recesses, newly installed tube lights glared green-white florescence down from low rafters. Detailed USGS maps of Wassateague County stuck with pins had been duct-taped to an old blackboard. A long, plastic-topped table held a fax machine, two telephones, stacks of paper, big red-spined volumes of federal statues. At another table Agents Detweiler and Keane of the Fish and Wildlife Service sat working on laptop computers at opposite ends, like a dysfunctional married couple at dinner. Agent Detweiler's jacket hung from a peg in an old board, the pearl-handled .38 glistening green as a garden snake in the green florescence.

She nodded stiffly when Doyle stepped through the low doorway. Agent Keane looked up from his computer, his long, cadaverous face more sorrowful than ever.

"At least you're not wearing pajamas this time," he said.

Doyle ignored this. "Nice office you've got here," he said. "If you like barns."

"We have an office at FWHQ in Washington," Agent Detweiler said, slightly offended. "This is our TCOP."

"Temporary Center of Operations," Agent Keane explained. "Convenient location, discreet landlady, and the rent is cheap. We've got an expense account for this case but it's not much, let me tell you."

"Fish and Wildlife usually gets the short end of the stick," Agent Detweiler said, with sudden vehemence. "We're not rich like EPA, those glamorous so-and-sos!" An embarrassed moment of silence followed this declaration.

Agent Keane cleared his throat. "Sorry, interdepartmental rivalry is not pretty," he said. Then, a long pause, in which Agents Keane and Detweiler exchanged a veiled glance.

"We can't tell you much," Agent Detweiler said.

"We won't tell you much," Agent Keane said.

"But we will tell you this." Agent Detweiler glanced down at her computer. "Case number 17447QD-0, which refers to the endangered Delmarva Peninsula Albino Fox Possum bisected by person or persons unknown and stuffed with seasquab —"

"— has now been expanded to include the investigation of multiple suspects besides yourself," Agent Keane finished.

Doyle looked from one to the other. "You two ought to spend time with other people," he said. "You're finishing each other's sentences. Give it up guys, that fucking possum's dead."

Agent Detweiler went beet red, seemed to struggle for a moment, but remained silent.

Agent Keane fixed Doyle with a doleful gaze. "We've learned to ignore your crude sense of humor," he said. "But to re-emphasize, that kind of language is not appreciated."

"You're wasting my time," Doyle said impatiently.

"All right," Agent Keane said. "We examined the material allegedly found adhered to the possum —"

"You're referring to the death threat," Doyle interrupted.

"— and subjected it to a thorough analysis."

"Forensic evidence suggests that this note was indeed fixed to the animal's left flank at some time subsequent to its dismemberment," Agent Detweiler said.

"We also identified three distinct sets of prints," Agent Keane said, "which we ran through the FBI's computer in Washington. All the prints came back with prior arrest records."

"Your own, of course," Agent Detweiler said.

"Teenage hijinks," Doyle said.

"Your partner, Ms. Maggie Peach," Agent Keane said.

This was an unpleasant surprise. "Maggie?" Doyle said. "What has she been arrested for?"

"That information is confidential," Agent Keane said uneasily. "Protected by right to privacy legislation."

"Not from you, apparently," Doyle said.

"It's the third set of prints we want to talk to you about," Agent Detweiler said. She pulled her chair directly across from Doyle's and straddled the seat, the way she'd seen cops do in the movies. Her thick, muscular thighs strained the grey flannel fabric of the trousers she wore today. Agent Keane moved up behind, a goofy grin on his face. They were getting ready for a crude imitation of the good-cop-bad-cop routine. Doyle experienced a *frisson* of *déjà vu* from his distant youth of petty larceny and drunkenness.

"The individual identified by the third set of prints has a rather more substantial criminal record than your own . . ." Agent Detweiler said, her voice trailing off as if Doyle was supposed to fill in the silence with a confession.

Doyle waited a long beat. Then he said, "So, who is it?"

"You don't know?" Agent Keane said, flexing his Herman Munster forehead.

"No," Doyle said.

"If you don't know then we can't tell you," Agent Detweiler said.

"Naturally," Doyle said, exasperated.

Agent Keane stepped forward and stood directly beneath the florescent light, which cast green monster shadows below his heavy brow.

"There are a couple of different scenarios that suggest themselves to us," he said. "First, that you and Ms. Peach and . . . this third party were involved in a conspiracy to slaughter an endangered animal, and that together —"

Doyle leaped up and his chair tipped back and clattered against the cement floor. He'd heard enough. "Did you people think about this at all?" He was shouting now. "Why would I plant a dead possum on my own property and then report it to the police?"

"That's only the first scenario, Mr. Doyle," Agent Keane said, attempting a reasonable tone. "The second scenario —"

"Wait!" Doyle waved his hands before his face as if to clear the air of a bad smell. "I don't want to hear the second scenario!" And he turned and ducked through the low door and back down the aisles of antique junk — every bit of which had belonged to someone who was now dead.

"We're watching you, Doyle!" Agent Detweiler's voice reached him, as he emerged from this spidery tomb into the glare of the parking lot. "Don't try anything funny!"

2

Doyle came into the bar forty-five minutes before Happy Hour and sat on his usual stool at the shadowy end and watched Maggie prep. She seemed innocent, bent over her pile of limes and lemons with a butcher's knife, rump thrust out for leverage as she leaned into each cut, half singing along with Merle Haggard on the jukebox, chewing on a toothpick — but was she as innocent as she seemed?

"Something wrong?" she said at last, looking up.

"One question, Maggie," Doyle said darkly. The red fishnet lights above the back bar blinking on and off in his face gave him a faintly satanic aspect. "You've got an arrest record. What for?"

Maggie stared. The toothpick fell out of her mouth. Her lower lip began to tremble. "How did you know about that?" she said.

"Never mind. Let's hear about it."

Maggie shuffled down to his end, an odd expression on her face that Doyle hadn't seen before. He tried to identify it and came up with a single word: shame.

"You really want to hear?" she said, in an unnecessary whisper. The place was empty.

Doyle wasn't so sure suddenly, but he said, sternly, "Go ahead."

Maggie scooped a handful of chipped ice out of the cooler and let it run through her fingers. "OK, buddy," she said after a painful moment. "I'll tell you. When I was fifteen, this cop bastard over in Wassateague caught me giving a guy a blowjob in the front seat of his car. It wasn't the first blowjob I'd given, it wasn't the last. In any case, the cop didn't —"

"Wait," Doyle interrupted. "Actually you don't need to tell me a thing."

"I'm telling you," Maggie said, angry all at once, " 'cause you asked, so just shut up and listen."

Doyle shut up.

"There I am working it and the cop bastard shines his flashlight into the car just as the dude is about to — you know — blow."

Doyle winced.

"So the cop knocks loud on the window and I pull back and, boom, it's too late, I get it right in the eye."

"Jesus," Doyle exclaimed, embarrassed.

"That's right," Maggie said. "And I ain't never been able to live it down ever since. It was all over town the next morning. I had to quit school 'cause of all the ribbing. Guys would come down the hall, rubbing their eye. Old One Eye, they called me that forever. Or Blinky or Winky, take your pick. Something like that can ruin a girl's life. Them half-assed fucks still tell sick jokes behind my back and it's been twenty years. That's why I come out here to Pirate Island in the first place and moved in with Buck, to get away from all that shit. Your uncle Buck, he knew the whole story and he never said a word. Not one goddamned word in all those years. The rest of them, they can go straight to hell."

"I'm sorry," Doyle said. "I had no idea . . ."

Maggie made a chopping motion that seemed to cut his words in two. "Now you know," she said, and she straightened her shoulders with all the wounded dignity of the Magdalene leaving a brothel for the last time, wiped icy hands on a dishtowel and went back to her limes and lemons.

3

The phone rang again late in the bar, not exactly three a.m. but close, and woke Doyle from a troubled sleep. Doyle let it ring for a while and it rang on with the particular insistence that could only mean death or disaster waited to be announced on the other end of the line. He had recently experienced enough of both — but in the end he roused himself, stumbled downstairs, and grabbed the receiver with both hands.

"What?" he shouted. The sound of his own voice startled him awake. For a moment, there was silence, then he made out the shallow rhythm of labored breathing on the other end.

"You must pardon an old man's sleeplessness," a raspy voice came faintly across the wires through the darkness, "but I never know when I'll have the breath to speak. Some days, I can barely lift a glass of water to my lips." The voice paused and Doyle thought he heard a deep, painful wheeze, which gave him just enough time to put a name to the voice, to conjure a lined, honest face with wisps of white hair standing towards the ceiling.

"My God," Doyle exclaimed. "I thought you were dead!"

"So did I," the voice said. "I waited, I prayed, but death would not oblige, most likely because there remain a few important things left undone. You must come out to the house tomorrow." Another wheeze, this one more like a sigh. "An urgent matter, I'd say, but more for you than me. Nothing's really that urgent for me anymore. You'll come?"

4

The house was nestled in a hollow in a grove of two-hundred-year-old cottonwood trees, its back against a clear running spring. A wrought-iron fence, carefully rust-proofed, separated the property from the spring, which had once been the only source of fresh water for the little brick town of Durrisdeer, partly visible through the trees.

Doyle parked the Cadillac along the road and crossed the footbridge over swampy ground and came up the drive to the house, a four-square, three-story red-brick structure of Georgian vintage, covered with the kind of ivy that takes a hundred years to grow. A black woman in her seventies answered the door. She wore a neat, old-fashioned maid's uniform, sweater over her shoulders fastened at the neck with a rhinestone clasp.

"How is he, Florence?" Doyle said.

Florence shook her head. "He's still alive's all I can say. Don't know how. Poor man's only got half a lung left."

She stepped aside and Doyle came into the house and she led him down the central hall to a room overlooking a quiet, mossy garden on the west side. The room had once been the library, but the books now stood in disarray, stacked in piles tall as a man in the corners to liberate several shelves for efficient-looking medical equipment in beige plastic casings. An adjustable hospital bed was in place where the reading table had once stood. An old man in a quilted robe sat in an armchair across from the bed with a weathered folio edition of Livy's *History of Rome* open across his knees. The only real indication of serious illness was the thin oxygen tubes leading into his nostrils and curved around his cheeks like a hussar's moustache.

"My father was always partial to Livy." The old man closed the book with the solid thump of heavy parchment and indicated a piano bench beside him, cluttered with papers.

Doyle moved the papers carefully and sat down. "You're looking good, Foy," Doyle said. "Just skinnier every time I see you. You need to eat, that's what."

Foy Whitcomb shook his head, wispy white hair so thin it seemed to float above his scalp.

"Skin and bones," he said. "I'm winnowing down for my passage into the next world. St. Peter's going to open the back door a crack just to see who's knocking so loud and I'm going to slip right in before he notices."

"For you they'll open the pearly gates and bring out the trumpets," Doyle said. "It's like Buck always said — you're the only honest lawyer he ever knew."

It was true. Millard Foy Whitcomb was perhaps the last lawyer in America to possess a fierce belief in the old-fashioned notion that law was not some corrupt compromise between the ideal and the real, but rather that law, properly administered, expressed the divine will. Law was no common tool to be used by one smart litigator against another: it was the sacred vehicle through which God's justice might express itself in an unjust world.

Whitcomb laughed soundlessly at this compliment. "You always were a good bullshitter, Tim," he said. "You . . ." but his next words turned into a long wheeze in which Doyle could hear the breath escaping from the man's collapsing lung like air from a punctured tire.

A moment later, Florence returned with a tea tray and a pint bottle of Old Granddad.

"He gets the tea," she said to Doyle. "Whiskey's for you. I know how you Doyles like to drink." She gave Doyle a familiar nudge and left the room.

Doyle poured the tea and emptied a shot of whiskey into his cup and made to screw the cap back on the bottle.

"Not so fast there, son." Whitcomb put a papery hand on Doyle's sleeve and drew the bottle over to his cup.

"Are you sure?" Doyle said.

"What does it matter now?" Whitcomb said, and Doyle poured and they both settled back with their whiskey-spiked tea. Whitcomb drank in a series of breathy gurgles and long pauses. His cheeks grew red from the whiskey and his breath seemed raspier than before. Doyle watched him over the rim of his cup, apprehensive. But Whitcomb smiled and rapped the morocco cover of the Livy with a bony knuckle.

"Time was, all the education a gentleman needed could be found in Livy and the Bible, with a little Homer thrown in for those who liked a side of poetry." He paused, and drew a long rattling breath. "I'm being strangled word by word," he managed, after a moment. "So I'll omit the pleasantries and come to the point."

"OK," Doyle said. He added a little more whiskey to the tea in his cup.

Whitcomb pointed out a weathered old briefcase on a chair across the room. "Would you be so kind?" Doyle got the briefcase and made to give it to Whitcomb but the old man waved him away. "No, you keep it," he said. "What's inside is yours alone. In fact, you might call it the true patrimony of the Doyles, for such it is indeed. Open it."

Doyle felt unaccountably nervous. He unlocked the briefcase and turned the latch. Inside was a grey piece of oilcloth and wrapped in the oilcloth an ancient manuscript, fifteen or twenty thick leaves written very closely in blotchy, crabbed characters. From the loopy script and the frail condition of the pages, he guessed eighteenth century or perhaps older. In a plain folder beneath the oilcloth was another manuscript, this one typed on onionskin in the recent past. Doyle looked up, baffled.

"What is all this?" he said.

Whitcomb opened his mouth only to emit a long, drawn-out wheeze. For a moment, Doyle was afraid he'd be left with a mysterious document and more unanswered questions.

"You are looking at the confessions of Finster Doyle, buccaneer and priest's boy, the progenitor of your line in America," Whitcomb said at last. "Or fragments thereof."

Doyle looked down at the pages again and experienced an odd dislocation that had nothing to do with the whiskey in his tea.

"You may ask how I came by such an extraordinary document," Whitcomb continued, now settling into a reasonable facsimile of breath. "As you probably know, the courthouse in Wiccomac contains the oldest series of court records in the nation, dating back unbroken to 1634, the year Calvert and his Catholics came into Maryland."

"I didn't know that," Doyle said.

"I was doing some title research over at the courthouse to support your uncle's case — this must be back in '54 — and I came across that document stuck in a sort of pouch in the binding of an old registry of deeds dating to the 1680s. What do I have here? I said to myself. Then the word Drogheda leaped out at me and I immediately knew that I had made a discovery of some historical interest."

"Drogheda?" Doyle said. This word had an ominous sound.

"Yes, your ancestor in his youth witnessed the terrible siege and massacre of the Irish at Drogheda by Oliver Cromwell and his Ironsides."

"I see," Doyle said, but he didn't.

"I don't mind telling you it took me nearly six months to puzzle out that convoluted mess of seventeenth-century script. Half of it's gone, the other half's completely illegible, the pages were unnumbered and the rest was in total disarray. My God, what a job that was! And keep in mind these confessions were set down in a prison cell by candlelight in the weeks before your ancestor's appointment on the gallows at Hampton Roads — sometimes in ink, sometimes in charcoal mixed with water, sometimes in a substance that might be blood. In any case I rightly handed the whole mess over to Buck — as you will see, it is to his descendants that Finster addresses himself in the narrative. Some years later — with your uncle's blessing, of course — I was preparing an annotated version for publication as a monograph by the Virginia Historical Society, so you will also find a typescript copy with some of my accompanying notes, unfinished, I'm sorry to say. I was never a man with much leisure time."

"Hell, you never even took Sundays off, Foy," Doyle said. "I remember coming out here after church and you and Uncle Buck working on legal stuff for hours while I played in the yard."

"Yes, pleasant memories," Whitcomb offered a weak smile. "And standing before the highest court in the state on your uncle's behalf to argue the case of Doyle's Pirate Island Goofy Golf vs. U.S. Park Service remains one of the great moments of my life." He paused and drew a long, painful breath that sounded like weeds sticking in his throat. This effort exhausted him all at once and his face went slack and Doyle knew the old man was reaching the end of his endurance.

"Maybe we should finish this some other time," Doyle said. "You've already done a powerful lot of talking."

Whitcomb shook his head. "It's now or never," he said, in a faint, creaking voice that caused Doyle to lean so far forward he was almost in the man's lap.

"When Buck knew he was dying," Whitcomb continued, "he entrusted the manuscript to me once again pending your return to these shores and I locked it in the safe in my office. But when I examined the document after Buck's death, I found that it had been trifled with, a small portion missing. Not much, just two pages. But in those two missing pages lie the root of your present predicament — by which I mean the gun battles, the arson, and other shenanigans I read about in the paper."

Doyle's mind was racing. "Any idea who took the pages?"

Whitcomb let escape a dry chuckle. When he spoke, his voice came out like a whisper from beyond the grave. "Only two people have access to the safe in my office — one of them's yours truly and the other's a vile, obese masturbating bastard!"

5

Doyle poured himself a glass of five-star Spanish brandy from a dusty bottle found stashed beneath the bar, the very bottle he'd sent to his uncle from Spain for Christmas about ten years ago, and tasted the sweet, languid afternoons of southern Spain, the soft brown hills rising behind Málaga, Flor's tawny limbs twisted in the sheets in the bed in room 212 of the Hotel Ibiza the year before Pablo was born, after a long night and early morning of drinking and dancing to the heavy beat in the never-closing discos there, filled with soap suds and casual carnality.

But all that was recent past. Now Doyle braced himself for an encounter with the past long dead, the past lingering in the blood, the unremembered sorrows that wrap their shadowy tendrils around the strands of DNA in the body's microscopic hollows, there to cling like strangling vines through the generations. Glass in hand, he mounted the stairs to Buck's room, briefcase pressed tight under one arm, and he could almost feel Finster's words beating through the leather casing and the intervening medium of three hundred years like a second heart against his ribs.

THE CONFESSIONS OF FINSTER DOYLE, BUCCANEER
with preface and explanatory notes
by
Millard Foy Whitcomb, Esq.

PREFACE

The broad outline of Finster Doyle's exploits as a buccaneer in the West Indies c. 1660–70, detailed in Esquemeling's remarkable volume *Buccaneers of America,* are well known and shall not be touched on here in any depth. The reader interested in sensational accounts of pirate massacres, or in details concerning the care and upkeep of seven wives, is urged to consult that famous work, continuously in print since the Leyden edition of 1685.

Concerning Finster's early life, however, almost nothing was known until the recent discovery of this fragmentary manuscript in the Wassateague County Courthouse in Wiccomac, Virginia, by the author of these notes.

The Doyles of Wassateague, VA, without a doubt descendants of the notorious buccaneer, have long maintained an oral history regarding their progenitor's adventurous life, certain aspects of which the surviving fragments of Finster's confessions corroborate. From lengthy interviews with William "Buck" Doyle of Wassateague, the writer of these notes established the following biographical details: that Finster Doyle's father died from an attack brought on by the consumption of copious amounts of alcohol while celebrating the boy's birth (c. 1633); that he was raised by his mother and seven sisters as the treasured only son in a family of women in and about the town of Drogheda in Ireland; that his maternal uncle (Fr. Francis Tyrone) being a priest of the Capuchin order attached to that order's establishment in Drogheda, the young, half-orphaned Finster was early on dedicated to the service of the Roman Catholic Church. By all accounts, Finster was apparently a pious and willing novice, a model student of Latin, and had also developed a precocious understanding of the theological arcana of the times. He would surely have been ordained a Capuchin priest and — such is Doyle family tradition — might have risen in time to the rank of Cardinal had fate not shown her callous hand.

In this case, fate descended on Finster in the person of Oliver Cromwell, Lord Protector of Ireland, still anathematized by the Irish people for atrocities perpetrated during the Unionist Wars of 1649–51. It is perhaps one of history's small ironies that Cromwell, the only son in a family of six sisters, raised by a stern but doting mother, was a man much like Finster Doyle. Many lengthy articles could be written by psychologists on the — perhaps compensatory — fierceness of men raised by women, but I digress. A word on that particularly bloody chapter of the Irish troubles might be appreciated at this point by the general reader.

In August 1649, an armada of thirty-five English ships carrying 12,000 men anchored at the mouth of the Liffey off Dublin and disembarked. At this time the English armies had just begun to uniform themselves in the brazen scarlet coats with which they later came to be identified throughout the world; what startling contrast the disciplined columns of red-coated pikemen and musketeers must have presented against the wild, barefoot soldiery of Ireland!

The political history of this distant era is complex indeed. In brief, during the English Civil War (1642–7) most of the Irish had sided with the Stuart King of England, Charles I. After Charles's execution and the establishment of Parliament's authority in England, various armies, both Catholic and Protestant, rose up in Ireland in support of the defeated royalist cause. Cromwell was sent across the Irish Channel to crush these royalists and subdue the country, which he saw as a barbarous wasteland, inhabited by drunken, priest-loving papists, wanton women, and wolves. His first military objective was the fortified city of Drogheda, which commanded the hilly country to the north of Dublin.

Drogheda fell under the jurisdiction of James, Earl of Ormonde, general in chief of the largest army in Ireland. Ormonde had instructed Sir Arthur Aston, commander of the Drogheda garrison, to hold out as long as possible against Cromwell's forces. As it turned out, Drogheda's Catholic garrison was greatly outnumbered; the other inhabitants of the town, mostly women and children and many priests and nuns, were unfit to bear arms. Drogheda was in those days something of an ecclesiastical center, containing an archiepiscopal palace, several churches, a cathedral, and the monastic establishments of the Dominicans, Franciscans, Capuchins, and Carmelites.

On September 11th, at midday, Cromwell reached Drogheda, immediately brought up his siege guns, and began pounding the ancient city walls, which quickly crumbled beneath the bombardment. Cromwell himself climbed down from his horse and, sword in hand, led the first assault on the Duleek Gate; a few hours later, at five in the evening, the English overran the Irish fortifications. Fighting continued all night long —

but for a close description of these terrible hours of darkness, fire and blood, we must now turn to the eyewitness recollections of Finster Doyle, then a frightened boy of fifteen.

[Note: The following text is presented exactly as transcribed from the original holograph manuscript. No attempt was made to correct Finster's original spelling, punctuation or lack thereof, erratic capitalization or syntax, all of which reflect the flavorful orthographic practices of the period. — MFW]

[pages missing]

. . . much screeminge from the Lower Towne, and the Sky seem-yngly illumin'd by Hellfire a Satanic Blaze consuming the Wicklowe Mountains and the very Heart of Irelande, then the awefull clatter of Musketrie againe and againe the screeminge. Presentlie did I turn to Father Tyrone, white-fac'd & trymbling in my voice and the fear lyke a thirst upon me. I begg'd him to fly with me to a place of saftey where we could hyde ourselves until the crisis was pass'd and the English had beene deefeat'd by our Noble Ormonde and gone back across the Sea unto thyr own Lande.

At this, the goodly Father laugh'd tho in no mockinge manner, and not in bytterness but with a timbre of gentle melancholy as a manne who knoweth the future will go badly for himself but also knoweth that the badness fit perfectly with the great inscrutible Plan of the Almighty which in the ende beyonde Time Itselfe shall worke ultimate Justice and Peace.

The Englishe will not leeve Ireland today or tomorroww either, says the goodly priest unto me. Indeed, they may never leeve at all as it please God, but remaine with us till the last Trump soundeth to scourge the Irish for theyr drunkennesse and lethargie. For indeed this is the curse of our race: to maintane a shrewd knowledge of the world yet a strange reluctance to cope with it. So this being the Will of God, let us go about the Towne and do what good we may for as wee Idle here in Safety there are some lyinge in their death agony upon the bloody road in need of the Extreme Unction of Holy Mother Church. And indeed what is the proper role for a man of God in a crisis such as this? To shew by deed and word to those who suffer that thyr sufferinges be not in vain and are known to the Almighty Redeemer who sees all and pities.

So Sayinge, this good priest donn'd the wide brimmed prieste's hat with purple tasseles which had been given unto him during his long sojourne in Rome by the Bless'd Pontiffe Himself as a way to shield his pale forehead from the hotte Roman sun and he hunge on himself a flask of Holy Waters and another of Sacred Oils over his shoulderes much as a Muskateere takes on powder and shot and he then took my hande sayinge Fear Not If God is with Us, Who Shall Stand Against Us? and thus arm'd with nothinge but our Faithe we ventur'd out into the war racked streets of the citie of Drogheda.

[*text illegible*]

. . . by this Time, the English Culverins and Demi-Culverins had done their Devil's workke and the English Ironsides turned the Irish Defense. By Intelligence later vouchsafed unto us we heard that Malodorous Devil Cromwell had himself in persone breeched the earthenwork entrenchments raised by Sir Arthur, and thus the Irish were driven beneathe the flail of this Devil towards the Mill Mount wherein they determin'd to make thyr Final Stand. We made our way downe St Johns in the Direction of the Butlers Gate as these terrible Eventes took place but a few streets distant, the clamour and crashing of battle all around and the night made blacker by thick Stygiane smoke from the burning houses of the Unfortnate Citizenry. We passed many scenes of Frenzie and Massacre of Women and babes lying bloody and stripp'd bare of clothing and in many cases missinge limbes or headdes and their bloode running in the gutteres like rain after a storm from the Sea.

The Dead mixt in with Dying and here and there Father Tyrone paused and did what little good remain'd to be done. He administer'd the Sacrament to those who had beene Mortally Wounded and lefte to die, he leaned close to many a bloody lippe and heard the secrets of hearts unburdened of the staines of life in this world. Listening, I hearde a mane confesse he had killed his brother over a trifle and hid the deed from all yxept God, I heard a woman say she had lain with many other men than her husband who had lov'd her more dearly than life and Who she had Basely Betrayed more times than she could counte, I heard another who deemed pious by all confessed that he beleeved in nothing his whole life and trembl'd now on the Brink of the Eternal as on the Brink of Utter Extinction. He had observed all the outwarde Signs but meanwhile robbed the Spirit of its Nourishment and for Him and all the others we pray'd kneeling in the Bloode and Gore and administered as best we could the last Grave & Sacred Mysterie.

Thus, Gradually, we made our way to Great Duleek Street to the Heart of the Fighting, and by this time the Defenders of the Mill Mount had been driven from their fortified Positions and the Slaughter was general, swirling around us like a Satanic carnivale of Madness and Bloode. Now the Dreadful Ironsides with Pike and Swords in hand did hack and stab through the ranks of the Fleeinge Irish the langth of the Thorough fare to the Lifting Bridge, which once crossed would leave the Upper Town and the Inhabitants thereof defensless including my Dear Mother and Sisters who did reside in that Quarter.

I prayd to God then that the Defenders of the Upper Towne would be grant'd the Wisdom to Draw up the Bridge thus leaving the fast running Byrne between themself and the Enemy, but no such wisdom was vouchsaf'd by God and Father Tyrone and I by this route crossed the waters of the river now red with the Bloode of the Irish easy as you please in the Van of the Attack unnoticed as if protected by an Angell on to the North Quay. Here we Came across the Bloody Corpse of Sir Arthur whose Wooden Leg had been pulled off in search of the Gold Coins rumor'd to be hid there but finding Nothing the Enrag'd Troopers dash'd his Brains out with the false Appendage.

Now across the River the Ironsides quickly broke into the houses of the Religious Orders like wolves among fowel and there began Killing priests and Friars with unspeakable Gusto and committing carnal outrages upon the bodies of the poor weeping Holy Women, but somehow again, Father Tyrone and I went about our business unobserv'd, even though he wore the purple girdled Pope's hat which fairly shouted This Is A Priest. Then In Batchelor's Lane, a comely young woman of that Place with long flowinge Hair undone and Bloode splatter'd Across her robes accost'd Father with much weeping and Entreaty.

To her Bared Breast she clutch'd a Babe which had seen no more than a day or two in the world, and she begged the Good Father for Baptism so it's tiny soul should not enter the Realm of Light Unshriven of the Sins of Adam. 'Tis Not Too Late, Good Priest, she cried. 'Tis Not too late for My Jemmy. Alas, the Infant was already gather'd into the skirts of the Holy Virgin Mother in Heaven, but this Woman proferr'd the carcass so piteously that Father Tyrone took it into his arms and we all knelt and he perform'd the solemnity of Baptism upon it. He then took his own Surplice and wrapped the Babe gently as in a shroud and handed it over to the woman and she Bless'd us and made the sign of the Cross upon herselfe and wander'd off into the Mayhem much comforted but never to be seen again by our eyes.

By and By, we reached the district of the Market Quadrangle and found ourselves again among our own People, all rushing in Great Fear and Disarray towards the Dark Spire of St Peter's Church and here in the Narrow Lanes, the press of men was so close we could not pause to perform any Holy Offices. And so Father T. and I rested beneath the great Stone Porch of the Tholsel and we stood quietly there in the Shadowes observing the sickening progress of the Retreat for many minutes, the tatter'd garments of our Irish troops giving way to the cleane Scarlet coattes of the English, cleane I say, no stained and covered with Bloode but not observable against that bright colour like the ruddy smocks of those that do butcher cattle for the Market.

Here it was, Lingering in the Porch that Father T. spoke to me of the inevitability of what must come to pass with the Prescience of a man unto whom compleate fore-knowledge of his fate has been vouchsaf'd which I would count a true Miracle of God, the first perform'd by Father Tyrone for certain that night. And I record the gyst of his conversation as followes.

I will die, says he to me and soon. As for you, yet you know it not, you are smiled upon by God and in posessione of Youth and Vigor will find a way to escape this Hell of Drogheda and the many snares and violences to come and live willy-nilly into the Next Age. His voice was Hollow and Solemn as like a Spirit talking as a Mortall Man, and it nearly froze my own bloode to hear him so.

I know you well and have lov'd you as a Son, he contynued, but I know also that you are despite your best designs weake in the Ways of Goodness, on account perhaps of being over cosetted by Your Mother and Sisters. You have seen much here tonight of Violence and Terror, methinks a full lifes Measure and the Desire for Vengeance will burn unquenchable Fire in your veins but you must resist this Impulse as a wile of the Devil and Stay your hand which if you Indulge it even once shall never tire of reaching for the Sword. To Strike when struck, this is not the way of the Redeemer. Now I urge you to think upon our Beloved Savior upon the Cross who could have called down the Wrath of the Universe upon the Romans and the Jews that day at Golgotha but instead asked his Father in Heaven to Forgive his very persecutors who knew nothing of the Vast Sin they were committing. This moment must come to Each Man, when the Greatest Forbearance is asked of us for the Lord's Sake and we must not Resist our Duty in the Matter. For when the Souls of All are called from theyr buryings on the Last Day, we must answer Verily have I Return'd the Fierce Blows of My Tormentors with the Love of my Heart. Do you understand these words, Dear Nephew? For despite what you have seen you must believe that All will be Rectify'd, the Guilty punish'd, the Just reward'd, the corrupted restored to purity, the pitifule and blody tale of Human History brought to its Just Conclusion at last.

Whereupon he finished this speeche, Father T. bade me kneel and placed his hand upon my head and I did feel I swear certain Weird Unearthly Emanations from the touch of his fingers. Swear this Vow, he said to me, Swear to God that you will not seek Vengeance for Drogheda upon any Livinge Man or Woman and I so Swore and swore again when he asked againe, but a greater Lie never passed my lips.

[*pages missing*]

. . . the Villaine reeked of Crippo or some such Vile Intoxicant with which he sought to veil his Soul from the Foul Deeds his hands were about to Commite. Then he seiz'd Father Tyrone by the hair knocking from his Headde the Pope's Hat and with the other hand drew his Dirk and drove it through the priest's Guttes once and again all the while uttering the Foulest imprecations against Poppery and all Priests.

Bless'd Father Tyrone Fell back to his knees, blood spouting from the mouth that had utter'd such wisdomes but at the last breath I swear a looke of gladdness pass'd upon his visage that made me recall his words of an hour before Do Not Despair, Death is A Gift and Ende to Earthly Suffering, and then he fell forward to the dirt and the odour which issued from his corpse at the moment of death was utter Sweetness like a field of Lillies in the Springtime: and this I consider the second evidence of Fr Ts Sanctity demonstrated upon that Dreadfull Night.

But the English trooper did not seem to smell this Heavenly Odor and quickly reached out for me and I saw my own Murder written upon his face. You're Next, Priest's Boy, he rored, but the drink had slowed his movements sufficient that as he reach'd out, I evad'd his Grasp tho Hot teares poured copiously down my cheeks over the Unjust Ende to so great a man who was now a Bonafide Martyr of the Holy Catholic Church. The Trooper swore an oath and stumbled on his owne feet and I leaped as if winged across the barrier and made off at a great pace down Sunday Street and was soon obscur'd in the Melee of maurauding Troops.

At this tyme, and not the first Occasion that dreadful evening. I bethought myselfe of my Mother and Sisters and now with Father Tryone gone I made my way in haste to our House in Pilgrims Lane so as to stand by their side in the hour of dire . . .

[*pages missing*]

. . . St Stephens steeple show'd itselfe on Fire, thus illumining the firmamente with the Red Light of Massacre. And so hidden as I was among the Chimneystackes on the roof, I could see clearly into the Courtyard below.

The troopers had gather'd my Mother and those Three Sisters re-maininge alive all in their sleeping gownes and huddled together, a tangle of loosed hair and weeping except for my Mothers strong Voice declaiming the Rosary and commending Her Soul to the Care & Mercy of the Deity. Then the Ironsides Captain who had enough of this Catholic Piety struck her on the Back of the Headde with his pike and she fell stunned to the Pavement then another trooper stuck her with his sword and the Pavinge Stones were soon covered with her Heartes Blood and she was no more. I did not weep at this foul crime for all weeping was gone out of me but these Mortal Blowes I felt into the very Rootes of my Soul.

Directly my poor Sisters let up such a caterwalling over my Moth-ers bloody corpse that it was horrible to hear, yet their lament ac-company'd by much gnashing of teethe did not coole the Hot Lust of the Troopers present yet maybe served to increase it. These Dev-ils laughing stripped the clothes from my sisters backs and there they stood white, gleaminge and naked upon the bloody grounde, faire and slim like unto willows in thyr Nakednesse as the Graces themselves in the Tragic moments preceding their ultimate De-spoilation. Ah my poor beautiful willowes. Ah my Dear Sweet Sisters who Now weep through all Eternity, who Cry out to God at the Outrages committed upon their Innocence.

I will not sett down the Particulars only to say that I watch'd the unfolding and Did Not close my eyes and in watching, my Heart filled with the Devil's Owne Blackness in which my Love for God was utterlie Extinguished and a roring came into my ears and all Father Tyrone's words of forbearance, his Saintly Council fled from my thoughts and I broke the Sacr'd vow in my heart and instead swore another to the Devil that should I escape this Storm with my life I would not forbear from killing any Englishman it rest'd within my power to kill, that indeed I would devote the Remainder of my Life to Killing any Englishman as I could and that I would not await the arrival of Devine Justice too slow, too slow, but with my own hands avenge the Cruel deaths of Father Tyrone, my Mother and Sisters. For presently, when the Troopers had satiated their Lusts in my Sister's Virgin Innocence, they took their great swords and sever'd the headdes from theyre bodies and thus more Doyle Blood darken'd the ground.

At this tyme in my agitation for seeing the abovementioned atrocities my foot dislodged a slate of the roofing which went clatteringe to the Abbatoir below. The Troopers espied my hiding place at this loude noise and the general alarm went up [and they] aimed theyr Arqebus and the balls hit the chimney bricks a hand's breadth above my Headde but makeing much haste I slide down the pitch and thence to the streete . . .

[*pages missing*]

. . . with the other dismal refugees in St Peters. But the square all around soon filled with the Ironsides like unto an army of red and angry ants crawling upon the dead carcasse of a bird. A call came to surrender from the English Captain. Lay Down Your Armes and You Will Escape with your Lives, said he. But the worth of English assurances had already been shewn that day at the Mill Mount where Sir Arthur and his Men had been Slaughtered despite what the English said. In Hell First, our Colonel called back, and the English said, In Hell it Shall Be, and a small Field piece was brought up and the Great door of the Church withstood not two batterings with the heavy ball and soon the English poured through the breach.

In the desparate fight which ensued I acquainted myself well by use of a brace of pistols stolen off a corpse and a short sword, killing my first man with a slash to the throat, the progenitor of many English victims to come. But the last vestige of the Irish myself among them had now been driven up the narrow steps into the steeple from which no attempt of the English could dislodge them. After a brief parley held in the square below the English decided to make of our redoubt a chimney. They then broke all the furnishings of the place, the pews, altar table etc. and arrang'd all the wreckage into a great bonfire at the foot of the steeple. This being done, they stood back to admire the conflagration and to allow the flames to worke upon the pitiful remnants of the citie they had destroy'd.

Soon the flames devour'd the outside wall, blistering the stone. Black smoke billow'd and poured upwards and it became like unto an Inferno in the narrow tower and about this tyme seemed very dubious as to which death would be the more desirable: death by leaping or death by flame. Many catching fire, leapt into the air screaminge terror on their lips falling to smash themselves on the stones below like soe many bundles of burning clothing. But I kept climbinge and clim'd at last unto the extremity, which is to say I fought my way up through the screaminge crush of smoke-blinde men and came out onto the roofe and thence to the very highest pinnacle, the iron crosse which had been set upon the Spire Pointe by the builders. From my vantage, the highest point in the citie, I could see by the light of many conflagrations the havoc wreak'd upone Drogheda now a ruine and a wildernesse and I raised my fist to Heaven and cursed God for allowing such damnable catastrophes to pass upon the Earth. Indeed, even the Byrne seem'd afire, its bloody water afloat with much burning wreckhage. Then black clouds pass'd across the moone as if this Heavenly bodie were in mourning and the stars too were obscur'd. I felte the winde upon my face and smelled the sea, glittering black and boundless on the horizon unseen and I wept many copious teers and curs'd Devine Providence, which had brought me to this fatale hour.

The flames were now catching at the heeles of my bootes and the very cross to which I clung had become as a hot poker new drawn from the fire. I heard a voice just below call out, I Burn Goddamn Me, I Burn, and it was as if my own soule cried out thus. Soon, I could hold fast no longer. I stood and flung my armes out as if to fly and said my Farewelles to the moon and the Citie wrecked below and my life and regretting only that I had not managed to kill more

English than the one, flung myself out into the Darknesse and the cinders and the pitiless night.

[*pages missing*]

. . . none among us bedraggled and beaten remnants of the Irish fettered under Guard in the Square who dared look over theyr shoulder at the black imprecating finger of St Peters spire where so many had met their Doom. Though the imprecation to my mind was againste the Almighty God Himself as well as the English, his miserable Tooles.

By and by the Fanfare was hearde and entering the square afoot like a Common Souldier the Lord Lieutenant Cromwell came followed by his Retinue and accompany'd by a great cheering from his Troopers and butchers of the night before and a great groaning from the captive Irish. Looking utterlie pleased with himselfe Cromwell first inspected his men who drew up proud in their Scarlet Coattes 'neath the gleaming of the sun from so blue a sky. And he said unto them many preatty things and treated them like his Children to his affections and made much compliments and told severall humerous stories pertaining to the unspeakable violence that had brought Drogheda low.

By and by this Devil Cromwell came to the remaining Irish some who did implore him for theyr lives in a most craven manner and some who did not. Cromwell then select'd by his own hand one of every ten to be put to death and the ranks were decimated in this manner, the men perish'd in a fusillade of balls from the Arquebus of the Musketeers. This Bloody worke being done, the Lord Lieutenant call'd to the Captain of the Guard saying, Show Me This Boy, the One Who Jumped from the Top of The Steeple and yet Escaped Unharmed. Not Quite Unharm'd, the Captain said, he has cracked a Bone In his Leg and cannot Walke. Nevertheless, Cromwell said, Let me See him. And the Captain led him to where I was fettered some distance separate from the Others.

Are You the Boy that Jumped? said the Lord Lieutenant in mildeste voice but I would not speak and the Captain brought the point of his blade against my bosome and said, Speak or be damn'd. I Am he, I said but I would still not looke into those Devil's eyes. Thereupon Cromwell lower'd himselfe to one knee and I could hear the Leather in his boots creakinge with the thick sound that fine new Leather has. Look at Me, Boy, he said and there was such a tone of Command in his Voice that I could not help but look.

He was a Big Ugly man plainly dressed in a buff coat with warts upon his face and a great stupid nose. He did not look like a Great Captain great as Alexandre or Caesar as some said, but his eyes were cold and hard as I've ever seen to this day in any othere man and blue like unto metal heated in the forge. He raised his gloved hand to the burnt steeple. You Jumped, he said, From that Promontory? I Did, I said for there seemed no point in lyinge. And what were the Thoughts in your head as you jumped? I wished that I Might Land upon the Headde of an Englishman, I said, and strike him dead to the Grounde. The Lord Lieutenant acknowledged my words gravely and his hard eyes blinked seemeingly wise as an owl.

Where is the Bone broken? he said. When I did not Answer the Captain again put his Blade to my throat. The Left, I said, Near the Foote. The Lord Lieutenant Cromwell then took off his gloves spot-lesse white and unstained by blood and rolled back his plain cuffes and cut my stokinge apart and took my leg in his hands and felt for the breake. Allay Your feares, he said. I Have Become a passing fair Surgeon in these many yeares of War, and he found the place and pressed down hard and I screamed out like a woman at the Sharp Pain but there followed a snapping sound and the pain was dulled to an ache and I felt my leg back in place againe. Have the Surgeon properly bind this Bone, he said to the Captain who sent a Trooper quick for the Surgeon. The Lord Lieutenant turned back to me and once again I found myself under the cold heat of his eyes.

Any Man leaping from such a Height, he again pointed out the steeple must surely shatter themselves to bits upon the paving as many another did last night. You survived with but one bone bro-ken. The Lord God Jehovah has surely saved you for a Special Pur-pose though the nature of his plans for an Irishman and Barbarian such as your selfe are Inscrutible as any He has ever Devis'd. Per-haps He seeks to fulfill some Covenant with You or through you with Others you shall meet in Future times. If so You must Seek to make your Life worthy of this Dispensation, Irish. And he paused and again I felt the murderous scrutiny of his clear blue eyes but heringe these Admonitions voiced by this cruel and Vicious Con-queror the Destroyer of my People proved utterlie inolerable: I leaned as far forward as my Fetters would allow and Spit upon his Boot of fine new Leather.

At this, the Captain raised his blade as if to strike me Dead but the Lord Lieutanant stayed the mortall blow. What Jehovah Hath preserv'd who are We to destroy? said he. But he stepped back and a terrible sort of merriment passed across his countenance. And yet my little barbarian I think you shall not have an easy time of it fulfilling the Lord's Destiny as a plantacion slave in the Barbadoes. And so saying, he rejoyn'd his retinue and accompany'd by clamorouse Fanfare marched quickly out of the Square, dissappearing from my Vision like the Devil in a puff of redd smoke at the Pantomime.

[Here a large number of pages are missing. Some details of Finster Doyle's subsequent adventures in the West Indies may be gleaned from Esquemeling and from Linch's *Description of the Island of Jamaica*, published by Blone in 1672. Ludlow's account of the Ironsides expedition in Ireland details the privations of the thirty survivors of Drogheda. Nearly four thousand human beings, almost every person inside the city walls without distinction of age or sex, were put to the sword by the English except for these poor wretches: forced to assist Cromwell's triumphant advance through their own country they were eventually shipped from the port of Galway to the island of Barbados where most perished within months from hard labor and tropical disease.

It may be helpful to remember that many slaves on plantations in the English-speaking colonies at this period were white Anglo-Saxons — indentured servants or criminals transported from the mother country. Here in Virginia, for example, enslaved Africans did not supersede indentured European laborers until after Bacon's rebellion of 1675–6.

Finster Doyle ended up as a slave on the indigo plantation of Everarde Kirke at Bathsheba in Barbados. Somehow he survived the tropical "seasoning" process that killed his fellow Droghedans, and over a period of years rose to a position of trust within his master's household. But this trustworthy demeanor was a ruse: Finster merely awaited the right moment. That moment came in 1657, so Esquemeling tells us, when Finster rose up and slew his master and mistress and five children while they lay asleep. He then boarded a pinnace already provisioned for the journey and made sail to join the colony of buccaneers at Tortuga.

By this act of violence, Finster Doyle set his course for the gallows at Hampton Roads twenty years later. His own account of the Kirke massacre is missing from this text, as is indeed any reference to his years of slavery except for the following fragment, which also contains some lovely passages of naturalistic observation:]

. . . and then sent by Master Kirke to the greene shores of the dis-
tante Islande called Cithycra by the Salvages of these parts and
Raleigh's Island by the English after the renown'd discoverer. The
aime of our expeditione here to be gatheringe fruit of the Rubra
Palm prized for salubrious effects upon those sufferinge with ague,
dropsey, heate of the bloode and other ailements. Free of my usual
toil in Master Kirke's fields on the bare sunnestruck headlandes of
Barbadoes, now the super-abundance of tropicale nature impressed
upon my hearte as one of the Glories of God's Creatione. In this
places I saw birds of red and azure and gold speaking from the
deepe Thickete as if with Human voice and by & by birds flock'd in
trees so green as to be taken for the very idea of greene itselfe.

I am as I write a miserable prisoner in a dank sell in the Virginias
as I have mentioned yet am still able to summon bright visiones of
some curious orange-faced Monkeyes who followed our progress
that forenoon upon the narrow path to the Interiore. One comicale
specimen came down off the trees and pulled the shiny brass but-
tones from Jasper's coate which he had set aside for a moment upon
a bushe. We made camp beneath a great knobby-rooted tree which
in Ireland hollowed out and pierced for windowes and doores might
make roome for several families to live in comfort. Dark quicklie fell
after the fashion of the countrie and came Peopled with strange
Cries, with croakings and cawing of Mysterious Animals that gave
us no little apprehension. In the morning . . .

[*text missing*]

. . . wee came at last to a great grene lake caught in a bowl at the pin-
nackle of the Mountain. The Medicinal fruits were to be found here
in the Foreste about the lake hanging from thicke vines embracing
the palms. Jasper and his man Collie and I and the other Slaves
spent all day and the next harvesting these fruits in many basketes
brought along for that purpose. On the seconde Day, just before the
falling of the Sunn we saw a multitudinous congregation of large
rosy-hued birds called by the salvages of these partes Flamingoes
descende out of the air and alight upon the green waters of the Lake.
For a bit of sport Jasper took up his Arquebus and filled it with lead
Pelletes and a single shot launched without effect in theyr directione
brought the birds rising up with much flexing of winges and anxious calles each to each in the Aire.

The sight was exceedingly beautiful; these rozy fowl, this green lake and falling sunlight; and I admit in contemplation of the Creator's workes I almost came to regret the bloody path upon which I had determined beyonde all human feelinge to set myself . . .

[*This regret did not trouble Finster Doyle for long. Soon after his reception into the Brotherhood of Buccaneers at Tortuga, he seized his first English ship, the* Endymion, *off the coast of Hispaniola. Upon its captain, crew, and passengers — among these several woman and children — he perpetrated such cruel atrocities as to earn him once and for all the respect of his fellow buccaneers and the enmity of all decent men. From this period of Finster's career, so ably described by Esquemeling, we have in his own words only the following fragment describing the capitulation of an unnamed English ship, probably c. 1662.*]

. . . other pirats thew themselves aboarde screaminge and whooping like salvages. The fight which followed was desperate and close and several of my men includeing Black Charlie who I regarded as a Brother fell beneath the last sally of the English sailors armed with Cudgel & Cutlass and two with Pistoles. Now one of the Officeres wearing a helmet & Cuirass like another Cromwell stood in command of a Sacker from which he fired a round indiscriminately which caused Great destruction both in our ranks and his owne: this piece of artillery put me in mind of the terrible guns with which the cursed Lord Lieutenant had breached Drogheda's walls and the thought made my eyes go redde and tearing off my leathere jerkin to expose my Lunges to the mortall blowes of Death should Godd will it I leapt down and struck this officer ere he aimed the Sacker a blow with my Cutlass across the face which split his nose in twain.

He fell with greate cry to the planks errupting blood and subsequently appealed to me for Mercy with the most piteous importunings. I stoode over him now as the Lord Lieutenant C. had once done to me, knowing a Life was mine to Give or take.

Mercy, wayled the Officer, Mercy. You Ask For Mercy, I said, Yet at the Reduction of Drogheda you showed no Mercy to the people, to my Mother and seven sweet Willowy Sisters. At this he fell to protesting: I Have Never been to the place you mention; during the Irish Wars I was a mere child. No, I said. You were There all you English were There, and I drove my Sword point through his Eye and out the back of his Headde which I then severed from its Trunk.

Holding this Grisly Specimen aloft I called to the English sailors to lay down their arms. They asked for a Promise of Clemency which I gave willingly then when they disarm'd I immediately gave the order for general Slaughter as was my Custom which we pursued till the gunnals ran red with Blood as the Byrne had done that Fatal Night Drogheda was brought Low.

[*Unfortunately none of Finster Doyle's impressions of Henry Morgan, the great buccaneer captain, survives in his fragmentary narrative. The concluding piece of Finster's confession seems to have been written in a fit of passionate remorse on the very eve of his execution at Hampton Roads and concerns the salvation of his soul. Whether this remorse is the genuine article or whether Finster wrote in some vain hope of clemency is now lost to history — known only to his Catholic God.*]

Now the shadow of the gallows lies heavy upon me. Lest tomorrow morn I am rescued from Cruel Bondage by a Band of Angels and flown away from the accursed Place I shall die a common Pirat and my neck feel the weight of my arse at ropes end. I lie shackelled in this dungeon by my ankles and in this dimness and the candles inconstant light as I scratch pen to paper one last time now may see my life whole and plain free from the Long Fever of Bloode which Overtook me the dreadful Night of Drogheda's reduction.

Long years have passed since them, Years of hating and Rapacious Plunder during which many towns have I sacked and destroyed and Castles taken and Ships looted and Burned and sent to the Bottom of the Sea with all Souls aboard and screaminge for Mercy unheeded. Yet still have I not managed to extirpate from the Inner Chamberes of my Heart the Sorrows of Loss though I dayly bathed myself in the bloode of Englishmen. I consider the violence committed against me and I consider the equally violent acts committed by my own hande and noe the balance is not redressed. For those who committed the First Sins against me are not punish'd by my hand but Innocents are punished in theyr place. And the soules of these Innocents wrongfully punished will fly about the World as like an evil flock of Rapacious Birds influencing those alive to inflict more violence upon the persons of other Innocents and so, gradually the World be drowned in Innocent Blood.

For now I see the dreadful Truth of Father Tyrone's words so long Ago: a Single Violent Deed is like unto a pebble cast into a still water and the ripples spreading therefrom the unending effects of this Bloody Deed upon the World and subsequent Generations of Men. Thus a Great Violence like a city sacked and destroyed is like unto a great stone cast into the same still water which does cause much Agitation and the water to overflowe its banks and borders and spread until it becomes like the Inundation of Noah but drowning Innocents not onlie sinners many leagues and many years distant. For such is the History of the Race of Man, violence begetting violence until all Goodnesse & Gentlenesse be washed from our lives like the Stain of Original Sin by the Sacramente of Baptisme. Yet if Goodnesse & Gentlenesse be a stain I do not find it now upon my own black soul.

That night of Droghedas reduction and the murther of my Mother and Sister was I shewn the True Way by Good Father Tyrone, Martyr & Sainte of the Church. He urged upon me the way of the Redeemer then and I denied Him to the peril of my Soul everlasting. Bad actions must be exchanged for Good, Violence for Gentlenesse I see now too plainly. Nor is this Capitulation of Pride Weakness but the greatest Strengthe. Only then shall His Dominion Prosper and his Sinful Children Walk forgiven in the Light of the Infinite. This is now my Prayer: May God Forgive me my trespass as I have not Forgive the Trespas of Others. May he Forgive English and Irish, Spanish and Dane. May he forgive Salvage and Christian who have Great need of Forgiveness, may he forgive all Doyles who are to Come in the years after upon this Bloody Ground called the Earth and show all the way to Salvation & Peace.

To Vouchsafe the Sincerity of the above testimonie I wish to diliver unto the hands of the Authorities of this Colony that which has been asked of me and which I have not revealed until now even under the direst Torture: Namely the place wherein I have hid my Treasure and those other Valuables acquired by Violence which I now renounce. I ask only that this Ill gotten Wealth be used for the Relief of Sufferinge among the Poor and I also ask that the account of my Terrible Adventures herein set down be delivered unto my Several Wives and Children now living among the Tribe of Oknontokok Salvages about the Isle called by these Salvages Wassanateaghe which lies in the Virginia Sound that my wordes might become a lesson for my sons who may thereby profit by my sufferinge and turne their feet unto the Righteous path and stay theyr Handes of Violence in Jesus name.

To this Ende, I have endeavoured plainly to mark on the ap-
pended Chartes the final Resting place of my Vesseles: The Poets
Grave interred on the abovementioned Islande at my Instigation by
these same Salvage tribe of Oknontoke, its resting place marked
carefully by me using sextant readings and sightings of moon and
stars and certaine observable features of landscape. The Monstrance
also, its belly full of the riches of the Peruvian Mines wrung from
the flesh of poor Salvages of that Country by the Spanishers rests
alas too deep under the Ocean's Fathoms her timbers cracked op'n
on a shoal of oysters lyke unto a Mountain and is not I think Re-
trievable by current Methodes. But just in case some comeing here-
afer might discover the means I will mark the approximate location
also upon a Seconde chart.

Againe, May God Forgve me I go to My just execution on the Mo-
row in hopes of Ressurection professinge Sorrow for the Evils committed by my Hande as I set down these last wordes near Midnight
this 16th Day of Sept. 1675.

5

By a strange coincidence, Doyle finished reading the confessions of
his ancestor the repentant buccaneer at exactly midnight. A cool wind
from the marsh disturbed the burlap curtains over the window open
over Buck's desk. A sinister moon shone upon the sawgrass rustling
ceaselessly down in the marsh. Doyle drained the last of his Spanish
brandy and felt the thick, abiding presence of ghosts in the room; not
just Finster himself but all the others, the martyrs of Drogheda, the
countless innocents brought low by the unquenchable fury of a pirate,
the untold slaughtered of the last three hundred years. The marsh
wind rustled the curtains now with a small damp sound that was like
the voices of the drowned, whispering their pitiful stories from the
bottom of the sea.

Doyle examined the ancient pages again. The maps were missing.
Pirate treasure maps. This sounded ridiculous, he knew, but what else
would you call them? The maps had been there when Foy Whitcomb

handed the manuscript to Uncle Buck years ago and were there no longer. The maps undoubtedly showed the presence of two seventeenth-century ships, allegedly carrying treasure, one buried close at hand, beneath the restaurant or the vacation cabins or the Beach Road or the golf course, a ship whose timbers lay disintegrating under dirt and sand and stones, under layers of irony and history. So this was the secret of the Doyles, that beneath their feet as they went about the mundane tasks of life — boozing, eating, bathing, shitting, talking on the telephone, making love, playing a relaxing round of goofy golf — lay the ark whence had sprung their generations in America. Thus, Doyle thought with a shiver, we walk on the bones of the ones who have gone before us.

6

Wiccomac Mews was a brand-new crescent of townhouses exactly two miles from the courthouse green, built against a nameless tributary of Wiccomac Creek and encircled by a high brick wall with a guardpost at the entrance but left unguarded at this late hour, the gate open and metal barrier raised. Doyle supposed the guardpost and the wall were more for show than anything else — status, these days, meant you could afford to live in high-security air-conditioned isolation — and he drove the Cadillac through the gates and parked in one of the two spots reserved for number 1127.

He stepped out of the car and crossed the neat square of lawn to the front door, painted blue and hung with one of those nondescript wreaths made out of dried twigs appropriate to any season in the suburbs. No lights shone, the blinds drawn tight. He rang the lit doorbell once, then rang again, this time long and insistent and a minute later heard a small voice on the other side of the door.

"Who's there?"

"It's Doyle," Doyle said. "I need to talk to you."

A hesitation, then the voice said: "It's one a.m. Call me at the office tomorrow."

"I'm selling Pirate's Island and getting out," Doyle lied. "It won't take long, just a couple of minutes."

Another hesitation, then the door opened a crack and Doyle saw a quarter of Slough's puffy face bisected by the security chain, one eye peering suspiciously through his glasses.

"You're selling Pirate's Island?" Slough said, his voice uncertain.

"That's right," Doyle said. "I've got Roach right here waiting in the car. You better open up."

Slough undid the chain, opened the door and saw the empty Cadillac facing the house, and realized there was just Doyle, and his fat cheeks trembled and he jumped back with a nimbleness that belied his bulk and tried to slam the door in Doyle's face. But Doyle caught the edge, and shoved it back hard and threw himself atop the fat man and both of them went over on to the beige carpet. Doyle felt his elbow disappear into Slough's stomach, an unpleasant sensation like sinking into Jello, and Slough groaned in pain and his face went ash grey and he ceased struggling all at once. Doyle pushed off the carpet and stood over the man.

"Don't move," Doyle barked. "Don't move a muscle."

The fat man lay there, chest heaving. He wore a plush monogrammed royal blue robe and monogrammed royal blue bedroom slippers; the spotless interior of his townhouse was utterly nondescript, decorated like an expensive hotel room with glossy institutional furniture and abstract prints no one would ever bother to look at.

"I want the maps," Doyle said, when Slough's breathing had calmed a bit.

Slough blinked. "I don't know what you're talking about," he said.

Doyle smiled, showing his teeth. He put his foot on the fat man's stomach and began to push down hard.

Slough made a choking noise and his face went red.

Doyle eased off a moment. "I'm in no mood for bullshit, Slough. I know you know who's got the maps because you had access to Foy Whitcomb's special files in the safe when he took sick, he told me so himself, and you saw the maps there and stole them. Am I right?"

"Absolutely not!" Slough gasped.

Doyle ground the heel of his shoe into the fat man's gut and felt the fat give way.

"The maps!" Doyle was shouting now. "Where are they?" Slough began to whimper; tears leaked down to stain the beige carpet beneath his ears.

7

Roach Pompton's octagonal palace stood in humid shadow on its pier overlooking the inlet. The main gate was closed. A faint bluish glow — the flicker of a television or the night-light for Roach's snakes and lizards — shone dimly from two long windows, otherwise the house was dark. Doyle followed the pier down to where it met the water. The tide was out, leaving a narrow ledge of green rock exposed. He grabbed the iron bars of the fence, swung himself around, found a toehold on the rocks, and inched along until he could gain a footing on the shingle, then swung on to the concrete lip below planters full of cactus that formed the base of Roach's garden. He crouched down and scuttled along beneath the planters to the porch, pulled himself up to the varnished wood, and made the tour of the eight-sided pile on his hands and knees, gently trying all the windows, which were double-paned and locked shut.

There seemed to be no way in but through the glass, which would undoubtedly set off alarms to wake the dead. Maybe Roach lived alone with his Jamaican harlot, maybe he surrounded himself with a private army of palace guards. Just now was not the time to find out. Doyle considered trying the windows again but his knees wouldn't stand up to more crawling and it didn't seem likely that he would find them unlocked the second time around. A fresh wind blew from the channel; the tide rose imperceptibly up the shingle. In the next moment, he realized he hadn't tried the front door.

8

Roach Pompton and Nomi lay in a naked heap of white and brown flesh atop the bedspread on the king-sized bed in the master bedroom, staring at a blue test pattern of a 1950s cardboard Indian in a feathered headdress on the television set in the vast entertainment console at the foot of the bed. The only light beside the television test pattern was a blue lava lamp, its globules of hot blue wax heaving and bubbling in the viscous medium. On a Chinese lacquer table next to the lamp was the ebony pipe and another brick of tar heroin, half unwrapped. Blue pills spilled from a silver pill box on the shiny black surface.

Suddenly, the test pattern of the Indian gave way to a giant blue eye, then a revolving blue mandala, then back again to the giant blue eye; obviously some sort of psychedelic video for the completely stoned. Roach's reaction to this monster oculus — a slight groan — was the only indication to Doyle that the man was still alive. Doyle stepped into the room, raised the African war club he had snatched off the wall in the living room, and swung it directly into the center of the eye. The television screen exploded in a shower of sparks and glass; the room filled with the unpleasant smell of burning plastic.

Roach rolled off the bed in slow motion and pressed himself into the corner by the closet, teeth chattering. The Jamaican didn't stir; she was still breathing but her soul had been swallowed into a blank stupor as if into the maw of a great beast; she had sunk to the blue addicts' paradise, that place beyond love or desire or even defecation, like death but not quite as final or as clean.

Doyle turned on the overhead light. "The door was open," he said, in a normal tone. "I let myself in. Hope you don't mind."

Roach stared, one eye twitching wildly. He didn't seem to understand what was happening.

"This doesn't have to be painful," Doyle said, once again eminently reasonable. "All I want is my maps back."

Roach opened his mouth and this sound issued forth: "Gah." Then his bladder emptied and a clear stream of urine darkened the rug by the bed.

"You are truly disgusting," Doyle said, disgusted. "Just how stoned are you, anyway?"

Roach offered a cretinous grin.

"Never mind," Doyle said. "I'll find them myself."

He went through the octagonal house room by room, turning on all the lights until he came to what looked like Roach's office. The room contained a drafting table, covered with tightly rolled blueprints, a desk, a computer, stacks of legal-looking documents, some as high as Doyle's knee, and heaps of papers like piles of leaves all over the floor. In the corner sat an old-fashioned wooden filing cabinet, decorated with glow-in-the-dark stickers of Captain Crunch and Petey the Sea Dog. Doyle smashed the lock with the African war club to find the drawers full of cash, freshly minted packs of fifties, and hundreds so new they looked counterfeit and, who knows?, probably were. The sight of so much money, hundreds of thousands perhaps, made him pause. This was Roach's mad money, the little bastard. Would he miss, say, twenty grand? Angry with himself for the thought, he kicked the drawers shut and pushed the cabinet over on to the floor. Then he mauled through the heaps of papers for a few minutes and gave up. He went back into the bedroom where Roach still squatted in the corner in a puddle of pee. Doyle pressed the blunt end of the club hard against the man's forehead.

"The maps or I knock your brains out," he said.

Roach trembled visibly at this, his twitching eye twitched up towards the club and twitched back. Understanding dawned faintly somewhere in the depths.

"D . . . Duyl?" he managed.

"That's right," Doyle said, and he yanked Roach out of the corner and pushed him down the hall into the octagonal kitchen. Roach slumped down on the tile floor, rubbery-skinned naked in the white kitchen light as Doyle banged around in the cupboards, then brewed a cup of coffee. Doyle poured a cup for himself and a cup for Roach, who brought the steaming liquid to his lips with both hands, like a French kid drinking a bowl of hot chocolate, docile and content.

When Roach finished the coffee, he seemed to have one foot in the world.

Doyle brandished the club. "The maps," he said. "Or else."

Without hesitation, Roach got up and shambled out into the white living room, his penis dangling limp and shrivelled in its thicket of hair. Behind a large Ashanti mask on the white wall was a safe with a digital lock. Roach worked the digital code and the safe clicked open. In there, in a manilla envelope marked Whitcomb, Kettle & Slough, Attorneys at Law, were two worn sheets of seventeenth-century paper bearing crudely rendered maps and markings in a crabbed hand that Doyle now recognized as Finster's.

"So you engineered all this mess," Doyle said, trying to understand, "because you thought you could dig up pirate gold on my land?"

Roach only offered another cretinous grin, but somehow Doyle understood: it wasn't money after all, Roach had plenty of that, he left wads of the stuff lying around like pocket change, but something grander and less tangible, call it romance, mystery. A child's dream of gold coins, diadems, rubies, strands of pearls, gold ingots all buried in an ancient chest surrounded by pirate skulls and mysterious bones — straight out of *Treasure Island*.

"You really think it's there?" Doyle said. "A fucking pirate ship?"

Roach wagged his head vigorously. "She took me," he said, in a clear intelligible voice, though his eyes were still half vacant. "She blindfolded me and took me there."

"She?" Doyle said. His mouth went dry. From another room in the house, in glass cages beneath the heat of an artificial sun, lizards and snakes nestled against woodchips and tropical plants in reptile slumber.

9

Maggie's lights were out. Her cabin, tucked into a massive bloom of yellow forsythia, lay in a sort of enchanted darkness, like the briar-haunted gloom in which Sleeping Beauty's castle lay obscured in Fairyland. Frogs sang from the darkness of the rushes nearby.

Doyle stepped up to the front door. The rubber doormat showed the

Tasmanian devil and the caption maggie's lair! He knocked loudly. Maggie's lights went on in an instant as if she'd been lying awake, waiting for his visit all along. A few seconds later, he heard the levering sound of the Winchester through the door. My God, Doyle thought, does she sleep with the damned thing?

"Hey, it's Tim," he called.

"What the hell do you want at this hour?" Maggie sounded angry. As always in Doyle's life, it was well past three a.m.

"I want to talk about the *Poet's Grave*."

A silence made more so by the chorus of frogs greeted this statement. "All right," she said, at last. "Just let me get decent."

A few minutes later, Maggie shot the bolt back and undid the latch, and Doyle stepped inside. She had tossed the penguin robe over the state of nature in which she slept and her hair was flat and oily. Doyle saw a pot of coffee bubbling on the two-burner gas range in the tiny kitchenette. These vacation cabins had been built in the latest style of two generations ago, with chrome fittings and fifties turquoise Formica and panelling of pale knotty pine, now darkened by the years. Maggie lived here like living on a ship: tight quarters had forced a clipped nautical neatness that reminded Doyle of Cap'n Pete's little cabin hanging over another inlet on the other side of the island. Clothes that would not fit into the tiny closet were neatly stacked in milk crates along the walls. The bare minimum of utensils was stored on the open shelf over the stove. Above the narrow bed in the sleeping alcove hung a large crucifix. A bank calendar with the days marked off in purposeful red Xs and a brown, mold-spotted print of a man duck-hunting — put up there by Uncle Buck back when the cabins first opened to the public — were the only items of décor on the walls.

Maggie sat on the quilted loveseat and pulled her robe over her knees. She looked muddled and puffy-faced. "Coffee up in a minute." She yawned.

"No, thanks." Doyle leaned against the pine panelling across the room, which meant he was only a few feet away. These cabins had always made him claustrophobic: there never seemed to be enough space for his shoulders.

"You heard what I said?" Doyle couldn't keep the edge out of his voice.

Maggie wagged her head in a mute affirmative. She had the

aggrieved air of someone accused of a crime for which they were not entirely responsible.

"Why didn't you tell me about the *Poet's Grave?*" Doyle said, struggling to stay calm.

Maggie hesitated. Then she said, "I don't know, just figured you knew. Then, when I figured you didn't know, I didn't want to tell you 'cause it seemed like our little secret, Buck's and mine. If he didn't tell you all those years he had his reasons, I guess."

"The secretive old bastard," Doyle swore.

"Maybe he thought OK, you're a kid and kids like to talk, and you'd tell someone just to tell and once rumors get around like that — holy shit, buried treasure — the place would have been overrun with all kinds of nutcases, shovels in hand. Then, when you got older, he was just waiting for you to come back, but you never came back, not while he was alive."

"So, how long have you known?"

"I've known for a long time," Maggie said quietly.

"Since when?"

"Since not too long after Buck and me started going out, I guess. One night he took me down there. It was real creepy."

Doyle felt a squeezing sensation in his guts. "You've been into the *Poet's Grave?*"

"More or less," Maggie said.

"You can you find your way there again?"

Maggie gave him a peculiar look. "What do you think?"

9

Golf-course statuary loomed against the moonless night like totems raised to pagan gods. Endangered possums scuttled in the underbrush beyond the storm fence, night birds gave lonely honks from the marshes. Maggie, in duckboots, stumbled over the cracked surface of the coquina path. The beam of her flashlight played across the plaster convolutions of the giant squid just ahead. "We should have put on the path lights," she said. "Just a flick of the switch. This is crazy."

"No," Doyle said. He couldn't explain it: they were like grave rob-bers in more ways than one — and grave robbers needed night, dark-ness, silence for their ghastly business. In another minute, they stood before the plaster battlements of Maracaibo. Maggie held the flash-light as Doyle put his shoulder to a wooden door in the northwest façade. The door creaked open on a storage room filled with mainte-nance junk — rolls of Plasti-grass, gallon cans of bug spray, dried-up cans of paint.

Maggie reached up, pulled a cord and the tight enclosure was filled with the glare of a hundred-watt lightbulb hanging on a wire from the ceiling. Doyle blinked at the jumble: in this harsh light it reminded him of the famous photographs showing the smashed, gleaming re-mains left by robbers in King Tut's tomb in the Valley of the Kings.

"Right," Maggie said. "Now we can see what we're doing. Or, I should say, *you* can see what *you're* doing. Because I'm not going down into that shithole for a million bucks."

She led Doyle over to a square of Plasti-grass laid like a rug at the cen-ter of the room and rolled this up to reveal a wooden pallet set into the ground, at the center, a heavy black iron ring. "That's it," Maggie said.

"That's what?" Doyle said, staring down at the ring.

"The main hatch of the *Poet's Grave*. Course, only the ring's the gen-uine article. Buck put that hatch in not too long after he built the golf course."

"All those years." Doyle smiled to himself. "All those tourists play-ing goofy golf and no one ever knew. They thought the pirate thing was just a gimmick to get a putter in their hand."

"Old Buck thought it was pretty funny, too," Maggie said. "Man had a twisted sense of humor, you ask me."

"Now what?" Doyle said.

Maggie pointed to a chain and hand winch from an old engine hoist fixed to a beam in the ceiling. Doyle put the chain through the iron ring, fixed the hook and jacked the winch till the chain drew tight.

"Better stand back," he said.

Maggie stood back and Doyle took the winch handle in both hands and pulled down hard; the gear caught and, with a shriek, the hatch pulled free from the earth and went swinging in the air a foot above shoe-level. A rich, loamy smell billowed into the storage room from the hole the hatch revealed. A centipede half as long as Doyle's arm undulated out from beneath the hatch into the darkness beneath a moldy roll of canvas.

Doyle lowered the chain, and heaved the hatch aside and stared down into the hole — no bigger around than a sewer cover, all mud and dark earth, its sides shored with timber and plywood. This was disappointing. He'd half expected to find himself looking into the interior of a ship preserved intact by some miracle from the seventeenth century.

"If you want to go down, go ahead," Maggie said over his shoulder. "I'm staying put. But you won't find anything. Just a lot of crud. Old Buck took what there was to take out of that pit fifty years ago, which was nothing much. There's less than nothing left now."

Doyle hesitated. The *Poet's Grave* smelled like the grave itself. Like rot and tree roots. "I've come this far," he said. He took a breath, squatted down, and swung his legs into the hole.

Maggie handed him the flashlight. "Good luck," she said. "And be careful. Stay on the first level, the other levels are unsafe by now."

Doyle pivoted off into the darkness and found himself at the bottom of a shallow well. From here, two tunnels just large enough to allow one man crawling diverged at right angles.

"Take the tunnel to your right," came Maggie's voice from above. Doyle looked up and saw her head haloed against the brightness of the bare bulb. "Always stay to the right and you'll end up back where you started from."

Doyle dropped to his hands and knees and crawled into the opening, with some difficulty keeping the flashlight pointed ahead. The beam illuminated a long, rooty tunnel, here as above shored with timbers and plywood. The air was foul and nearly unbreathable. He crawled along for some distance and he had the unpleasant sensation that he was crawling through the bowels of some vast decomposing buried possum. After a few minutes of this exercise, he wanted to turn and go back, but it was easier to crawl forward and he continued along until he came to a place where the shoring had given way, the tunnel collapsed on itself. He backed up slowly and took the first right turning. Along the way he saw nothing that shouldn't be present in the depths of the earth: roots, worms, larval cicadas secreted in their burrows awaiting a hot summer still several years to come. There was nothing here, he told himself. Just empty tunnels in the ground, a mad folly of his uncle Buck — a man known for his pursuit of folly. Then he nearly fell across an iron something partially blocking his path.

Doyle inched forward to examine this protuberance with his flashlight. It was the breech end of a cannon, its muzzle firmly buried in the earth. Someone had treated the exposed metal with a rust inhibitor, and by shining his flashlight at an oblique angle, Doyle could just make out a lion and castle — the arms of Aragon and Castile, still featured on the Spanish national flag. A Spanish cannon! He clambered over this demi-interred piece of ordnance and went forward until he felt fresh air on his face. Then he was back in the well coughing and spitting dirt and there were Maggie's strong arms reaching down to help him up to the world again.

10

"I didn't believe it either," Maggie said.

They were sitting in the bar, Maggie with a cup of coffee, Doyle with a bourbon and soda. Tunnel muck caked his hair, stuck to his skin. He still felt clammy from crawling around in the belly of a ship dead and rotted to nothing three hundred years ago.

"Then Buck took me down and showed me that cannon and some other things," she continued, "and I guess I had to believe him but shit —"

"Like what other things?" Doyle interrupted.

"Like nothing interesting," Maggie said irritably. "Like bits of wood, like rusty old metal rings and a shoe buckle that fell apart when he brought it up. But it's down there, all right. The whole damned boat, or what's left that hasn't done rotted away, which is precious little." She paused, a vague smirk on her face, anticipating Doyle's next question.

"So there wasn't any . . . treasure?" Doyle stumbled on the word. "Didn't Buck —" But he was cut short by the high shriek of Maggie's laughter.

"You too!" she said. "All of you! Like a bunch of fool kids in a pirate movie. Buried treasure only happens in your dreams, buddy!"

"Listen," Doyle said hotly, "Finster's confession distinctly mentions *treasure and other valuables* — I believe that's the exact phrase. Why else would Buck dig all those tunnels?"

"Buck dug all those tunnels because he was Buck and the stubbornest damned SOB you ever saw," Maggie said. "He dug for years all under the golf course, which is one of the reasons some of the putting greens are out of whack and he never found a single gold coin. He was still digging when you was a kid. You ought to remember. He said you used to ask why he came out of Maracaibo all covered in mud. You remember that, right?"

Doyle thought back and summoned a single image from the depths — Buck wiping mud off his face with a red bandanna — though this was somehow mixed up with a glimpse of one of the early Mercury rockets shooting into space like a silver bullet on the old black-and-white rabbit-ear TV on the shelf above the bar.

"So when Buck kept on not finding anything down there, year after year," Maggie continued, "he put down his shovel and went to have a look at some old government papers somewhere and it turned out the treasure the *Poet's Grave* was carrying was nothing but pipe tobacco."

Doyle pressed Maggie to explain further and she succeeded in recalling most of the things Buck had told her about his investigation. According to seventeenth-century records found by Buck at the archives of the Commonwealth in Richmond, the last prizes taken by the *Poet's Grave* were two heavily laden vessels of the Virginia tobacco fleet — the *Ramona* and the *Juno* — bound for the markets of London. The ships had carried between them three hundred hogsheads of Virginia's finest tobacco, in those days used as currency in the cash-poor colonies. Three hundred hogsheads of tobacco disposed of properly in Europe would have been enough to make a very rich man of Finster Doyle. As it was, the tobacco just rotted to nothing in the broken hull of the *Poet's Grave*, eaten away by worms and earth and time.

"That's the funny part," Maggie said, and she laughed. "Tobacco. Don't you think that's funny?"

"Funny," Doyle said glumly.

"Old Buck digging away down there in the ground like a goddamned mole for years looking for a bunch of rotten tobacco."

Doyle finished his bourbon and soda and set the glass on the bar. "Of course, Roach Pompton wouldn't have known any of that," he said suddenly, and he looked Maggie in the eye. "Am I right?"

Maggie blinked and looked away.

"Why don't you tell me what happened there?" Doyle said.

"It was my fault, really, for bitching that I never got to go on a vacation." Maggie squirmed uneasily. "So Buck gets sick of my bitching and decides he's going to take me out west to see the mountains, come hell or high water. I always wanted to see the mountains. But we didn't have any money so . . ."

"So?"

"So somehow Roach got his hands on the maps —"

"Slough," Doyle interrupted. "He took them out of Foy Whitcomb's safe."

"That asshole lawyer," Maggie swore. "In any case, Roach comes on down here one day in his SUV and talks to Buck and says he wants to buy the whole place for a couple of hundred grand just like that. Buck thinks this is pretty weird and tells him so, on account of the fact that development is not allowed and Roach is into developing the hell out of everything, then Roach lets on how he knows about the maps. Buck's thinking fast during all this — what we got here's rotten tobacco but Roach doesn't know it. So on account of Buck's illness it's me that's got to get Roach blindfolded and take him down through those goddamned tunnels and when he comes up for air the bastard's got gold doubloons in his eyes and he goes in to see Buck. 'You can't find anything with tunnels,' he says to Buck. 'You've got to raze the whole golf course, excavate the whole damn place with a backhoe.' 'Not while I'm alive,' old Buck says to him, 'but I'm sick, won't be too long now.' So they cook up a secret deal then and there — Roach hands over thirty thousand in cash for exclusive rights to the maps with the understanding that after Buck's demise, he's got first dibs to buy the land from me or you or the bank.

"Of course, Buck didn't ask my opinion about any of that bullshit. I'd have said no way, I'm never selling this place — it's home and you don't sell home. But that was how he worked, never asking nobody nothing, especially not a woman. So Buck got his thirty grand and we went and saw the mountains and had a pretty good time, but as it turns out in light of recent events, such as dead possums and fires

and gunfights, he just opened up a can of worms for us that's left behind because what's the use of having maps to buried treasure on
somebody else's property? There, that's the whole goddamned story.
Satisfied?"

Doyle rose from the stool, dried mud flaking to the floor. No, he
wasn't satisfied. Something was missing from this tale, some important element, he just couldn't say what. He questioned Maggie closely
until he was convinced she had told him everything she knew, then he
knew she didn't know everything. What next? After a while, dawn
showed out the big window of the bar, a hesitant pinkish-grey light
rising above the black pinnacles of the pines.

11

Memorial Day. Rain. But the Wassateague Town Volunteer Fireman's
Memorial Day Carnival, one of the bookends of the summer beach
season on the island, would proceed as scheduled.

The Tilt-a-Whirl flashed its lights against the sodden, rain-black sky.
Steam rose from the burping generators. A few tourist kids, wearing
nylon bike gear, huddled together in the dripping wire baskets of the
Alpine Plunge. Electrical cables snaked dangerously across the mud
and straw of the midway. In the open bays of the fire station across the
fairground, the volunteer firemen in their blue fatigues needlessly polished the massive steel wheels of the engines. The townies sought
refuge from the downpour at the hoop-toss concessions or beneath the
beer tent, its pregnant canvas bulging with rain.

Doyle saw Harold at the shooting arcade, a pellet-firing sub-
machine-gun butted against his shoulder. Shoot the red paper star
completely out of the target with one burst and you would win something utterly useless: a cheap blue animal stuffed with Styrofoam
beads, not a tiger or a lion but something in between; a huge foam
rubber hand showing the nasty finger with the slogan *I'm Number
One!* printed in gold letters across the knuckles. But this game was
harder than it looked. Doyle stood back and watched the kid lose fif-

teen dollars for a prize not worth fifty cents. Then he went up and laid a friendly hand on his shoulder.

Harold jumped around and would have swung the pellet machine-gun in Doyle's direction, had it not been chained to the counter.

"Hey, be careful with that!" the attendant yelled. Doyle held up his hands and backed away. Harold's eyes were red and stoned-looking; the sharp pungence of cannabis hung about his wet clothes.

"You're wasting your minimum wage, kid," Doyle said. "Come on, I'll buy you a hot dog."

"I'm not on duty, man," Harold said. "I'll spend my fucking minimum wage any way I fucking feel like."

"OK, pardner," Doyle said. "You're on your own." And he backed out into the rain.

Tonight Doyle wore Uncle Buck's pork-pie Stetson and the enveloping gangsterish Mackintosh, which kept most of the wet off his clothes, except where it leaked along the seams. His shoes were sensibly encased in a pair of Buck's black rubber galoshes over Buck's black and white wingtips. He ran into Maggie coming across the midway. Her feet were bare, caked with mud like the paws of a possum. She was drunk tonight. Doyle had never seen Maggie drunk before and the sight was somehow shocking. A pair of very brief cut-offs and an extremely tight T-shirt stuck to her sodden curves. Her bleached hair hung dripping against her head. She grabbed Doyle's sleeve. "Come on, Al Capone," she said. "Let's go on the Tilt-a-Whirl. I've got tickets!" She waved four bits of paper in his face, grinning, happy as a kid.

"No, thanks," Doyle said. "Not in this weather. Anyway, carnival rides make me sick."

She stuck out her tongue and ran off towards the dripping rides, stalled at the moment for lack of customers.

A few minutes later, Doyle found himself pressed in with the crowd — entirely male — at the open-fronted shed that contained the wheel of fortune. The close smell of damp, unwashed bodies, cigarettes, and male flatulence assailed his nostrils. The wheel itself was about five feet in diameter, the inner rings painted with Masonic symbols and signs of the zodiac, the outer with a democratic deck of cards excluding the jack, queen, and king. The maximum bet was a mere dollar a spin, but the men gambling here showed the same grave, contentious attitude of gambling men everywhere; they might have been in Vegas, rolling the bones for thousands. Now, they threw quarters on to the felt pad, the wheel spun to a quick ratcheting sound, and when it came to a stop almost everyone lost, wagered quarters swept by the attendant into a trough behind the counter. Doyle caught the fever and put three quarters on a red ace and lost, two more quarters on a black deuce and lost again. The attendant, a lanky young man wearing a T-shirt, exposing sinewy, tattooed arms, climbed up on a box and peered over the head of the gamblers.

"Listen, you high rollers," he called, "unless there is a peace officer present, I am prepared to raise the minimum wager to five dollars a spin!" A general hoot of approval followed this suggestion, and in an instant, five-dollar bills were strewn across the green felt. Doyle produced a five from his pocket and played the black eight.

"And around and around she goes," the attendant called, jingling the change in his apron. The wheel spun, slowed, teetered against the pointer and snapped into Doyle's black eight. He felt the primal surge of adrenalin and, eyes glittering, watched as ten five-dollar bills were added to his one on the green felt.

"Lucky bastard," an Irish voice said in his ear.

Doyle spun around, instantly put on his guard by the Irish accent, to confront a pair of dark pop-eyes staring up at him. The eyes belonged to a tweed-capped homunculus, a hairy little man who came no higher than Doyle's shoulder. There was something sinister about the man's demeanor, as if he knew a couple of things Doyle didn't know and wasn't telling, and this knowledge made him as tall as he needed to be.

"It's nothing," Doyle said. "Just beginner's luck."

"No, I think you've got the touch," the little man insisted. "Put a fiver for me on something there, would you, big man? Any number will do." He held up a rumpled five dollar bill.

Doyle hesitated, then took the bill and tossed it on the nearest ace. For himself, he played a red two, a black ten, and a red ten. The wheel spun, the little man lost. Doyle's black ten came in and he won another thirty dollars.

"There you go again," the little man said. Suddenly, Doyle felt himself pinned against the counter. A hulking bruiser wearing a see-through plastic rain slicker over a leather motorcycle jacket pushed up and wedged himself directly behind them. The bruiser reached into the pocket of his jeans, pulled out a fistful of crumpled fives, and dropped them on the felt.

"Get a tip from the lucky bastard here, Jesus," the little man said, pointing to Doyle.

The man named Jesus shot Doyle an unreadable look and grunted. Doyle began to feel claustrophobic, nervous presentiment quivering up his spine. He put a dollar down for the next round but when the wheel spun didn't wait to see what came up — instead, he turned quickly and elbowed out through the crowd. He stepped on someone's toes, stumbled into someone else, a curse or two was thrown after him, but he was not followed. He splashed off quickly across the midway to the beer tent, bought himself two pints of National Bohemian with his winnings, and sat down at one of the long, vinyl-covered picnic tables in the back.

A sinister atmosphere pervaded this carnival tonight — it was the rain, of course, and the fact that carnivals are sinister at the best of times — and, once again, Doyle had the feeling that conspiracies were being hatched out there in the darkness, that he was caught at the center of something more than just Roach's lust for buried treasure. The Irish voices didn't help. Since when had there been so many Irishmen in Wassateague? The bumper cars bumped and crashed in the garish arena on the other side of the tent and now the Tilt-a-Whirl tilted wildly to the fast scream of electronic carnival music. He had a headache. He would finish his beers, go home to bed.

"If it isn't the old gunslinger himself!"

Doyle looked up. Roach Pompton stood at the end of the table, long, sallow face lizard-like in the dim light.

"Drinking for two, Doyle?"

Doyle didn't respond. Roach threw his skinny ass down on to the bench and put his elbows on the table. He didn't have a beer. He pulled out a pack of cigarettes, lit one, and set down the pack upright as a tombstone.

"You've got ten seconds," Doyle growled, "before someone's going to have to pick up the pieces."

Roach's lizard mask slipped to reveal a slightly hurt expression, but he leaned forward and tried to make his voice tough; instead, it came out all quivery around the edges. "Usually I kill someone for doing what you did the other night."

"Kill away," Doyle said.

"But you're a hard guy to kill, aren't you, Mannix?"

Doyle shrugged.

"Because if that's what you think, you're wrong. Everyone can be killed. You had no right to bust into my house like that and bust my television and take those maps and I'll tell you why — your god-damned uncle sold them to me two years ago. Thirty grand, I paid."

"Then you got ripped off," Doyle allowed. "Nothing in the ground there but dried-up old tobacco."

"Yeah, I found that out the hard way," Roach said bitterly. "I hired a research guy who went to the Admiralty in London and dug through a bunch of historical papers and that cost me seven grand more."

"You got ripped off again," Doyle said. "Buck did that work for nothing at the archives in Richmond."

"So I figure that's thirty-seven grand you Doyles owe me now," Roach blew an unsteady plume of smoke into the wet air. "But I'm willing to forget the debt if you'll just wise up and fucking sell that fucking place. Two hundred and fifty grand, and all debts forgiven. Now, that's one fuck of a great deal. What do you say?"

"No." Doyle didn't hesitate. "I wouldn't sell to Bracken and I certainly won't sell to you."

"I don't know any Bracken," Roach said.

"Sure you don't," Doyle said. "So the Royal Blue Cola stand thing was nonsense, a scam."

"A scam." Roach wagged his head unconvincingly.

"So now there's no treasure and you know it but you still want my land. Why?"

Roach swallowed hard. An urgent tone crept into his voice. "There are other parties interested here for reasons of their own, that's all I'm going to say. And these other parties, you don't want to mess with. They're real hard cases, not regular pushovers like me."

Doyle drained the dregs of his first beer. "Would some of these hard parties of yours hail from Delaware?"

Roach blinked. "Maybe. Then again, they might be from all over."

He glanced over his shoulder into the rain as if looking for someone. "So after Buck died, I called Maggie in good faith to say, hey, time to exercise my option, and you know what that fucking slut did to me? That fucking slut fucking hung up the fucking phone in my ear!"

"Wait a minute!" Doyle set his second beer half drunk on the table. "Don't call Maggie a slut again."

"You've got to be kidding," he said, incredulous. "There's one slut's blown half the town —"

Doyle rose, lunged forward and caught Roach on the left side of the jaw with his right fist. He was off-balance, so the blow wasn't much, but it landed with sufficient force to knock Roach off the bench on to the beer-fouled straw.

Roach scrambled up, hand to his cheek, eyes wide and hurt. "You shouldn't have done that, Doyle," he said, an unmanly sob rising from his voice. "That was the last mistake you'll ever make." And he turned and stumbled off into the rain.

Doyle settled back down and finished his beer. Then he put his wet Stetson on his head and snapped the brim and went out into the rain to look for Maggie. The rides were situated at the far end of the midway, in a grove of stunted pines. Doyle stood at the painted metal barrier and watched the Tilt-a-Whirl loop into the wet sky, driven on by a peculiar, exhausted music. Squinting up, he thought he saw Maggie's bare, white flank up there at the top of the parabola, and so he didn't notice the two men until they were right beside him.

"You lost my money, lucky man!"

It was the Irish homunculus from the wheel of fortune, the little man's tweed cap beaded with rain, black-pop eyes staring out of the shadow of his face.

"I think this lad owes me a fiver. What do you think, Jesus?"

The hulk in the plastic raincoat stepped up from behind and pulled a leathery something from his pocket. Doyle recognized what it was — a woven leather sock filled with lead shot — in the half-second before it smashed against his temple, just north of his ear. A shower of sparks exploded in his head and he went limp and fell to the ground. Only vaguely did he feel the big man named Jesus kick him hard in the ribs with his motorcycle boots; only vaguely did he feel the two men drag him through the mud and wet pine needles to the access road on the other side of the grove, where a long, dark car sat idling in the rain.

12

A blackness peopled with crawling things. One shoe off, one sock missing and something — ants? — biting Doyle's bare toes. This was the painful sensation that woke him out of his delirium far enough to realize that he lay on a mattress on the cement floor in a windowless room somewhere he'd never been before. The room had the close, damp, cement smell of a basement, and the faint sound of voices from somewhere above reached him in muffled echo. His arms and legs felt rubbery and weak, and he lay there without moving, concentrating on the ants biting his toes and trying to remember his name.

A little while later, the ants moved up from Doyle's toes and began biting his arms and his face, and he gritted his teeth to keep from screaming. He thought about Pablo for a long time and felt the empty spot in his heart where the boy had been. Then he thought about a nice cool glass of bourbon with shaved ice and a little mint and sugar, but there was no bourbon or mint or sugar, and certainly no shaved ice, and the delirium claimed him again and now he was on a carnival ride with Maggie, who was buck naked, her wet hair streaming back, her breasts flattening out as the metal car flung itself against gravity into the night and the rain. Doyle groaned aloud with each lurch of the car, then he thought about Pablo again and for some reason remembered a kids' book they'd bought together at the English-language bookstore in Madrid, and he began repeating a remembered fragment of text aloud to himself, just to hear his own voice and to remind himself that he was still alive. "My teeth are gold, my hat is old, my shoe is off, my foot is cold, I have a bird I like to hold." Doyle liked the hollow way his voice sounded in the dark room and he kept repeating these lines sometimes soft, sometimes loud then louder until he was screaming at the top of his lungs: "MY TEETH ARE GOLD, MY HAT IS OLD, MY SHOE IS

OFF, MY FOOT IS COLD, I HAVE A BIRD I LIKE TO HOLD!" And he kept screaming and after a while a thin wedge of light shone from beneath a door at the far end of the room and he heard angry voices coming closer. A moment later, the door flung open and overhead lights flashed on bright as the sun after all that darkness and Doyle quieted instantly and lay still, but watching through his lashes as two men came into the room.

"This bastard's strong as a fucking horse," said one of the men. An Irish voice. "We've shot him up with enough shit for an army."

"Another dose?" the other one said. Also Irish.

"I don't know," the first man said. "Might be dangerous."

The second man carried a small black vinyl case. He unzipped the case and removed a long, glittering hypodermic needle and a small bottle of clear liquid and began to fill the needle from the bottle. As he was doing this, Doyle recognized the man's pop eyes and bulbous leprechaun face from the Wassateague County Volunteer Firemen's Carnival — how long ago, he couldn't say. It seemed he'd been lying in that room in the dark forever.

The homunculus held the hypodermic up to the light and tapped the shaft for bubbles, neat as any registered nurse, and leaned over and took Doyle's arm by the wrist. "You want to help me, boyo?" he said to his companion, he held out a rubber thong to tie up Doyle's vein.

But the latter stepped forward and pushed him aside. "Hold a minute," he said softly. "You're too happy with that shit." This one he leaned down and slapped Doyle's cheeks hard, harder, seized his arm from the homunculus and let it drop. Doyle managed not to move, not to breathe, picturing for some reason the desiccated bones of Colonel Brodie Deering lying in the darkness of the tomb, all rot black and rust red. Doyle's tormentor stood back and grabbed the needle from the homunculus and squirted out its contents and zipped it back into the case.

"We wouldn't want to kill Mr. Doyle here," he said softly. "Not till the Old Fruit gets back from Philadelphia and gives us the say-so."

Doyle listened to the man's soft voice, and through his eyelashes saw the light glimmering off his slicked-back hair and visited again that night out on the Toquonque pier and the Whitneyville-Walker Colt going off like a cannon and the soft Irishman holding up his hands and trying not to be afraid.

"We don't want him screaming again either," the homunculus said angrily. "There's guests coming, Feeney. Try to put aside your fucking arrogance for once and listen."

The soft Irishman called Feeney reached out and calmly back-handed the homunculus across the mouth, a tight, popping sound that echoed off the cement walls. "Enough bloody lip, you odious little midget," he said, in his soft voice.

"I'll kill you for that one day," the homunculus said, trying to sound like he really would — hard to do while wiping a trickle of blood from his chin with a trembling hand.

"One day I'll kill myself." Feeney laughed, and the two men went out and the door slammed and the lights went out and Doyle was sunk in darkness again. He lay there for a while, listening to himself breathe, and almost slipped back to the terrible place where the ants were biting his toes but something on the low ceiling, something he'd seen through half-lidded eyes, made him get up. He rose to his knees and soon he was standing, the darkness reeling around his head, full of sparks and fire like constellations wheeling around the pole, and he reached up to the ceiling and put a hand on the thing he had seen there: the spigot of a sprinkler system with neat little heat-sensitive prongs around the nozzle, like the cilia of an exotic flower.

Holding on to the pipe to steady himself, Doyle reached into the deep pocket of his uncle Buck's trousers and found a box of matches nestled there against his leg. He shook the box and heard a faint rat-tling sound — there were only a couple of matches left. He struck the first, held it up to the heat-sensitive prongs, but the match sputtered and went out. Darkness again. He struck the second match and this time lit the matchbox itself and held flaming box to prongs and soon there was a gurgling sound and a mechanical whirring and a great whooping alarm from somewhere above and in another moment he was hit in the back of the head with a blast of cold water and the small room was filled with its own violent rainstorm.

Doyle jumped back against the wall beside the door and began to howl. Soon he heard loud cursing from the other side of the door and the sound of keys but this time when the door flung open he was ready. He lunged forward, putting his shoulder into it, an old football move that caught the homunculus square in the center of his chest.

The little man went down with a solid thump and a painful exhalation, and Doyle slid around him wetly on the wet concrete and went scrambling out into a long, low basement big as a warehouse, piled floor to ceiling with case after case of Royal Blue Cola. Feeney, not calm at all, was running towards him down the narrow aisle formed by two cola buttresses, a semi-automatic pistol in hand.

Doyle dodged down another aisle and careened into a wall of cola cases, which gave way before his weight as if full of air, and ran to the far end of the room where a set of concrete stairs led up to a metal door. He flung himself up the stairs and through the door, and found himself in a large, brightly tiled kitchen where a fat man in a chef's toque was stirring a large pot of something on a stove, all sparkling chrome and brushed aluminum. The chef stared.

Dripping, Doyle grabbed a sharp Japanese carving knife out of a butcher-block holder and waggled it in a manner he thought might be menacing. "Which way's out?" he managed, his voice a painful croak.

The chef gestured towards a swinging door across the room and Doyle dropped the knife and slopped through this door into a dining room, where a huge table was laid with a white tablecloth set with dishes and crystal and napkins folded to resemble little swans. Then he heard shouting from the kitchen and ran through the dining room into a central hallway just about wide enough for an army that seemed to be full of the lilting trill of something very sweet and classical played on a nicely tuned piano.

At the far end of the hall a big doorway with a fanlight overhead admitted the gray light of the outside world. Doyle swung towards this light, then the piano music stopped abruptly and he heard a voice call his name and it was a voice he knew. He swung back to see Bracken rise from the bench of a grand piano in a room across the hall to his left that was all carpet and chandeliers.

"Timmy!" Bracken said again, and she sounded upset. Her face white, she held a hand at her throat, rather prettily, it seemed to Doyle. She was dressed for a fancy party in an off-the-shoulder black dress, diamonds at her ears, at her wrists.

Doyle blinked and felt himself wearying all at once and thought it might be nice to lay his head right there on Bracken's breasts for an hour or two. Then a big man wearing a see-through plastic rain-slicker over a black leather jacket stepped out of nowhere and caught Doyle in the throat with a plastic-coated leather-clad elbow.

Doyle heard Bracken screaming as he went down, gasping for breath. Jesus, he remembered. The man's name is Jesus, and Doyle shouted it out loud, "JESUS!" a sort of prayer uttered to oblivion as he hit the floor and the darkness came again with the ants waiting.

13

The second room was very different from the first. The walls were hung with nineteenth-century hunting scenes and nicely framed copies of Piranesi prisons and the room was furnished with expensive leather furniture and a massive mahogany secretary full of big leather-bound books. Wooden blinds drawn halfway down the tall windows let slip the deepening blue of twilight. Doyle found himself lying on a button-pleated leather couch, hands and feet shackled with steel cuffs. His clothes were damp and clammy, his head hurt, and his vocal cords burned where he had caught Jesus's elbow, but the ants were gone. He tried to twist his legs to the floor and felt the cuffs ratchet tighter and cut into the skin of his ankles. His mouth tasted like something had crawled in there and died. Then, for some reason, he squinted up at the secretary and tried to make out the titles of the books, but his vision went blurry and he gave up.

"You can't read them," Bracken said. "They're fake. Hollow. I think they keep ammo inside or booze."

Doyle turned his head painfully to see Bracken sitting in a club chair across from the couch, her bare feet propped on a leather ottoman, her black dress bunched up around her knees, smoke curling from a cigarette between her fingers towards the ceiling. Then he felt the imaginary ants again, biting him beneath his damp clothes, and he grimaced and closed his eyes.

"What?" Bracken said, frowning.

"Nothing." Doyle's vocal cords felt scraped and bruised. He held up his shackled wrists. "You've got to get me out of these."

Bracken looked away. "I can't," she said, to the twilight beyond the blinds.

"Why not?" Doyle said.

"I just can't," Bracken said. "Besides, I don't have the keys."

"Who's got them?" Doyle said, his voice gaining strength.

"Oh, shut up," Bracken said, and she stubbed out her cigarette in an ashtray on a small table beside the chair, angry suddenly. "You got yourself into this situation, you get yourself out. You should have sold Pirate Island to me when you had the chance. We'd be in New York right now, the both of us, having a couple of martinis at the Cabala Club in SoHo, then home for a nice long fuck. Instead you play hard to get, and on top of everything else you manage to turn me into a fucking criminal! Thanks to you, the Feds are very seriously after me for some sort of immigration shit."

"Sorry to hear that," Doyle said.

"You're a real jerk." Bracken pouted. "All I wanted to do was grow some goddamned strawberries."

"With slave labor," Doyle said.

"What do I know about Mexicans?" Bracken wiggled angrily. "I can't even speak the language! I hired Enrique, he brought his own Mexicans. How was I supposed to know what was going on?"

"You got eyes, right?"

"Oh, fuck you."

"He was starving them, torturing them," Doyle persisted.

Tears sprang to Bracken's eyes. She bit her lip and for a while neither of them spoke. The light beyond the blinds faded to night. Bracken lit a lamp with a green glass shade, crossed her legs, uncrossed them. She didn't seem in a hurry to go anywhere but she wouldn't look at him. Gradually, Doyle became conscious of great thirst. "I could really use something to drink," he said. "A nice bourbon mint julep."

"What?"

"Just something to drink," Doyle said. "How about some water?"

"No," Bracken said. "Suffer."

Doyle waited and she threw up her hands and stalked out of the room through a heavily padded door and came back a few minutes later with milk in a large plastic sports cup, a straw, and a package of Oreos.

"Can you sit up?" she said.

Doyle swung his legs over the edge of the couch with some effort, heaved his body around, and twisted himself into a sitting position. Bracken sat beside him and held the straw to his lips and he drank the milk greedily. Then she popped an Oreo into his mouth and wiped crumbs from his chin with her fingers as he munched. The cuffs around his wrists weren't so tight that he couldn't feed himself, but he didn't mind the attention.

"Double stuffed," Bracken said, offering another Oreo. "The best kind."

Doyle shook his head. "They're going to kill me, you know that," he said.

"Don't be ridiculous," Bracken said, but she looked away.

"They've tried twice already," Doyle said. "And I shot one of their guys. They've got to get me for that." He paused. "But who are *they*?"

Bracken sighed. "Just wait and see," she said.

"I think you can tell me what's going on," he said, trying to keep his voice steady. "You owe me that much."

Bracken got up abruptly and wandered over to the chair she'd been sitting in earlier. She threw herself down and put her feet up on the ottoman and began twisting her long, elegant fingers together.

"I tried to help but you wouldn't listen," she said. "Now it's too late. I'm helpless, at their mercy, just like you. You've got to understand all the crap that went down —"

"Arson, kidnapping, attempted murder," Doyle interrupted.

"— wasn't my fault."

Doyle smiled grimly. "Sure, baby," he said. "You're just like a leaf, blown from gutter to gutter."

"And you're a mean bastard," Bracken said hotly.

Doyle turned his face to the leather cushion. "Get out of here. If I'm going to die in this room, I don't want you stinking up the air."

Bracken colored, got up, and stalked out, slamming the padded door behind her. But she came back in, not fifteen seconds later, and threw herself down on the chair again, green light from the green-shaded lamp reflecting along her bare shoulder.

"What do you want to know?" She lit another cigarette.

"Everything," Doyle said.

"You've got to ask specific questions," Bracken said. "Start at the beginning."

"All right," Doyle said, looking directly at her cleavage. "Why are you wearing that dress?"

"There's a dinner tonight," she said. "Fantucci's going to be here and some other big shots."

"Who the hell's Fantucci?" Doyle said.

"Fantucci's governor of Delaware," Bracken said, impatiently. "You're in Delaware."

"Delaware." Doyle winced. "I should have guessed."

"But Fantucci's just along for the ride. The guest of honor is William J. Donovan."

Doyle thought for a second. The name was a famous one. "You mean Donovan the tenor, from Ireland. That Donovan?"

"You got it," Bracken said. "He's singing for the Old Fruit."

This was the second time today Doyle had heard this expression. "Old Fruit?" he said.

Bracken shot him a look. "He's the boss," she said. "The big cheese."

"Fruit, cheese," Doyle said, annoyed. "Does this bag of groceries have a name?"

Bracken sighed deeply and for a moment, it didn't seem she would answer. "O'Mara," she said at last, emphasizing the name in a way that sounded like it should mean something special.

Dole racked his brain but couldn't come up with a single association. Who was this O'Mara — presumably an Irishman — that he could command the presence of governors and world-famous tenors and wreak havoc up and down the Eastern Shore?

"Never heard of the guy." Doyle shook his head at last.

"You've got to be kidding," Bracken said, incredulous. "Fergus O'Mara, the heating and air-conditioning king! You've seen those obnoxious ads, they're all over TV, right? You've seen his trucks with the big fat inflatable leprechaun on the roof, they're absolutely everywhere. The man either owns, services, or installs every air-conditioning unit between here and St. Louis, and that includes houses, office buildings, hotels, cars, trains, and airplanes. You name it, O'Mara cools it down."

"Heating and air-conditioning?" It was Doyle's turn for incredulity.

"Mostly air-conditioning, which is huge business now that the world is turning hotter than the fucking sun because of global warming."

Doyle was dumbfounded. He didn't know what to say. He opened his mouth and closed it again. Air-conditioning.

"You wanted the dope," Bracken said. "Now you can't take it."

"No," Doyle said, confused. "I just don't get what you're telling me. You're going to have to try again, very slowly."

Bracken stubbed out the end of her cigarette and immediately lit another. "Let me put it this way," she said. "It's all about CFCs."

Doyle nodded blankly.

"Something floro-carbon," Bracken continued. "It's a gas, like freon. The basic ingredient in all air-conditioners. Very illegal to manufacture here because it absolutely destroys the fucking ozone, but the stuff has got to come from somewhere if you want to air-condition your house. So they smuggle it in from places like China where the Chinese don't give two Chinese shits about the environment — those people can live on a pile of radioactive slag and it wouldn't bother them. But it's not so easy to smuggle things around here, these days, in case you haven't noticed, with the whole coast built up to within an inch of the beach. So," she fluttered her hands in the air, "that's where you come in." And she settled back and took a deep breath of her cigarette as if she had told the whole story.

Doyle still didn't get it. "I still don't get it," he said.

"Christ, you're dense, Timmy," Bracken said. "And I thought you were a smart guy."

At that moment, a loud crackling static filled the room and an Irish voice boomed out from somewhere, like the announcement for a gate change at Shannon Airport, "Bracken, are you there, darlin'?"

Bracken sat up, startled, and stared at the ceiling. Doyle followed her gaze to a speaker concealed in the coffered paneling.

"I'm right here, sir," she said, unnecessarily loud.

"Fantucci's due any minute," the voice said. "Get your ass down here and stick your tits out and act sexy." Then there was an ominous chuckle. "How's our friend Doyle? Any trouble?"

"No, sir," Bracken said. "He's just fine."

"Not for long," the voice said, and clicked off.

Bracken stood, smoothing out her skirts. "Got to run," she said, and turned towards the door.

"Wait!" Doyle called after her. "What does that," he gestured towards the ceiling, "have to do with Pirate Island? You still haven't told me."

Bracken made a face. "Brother, you really ought to look at a map sometime."

Then she opened the padded door to the sound of conversation and laughter coming from another part of the house, slipped out, and closed it behind her again. Doyle was left alone and in silence. Now he couldn't hear any sound, except the beating of his own heart and the faint, sad chirping of birds from the night beyond the window.

14

After a while Feeney and Jesus came in and hefted Doyle up a narrow back stairwell to yet a third room — this one large and shabby, dominated by a projection screen TV and a snooker table. The room had a smoky boys'-clubhouse sort of feel, its scuffed walls decorated only by white streaks of spackling and black smudges. A half-dozen misshapen lumps that were beanbag chairs sprouted from the floor like large vinyl mushrooms. Doyle couldn't remember the last time he'd seen a beanbag chair. Greasy pizza boxes, cheap porn magazines, and bottles of beer lay strewn about. The homunculus and another man sat around a folding table playing poker in such a droopy manner it made Doyle think of the roadside tapestry of card-playing dogs Uncle Buck had hanging in the bar years ago.

Feeney undid the shackle around one of Doyle's wrists and attached it to an elbow of protruding heater pipe and sent him sprawling down on a beanbag chair against the wall. Then he and Jesus went over to sit in on the poker game. The projection screen TV was tuned to the AlternaNet Sports Cable Network with the sound off, a show that cut rapidly between a jai alai game in Miami, Irish football in Cork, and a curling tournament in Saskatchewan. Doyle felt oddly detached from his surroundings, some rubbery after-effect of the dope they'd had him on. From the depths of his beanbag chair, he stared up at the projection screen TV for a long time, his mind — perhaps inspired by the huge, kinetic images of athletes in motion — conjuring ancient warriors, interminable battles for high-walled, dusty cities.

An hour went by.

At last, Feeney stood from the table and threw down his cards. "I'm out, gentlemen," he said in his oily-smooth voice. He came over to Doyle's beanbag chair and crouched down. "You need anything, Captain?" he said.

Doyle concentrated and shook himself out of his lethagy. "How about a beer?" he said.

Feeney cocked an eyebrow. "I don't know, you might crack me over the head with the damned bottle." But he went across the room to a small, battered refrigerator and withdrew two bottles of Murphy's stout. He opened them and passed one to Doyle.

"*Slainte,*" he said, and drank.

Doyle lifted the bottle with his free hand, rim clattering against his teeth. He finished the contents in three long swallows and afterwards felt much better, part of the world again.

"So, you guys are some kind of heating and air-conditioning repairmen?" Doyle said, when he could speak clearly.

Feeney let out a shrill bark of hilarity. "What do we know about heating and air-conditioning?"

The homunculus looked up, one pop-eye glittering madly. "Not a damned bloody thing, more's the pity."

"You might call us security," Feeney said.

"You might call us garbagemen too, if you've a mind," the homunculus muttered to his cards.

"Ah, dear Captain," Feeney said, "our midget's bitter. Comes from being a wee little man all his miserable life."

"Fuck you to Sunday," the homunculus grumbled, and went back to his game.

A minute later the door swung open to the corridor and two brittle flowers in ball gowns blew in on a gust of warm, dinner-scented air. Faintly, from downstairs, could be heard an Irish tenor, impossibly pure, raised in song. One of the newcomers was Bracken, the other a tall, striking blonde. The blonde carried a half-empty bottle of Irish whiskey and she and Bracken were giggling drunk. The blonde passed the bottle to Bracken, who took a long swallow and came up gasping. "God," she coughed, pounding a knuckle against her chest, "I didn't need that one bit."

Then the blonde took the bottle back and without warning pitched it hard at the three men playing poker. "Think fast!" she called. The homunculus dropped his cards and ducked. Jesus looked up at just the right moment, reached out and caught the bottle in his big hand. He set it on the table, still half empty, and went back to his game. Somehow, not a drop of whiskey had been spilled.

"That wasn't so smart," Feeney said. "One of these days you're really going to hurt somebody."

The blonde flashed a contemptuous look, pushed Feeney aside, and stepped over to where Doyle lay in the beanbag chair. For a long minute she stood studying him with a critical eye.

"Hello again," Doyle said. He recognized her now — the stoned film buff from Bracken's party, the one he'd put to bed on the pile of coats in the hall.

"Hello, Gunslinger," the blonde said.

"Call me Tim," Doyle said. "But I didn't catch your name last time. You were too stoned."

"Meena," the blonde said. "But don't think I forget things, just because I get a little squiffed."

Bracken came up behind her and leaned against Meena's shoulder. "How are you doing there, Timmy?" she said sheepishly.

"About the same," Doyle said.

"He's pretty, I'll give you that," Meena said to Bracken. "But from where I'm standing, he doesn't look like much."

"Wait till he gets his pants off," Bracken giggled, "and pulls out his gun."

"There'll be no removing the prisoner's pants unless I do it myself!"

It was the Irish voice Doyle had heard on the loudspeaker in the library. Feeney stiffened visibly, the men at the table folded their cards and sat up straight: their game was over. A trim, middle-aged man with a red Irish face strode into the room, followed by a thin, mincing youth in a frilly shirt like a flamenco dancer and very tight pants. The red-faced Irishman wasn't much taller than five-five, but his demeanor suggested that, like Napoleon, he was used to commanding the respect of those much taller than he. He was about sixty, his hair a neat plantation of perfectly lifelike dyed black follicles, his eyes a sleety blue that seemed to drop the ambient temperature. He was flamboyantly gotten up in a winter-green Tyrolean jacket trimmed with embroidered panels at collar and cuffs, a powder-blue silk shirt, and a wide red and yellow polka-dotted tie that wouldn't have looked out of place on a circus clown. Gold hoops much like the ones worn by Mr. Clean on the bottle dangled from each ear. The overall effect was absurd, but somehow the Irishman was able to pull it off. Doyle didn't need to be told: this was Fergus O'Mara, the Heating and Air-conditioning King.

"Da," Meena said, "meet the famous gunslinger."

O'Mara came over and, without warning, kicked Doyle viciously in the thigh with a thick-soled black shoe.

Doyle cried out in pain.

"That's to let you know who's boss around here," O'Mara said.

"Next time why not just tell me?" Doyle said, rubbing his thigh.

"You're a real wisecracker, aren't you, Doyle?" O'Mara said. "We don't have much use for wisecrackers around here, do we, boys?"

The men at the poker tables wagged their heads.

"Great," Doyle said. "Because I'd like to go home now."

"More wisecracking," O'Mara said. "Feeney, club the bastard."

Feeney pulled back his sleeve and made a fist. Doyle steeled himself for the blow, but before it fell, the thin youth intervened.

"If there's going to be violence, Fergus, I'm going to bed," he said in a voice that sounded like a toy poodle in a cartoon.

"You'd better be off then, darling." O'Mara rose to the tips of his toes, the thin young man bent down, and they shared an open-mouthed kiss. This was the last thing Doyle had expected. O'Mara turned back just in time to catch the look of surprise cross his face.

"That's right, I'm a man who loves men," O'Mara growled. "Do you have a problem with that?"

"Hey, whatever works for you," Doyle said.

O'Mara kicked Doyle hard in the thigh again. Doyle's ears rang, he saw spots. He shook his head and his vision cleared.

"Next time, keep the sarcasm out of your voice, cunt," O'Mara said.

Doyle thought it best not to respond. The thin youth hurried out. Bracken feigned a disinterested yawn. "Past my bedtime," she said.

"Excuse me, folks." She wouldn't meet Doyle's eyes as she left the room. Doyle watched her go. She had always been bad, he thought bitterly, rotten in all the places that counted most, like a beautiful house whose foundations had been eaten away by termites. Good riddance.

"Let's get down to business." O'Mara nodded. "Do you know who I am, Mr. Doyle?"

"Sure I do," Doyle said. He couldn't resist: "You're the heating and air-conditioning queen."

O'Mara's face went blotchy and Doyle knew what happened next was probably going to hurt. But at that moment Meena threw back her head and laughed loudly, all out of proportion to the joke, it seemed to Doyle. "That's rich!" she said. "Doyle, you're a damned comedian!" She couldn't stop laughing and at last tears came to her eyes.

O'Mara watched her laugh and his jaw relaxed; and the pressure seemed to lift all at once. He knuckled his hands into his pockets. "All right, daughter," he grumbled, "it wasn't that funny."

Meena stopped laughing and wiped the tears from her eyes. Then she knelt and took a fistful of Doyle's hair. He felt her cool fingers against his scalp and a corresponding jolt between his legs. She seemed to be considering something. She pulled his head back and looked directly into his eyes.

15

The bathroom window stood open a crack. Darkness and cool night air seeped gently over the ledge and touched Doyle's limbs where they protruded from the warm water of the tub. Steam glazed the mirror, sweated droplets down a Commedia dell'Arte scene printed on the shiny wallpaper. There was Pierrot offering Columbine a stolen rose, Scapino picking a pocket, and Dr. Erasmus with his *pince-nez* spectacles and tall professorial hat. Doyle inspected the clumsy needle marks tracking down his veins along the inside of both elbows. How long had he been out, lying in the darkness in a small room hidden behind ten thousand cases of RB Cola, doped up, haunted by ghostly insects? Days, a week? Had Maggie bothered to notify the police?

Then the bathroom door opened and Doyle slid down in the water and floated a washcloth over his privates. It was Meena. She wore a white silk robe printed with blue Japanese flowers and nothing underneath. Her nipples showed dark circles through the thin fabric. She came over and sat on the edge of the tub.

"Modest, aren't we?" she said in a low voice and reached under the washcloth and took him in her hand.

"Tell me one thing," Doyle said, gasping, "how often do you rescue men your father kidnaps and —"

"Let's not talk right now," Meena put a finger over his lips, "or I'll start having second thoughts." And she leaned down and kissed him and somehow Doyle's hand found its way to her breast, then the Japanese robe was on the floor and she was on top, moving against him in the warm water.

Afterwards, the water began to cool and Doyle's fingertips wrinkled to prunes. Meena lay against him in moist, companionable silence. She reached up and turned the hot-water tap with her toes. The sound of the tap running echoed loud as a waterfall in the closed room.

"The answer is never," she said.

"Huh?" Doyle had drifted off a second.

"I don't sleep with every poor creep my father kidnaps. Just you, actually."

"Why?" Doyle said.

"What do you want to hear?" Meena said. "That you look like Mitchum? That Bracken said you were great in the sack? That you reminded me of a lost dog? I have a soft spot for lost dogs, you know."

"Woof," Doyle said.

She rose out of the water suddenly and got out of the tub, and Doyle watched the water running off her curves. Then she wrapped herself in a towel as thick as shag carpet and left the bathroom.

Doyle soaked a few minutes longer, got out, dried off, went into the bedroom, and crawled into the big bed, covered with a white down comforter, where Meena lay with the lights out. The room was large and airy with tall ceilings and undraped windows that looked out on a dark wood and a thin wafer of moon. Stuffed animals, their hard glass eyes glittering, watched from the cushions of an easy chair across the room as Doyle and Meena fucked again. The second time, most of the punch had gone out of the act. Doyle felt disoriented and sore and barely managed to finish.

"You don't love me," Meena said, when it was over.

"You're funny," Doyle said. "But thanks for saving my ass."

"It's not saved yet," Meena said. "Your fate is still uncertain. Da said he's got to sleep on it. We'll have to see in the morning."

Doyle was quiet for a few minutes. Here he was on Death Row and a prostitute had just been brought into his cell by the prison guards. No, that wasn't charitable: the situation was more like Pocahontas and John Smith. Shadows moved across the ceiling. Best try to think of something else. "Your father's into smuggling CFCs, am I right?" he said at last.

Meena hesitated. "How did you know that?"

"A little bird told me," Doyle said. "Now, I admit Pirate Island would make a great place to land some heavy contraband — but there are other places. So the question is, why me?"

"Your place was just the perfect place," Meena said. "Filled all the particulars nicely. That's what the man said."

"What man?" Doyle said.

Meena frowned into the darkness. "Da's man in Wassateague."

"Who's that?" Doyle tried to sound like he didn't really care to know.

"None of your business," Meena said, and she rolled over and went to sleep.

Doyle lay on his back and tried to think things through but in another moment he, too, fell asleep. At some point in the dark hours of the morning, he was visited with dreams of maps and coastlines like the ragged edges of torn paper blowing in the wind.

16

At the far end of the long table Fergus O'Mara, the heating and air-conditioning king, sat eating French toast with his daughter. Doyle came into the dining room from the hall and limped down the length of the table. He still wore just one shoe. His galoshes were gone. The vintage suit he'd been kidnapped in was tatters. Uncle Buck's Stetson hat and the leaky Mackintosh were gone, he was sore, beaten, and probably doomed, but he felt for reasons he couldn't say rather spry this morning.

"What do you want down here, cocksucker?" O'Mara said, looking up.

"My shoe is off, my foot is cold," Doyle said. He pointed to his bare foot against the carpet.

O'Mara looked baffled, but Meena leaned her head back and let out a laugh like a shout.

"You're a funny man, Mr. Doyle," she said. "That's from *One Fish Two Fish,* isn't it?"

Doyle grinned. "I'm hungry," he said.

"You've got some fucking brass, Doyle," O'Mara said to him, "I'll give you that. And you make my daughter laugh, which isn't an easy thing to do." He pushed an unseen button, and a moment later, the homunculus appeared out of the kitchen wiping his hands on a stained apron.

"Another plate of French toast," O'Mara said.

The homunculus levelled a pop-eyed blinkless stare at Doyle, then disappeared back into the kitchen.

Doyle sat down beside Meena. She leaned over and kissed his cheek. She was wearing a Harvard Business School sweatshirt and sat cross-legged in her chair. Her hair was pulled back in a crisp collegiate ponytail. "You don't mind?" she said in his ear.

"What?" Doyle whispered back.

"The kiss."

"Not at all," Doyle said.

"No whispering!" O'Mara slammed his fist on the table. "We were just discussing your fate, Doyle," he said. "And there's a couple of basic problems. First, you're a stubborn, hard-to-kill cocksucking bastard who doesn't know what's good for him. Second, you shot one of my boys and that's something I can't countenance. You're going to have to pay for that one."

As these ominous words were spoken, the homunculus appeared

once again from the kitchen, plate of French toast in his hand. He dropped it down in front of Doyle without ceremony and the plate made a rude clattering sound on the glossy wood of the table.

"He kidnaps," Doyle said. "And he cooks."

Meena giggled.

The homunculus approached O'Mara with something like a bow. "May I speak plainly, sir?" he said.

O'Mara said nothing.

"This one's trouble," the homunculus said. "I'd off him right now and not waste any time with a good breakfast."

O'Mara accepted this advice with a grave nod. Doyle ate a few bites of the French toast, which tasted fine, then his mind was invaded by an image of the little man blowing his nose into the batter and he put down his fork.

"How is he, the guy I shot?" Doyle said.

"He's been invalided out of my service," O'Mara said. "He'll live, but he's of no use to me anymore, which is the same as being dead in my book. So, in effect, I've lost one top-quality trigger man, which is where you come in." He jabbed his fork in Doyle's direction. "This is how you square your debt to me and get out of here walking and talking and wearing your own skin. Listen carefully, I have a little job for you, I want you to get someone for me. He's a hard man, one of the hardest. He actually had the balls to steal some of my money, and by a coincidence that in no way surprises me, his name also happens to be Doyle. But for your sake I hope he's no relation because you might very well have to shoot the bastard."

"Doyle?" Doyle said, his heart sinking.

"Correct," O'Mara said. "And whether I've got the right Doyle for the job remains to be seen."

"Let me get this straight," Doyle said. "You want me to find someone named Doyle and bring him here so you can kill him."

"We've got a few questions to ask him first," O'Mara said. "Such as where's my money. And don't you worry about finding him, that's our part of the bargain. We don't know where he is tonight, but we know where he's going to be tomorrow night. All you've got to do is go down and get him. I'll make it easy on you. I'll send a couple of my boys along to show you the way."

Doyle stared down at his plate. He felt Meena's eyes on the side of his face.

"If you refuse," O'Mara continued, "you'll be killed today, right after breakfast. If you fail or change your mind or go to the cops, you'll be killed later at a time convenient to us. Then we kill that slut who works your bar and we'll purchase the shithole from the courts for a song. However, if you succeed in bringing Doyle to me here, alive, I am prepared to write you a check for two hundred and fifty thousand dollars in exchange for all your deeds and easements, and don't worry, we'll have everything done all nice and legal, drawn up proper by my lawyers."

The heating and air-conditioning king rose to his full height, which wasn't much, but the power he wielded conferred a stature not related to mere feet and inches.

Doyle stood slowly. "You can't force me to sell my property," he said, through his teeth. "It's against the law."

O'Mara cracked a smile that was more like an evil leer. "You *are* a funny man," he said, in a calm tone more ominous than all his threats. At this, Meena jumped out of her chair and dragged Doyle from the room.

17

They sat on the front steps, waiting for Feeney to bring the car around. The labyrinth in which Doyle had been imprisoned was a massive neo-Flemish pile, all gables and dormers, built in reference to Delaware's first Dutch settlers for a relative of the Roosevelts in the 1920s. The sky was blue above a manicured forest of oak and chestnut. Doyle thought of summer, of the happy smell of sun-tan lotion and beer, the tanned summer crowds, and what remained to be done to get the golf course ready for June. He could forget about all that now.

Meena nestled closer and took his hand. He wore a spiffy Italian sports jacket, new pants, shoes, all of which fit him perfectly — courtesy of one of O'Mara's thugs.

"You got off easy, if you ask me," she said. "One little job, then you're free."

"Great," Doyle said, but he couldn't keep the chagrin out of his voice. "Uncle Buck built that property from nothing, from woods and swamp with honest sweat and the GI Bill and a dream of goofy golf under the arc lights. It's all I've ever had, if you want the real truth. I ran a restaurant in Spain once, but what did I know about restaurants, really? That was my ex-wife's game all the way. All I did was tend bar and smile at the customers. And now I'm just supposed to hand over my patrimony to a —"

"Don't," Meena shook her head.

"— diminutive gay thug and be happy about it?"

"Life is tough," Meena said, letting go of his hand. "And not very safe. Look at it this way — Da could have had you hauled off and turned into catmeat and he still might. So after you do what you have to do and get your money, I'd move somewhere far away. Ever think of San Francisco?"

"Never heard of the place," Doyle said.

A warm wind rustled the tops of the trees; the wide leaves of the oaks looked impossibly green in the sun. "I've always wanted to go to San Francisco," Meena said wistfully. "Ever since I saw *Vertigo*. Never been."

"Tell me something," he turned to Meena, "I know this is America and all that but how exactly does one Irish immigrant son-of-a-bitch go from heating and air-conditioning to a life as one of the big shits of organized crime?"

"Da's not a monster, you know," Meena said quietly. "He's just a businessman who's been forced to use hard tactics by the demands of the market. Crime and capitalism go together, I learned that much at business school. As for the heating and air-conditioning part, he took a correspondence course in heating and air-conditioning repair in New York when he first came to America forty years ago and worked his ass off every day ever since. Any other questions?"

"Yes, how did you happen? I mean with the king's sexual preferences and all."

Meena flushed. "In the usual manner," she said. "Not with a turkey baster, if that's what you're thinking."

"What about your mother?"

"Dead," Meena said, looking away. "A long time ago."

A moment later, a black Mercedes 320 with cartoon eyes crunched up from the vast, Flemish-gabled garage at the back of the house and pulled to a stop in front of the steps. Doyle couldn't see a thing through the windows, tinted the shade of burning tires.

Meena kissed him and handed him a business card with the number of her cell phone scrawled across it in red ink. "This is goodbye," she said, "but it doesn't have to be. I'd still like to visit San Francisco." Then she turned and went up the steps and back into the house.

Feeney stepped out of the Mercedes, came around, and opened the massive door for Doyle. "Lucky fucking bastard," he said, under his breath.

But Doyle still didn't think he was so lucky. And as he climbed in he saw Jesus, glowering from amidst the sharp creases of his plastic raincoat, hunched in the back seat. Feeney closed the door and got in the driver's side, and they took off down a long drive through the oaks, then south along narrow Delaware highways into Maryland, past the chicken farms and one-pump gas stations in silence all the way to the Virginia line.

"Where are we going?" Doyle said, after a while. Feeney didn't answer, and fifteen minutes later, they crossed the causeway, and an hour after that the Cape Charles Bridge in the rush of interstate traffic, America spreading in uncertain light to the horizon ahead.

part five

THE RIGHT
DOYLE

BEYOND THE STREETCAR *lines and the imperial palms bordering Ocean Avenue, Los Angeles stood in thick brown haze, the skyscrapers along Grand and Alvarado downtown bare silhouettes, the low neighborhoods of tidy bungalows shadowy beneath overhanging palms, the distant scrubby hills vague scribbles, the department stores full of women shopping half-effaced from just a mile away, the unseen restaurants full of women eating lunch. Yes, women in clean dresses with nails done and skin gleaming and shoes patent leather and, God, why not orchids in their hair? Women perfumed from head to toe and walking up and down the sunny brown sidewalks arm in arm and riding the streetcars just to ride, and behind the wheels of brand new automobiles on the Golden State Freeway and talking on the telephone, their red lipstick lips barely half an inch from the receiver, and sitting on bamboo stools having a drink maybe soon, at dusk in this very bar, as a dying ocean breeze rustled their skirts and blew sun-withered fronds along the esplanade. Now, just across the neat yellow apron of beach, the Pacific flexed in blue-green vastness and the sound of women laughing somewhere else drifted over the sand faintly dusted with city soot and planted with striped umbrellas and pastel cabanas: It was August 6, 1946, late afternoon, and the war was finished all over the world.*

Jack Doyle sat on the patio of Don the Beachcomber on the beach in Santa Monica drinking his first Atomic Bomb Cocktail — an explosive mixture of strong Demerara rum, both light and dark, and various fruit juices invented that morning by the Chinese bartender to celebrate the levelling of Hiroshima exactly one year before. The Chinese bartender was born in Nanking and had not found it in his heart to forgive the Japs for what they had done there to his family in 1938, and he made the cocktail bright red with grenadine to symbolize the innocent blood of the Chinese people and priced them on special at fifty cents all day long to remind everyone who ordered one how horribly, and with what just finality, the

Japs had been defeated. Imagine a single bomb taking out a whole city in a puff of yellow smoke like a magic trick! Only no one understood the symbolism except the Chinese bartender, and he didn't bother to explain. But Jack Doyle didn't care about any of that any more. The war was over for him, completely over; even thinking about the war being over was yesterday's business. Earlier that afternoon, at 1400 hours exactly, he had been honorably discharged from the United States Marine Corps at San Pedro, paid off not in GI script but in good U.S. greenbacks and he marched out the gates and, within full view of the sentries, took off his uniform — pinned with the Purple Heart and combat ribbons won for fighting through the lush green hills of Pacific islands whose names he also earnestly desired to forget — stripped down to his undershirt and regulation boxers and regulation socks and balled everything up and stuffed it into the large wire trashcan placed there, so it seemed, for just such a purpose.

The sentries hooted and laughed. "Nuts to you too, Mac!" one shouted, but Jack didn't care because his war was over forever and he marched Marine double-time up a block or two in his underwear, thankfully without meeting a cop along the way, and into a men's store and told the clerk, "I need a suit of clothes, mister."

The clerk nodded, unimpressed, as if discharged Marines in underwear came into the store every day demanding clothes, and he sold Jack the most garish civvies in Los Angeles: a brown and yellow Hawaiian shirt hand-embroidered with red demon-god masks, green trousers pleated and cuffed and baggy as zoot-suit pants, a pale yellow sport jacket with extra-sporty wide lapels, beige socks with clocks on the ankles, and sandals.

Thus attired, Jack sauntered into a nearby tobacconist and bought three seventy-five-cent Cuban cigars and got on the first red streetcar that came along and took it up the coast all the way to Santa Monica where he hopped off and walked down to Don the Beachcomber's, a sprawling, open-fronted bar made of bamboo, driftwood, and thatch, planted on stilts in the sand. He'd read about the place in a movie magazine once — Myrna Loy went to Don's, Jack remembered from the magazine, so did Carole Lombard. Ronald Colman and Jack Benny had also been seen there. Of course, that was a long time ago in another world, before the war. Carole Lombard was dead and Myrna Loy lived in New York.

Jack took a seat at one of the little round bamboo tables on the patio, lit up one of his seventy-five-cent cigars, and ordered a cocktail, it didn't matter which one — the Filipino waiter recommended the Atomic Bomb, on special at the moment — and Jack nodded, OK, and put his mind to the great work ahead: finding a woman. Not just a woman for one night but a woman for the rest of his life.

Jack had been among the last Marines discharged from service in the Pacific — a million men had come home before him — and he was worried now that all the women might be taken. But then the hard California light softened and slanted into the sea and dusk brought the women out of the offices and out from behind the glass counters of shops, and they took the red streetcars down to the beach and here they were now, coming across the sand on the little path laid with boards, and soon there was a lovely fading blue in the sky, beautiful and faintly starry over the ocean, and the place was filling up with women, bracelets jangling against tanned wrists in mysterious music, lipstick marking the soggy ends of their cigarettes.

At Jack's signal the Filipino waiter came out to the patio. "Give me another one of these," Jack said, pointing to his empty glass.

The Filipino shook his head. "Don says only three Atomic Bombs per customer on account they too strong," he said. "You already have four. How about a nice cold beer?"

"Say, what kind of a cockeyed bar is this?" Jack said, then he paused. "Where are you from, boy?"

"Manila," the waiter said.

"I was in Manila, you know," Jack said. "In 1941 with MacArthur." This was a lie. "I was on Corregidor and Bataan and Palau too." This was not a lie.

"You and everyone else." The Filipino waiter rolled his eyes: a million GIs had come into Don's in the last year and every last one of them wanted one drink over the limit.

Jack saw he wasn't getting anywhere with the patriotic line and he wasn't drunk enough yet for a fight. "All right," he said. "Anything but beer. I had enough of that in the service."

The waiter went away and came back with a tall glass afloat with fruit and paper umbrellas, a drink he called a Sumatra Kula, light and refreshing, he said, which Jack tasted and found no lighter or more refreshing than the Atomic Bomb. In fact, all the drinks at Don's tasted exactly the same to him, strong mixtures of rum, rum and fruit, with only the fruit varying a little from drink to drink. But the drinking was only something to keep himself busy while he watched the women coming down from the city: some in pairs, some in tight, gossipy groups, some with men still in uniform, a few single and shifty-eyed with plenty of makeup and obviously on the prowl. Blondes, brunettes, redheads, skinny, fat, and in between; women who knew what they wanted and would get it, women who didn't know what they wanted and would still get it, women who didn't want a thing but would get it just the same.

And as he watched, Jack knew for certain — though he couldn't say exactly how — that among them tonight was the woman he would marry.

The sky went dark and indistinct, the fresh-looking stars seemed to fade all at once. Colored Tiki lights came on over the bar; a few white yachts anchored in the swells out beyond the pier glowed faintly in the darkness. Jack noticed a sign hanging over the door to the men's lavatory that said, WELCOME HOME HEROES, and thought, Some wise guy thinks he's funny.

A few minutes later a short, serious Hawaiian man with a small guitar and a half-dozen leis strung around his neck, set up on a couple of soapboxes on the patio and played the guitar and sang a few nice Hawaiian numbers — "Mana Loa Lady," "Calling the Wanderer to Return," "Queen Maha'e" — but no one paid any attention and he took his guitar and went away. After that the Chinese bartender put a record on the phonograph behind the bar. It was the Sunset Royal Entertainers, an old Negro group Jack had seen at the Alhambra Theater in Baltimore once before the war; the music was smooth, crooning, somehow redolent of bootleg gin and private railroad cars and fishing trips with tipsy gentlemen high rollers — an America that was gone forever.

Jack closed his eyes to the music, expecting nostalgia, but was instead swept with a wave of nausea like the bitter taste of the atabrine pills they had given him for malaria in the jungle; he saw the landing on Tarawa again and the bloody beach and the bodies of his comrades bloating in the heat and the nightmare flak exploding in the night sky over an unnamed lagoon filled with corpses and heard the screaming of the wounded and felt the fear of the Japs out there in the darkness ubiquitous as sweat. Then he opened his eyes again and there she was, the woman, coming up the steps to the patio with a fresh-faced young ensign in his ridiculous summer dress whites, white shoes, white hat, everything white as the milkman, probably fresh out of a V-12 program somewhere and disappointed the war was over before he could get to it — as if there wouldn't be another war and another until the end of time. The ensign led the woman over to a table in the corner near the bamboo fence and went up to get drinks at the bar. Jack stared at her openly; she saw him staring, met his gaze for an instant, and looked away.

She was tall but nicely round, with long, tanned legs, her dark blonde hair piled up in a complicated pompadour; she wore an expensive-looking polka-dotted dress and matching spectator pumps; a cute little blue hat perched on her hair, a fleshy-looking orchid drooped from the polka-dotted fabric over her left breast. Her eyes were green and curious, her skin, freshly powdered, looked cool to the touch. Jack couldn't get enough of looking at her. He liked the way she pulled her gloves off finger by finger, he liked the way she lit a cigarette then shook the match out very slowly as if she had all the time in the world. She fidgeted beneath Jack's intense scrutiny; she crossed and uncrossed her legs and Jack heard a faint musical tinkling that made him catch his breath: there, around her ankle, a thin, elegant anklet with a charm dangling from the chain.

Heart thumping, Jack stood up and went over to the bar, through the crowd to where the fresh-faced ensign was still waiting for his drinks in the crush at the rail. Jack took the kid hard by the elbow. "Can I speak to you, Ensign?" Jack said. "It's important."

The ensign turned to him, startled. "I'm waiting for my drinks," he said, in a slightly effeminate, high-pitched voice. "Anyway, do I know you, mister?"

"Marine Sergeant Jack Doyle, sir, honorably discharged, 1400 hours today."

"All right, Sergeant, what is it?" the ensign said, all the freshly learned superiority of rank in his tone.

"It's something . . ." Jack hesitated, ". . . something about the war."

Jack steered the ensign into the breezeway that led to the garbage bins out back and there, without warning, twisted around and delivered a powerful blow to the ensign's gut, slamming the startled boy back against the wall and knocking the wind out of him. The ensign's white hat spun off into the filth by the trash cans. Jack held him there against the wall with an elbow at his throat.

"I'm really sorry about this, sonny," Jack said, through his teeth, "but the girl you're with is the girl I'm going to marry. I don't suppose she told you that, did she?"

The poor ensign looked at Jack with frightened eyes. He couldn't speak with Jack's elbow pressed into his Adam's apple; Jack lifted off a bit and the ensign gasped for breath. "I didn't know . . ." he managed, then Doyle reapplied the pressure.

"On Tarawa I slit a surrendered Jap from chin to rocks with a bayonet and scooped his guts out with my bare hands just to teach the bastards a lesson, got that?"

The ensign stuttered incomprehensibly.

"Four years of hell in the Marines and all my best pals dead and I'm not about to let some snotnose kid just out of fucking OCS make time with my fiancée. Do you understand me, sir?"

"I didn't know, I swear!" A tear trickled out of the corner of the ensign's eye and down his nose. "I met her at the counter at Schwab's, we made a date, that's all."

Jack felt sorry for the kid and stepped back. "Get lost," he said, "before I break your teeth."

The ensign stooped to retrieve his ruined white hat and stumbled down the breezeway past the garbage cans and ran up the beach to the stairs leading to Ocean Avenue.

Jack watched him go, went back to the bar, and got two Hawaiian Sunset cocktails from the bartender and walked over to the table where the woman still sat waiting for her date.

"I'm with someone," the woman said, looking up at him with her green eyes. But she didn't seem surprised when he sat down with the drinks and handed her one.

"Your boyfriend had to go home to his mother," Jack said. "He asked me if I wouldn't mind taking his place."

The woman didn't say anything to this. She took the drink and put the straw to her lips.

"What's your name, honey?" Jack said.

"Barbara Stanwyck," the woman said.

"Never mind, tell me later," Jack said. "I'm Jack Doyle."

"You from the south?" the woman said. "Because you sound like a hick."

"Wassateague, Virginia," Jack said. "A little island off the coast of nowhere. I'd tell you all about the place but you'll see it soon enough."

"What's that supposed to mean?" the woman said, frowning.

"It means I'm taking you home to meet the folks," Jack said, "after we're married," but he smiled like this was a joke. "What about you? Where are you from?"

The woman hesitated. "New Mexico," she said. "Albuquerque." This was a lie and Jack knew it. He watched the red liquid rise through the clear straw to her lips. She swallowed, then swallowed some more and looked down at the jagged white scar that bisected the Marine tattoo on his arm.

"You were overseas?" she said.

"Just doing my patriotic duty," Jack said.

"Where?"

"Horrible places," Jack said. "Mosquito-ridden specks no one ought to ever have heard of. The last horrible place was Iwo Jima."

"That's where they raised the flag," the woman said. "Where they took that picture for Life."

"Yeah," Jack said. "Get a good look at that picture next time. I'm the last guy on the pole. The guy squatting in the mud."

"Are you really one of the guys in the picture?" the woman said, her green eyes wide.

"Absolutely," Jack said. This was another lie, though just barely. He had been on Iwo Jima where the Japs fought from caves like wild animals, like bears, and had to be burned out with flame-throwers; but when they raised the flag on Mount Suribachi he was down at the foot of the hill in a foxhole crapping his guts out with dysentery.

The woman finished her drink. More drinks came. Watching her sucking hard on the straws, Jack was cursed with a painful erection that would not go away. An hour passed this way, drinking and talking, with Jack doing most of the listening and looking for a way in.

The woman's real name was Clara Lavalle, she was twenty-two, Catholic, from a rich Pasadena family. Her father owned a few dozen oil wells and a modest fleet of tanker trucks. So much the better, Jack thought. She had gone to Mother of Angels College with the Marymount nuns for a while, then dropped out, sick to death of the nuns, of books and classes. She had been engaged five times in the last four years to various soldiers, sailors, and airmen and didn't care who knew. She had written dear-John letters to all five. One of them killed himself, she added, but she really didn't think it was her fault. She liked to drink. She was trouble. Self-indulgent and spoiled, rich, well fed, nicely dressed, and utterly untouched *in any real way by a war that had killed half the world, which for her had been a big playground full of men in handsome uniforms.*

Exactly what Jack was looking for.

Finally, around ten o'clock, Jack had heard enough of Clara's chatter. He reached down and took hold of her ankle, the one with the anklet, and pulled it up across his knee and Clara let him do it. "So what's this?" he said, tinkling the charm with his finger. The charm on the anklet wasn't a charm at all but a worn old Seated Liberty dime with the date 1841 barely legible and a tiny hole drilled through the top.

"That's my grandmaman's gris-gris," Clara explained. "Grandmaman was from New Orleans and down there they used to believe in all this hoodoo stuff. Wearing a silver dime around your ankle is supposed to," she leaned across the table and lowered her voice to a whisper, "make you more attractive to men."

"You don't need any help in that department, sister," Jack said. He bent down and kissed her toes.

Clara giggled and pulled her foot away. "Fresh," she said. Then she finished her second Hawaiian Sunset and switched to Cuba Libres and asked him to tell her a story about the war. "A real story," she said. "None of this red-white-and-blue heroism stuff."

"Believe me, you don't want to hear any real war stories," Jack said. "They're not for your pretty ears."

"No, really, I do," Clara said, peevishly. "I can take it. Just try me."

"OK." Jack sighed. "Here's one. We were in Bilakau, a miserable scrap in the Solomons, and there was a tribe of buck-naked savages who lived in the jungle and helped us beat the Japs there. The captain became friends with the old chief and when the action was over the whole outfit got invited to a kind of victory dinner. You want to know what they served?"

"Sure," Clara said.

"Actually, I don't think you do," Jack said.

"Shut up and finish the story," Clara said.

"OK," Jack said. "Thing was, this tribe didn't know a thing about cooking. They ate all their food raw because they didn't know about fire and didn't know that food is supposed to be hot. So in the morning they fed a whole bunch of rice to a pack of starving dogs. Then dinner time came and everybody sat down hungry and ready for roast pig or something but instead they brought in the dogs and hacked their stomachs open and started

eating the rice right like that, half digested out of the dogs' stomachs, and we were supposed to join in. That's cooking on Bilakau for you."

Clara looked green. "You made that up," she said. "That's really awful."

"I told you," Jack said.

"Did you eat the rice?" Clara said.

"No," Jack said. "The captain told them it was against our religion or something and we ate bananas and coconuts and afterwards we got to go to bed with the chief's daughters."

Clara didn't seem shocked by this. She sucked on her straw thoughtfully. "What were they like?"

"Not bad, considering," Jack said and reached down and caught Clara's ankle again and held it in a firm grip. "Listen to me, Clara. I love you. I loved you the minute you walked up here with that kid in the milkman outfit, you and your green eyes, and your ankle bracelet, and your polka-dots, and I want to go to bed with you now, tonight. The last four years I've only been with the kind of woman you meet in a war, the kind that go with Marines who aren't officers, and by that I mean prostitutes and half-starved sluts, and you're the first beautiful clean thing I've seen since I left home. So I don't know how to say this any other way but here it is — let's go somewhere right now and get married and go to a hotel and make love all night and all day for the rest of the week and for the rest of our lives. What do you say?"

Clara was too astonished to respond and Jack didn't give her the chance. He lurched across the table and kissed her, crushing the orchid against her breast, and kissed her again, and they got up and went up the beach and found a motel on the seedy end of Ocean Avenue called Happy Clam Bungalows and made love in the squalid little cabin all night long and all through the next two days, forgetting all about the Justice of the Peace for the time being. Things like this happened right after the war, when the world had seen enough of death and people were trying to make up for all the carnage with energetic and continuous lovemaking, and there was a happy, libidinous humming in the air that was the sound of men and woman everywhere entwined in carnal embrace.

As it turned out, Clara wasn't a virgin by any definition of the word and not as clean and inexperienced as Jack would have liked, but it didn't bother him as much as he thought it might. And when they had exhausted themselves thoroughly with making love, on the third day at noon, they put their clothes back on and emerged from the stale sex reek of the cabin at the Happy Clam and walked up Ocean Avenue in search of the Justice of the Peace they had forgotten about two nights before.

Eventually Ocean Avenue turned into something else and Santa Monica became a rundown little Mexican neighborhood threaded through with overgrown canals, where all the houses were stucco and built in an odd, half-gingerbread style that somehow reminded Jack of snapshots his brother Buck had sent from the war in Italy.

"Venice Beach," Clara explained. But it was all a strange adventure to Jack: they had entered a secret country hidden within the confines of mundane Los Angeles that belonged only to them on their wedding day. They stopped into a Mexican bar for a cerveza and Clara spoke in Spanish to the bartender, who directed them to a narrow street that led to the beach and to a pink house on that street, its front yard wild with banana trees and jacaranda and big bushes in blossom with drooping blue flowers. A hammock hung between two columns of the porch, and in the hammock a Mexican man lay fanning himself. He had, so he explained to Clara in Spanish, the honor of being the Justice of the Peace for the district.

The Justice of the Peace's wife, a melancholy, grey-haired Mexican woman who reminded Jack of his grandmother, was so charmed by Clara's beauty and Jack's easy manliness that she went out to the porch, clipped a few blue flowers for a bouquet for Clara, and insisted on inviting them to share their Mexican lunch of frijoles and fried tortillas free of charge after the ceremony, after Jack took Clara in his arms and kissed her and promised to protect and love her in sickness and in health for the rest of his life.

Later, the newlyweds went back up to Santa Monica on the streetcar and caught a Yellow Cab from Ocean Avenue all the way up the foothills to Pasadena, to the dark-shingled, twin-turreted home on Kearny Street where Clara had grown up and where her parents lived in another world of well-tended lawns, polite servants, and bridge parties. Of course, her parents took an immediate dislike to Jack when they found out he was a nobody without a penny to his name, not even an officer, some common ex-Marine GI from some little hole in Virginia, and they tried to convince Clara to annul the marriage — which might have been the happiest solution for everyone in the end — but she refused, too busy making love and drinking and dancing with her handsome new husband to notice their utter incompatibility.

But despite the unfortunate complications of later years, despite all the unhappiness to come, and the terrible fights and the long, bitter hangover mornings and the cheating and the tears and the divorce, they would always have the first beautiful evening at Don the Beachcomber's, and the three sumptuous days of lovemaking at Happy Clam Bungalows, and the single bright afternoon of their wedding, when they ate lunch with the Mexican Justice of the Peace and his wife, and afterwards walked down to the beach hand in hand and took off their shoes and kissed each other tenderly on the sand.

1

CROSSING INTO ALABAMA just before dawn, Jesus had to stop for a leak. This was no more than fifteen minutes over the Georgia line, in the reedy northeast corner of the state, in the vicinity of Opalika but not quite. The big man signalled his need by pounding on the back of the driver's seat with his fist and uttering a loud guttural croak, waking Doyle out of the restless slumber that had enveloped him like a fog since South Carolina, the back of his shirt collar damp and the corresponding patch of leather headrest slick with sweat. Feeney veered the Mercedes down an exit ramp then down a road, mostly dirt and potholes, to a rickety little truck stop, bright with fluorescent lights. A dozen big rigs sat rumbling ominously in a gravel lot to the left of the pumps; on the other side, a field completely taken by creepers disappeared into a scraggly forest of pine. Feeney pulled up to the pumps and Jesus jumped out before the car stopped rolling and ran off into the creepers and the darkness.

"Freak can't even piss in a toilet like a civilized person," Feeney muttered, then he got out and began filling the tank.

Doyle went into the truck stop and paid seventy-five cents for coffee in a Styrofoam cup from a pot that looked like it had been sitting there for two weeks and came out and grimaced as he drank it and blinked up at the flickering fluorescent tubes over the pumps. A disquieting wind ruffled the creepers. He turned idly and looked at the car, a new black Mercedes 320 sedan, much like any other new black Mercedes 320 sedan, no doubt, but he knew suddenly that he'd seen this particular vehicle before. Then he walked around to the pump where Feeney was topping off the tank. The Irishman withdrew the nozzle carefully with a rag so as not to spill even a drop on the Mercedes' glossy black paint.

"You ever lend this car out?" Doyle said.

Feeney shot him a curious look. "I think you got the wrong business, boyo," he said. "The Old Fruit does heating and air-conditioning, not car rentals."

"Seems to me I know this Mercedes," Doyle said. "A man named Slough behind the wheel. Ever run into him?"

Feeney curled his lip. "Can't stand that great fat bastard," he said.

"So you know him," Doyle said.

"Works for the Old Fruit." Feeney shrugged. "His attorney. It's no secret."

O'Mara's man in Wassateague, Doyle thought grimly. That fat spider was at the center of everyone's web.

A silence followed, in which they heard the sound of Jesus thrashing somewhere in the creepers and the small grating of unfamiliar insects.

"I think he's back there taking a crap," Feeney said at last. "Ever ask yourself what's wrong with the bastard?"

"No," Doyle said.

Feeney tapped his temple with his middle finger. "He's loony," Feeney said. "Utterly daft. His mother was a godawful drunk — he doesn't talk, you know, more than a few words. Something wrong with his head. But he's a genius at — let's call it artful persuasion. I've seen the man do a few things to a guy with a pair of pliers you wouldn't ever want to see again . . ." He shivered.

A few minutes later Jesus emerged from the creepers, his face slack.

"Hey, Jesus," Feeney said, "the Gunslinger here said he wants to hear you sing 'Roisin the Bow.'"

"I said no such thing," Doyle began. But Jesus puffed himself up, opened his mouth, revealing a withered tongue and a row of yellow teeth, gave one loud bleat and shut it again, apparently satisfied with his performance.

"That's one of the lad's little tricks." Feeney chuckled. "Like a fucking performing seal."

Then they got back into the car, green fluorescence from the truck stop shimmering across the windshield, and a few minutes later were back out on the highway, and Doyle saw a sign that listed the mileage to Mobile, Biloxi, and New Orleans in that order, the first still hundreds of miles away.

"Where are we going?" he said. "I think you can tell me now."

Feeney shook his head. "Might be Mexico, might be the next town."

"You're an asshole," Doyle said.

"No, it's psychology," Feeney said. "The Old Fruit doesn't want you knowing what you got to do till you got to do it."

"I already know," Doyle said. "Get Doyle."

"Yeah, but it's the details that will stick in your throat."

Morning came up hard and bright, and they passed through red-brown fields flecked with white puffs of cotton plants, stands of live oak hung with Spanish moss, creeper-covered shacks. They passed Shorter and Mount Meigs and came into the parched-lawn suburbs of Montgomery, the golden dome of the state house ablaze in the distance. Doyle wanted to sleep now but couldn't with the truck-stop coffee humming in his veins and this violent southern light in the sky, which was bright blue and vast, hawks gliding on the currents above the trees.

Feeney fiddled with the CD player and selected another track of the mournful Celtic music he'd been listening to off and on since Delaware. Jesus hit the back of the seat and gave a tight groan.

"The monster's sick of my tunes," Feeney said to the CD player.

"Ditto," Doyle said.

Feeney cranked the volume to ear-splitting level. "Fuck both of you!" he shouted. "I'm driving, I say what goes!" and he stepped down on the accelerator and the Mercedes surged forward towards an unknown destination further south.

2

The Gulf Sands Tropical Motel, a series of decrepit sea-blue cement blockhouses dating from the 1950s, sat atop a weedy eminence half sand, half oyster shells, just across a disused railroad siding fifty yards from the Gulf of Mexico. It was the kind of place where prostitutes were strangled by baby-faced men not entirely comfortable with their sexuality, where drug deals went awry and mysterious Cubans came and went in the night. A dirty little two-lane road connected it to 90 and the highway to Ocean Springs and Biloxi; for Doyle it was no place at all, a waiting room.

They pulled into the parking lot just after two in the afternoon; the cabin at the end of the row, number seventeen, had been reserved in advance. As Feeney registered in the office — a bare concrete cubicle protected from the rest of the world by a steel door and foot-thick bulletproof glass — Doyle got out of the car and stood on the hot apron and stared out at the calm expanse of gulf and breathed the briny smell of salt water and wondered what would happen next. A sharp wind blew sand against the faded pine shutters.

A few minutes later, Feeney lounged in the doorway of number seventeen, his jacket off, square-handled Ruger roosting casually against his ribs.

"Why don't you come in and get yourself some rest, Gunslinger?" he said. "You've got a rough night ahead."

The sound of Jesus snoring already echoed from the dim, stuffy interior.

"No, thanks," Doyle said. "I'm going for a walk." He gestured to the narrow strip of rubble-strewn beach the other side of the railroad tracks.

"I think not," Feeney said. "You stick close where we can keep a good eye on you."

"I've come this far," Doyle said. "I'm going to run off now?"

He turned and walked to the tracks and stepped across them and came out across the sand, picking his way around crushed plastic bottles and other trash, and sat down and took off his shoes and rolled up the cuffs of his pants. A yellow foam flecked with cigarette butts marked the high tide. He waded into the piss-warm water to his ankles and stood squinting out towards the indistinct horizon. The breeze blew off the waves, thin white clouds sailed above, birds he didn't recognize dove into the surf. Somehow, this seemed like the end of the line. Why didn't they just kill him now and get it over with? He stood there stiffly, half expecting the deadly squiff of the silencer, a discreet bullet in the back of the head, his body left to drift facedown in the surf.

But the bullet didn't come and he splashed around foolishly in the water for a few minutes till his toes brushed against something soft and squelchy, then he jumped out and walked along the hard wet sand and came to a place blocked from view of the motel and railroad tracks by a dune. He lay down there on the other side of the dune, and fell asleep and, in dreams, visited again the shabby white-walled room — was it the Hotel Gallego in Madrid? — on the morning of his second day out of New York with Flor in Spain years ago, warm Spanish light slatting through green metal shutters and her taut body heaving beneath his own.

The act didn't last very long, but it was fierce and exhausting and afterwards he felt giddy lying in bed beside the woman he loved in a strange city in a country he did not know. Then Flor began whispering odd Spanish words in his ear, *"escoba* — broom, *cuchara* — spoon, *colinabo* — rutabaga, *riñónes* — kidney, *desesperar* — despair, *primavera* — spring, *nieve* — snow,"* to continue his Spanish lessons, she said, but no, that wasn't the truth — just to feel the pressure of her lips against his ear.

The dirge reached them like that, lying close in sticky communion, the deep, mournful bleat of horns, the grim pounding of a single drum, and Flor ceased her whispered vocabulary and cocked an ear like a cat as the music grew louder.

"What's that?" Doyle said, apprehensive.

Flor rose, and shook out her black hair and folded back the green shutters to the tiny balcony, little more than a ledge suspended over the street. Petunias and irises grew in a tangle from a terracotta pot out there, and morning sun shone on the purple and pink petals and on the curves of Flor's body. Doyle watched from the bed. Naked, she pressed against the railing to get a better view.

"Come see," she said, and he kicked off the sheet and stood beside her as a funeral procession turned the corner below: a narrow white coffin borne by six men wearing white robes and pointed hoods like Klansmen, red Maltese crosses on a mantle hanging from their shoulders. The five-piece brass band following this doleful procession also wore white robes and hoods, with special holes cut out for their instruments. There was no one else in the street, just the hooded men and the coffin. Flor crossed herself; the hooded men bearing the coffin drew nearer so slowly it seemed they must be moving in another world.

"Why isn't there anyone else?" Doyle whispered. "Where are the mourners?" He felt a cold wind against his privates.

"The men in the robes are monks," she whispered, "who swear a vow never to speak on this earth unless addressed by an angel or God Himself. One of their brothers has died and they carry him to the Campo Santo to be buried."

When the procession passed just below, as if on cue the monks looked up at the man and the woman standing naked as Adam and Eve on the balcony looking down — and this is what Doyle saw now in his dream, the morning sunlight on the irises, on Flor's breasts, on the hooded men, on the white coffin gleaming like snow, like a strip of paper on which nothing has been written.

3

The Mercedes was stuck in traffic on the access road along the sea-wall. Ruby taillights curved in an unbroken line towards the white dome of the Biloxi SunCoast Arena a half-mile ahead. The long fingers of spotlights trailed obscenely across the dark, pendulous knobs of low-lying *mammato cumulus*. A faint last flush of sunset showed beneath the clouds, then faded out all at once. As the Mercedes crept closer, Doyle could make out the words on the massive banner hanging from ramparts just beneath the dome: FLIGHT NIGHT.

"Who's fighting?" Doyle said, breaking the silence.

"Esposito and Fleming," Feeney said. "Esposito's a spic, Fleming's a nigger — always makes for a good fight. If Esposito wins tonight, he's got a shot against de la Hoya at the Garden in two months. But why am I wasting my breath? You're not here to see the fight, re-member?"

"Right," Doyle said.

Feeney was fiddling with the climate control, setting and resetting the digital thermostat, not paying attention to the car ahead, which came to a sudden stop. He hit the brakes, tires grabbed at damp asphalt; the big car lurched forward and skidded to within an inch of the other's rear bumper. Feeney punched the wheel with his fist and jerked sharply towards Doyle.

"Why didn't you say something, asshole?" he shouted.

"I think you're the one driving," Doyle said calmly.

Feeney pulled the Ruger out of his jacket and put it to Doyle's temple. "Get out and walk before I put a bullet in your brain, you fucking smartlipped cunt!"

Doyle got out and slammed the door and started walking. Feeney buzzed down the window. "The bar on Concourse C, asshole," he called. "One hour."

Doyle walked down the strip of bare dirt between the cars towards the arena rising from its parking lot like a huge mushroom out of mold. The men and women in the cars he passed reflected the ethnicity of the fighters. Most were black, like Fleming, and looked like they were dressed for an evening on the town in a 1930s movie. Doyle saw the sheen of satin lapels, snap-brim hats, big jewelry, and, improbably, fur. The tinny horns of Mariachi came from the occasional pickup decorated with the Mexican tricolor. He reached the arena ten minutes later, gave half his ticket to a man in a red sport jacket at the turnstile, took the crowded escalator up to Concourse C, and found the bar, an Irish-style pub called the Pugilist which, despite the thirsty crush of spectators on the concourse, was empty. A painted sign just inside the door depicted two old-fashioned white boxers with handlebar moustaches facing each other in the stiff-armed, feet-planted stance of the nineteenth century.

Doyle came in and sat at the bar, and the bartender, a jowly, beef-faced man wearing a white short-sleeve shirt and bow-tie, put down the racing sheet he was reading and stepped forward. Doyle knew he was Irish before he opened his mouth.

"What can I get for you?" the bartender said.

Doyle told him, and the bartender poured a shot of bourbon and pulled a pint of Guinness slowly over a slotted spoon and set them on the counter.

"Where is everybody?" Doyle said, looking around. "I would think you'd do big business tonight."

"Them kind's not wanted in here," the bartender said. "High-stepping bucks and hootchie mamas not my preferred clientele, if you know what I'm saying."

"You were expecting the ballet crowd?" Doyle said.

The bartender scowled and went back to his racing sheet.

A few minutes later, Feeney came in and sat down two stools away from Doyle. "Guinness, Sean," he said to the bartender.

The bartender put down his racing sheet again and picked up a pint glass.

"You meet my man Doyle here?" Feeney said.

Startled, the bartender jumped around and made a quick move for something under the bar.

"Calm yourself, boyo." Feeney laughed. "This one's the wrong Doyle. The right Doyle's upstairs in the Greek's skybox. Or, at least, we think he is."

The bartender relaxed. "So how you going to get him out?" He handed the pint across the bar to Feeney.

"How we get Doyle out is up to Doyle here," Feeney said. He took a long drink of his pint, wiped his mouth on the back of his hand, and turned his stool till he was facing Doyle. "Here's your instructions, jerk-off." He grinned. "You only get them once, so try listening with both ears. Very simple — you go up to the VIP skybox on Concourse F, get Doyle away from the Greek, and bring him down to this bar. That's the hard part. I don't care how you do that, only thing is the bastard can't be dead because there's some questions we got to ask him first. Here's the easy part. Through that door," he pointed to a grey metal fire door against the far wall, "is a corridor. Down that corridor is an elevator. You get Doyle into the elevator and press SB, which means sub-basement. I've got the car down there now, parked on the far side by the garbage, and I'll be waiting. You stick him in the trunk and we drive back to the Sands where, just about now, Jesus should have his equipment all set up and ready to go."

"Equipment?" Doyle said.

"That's right," Feeney said. "Tools of the trade. Dental drills. Electrical doo-hickeys you clip on to a poor man's scrotum to give him a nice little jolt. Surgical saws, you get the idea. Jesus is a fucking expert. A real craftsman, isn't he, Sean?"

The bartender nodded. "You might call him the *idiot savant* of torture."

"What happens then?" Doyle said.

Feeney gave a sharp-toothed grin. "Then we ask our questions, we get our answers, which we verify as accurate by means of a phone call or two, and when it's over you take him down to some little spot along the gulf and finish him proper."

"Me?" Doyle said. He swallowed hard.

Feeney made a gun out of his thumb and forefinger. "A shot to the back of the head I find works best," he said. "But you probably already know that, don't you, Gunslinger? You drop him in the drink and we drive back to Delaware."

"Great," Doyle said. "At least you guys are door-to-door gangsters."

The bartender cleared his throat. "There's one problem with all that," he said. "The Greek's got a guest list tonight and they're checking the door damn careful, like."

"Logistics." Feeney tilted his sharp chin to the ceiling, as if addressing someone suspended from the acoustic tiles. "Logistics don't interest me one bit. Like I said, how it's done is all up to our friend Doyle here. The man's famous, you know. Quick with a gun, quick as hell. I should know, I seen him work. You remember poor old Gallagher?"

The bartender nodded.

"It was our friend here done that one."

The bartender shot Doyle a black look.

Doyle stood up and held on to the wooden lip of the bar to still the shaking in his hands. "So how do I recognize the man?" He tried to keep his voice calm and tough.

"That's the easy part," the bartender said. "You've got one Irishman, one Greek, and a room full of piccaninnies. Let's see if you can spot the Irishman."

Feeney reached into the pocket of his jacket, pulled out another automatic pistol, this one a .22 Beretta, and slid it down the bar. "You're going to need that, Gunslinger," he said.

Doyle looked down at the stumpy weapon, its muzzle pointed directly at him. He picked it up gingerly, weighed it in his hand. This pistol felt light and inconsequential somehow, with none of the heft or portentousness of the Walker Colt that had once helped win a war against Mexico. This wasn't a weapon, just an evil little death made by machines from alloy, carbon, high-density plastics and dealt out by thugs and cowards.

"No, thanks," Doyle said, and put the gun back on the bar.

Feeney and the bartender exchanged glances.

"Just how you expecting to get the bastard down here, then?" Feeney said.

"I'll ask nicely," Doyle said.

4

The black man checking names at the velvet rope was one of the largest human beings Doyle had ever seen in person, over six-and-a-half feet tall and nearly as wide — what wasn't fat was certainly muscle — with a small head sitting atop all that bulk like a grapefruit on a weather balloon.

"Let me guess," Doyle said. "They call you Tiny."

The big man fixed him with a humorless stare. "Name?" he said.

"Doyle," Doyle said.

The big man ran his eyes down the list on a clipboard in his hand.

"You already done come in here once, Doyle," he said. "I got an X next your name."

"I'm coming in again," Doyle said.

The big man asked for Doyle's ID and Doyle produced his expired Spanish driver's license, which listed his address as Calle Mercado, Málaga, and the big man studied it with cross-eyed intensity.

"You Mexican or something?" he said, handing it back.

"Something," Doyle said.

"I got to warn you, it's a Fleming crowd in there. Marcus our boy. Don't go getting in any trouble now."

"OK," Doyle said, "thanks for the advice," and he stepped around the big man and crossed over the velvet rope and entered the Greek's VIP skybox, a large room with one glass wall overlooking the arena and the ring small as a postage stamp far below. The place was packed with spectators — largely black, but despite what the bartender had said, Doyle saw several whites, none obviously Irish. Most of the spectators were pressed against the window, gaping out at the action on a TV cube the size of a house suspended from the center of the dome.

A loud bell went off and the warm-up bout entered the third round. The fighters, a sleek-looking black man named Shabazz and a pale pink hulk named Wheeland, appeared entirely mismatched. Doyle didn't know much about the fight game, but he could tell Wheeland, staggering and puffy-faced, was losing badly. Shabazz danced around him, landing quick jabs, in control, looking for an opening that would end the fight. Doyle edged over into the corner by the window where he could get a better view of the crowd. How would he find Doyle in this mess?

"Only thing white boy's got is he won't fall down," one of the spectators was saying.

"Look at Shab go," another spectator said.

"Shit, I could clean up that pink mofo sonofabitch myself," a third spectator said.

"You mama could clean up that pink mofo sonofabitch," the first spectator said. "Two hands behind her back."

"Like to see that one," someone else said, laughing.

A small, attractive black woman in a tight mini-dress made of snakeskin-patterned Spandex turned to Doyle. She came up to his chin and Doyle found himself staring down at the top of her breasts and liking what he saw. She had smooth dark skin the color of a library table and big black doe eyes.

"What's wrong with you white boys?" she said coyly. "Just can't fight worth a damn."

"That's easy," Doyle said. "We've given up."

"Glad to hear one of y'all finally admit that," the black woman said, and she grinned.

"What's your name?" Doyle said. But at that moment a shout went up from the crowd and Doyle looked down to see a pink ant hit the canvas below. The black woman shrieked and jumped a foot off the ground. Instant slow-motion replay on the television cube showed the fatal blow, a cross-cut right full on the jaw, Shabazz's muscles glistening, and the mouthpiece flying from Wheeland's teeth in a spray of spittle and Wheeland crumpling in a foamy heap.

"Seven! Eight! Nine!" the referee's voice came booming over the PA system. "Ten!" and the SunCoast Arena erupted in a roar heard halfway to Biloxi.

"Indonika Pinkney," the woman said, when the roaring had subsided. "That's my name."

"Indonika, do you know a man named Doyle?" Doyle said.

Indonika studied him for a long moment. "You looking for trouble?" she said at last.

"Just looking for Doyle," Doyle said. "Matter of life and death."

Indonika shook her head sadly. "You looking for trouble, mister, plain enough," she said. "Anyone looking for Doyle looking for trouble. I'm going to ask you something and don't you lie to me. I know when people are lying, it's a gift. You a good man or a bad man? And I don't mean go-to-church-Sunday kind of good, I mean don't-sell-my-friends-to-a-nigger-for-a-dollar kind of good. Got that?"

"I'm on the side of the angels," Doyle said, with all the sincerity he could muster. Indonika thought about this, her black eyes narrowing. Down in the ring, men in white jumpsuits were mopping blood off the canvas in preparation for the final contest.

5

The Greek's VIP-VIP skybox was a small intimate room off the larger one, coolly air-conditioned, its walls upholstered in white leather, the furniture white leather and chrome. About fifteen guests milled about, talking in hushed voices, cocktails in hand. Behind a bar in one corner a discreet young man in a spotless tuxedo shirt stood waiting. Indonika stepped up to the bar. "Give me a Remy Martin," she said.

The young man offered a wan smile and poured out the Cognac with all the gravity of a priest pouring the communion wine at mass.

"Is he here?" Doyle whispered.

"Be cool!" Indonika whispered sharply.

She gestured towards a white leather couch facing the glass wall. There, a broad-shouldered white man, his arms around two young black women, sat staring out at highlights of the Shabazz–Wheeland fight on the giant TV cube. The women were caricatures of sex in skimpy dresses that barely reined in their ample flesh; the man was positioned in such a way that Doyle could see only the back of his head. An older white man, about sixty, was seated in a deep-cushioned club chair adjacent to the couch, his salt-and-pepper hair pulled back in a ponytail to reveal sharp, leathery Hellenic features. He wore a brightly figured silk shirt open to white chest hairs matted with gold chains in the disco style of twenty-five years ago. Obviously the Greek. Doyle had seen men like him before, on the terrace of El Rey in high season, dining with women young enough to be their daughter's friends and probably were. These men were what the French called *un numero,* a player; they littered the beaches from the Costa Brava to the Côte d'Azur with their skimpy bathing suits and Ferraris and cell phones, grown rich from questionable undertakings, from the weaknesses and vice of others. But this particular *numero* had something, a melancholy look in his eye, as if he had just realized that all of it — the Ferrari, the fast money, the pubescent mistresses, even this skybox — was worth nothing at all. Ashes.

Indonika took her drink from the bartender. "Stavros," she called to the man in the club chair, "I brought a friend."

Stavros jumped out of his chair, enraged in an instant, and came over to the bar in two long steps. "How many times I tell you, Indonika, this is like my private home here? Public party's next door. You don't bring a stranger to my private home without a special invitation." He caught Doyle's elbow in a rough grip and pushed him back towards the door. "Out, my friend."

Doyle pulled his elbow away. "I need to talk to Doyle," he said, loud enough for Doyle to hear.

The Greek flashed a glance at the couch. Doyle didn't stir or look around. "He's busy right now."

"It's very import —" Doyle began, but the Greek put his hands against Doyle's chest and pushed. Doyle staggered into the bar, highball glasses ringing together like crystal bells.

"Hey, Doyle," Doyle called out, "O'Mara sent me."

The man on the couch stiffened visibly, muscles in his shoulders tensing. Then he slowly turned around.

6

The two Doyles stepped out on to the concourse, deserted in the last minutes before the title bout. The escalators made hollow clanking noises for seven levels down. Even Tiny had abandoned his post at the velvet rope.

"Say what you got to say quick, like," Doyle growled in a heavy accent Doyle knew for a Connaught brogue. "I got a couple of quid riding on this fight and I'm not about to miss it for the fucking Old Fruit or anyone else."

"I'm afraid you're going to miss a lot of things in the near future," Doyle said, and he told Doyle about O'Mara, about Feeney downstairs smoking a cigarette in the darkened interior of the Mercedes parked in some nether region of the Biloxi SunCoast Arena visited only by dog-sized rats and garbagemen; about Jesus waiting now in a remote concrete-block motel cabin, torture implements spread out neatly on a towel on the bed as the quiet waters of the gulf rubbed up against the dirty shore.

Doyle listened and his face grew pale. He was a man of about Doyle's height, a bit broader in the shoulder, perhaps, but with the same dark hair and sleepy-eyed expression suggestive of the young Mitchum and the same slightly crooked nose. They might have been cousins, brothers. Tonight, he was dressed like a sport in a long Guyabera shirt of a garish floral pattern, silvery-grey trousers, expensive Italian loafers without socks.

"This man Jesus," he said, when Doyle was finished. "Does he speak?"

"Not really," Doyle said. "He grunts. He seems dull, slow —"

"No," Doyle interrupted, a shudder passing across his even features. "He's not slow, not at all. He's fast, deadly as a snake."

"So what are you going to do?" Doyle said.

"No, what are *you* going to do, boyo?" Doyle said. Just then, a muffled roar reached them from the arena. The fighters had stepped into the ring. Doyle rolled his eyes towards the sound and began back-ing away. "Like I said, I got a couple of quid —"

"Wait a minute," Doyle cut him off. "I came all the way from Vir-ginia with two thugs riding my ass just to let you know the score. Now I need a favor."

"What kind of a favor?" Doyle said, wary.

"I need you to help me get a man into the trunk of a car. Can you handle that?"

"Is he dead?" Doyle said.

"Alive, unfortunately," Doyle said. "A dead guy I could handle on my own."

Doyle hesitated. "How about I see the fight through first?"

Doyle nodded, OK, and the two men went back through the door to the Greek's VIP-VIP skybox. The fight was still in the first round. Spectators jostled for position against the window. Indonika and Doyle's two women were up on their fuck-me heels screaming at the vast image of Fleming on the giant TV cube, drops of sweat on his video forehead at least two feet across. On first glance, the fighters seemed evenly matched: they danced around each other throwing el-egant punches at the air. But Fleming's dark flesh soon ran with mois-ture; Esposito somehow stayed cool, dry as powder.

The Greek slumped in his club chair unmoved, chin resting on his knuckles; the women screamed themselves hoarse. Doyle came around and took his former place on the couch just as the bell went off and the round was over.

"Next round watch Esposito doesn't finish him off," Doyle said to the Greek.

The Greek shook his head. "It is a decision, my friend. Esposito, of course, but a decision. And I say it goes the distance."

"Next round." Doyle grinned. "Knockout. Care to pump it up a thousand?"

The Greek stroked his moist lower lip with one nicotine-yellow finger. "Done," he said. Then he glanced over his shoulder at Doyle leaning back against the bar. "You still here?" he called, his manner vaguely threatening.

Doyle came over and sat on the arm of the couch. "As it turns out I'm a friend of Doyle's," he said.

The Greek raised an eyebrow.

Doyle nodded. "Man come a long way to do me a good turn."

The Greek seemed to relax. "Then you are welcome here." He held out his hand and Doyle shook it. Then the bell went off for the second round and Esposito came charging out of his corner with the air of a man determined to put an end to a bad habit. Fleming reeled under this onslaught and, to much screaming from all sides, was driven against the ropes. He fell to one knee, knocked down by a classical left-hook-upper-cut combination. Esposito danced away, barely winded. Fleming was up after three but the round was over and an egg-sized purple swelling had suddenly appeared over Fleming's left eye.

"He's hurt!" Indonika shouted, nearly hysterical.

"They ought to stop the fight!" one of the other woman screamed, and pounded her fist on the thick glass. "Stop the fight! Stop the fight!"

The Greek smiled. "They think it's real," he said wearily.

Presently the referee stepped into the ring and announced a standing eight count. He took Esposito's gloved hand and lifted it in the air and a dull, ambiguous noise rose from the crowd.

The Greek made a disgusted gesture. "Standing eight. What do we do with that?"

Doyle rose from the couch. "Not a knock-out, not a decision," he said, "but I got the round right. What say we split the difference?"

The Greek seemed pleased with this suggestion. He removed a wad of cash from somewhere, peeled off four thousand-dollar bills and handed them to Doyle without comment. There followed a general movement towards the door; hip-hop could already be heard from the VIP skybox.

"You done found your Doyle," Indonika gave Doyle a playful slap on the arm, "so why don't you come in and dance?"

"Wish I could," Doyle said, regret in his voice. "Next time."

Indonika flashed a red-lipped parting glance that almost made him blush, turned with a shrug of hip and was gone.

In another minute the Greek's VIP-VIP skybox was empty, except for the Greek himself and the two Doyles.

"My friend, I think you are going away," the Greek said to Doyle, heavily.

Doyle folded the thousand-dollar bills into the pocket of his Guyabera shirt. "Don't talk a lot of rubbish, Stavros," he said, but he wouldn't meet the Greek's eye.

"Then you will come out on the boat tomorrow." The Greek brightened. "We'll have a little party for no reason at all."

"Not tomorrow," Doyle said. "Excuse me for just a second," and he turned and followed the women into the next room and Doyle and the Greek were left alone.

The Greek folded himself miserably into his club chair. Suddenly he looked like any old man in baggy clothes. He levelled a sad-eyed gaze at Doyle. "You are going to take my friend away," he said. "For this I should kill you."

"I'm just borrowing the man for half an hour." Doyle held up his hands.

The Greek didn't seem to hear this. "Women I can have," he said, "as many as I want. Just flash some money around and, pouf, there they are, wearing bad perfume and cheap dresses that show everything but their snatch. Friends, though, that is very hard."

"Yes," Doyle agreed.

The Greek took a string of black worry-beads out of his pants pocket and entwined them around his fingers with an unconscious gesture that seemed second nature to him. "I am from Cyprus," he said. "Famagusta is my city. Years ago, there was a war in Cyprus against the Turks. Of course, there is always a war in Cyprus against the Turks, but in this war a very old, very famous church stood halfway between the Greek and Turkish army and they were both fighting for this church. My little brother was a patriot, very brave, very stupid. He climbed up to the top of the church and put a Greek flag there and then," he shook his head sadly, "the Turks shot him down. I saw this happen. He fell like a stone and his head split open on the ground. Doyle, he reminds me of my brother. I think, maybe, if . . ."

But he didn't say any more. The quiet clacking of the worry-beads took the place of speech. After a while, Doyle got up and went out to wait on the concourse for Doyle. A massacre, a melancholy Greek, another forgotten war half-way around the world. The same old tragedy, each crime a stone, enough stones thrown into the water to engulf the world.

7

The sub-basement of the Biloxi SunCoast Arena was a vast, empty, underground rotunda, its concrete floor oil-stained and sticky with hydraulic fluid. A foul subterranean wind blew scraps of paper — old ticket stubs, wrinkled pages of programs for sporting events long past — over the concrete like dry leaves. Massive dumpsters and a dark car parked between them lay in the gloom on the other side.

"A disturbing thought just occurred to me, boyo," Doyle said, presently. "How for fucksakes do I know I'm not the lad to be stuffed into the trunk?"

"Good question," Doyle said.

"And the answer?"

"I told you the truth," Doyle said. "If you didn't believe me, you wouldn't be down here now."

Doyle grunted. "So how we going to do this, MacArthur? Got a plan?"

"Simple," Doyle said. "We get him out of the car. Knock him over the head, stick him in the trunk. How does that sound?"

Doyle didn't answer and the two Doyles advanced cautiously around the perimeter, sticking close to the massive concrete pylons supporting the walls.

"They could flood this bloody place and float a couple of battleships," Doyle said, after a minute.

"The Romans already thought of that one," Doyle said, remembering a fragment from Suetonius' *Lives of the Twelve Caesars*, something he'd read in college at Hampden-Sydney years ago. "Mock sea battles. They filled the Colosseum and forced convicts dressed like sailors to fight to the death with swords and catapults."

"Them Romans knew how to have fun," Doyle said, chuckling.

Edging along from shadow to shadow took some time; at last they reached the dumpsters. The grill of the Mercedes and the cartoon-eye headlamps could just be made out, peeking from between the two closest.

"Now walk ahead of me," Doyle said. "Hands behind your back."

Doyle clasped his hands behind his back and Doyle fell a step or two behind him.

"Good," Doyle said. "Now hang your head. Stagger a bit — you're in pain, a prisoner. I've just given you a good beating."

"That'll be the day," Doyle muttered, but he hung his head and staggered.

"Feeney!" Doyle called, his voice echoing thinly in the vast space. "I got your boy! Come out and get him!"

The Mercedes' cartoon eyes flashed on, blinding the two Doyles.

"Did you say the bastard was armed?" Doyle said in a low voice.

"I didn't," Doyle said, "but he's got a Ruger in his pocket."

"Thanks for telling me," Doyle said.

Then came the sound of the Mercedes door opening and the soft scrape of a shoe on concrete. "You did it, for fucksake!" It was Feeney's voice.

"Looks that way," Doyle called.

"Bring him on now, nice and slow," Feeney said.

"Get the trunk open," Doyle said, drawing nearer. "We'll put him in the trunk."

"You're a hard man, Gunslinger." Feeney chuckled. He took the keys out of his pocket, pressed a button, and the trunk lifted with a smooth, unlatching sound. Doyle staggered up to the Mercedes, Doyle just behind. The headlights threw long shadows across the oily concrete; the atmosphere was thick with heat and the suffocating sweet smell of decomposing garbage. Feeney reached up, took hold of Doyle's jaw with his fingertips, and shook the man's head back and forth violently.

"We finally got you, Billy," he began. "The Old Fruit —" Then Doyle swung a fist from behind his back and caught Feeney square between the eyes. Feeney cried out and fell against the Mercedes' bumper. He tried to scramble up but slipped on the oily floor, and Doyle threw himself down and twisted Feeney's arms back.

"Get the gun," Doyle growled.

Doyle came around quickly, reached into Feeney's torn jacket, and pulled out the Ruger, which he immediately threw overhand into the dumpster.

"Just why did you do that?" Doyle said, angry. "We could have used that gun!"

"Don't like guns," Doyle said. Then he went around to the open trunk and came back with a pair of extra-long jumper cables and tossed them down. "Secure him with these," he said, remembering in a flash eight hours of terror in the rural Delaware dark tied to a tree by another Irishman and thought these bonds a kind of poetic justice.

Feeney didn't make a sound as he was hogtied with the jumper cables and gagged with a dirty rag. He didn't start kicking until they had put him in the trunk and slammed the lid. The thumping and moaning could be heard from inside the car, even with the radio on.

"Maybe he's claustrophobic," Doyle said. He was driving; they were stuck in slow exit traffic along the seawall, the gulf near, awash in darkness.

"So what do you think you're going to do with the bloody bugger?" Doyle asked. "Keep him in the trunk like a spare tire?"

"I don't know," Doyle said.

Doyle took a bent cigarette out of his Guyabera shirt and lit it with the dashboard lighter. "Only way's to kill him," he said softly. "Otherwise he goes running off to O'Mara and you're a dead man."

"You let me worry about O'Mara," Doyle said, sounding tough.

Doyle cracked the window and blew cigarette smoke out into the night air. "You're a cool one," he said.

"You heard what they call me," Doyle grinned, "for reasons I won't explain."

"Right," Doyle said ruefully. "Gunslinger without a gun."

8

A half-hour later they were clear of fight-night traffic, and twenty minutes after that, shooting north on 49 towards Hattiesburg. At Saucier, at Doyle's instruction, Doyle turned up a bumpy park road into the DeSoto National Forest. Doyle drove another twenty minutes, turning off the park road and up a narrow trail just wide enough for the car, hemmed in by the huge, gnarled trunks of live oak, Spanish moss trailing from the branches eerily like a woman's hair.

"This is as good a place as any, boyo," Doyle said.

Doyle stopped the Mercedes, its headlights catching the glitter of water down the slope between the trees. The two Doyles got out, went to the trunk and lifted the unfortunate Feeney out on to the road. Doyle removed the gag and Feeney retched into the dirt. "Goddamned rag soaked with petrol," he gasped, spitting. "You cocksuckers nearly asphyxiated me."

"More's the pity we didn't," Doyle said. "You'd be dead right now if it was up to me, but," he jerked his thumb towards Doyle, "you know these Americans. Soft-hearted eejits."

Feeney looked up at Doyle from where he lay in the dirt and saw something in the man's eyes that made him afraid. Then he laid his head down and closed his eyes and began to recite the Lord's Prayer under his breath.

"Oh, this is too bloody pitiful," Doyle said. "The bastard's found religion in his final hour. I can't stand it."

But Doyle squatted down, undid the jumper cable restraints, and helped Feeney, trembling now, to his feet.

"What are you going to do with me?" Feeney said, whimpering.

"Absolutely nothing," Doyle said.

Behind him, Doyle uttered an exclamation of disgust to the night.

"Now remove your shoes and pants," Doyle said.

Feeney hesitated, then he saw Doyle was serious and removed his shoes and then his pants one leg at a time and stood pantless in stockinged feet on the dirt road.

"Boxers too," Doyle said.

"No," Feeney protested. "Have pity, for fucksakes!"

Doyle made a threatening gesture and Feeney removed his boxers and pulled his shirttails down over his bare ass.

Doyle tossed Feeney's shoes, pants, and boxers into the trunk and shut it. Then he got back into the car and closed the door and Doyle followed. Feeney spun around, staring with frightened eyes at the dark shapes of the trees.

"Hey!" he called. "You can't just leave me here half-naked in the fucking wilderness!"

Doyle buzzed down the window on the passenger side. "Remember, boyo, moss grows on the north side of trees. And all rivers end up in the bloody ocean, eventually. And watch out for bears or you just might get your tiny widget bitten off."

Doyle put the car in reverse and began to back down the path, but Feeney ran after them, waving his arms wildly. Doyle stopped; Feeney came up to the driver's side, out of breath.

"I've got to know what's to happen to Jesus," he said.

Doyle thought for a long moment. "I guess he'll just get tired of watching TV in the motel and go home," he said.

Feeney shook his head. "The poor bastard's got the brain of a child —"

"Yes, an evil child," Doyle interrupted.

"He'll just sit there staring at that telly until someone comes and fetches him," Feeney said, sounding desperate. "He doesn't know how to get food, he can't talk, for fucksake! He'll perish!"

"Let him perish." Doyle buzzed the window up and reversed the car quickly out on to the park road, the headlights touching Feeney, forlorn up the trail, nothing on his bottom half except for his socks, arms at his side, closed in by darkness and the thick, scarred trunks of the trees.

When they were out on 49 again, headed south towards Biloxi, Doyle turned to Doyle from the passenger seat and told him where he wanted to go.

9

The lights of New Orleans showed as a green haze in the sky to the west. They crossed the Mississippi on a wide modern bridge lit bright as daylight. On its own, the Blaupunkt found a Cajun station from a parish deep in bayou country and the happy scratching of accordion and fiddle made itself heard through the static of the night. Doyle leaned back against the headrest in the passenger seat and pulled another bent cigarette out of the pocket of his Guyabera and cracked the window.

Doyle took his eyes off the road for a moment and studied the Irishman's calm profile. "Tell me something," he said. "How did you get mixed up with O'Mara in the first place?"

They were riding above the low-lying suburbs now, a vague landscape of seedy, one-story bungalows, levees, and barely restrained verdure, then suddenly a white cemetery with row after row of aboveground tombs and marble angels gleaming in the moonlight.

"I used to be a gambler," Doyle said, blowing smoke against the window. "This is back in Dublin some years ago. But I suppose gambler is too grand a word. More like small-time punter, professional bullshitter, but always something to do with the cards or the horses. Then I met O'Mara because everyone in my line of work meets O'Mara sooner or later, and I came over to the States and crash-landed on the bastard's planet, you might say, and he offered me a job. And in the man's employ I became someone else, someone I really didn't like at all."

"Who was that?"

"I mean a dirty, disgusting stooge, a button man, a bazooka. Myself, I always liked the term bazooka." Doyle grinned. "Has a sort of military ring, don't you think?"

"OK, you're a disgusting bazooka," Doyle said. "How long?"

"Five years working for that rat bastard," Doyle said glumly.

"Five years is a long time," Doyle said. "It must not have been too disgusting."

"Let me put it this way," Doyle said. "Do you know 'Whiskey in the Jar'?"

Doyle thought for a moment. It was one of the old Irish chestnuts. Uncle Buck used to blast the Chieftains version on the jukebox in the Parrot Cage every St. Patrick's Day.

"You mean the song, right?"

"Right." Doyle cleared his throat and sang in a reasonable tenor: *Some take the life in the carriages a-rolling; some take the life in the hurley and the bowling; but I take the life in the juice of the barley and courting pretty fair maids in the morning bright and early* ... He stopped abruptly. "Now, that's philosophy," he said. "Man's life in the world in three lines, fucking beautiful, if you think about it. For me, it was always the carriages a-rolling. I always wanted to be where the action was, something going on, something fast and dangerous, and wherever O'Mara was, the game was fast and dangerous and the governor to dinner too for a little glamour and just enough gun-play to keep you on your toes and women, beautiful women, to take your mind off the dull hours if you wanted them — which brings me to your problem, my friend." He cast an assessing eye at Doyle. "It's the latter with you, ain't it? I can tell — whiskey and women. Trouble, that pair."

Doyle grinned despite himself. "Maybe," he allowed.

"But then the game got rough," Doyle continued. "The Old Fruit got involved in some nasty business and I found myself doing a couple of things in the line of duty I didn't want to do, couple of things that turned my stomach. Got so I couldn't bear the sight of my own face in the mirror. Finally I couldn't take it any more and one day I saw my chance and took some money and took off. O'Mara's been after me ever since."

"How about just giving the money back?" Doyle said.

At that moment, a truck full of chickens roared past in the left lane, blowing a trail of brown feathers in its wake.

"Money's gone," Doyle said, when the truck had pulled ahead. "Spent. High living, unwise investments."

"How much are we talking here?" Doyle said.

"Never mind," Doyle said. "Enough to keep me awake at night, dreaming about how much I used to have."

They came down the Airline Highway through Kenner, the landing lights of circling aircraft hovering in the green sky over Moisant Field. It wouldn't be long till dawn turned the brown river gold and the city woke to another bleary morning. Doyle pulled up the access ramp to the terminal and followed the sign marked departures. He pulled over to the curb in the standing lane and, as a gesture, got out and opened the door for the Irishman.

"You're a gentleman, sir," Doyle said. He stepped up on to the sidewalk and stretched, Guyabera shirt billowing in the warm night wind, and reached into his pocket for another cigarette. He seemed in no hurry to get where he was going.

"The Greek will be disappointed," Doyle said.

"Pity the poor Greek," Doyle said. "He's a good man, but a little sad as the old tyrant approaches."

"Which old tyrant is that?"

"Death, man, death." Doyle smiled grimly, as if he was on intimate terms with that specter. "He's got something wrong with his guts, I don't know what exactly, but it won't be too long now. One or two years at the most."

"Poor bastard," Doyle said.

Doyle shrugged. "Well . . ."

"So where are you going?" Doyle said.

"Anywhere away from O'Mara," Doyle said. "Anywhere the game's fast and the stakes are high." He tapped his back pocket. "Always carry my passport. This time I'm thinking the Orient. Macao. Singapore. Bangkok."

Doyle was impressed. "The Orient, just like that?" he said. "No luggage, no toothpaste. Just a gaudy shirt and a shiny pair of pants."

Doyle grinned. "I travel light, brother."

And Doyle envied the man for this lightness, for his ability to blow with the wind to the other side of the world and be at home wherever he landed. He'd had that ability once himself, but no longer. He thought of Pirate Island now, washed by the shallows of another coast, and longed to be there, to feel the same old sandy ground beneath his feet and hear the familiar marsh grass rustling in the same ocean wind.

"Listen," the Irishman said, serious suddenly, "I've got something for you. A little secret that might give you a card to play in the Old Fruit's game. You know about his damned poison-gas smuggling, right?"

"The CFCs, the freon," Doyle said.

"That's the shit," Doyle said. "Know how he gets it into the country from China?"

"No," Doyle said, listening closely.

"The fucking Old Fruit bought a broken-down can factory somewhere in Virginia, I think, that used to make some sweet teeth-rotting soda pop."

"Royal Blue Cola," Doyle said. "The factory's in Ainsley."

"That's the stuff," Doyle said. "So the Old Fruit starts making the cola again and selling it cheap and taking a loss, but here's the clever part. Half the cans go out empty to China where he's got another can factory, and they come back filled with the poison gas. He's a smart

Old Fruit, all right, only where does he keep his precious cans filled with poison gas, that arrogant fuck?"

Doyle knew but didn't say anything.

"In a concrete bunker in the basement of his fucking castle in Delaware. In other words, right in his own fucking house. Back in the old days when I was chief stooge over there I used to tell him, 'you got to find someplace else to keep your poison gas,' but he just laughed at me. 'Who's going to touch the king?' he said, the arrogant bastard."

Doyle nodded solemnly. "Thanks for the tip."

"OK," Doyle said, and the two Doyles shook hands. The automatic doors opened with a pneumatic snort and they could hear the loud-speakers crackling with urgent, garbled announcements for the first departures of the morning. At the last second, Doyle stopped and turned around. "By the way, what's your name, brother?" he said.

Doyle grinned. "Doyle," he said. "Tim Doyle."

The Irishman's jaw went slack. "You're shitting me," he said.

"No," Doyle said. "I'm not."

Doyle gave an ironic little laugh. "Good luck, then, brother Doyle." Then he turned and disappeared into the brightness of the terminal.

10

Doyle charged up half the continent possessed by something like white-hot rage, his mind working out all the possibilities. He crossed wide rivers and bare trickles that nonetheless required a bridge, he passed through brown country and green, cities and suburbs, rural wastes of abandoned family farms and well-tended corporate fields, raced dangerously over the speed limit through three or four states, the Blaupunkt searching the bands for a radio station that wasn't red-neck warbling or farm reports; and it was all the same highway all the way, a blur of headlights and tractor-trailers roaring by and SUVs and cars and gas stations and bright plastic franchises selling the lard and grease Americans take for food.

At nine in the morning, Doyle grew weary and longed for the sweet taste of bourbon. Then later, charging through the last of Tennessee, he longed for it again, this time with a sprig of mint on ice, and he felt the dead, stupid bone-weariness in his limbs — the only sleep he'd gotten in thirty-six hours on the beach between the dunes by the motel — but he beat back the exhaustion somehow, his thoughts racing faster than the Mercedes, and he was in Virginia as dusk fell across the mountain ranges like a curtain, the big car sweeping up the hills and at last down to Tidewater again and across the great bridge to the peninsula and up 13 unknowingly over the ancient lost burial grounds of the Oknontocokes past chicken farms and tomato fields into Wassateague County, his heart pounding, pumping blood to his furthest extremities, to the tips of his fingers and the tips of his toes in preparation for the ordeal ahead.

11

The *Chief Powhatan* rested steady as a barge at its moorings in the still night. Doyle came down the pier to the yellow cabin poised over the dark waters of the inlet and heard a familiar creaking from behind the screen in the darkness and the wiry old man appeared at the screen door, set his shotgun aside, and pulled the latch and Doyle came on to the porch.

"You coming at this hour of the night there must be trouble," Cap'n Pete said.

"There is," Doyle said.

Cap'n Pete reached up and touched the religious medals in his hat. "All right, what is it?"

Doyle told him and the old man waved him into the shipshape little house to a steel door locked with a large, impressive combination padlock. He unwound the combination number by number and the lock dropped and he pulled the door open and switched on the light and they stepped together into a windowless room, its walls completely covered with antique guns — hundreds of them, enough to outfit a small nineteenth-century army — set on racks or hanging on pegs or lying side by side on narrow felt-covered shelves. The room smelled of fresh oil and old varnish, with the ominous, faintly satanic hint of sulphur under everything. A state-of-the-art dehumidifier clicked away like a Geiger counter on the floor.

Doyle gave a low whistle. "Quite an arsenal."

"Yes indeed," Cap'n Pete said proudly. "It's the most extensive collection of its kind in the state of Virginia outside the NRA museum up in Fairfax County. We go all the way from this," he indicated a splendid ivory inlaid wheelock arqeubus, circa 1620, "to the dawn of the cartridge era which, for the sake of argument, I'm calling 1860. My best guesstimate is, sold off at auction, the whole thing's worth nearly three hundred thousand, maybe more. At least, that's what my insurance policy says. But I'll never sell." He repeated for emphasis, "I'll never sell. Now you know why I sit out there with my shotgun most nights. I'm known to collectors all over the country. And collectors are strange birds. All someone has to do is back a truck up to the pier some night and everything's gone."

"I see your point," Doyle said.

"Obviously some of these pieces I won't let you touch, pristine museum-quality weapons — it would be a crime to load and fire. But that still leaves a lot to choose from. Just state your preference."

Doyle looked around, bewildered. Bluing shone dully off the engraved cylinders of Colt's repeating pistols, off the elegant long barrels of Kentucky long rifles. "Something more or less modern," he said. "And small."

The Cap'n nodded, his mind working. In no time at all, he came up with a model 1861 Police Colt, converted for cartridges — a beautifully balanced piece that, unlike Feeney's Beretta, felt right in Doyle's hand.

"A favorite of the frontier lawmen," Cap'n Pete said. "Fast pulling and straight shooting, good for those tight spots." Then he handed over a box of cartridges, and the two men went out of the little house and up the pier to the road.

"That your car?" Cap'n Pete said, when he saw the black Mercedes.

"It is now," Doyle said. He stuck the Police Colt into his belt.

"Don't shoot yourself in the privates," Cap'n Pete said, alarmed. "Wish I had a holster for that but I don't. Maybe I could rig up . . ." The high melancholy cry of a loon interrupted his ramblings from somewhere across the inlet. ". . . something from —"

Doyle cut him off with a gesture.

"Anything else I can do?" Cap'n Pete persisted.

"No," Doyle said, backing towards the car.

"How about a prayer?" He reached up and touched his hat.

Doyle thought of Finster's prayer for an end to violence only after a lifetime of using violence for his own purposes and shook his head.

"Not right now," he said. "Maybe later."

12

When Doyle got back to Pirate Island at last, around three a.m., there was a message blinking on the machine behind the bar. He listened to the message and dialed the number left there and the phone rang twice and a female voice answered.

"What do you want?" Doyle said, in a tight voice.

Bracken hesitated. "This is my cell," she said. "Can't talk here. I've got to get to a better place. Call back in five," and she hung up.

Doyle wasn't going to call back, but he did.

"How was she?" Bracken said, when she picked up.

"Who?" Doyle said.

"Meena, honey," Bracken said. Doyle could hear her smoking on the other end, the soft pauses for exhalation. "I want you to know we're even now. I threw that slut into your lap and here we are talking peacefully on the telephone."

Doyle didn't understand. He said so.

"I spent two days laying it on thick, telling the bitch what a great lay you were, what a fucking machine and so on, and sooner or later I knew she'd have to find out for herself. And I knew if she found out for herself, she'd get you off her daddy's shit list just to rub my face in the whole thing and also because she's a sensitive little bitch, soft as an oyster beneath that hard exterior. See, I've known Meena for a long time now, and whatever I have she's got to have . . ." A smoky pause. "So I hope you appreciate my little ploy. Because it saved your ass."

Doyle didn't know what to say. This story seemed implausible enough to be true. Then again it could be Bracken weaseling her way out of her own guilt as usual.

"Thanks," he managed in a flat tone that reflected his ambivalence.

"Be that way," Bracken said. "See you in the next life."

"Wait," Doyle said, in the last half-second before she hung up. "What are you going to do now?"

Bracken blew more smoke. "I'm going to Mexico with Enrique, if you want to know."

"You're kidding," Doyle said.

"Why not? He absolutely worships me. Says I'm a white goddess. I remind him of Rita Hayworth, who was, ironically, half-Mexican. Anyway, I'm sick of this country. The problem with America is too many annoying little laws. And if I stick around, one of them is going to fall right on my head. I've talked till I'm blue in the face to those bureaucrats at INS. I explained I had no idea what was going on and they fed me that old saw about ignorance being no excuse, just like grade school again. It's five years inside for me, no matter what happens, my lawyer told me that much. Well, honey, in five years, I just might be dead. In Mexico, things are more natural, which is to say, there's more room to wiggle. You don't like a law, just pay somebody in the government to make it go away."

"But what happens to the Hundred?" It was all Doyle could think to say.

"The Hundred can sit and rot," Bracken said. "With all the doors and windows open and the wind and rain blowing down the hall. I always hated that old place. Too much history, most of it bad. Bye-bye, honey!"

"Wait —"

She hung up.

Doyle leaned heavily against the ice cooler and imagined Bracken living in some grimy Mexican border town behind the stuccoed walls of an armed compound, the plaything of uncouth men, their brown hands upon her pale, wintry flesh. She'd fallen a long way since college — the night they met years ago at Sigma Nu when she had peeled off her clothes and leaped naked and beautifully drunk off the ballroom mantel into anyone's arms that just happened to be Doyle's — and he supposed she'd keep falling and prayed for her sake she'd never hit bottom.

In a way, he thought, Bracken was merely following the trajectory set a long time ago, the forgotten afternoon Colonel Brodie Deering marched the first African slaves in chains down the gangplank of one of his ships into the wilderness he intended them to clear and harvest beneath the inducement of the lash.

Doyle held the receiver to his heart for a moment, as a man holds his hat out of respect for the dead, then replaced it gently on the cradle and went upstairs to his bedroom and got between the sheets and slept for the next fourteen hours.

13

Over the long day's slumber a voice came in dreams as if whispered into his ear by an obliging goddess. Doyle awoke the next evening, groggy from all that sleep, and followed the goddess's secret whisperings straight down the hall to the storage closet at the far end and rummaged around in there through successive layers of junk until he dug up a battered box from his college years marked "Books, Etc." He broke open the brittle nylon tape and right there on top found what he needed to find — a tattered black-spined Penguin copy of *Plutarch's Lives of the Noble Romans*. He took the book back down the hall and got back into bed and read again "The Life of Marius," Plutarch's short biography of the cruel, brilliant Roman general and politician who shaped the Roman legions into the great weapon that subdued the world.

Marius rose from obscure country beginnings to become one of the Republic's great men, which meant he led a life of cunning and cruelty, forced both in political and military life to defend himself against powerful enemies in situations where the odds were always against him. At one point Marius, caught in a political struggle between certain aristocratic senators and the popular tribune Saturninus, invited both parties to his rambling old villa near the Forum. He let the tribune Saturninus in through a door at the back of the house and installed him in a secluded room; meanwhile the senators were admitted through the front door. Then, as Plutarch says, *Marius pretended to both parties that he was suffering from diarrhea and kept running from one end of the house to the other, dealing now with the nobles and now with Saturninus and making mischief between them to save his own skin.*

Exactly, Doyle thought.

He read this passage twice, closed the book, and tossed it to the floor beside the bed. Then, when he had everything straight in his mind, he got up, splashed some water on his face, slipped his feet into Uncle Buck's carpet slippers, put on the man's World War Two coat, and went down into the bar to make the necessary telephone calls.

14

The last call Doyle made was to Meena's cell. She was driving somewhere — Doyle could hear the swoosh of passing Delaware telephone poles in the background.

"Meena speaking."

Doyle let a second elapse.

"Hello?"

"Hey," Doyle said, trying to find his most seductive voice. "It's me."

"Who's me?"

"Doyle," Doyle said.

"Doyle?" Meena sounded shocked.

"That's right," Doyle said.

"I'm fucking amazed you're still alive," Meena said. "Da's really pissed. He wants his car back and he wants your head on a plate."

"Yeah, how is the old AC king?"

"Like I said, pissed. It seems you left poor Feeney with his pants down in the woods."

Doyle couldn't suppress a chuckle. "Yeah, I did."

"You're a funny, funny man, Doyle." Meena didn't sound amused. "Unfortunately you're also a real dead funny man. Why did you do it? You had everything wrapped up —"

"Listen, we can talk about all that bullshit later," Doyle interrupted. "In bed. Right now, I want you to come to San Francisco."

"What?"

"That's right, I'm in San Francisco," Doyle said, and he glanced out the window at the crushed shells of the parking lot and the oozing trunks of the pines across the way. "It's beautiful here today, sunny and cool. At this moment, I can just about see Berkeley across the bay. Wait, there's a regatta going on — four white sailboats with rainbow sails just skimming along down there. If I press my nose to the window, I can see a streetcar coming up Hyde. And the bed is huge. A four-poster canopy and," he invented this detail on the spot, "the underside is embroidered with stars."

"You're kidding, right?" Meena said, her voice wavering.

"No," Doyle said. "I've got the Sequoia Suite at the Humboldt Arms B and B in San Francisco, that's where I am right now. And I've booked a flight for you first class, leaving tomorrow out of BWI. I want you on that flight, baby. And I'm going to be waiting here with an armful of roses and a bottle of champagne. What do you say?"

No response. Doyle didn't hear the telephone poles any more: she had pulled over to the shoulder in stunned silence.

"Meena?" Doyle said. "Are you there?"

"I'm here," Meena said, after a moment. "I'm just wondering whether you're crazy or not."

"Listen," Doyle said. "You're the one who was talking about wanting to see San Francisco. Well, here I am. Waiting for you."

"You're pretty bold," Meena said. "What if I send Da and a couple of his goons in my place?"

"My life's in your hands," Doyle said. "But I don't think they'd enjoy themselves here as much as you would."

Meena lapsed into another long silence.

"Come on," Doyle said, cajoling.

"First class?" Meena said weakly.

"Yes," Doyle said. "Nonstop. Cost me $2,500. We'll have a beautiful week together and maybe figure out how to make up with your da and what to do with the rest of our lives. What do you say?"

Now, Doyle heard Meena's steady breath. When she spoke again, her voice was soft and she sounded happy, and he felt sorry for all the lies, but they couldn't be helped.

15

Later that night, Doyle finished oiling and cleaning the lever and pulleys on the Trap-O-Matic at Maracaibo. He tested the lever twice: each time the Plastigrass heaved wildly and he smiled to himself, remembering the shrieks of the tourists caught by this contraption in the old days.

Then, he withdrew Cap'n Pete's Police Colt from his toolbag, unloaded the cylinder, tied a piece of string to the trigger guard, and secreted it just beneath the carriage of the cannon closest to the lever, arranging the end of the string so it trailed back along the breech. He pulled the string once and the gun spun out and was in his hand, hammer cocked, maybe six seconds later. Doyle practiced this move two dozen times, eventually cutting down the time by half. Then he reloaded the cylinder and replaced the gun in its hiding hole, and turned around to see Maggie standing there leaning against the battlements, by the top step, watching. Damn, that woman was quiet.

"I won't ask you what you're doing," she said. "I don't want to know. But I would like you to tell me where the hell you been for a week. I called Smoot, you know. Filed a missing persons. I thought for sure you were dead."

Doyle was touched by the teary tremble in her voice, by the look of concern. "I went to Delaware," he said. "Then to Alabama."

"Shit, you been all over the country," she said. Then she paused and looked down, and even by the faint light of the moon, he could see a blush come to her cheeks. "You been with *her*?"

"Who's that?" Doyle said.

"That crazy-ass bitch."

"You mean Bracken," Doyle said. "No. She took off for Mexico."

"Good riddance," Maggie said.

Doyle ignored this, then he told her about what was going to happen in the morning.

16

The heavy rumble of official vehicles came up from the beach road just as light broke the treeline, followed by doors slamming and the sound of voices and the thud and clatter of heavy equipment being dragged up on to the porch, across the bar, and into the restaurant — and soon enough, over all this muffled uproar, the high complaint of Maggie's voice rising through the floor. Doyle got up, found his uncle's slippers and coat again and put them on over his pajamas and went downstairs into the bar where he made himself a pot of coffee.

He drank two cups quickly and, thus fortified, strolled through the swinging doors into the old restaurant with all the insouciance of an aristocrat in a country house who has woken to discover a large party of his friends, expected for dinner, has instead arrived for an early breakfast: The dusty old dining room, with its cracked, high-backed vinyl booths and checkerboard linoleum tile floor and framed pictures of famous local fishing boats on the wall, looked like it had been turned into the nerve center for a commando raid, which was, in fact, the case. Agents Detweiler and Keane, wearing SWAT team combat fatigues, were setting up a complex-looking digital recording device on a table at one of the vinyl booths. Six other agents of the Fish and Wildlife Service, wearing body armor over their fatigues, were busy checking their armaments — deadly-looking MP5 assault rifles — or tightening the laces of their matte-black combat boots. One of the tables had been given over to a flat metal box containing spare fifty-round ammunition clips and tear-gas canisters stacked as casually as cans of orange juice.

In the midst of all this Maggie — brightly scrubbed and wearing a clean, frilly apron Doyle hadn't seen before — circulated with a tray of coffee and donuts.

"Why, thank you, miss," one of the Fish and Wildlife commandos said shyly, taking a French cruller from the tray. He sported a clipped law-enforcement mustache and the aw-shucks attitude of a cavalry officer courting a schoolmarm in a Western.

Doyle cleared his throat, and another agent dropped his coffee to the floor and swung towards him, assault rifle locked and loaded in a bare second.

"Not me," Doyle said, peevishly — although from a professional standpoint he admired the man's speed. "I'm one of the good guys."

The agent looked to Agent Keane for confirmation of this fact. Agent Keane nodded reluctantly and the F and W storm trooper lowered his rifle and leaned down to mop the spilled coffee off the linoleum with a rag.

"Your guys seem a little jumpy today," Doyle said to Agent Keane. "I'm not sure coffee is such a good idea."

"Good morning to you, Mr. Doyle," Agent Detweiler said, with mock cheeriness. "Glad to see those pajamas again."

"Just got out of bed," Doyle said. "It's five a.m."

"We wouldn't want it any other way," Agent Detweiler said, smiling. She seemed lighthearted, happy, in anticipation of the carnage to come.

"You guys preparing for a riot here?" Doyle said.

"Possibly," Agent Keane said.

Doyle came over to the table where Agent Detweiler was making the last adjustments to the digital recording device, its control panel a bewildering arrangement of dials, switches, and oscillators. "Does it work?" he said.

"Absolutely," Agent Detweiler said. "You want us to fit you with the wire now or later?" She indicated a device no larger than a cigarette pack nestled in a foam fitting in a steel box.

"Later," Doyle said.

"You're looking at the latest in personal-surveillance technology," Agent Keane said proudly. "The Panex AR200."

"OK," Doyle said.

"It sends signals, of course, but can also receive them," Agent Keane added. "Watch this." She hit a button on the control console and the cigarette pack made a loud buzzing noise and nearly bounced right out of its steel box.

"You think you can turn that effect down?" Doyle said.

"Don't worry, we'll turn the sound off completely," Agent Keane said. "You'll feel the vibration, that's all."

"When we're ready to move in, we'll send you three quick signals," Agent Detweiler said. "You'll feel the device vibrate then pause, vibrate then pause, then vibrate. After the last vibration, we will move out quickly and efficiently and take our man."

Doyle felt the back of his neck tingle. "What if there's gunplay?" he said uneasily. "Don't you think I should be armed?"

"Absolutely not!" Agent Keane said. "This is a Fish and Wildlife Service operation. Regulations strictly prohibit the arming of civilians in any action of this kind."

"So it's OK for me to get shot at," Doyle persisted, "just not to carry a gun."

"In the event of gun-play, as you call it," Agent Detweiler said drily, "just keep your head down."

"Great advice," Doyle said.

"Now," Agent Keane unhooked a portable phone from his belt and held it out to Doyle, "make the call."

Doyle shook his head. "The man's asleep in climate-controlled comfort until at least eight."

"Are you so sure she's going to go through with it?" Agent Detweiler smirked. "We're leaving a lot up to your charms, aren't we, Mr. Doyle?"

Doyle didn't say anything. He ambled out to the porch and sat on the swing with another cup of coffee and stared out at nothing. After a while, Maggie came out with a heap of frosted crullers on a paper plate and sat beside him on the swing.

"Done feeding the troops?" Doyle said.

"Nice guys," Maggie said. "Clean-cut, polite. Not like you."

"Yeah," Doyle said, taking a cruller off the plate. "I need a haircut."

"Are you ready?" Maggie said.

"For a haircut?"

"No," she swallowed hard, "for the game."

"I suppose so," Doyle said.

"When was the last time you played?"

"I played last month," Doyle said. "Against myself. I won."

"That's not good enough," Maggie said. "Get out there now and practice."

"Don't be ridiculous," Doyle said. "It's a subterfuge."

"A what?"

"Never mind."

Maggie seemed anxious, fidgety. Then she put her hand on Doyle's knee. "Don't get yourself shot, asshole," she said and leaned over and kissed him on the lips, a hard, open-mouthed kiss, frankly erotic, and Doyle was too stunned to resist and he felt her hand creeping up beneath his robe and felt himself respond there.

"Hate to interrupt you, kids." It was Constable Smoot's voice. Maggie sprang up, embarrassed, and hurried back into the bar, screen door slamming in her wake. Constable Smoot stepped up on the porch with a heavy tread. "Looks like you got some live-in trouble there, son," he said.

Doyle blinked up at him, a little dazed, still feeling the heat of Maggie's kiss. "That's news to me, Constable," he said. Then: "I didn't hear you drive up."

The constable sat down and popped one of Maggie's crullers into his mouth, crumbs falling on to his khaki uniform. "Deputy dropped me off up at the road," he said. "Wouldn't want a cop-cruiser sitting in your parking lot, would we?"

"Right," Doyle said.

The constable ate a second cruller thoughtfully. Then he stood up and set his trooper hat squarely on his head. "I better go in and meet the government," he said. But when he reached the screen door he stopped and turned around. "Think you can get your man?"

"I don't know," Doyle said.

"Anyway, I appreciate you calling like you did," Constable Smoot said. "Otherwise it wouldn't have looked too good for the department in the papers. Local law enforcement's got to be in on a bust like this."

"No problem," Doyle said.

"Just the same, if you survive — which you just might, given your moxie — I think you'll find this department more cooperative from here on out."

"You mean you'll send my juvenile records back to Wiccomac?" Doyle said.

"Maybe." Constable Smoot grinned. "Anyway, good luck, Tim. I'll say one thing, you certainly make life interesting around here." And he turned and went inside.

Doyle sat out on the swing a while longer, munching the last donut. The first hesitant traffic picked up along the Beach Road, early birds in bathing suits out to catch tepid, early June sunshine. The beach season on Wassateague was just beginning; in another couple of weeks, that road would be jammed with cars full of tourists, some of them no doubt stopping for a few rounds at Doyle's Pirate Island Goofy Golf. With this happy thought in mind, Doyle brushed the crumbs off his lap and went inside to be fitted with his wire.

17

Everyone sat along the bar, watching: Agents Detweiler and Keane, the Fish and Wildlife storm troopers, Constable Smoot and Maggie — who at the last minute had decided to make herself a Bloody Mary and was now sucking absently on the celery stalk.

"This doesn't make me very comfortable," Doyle said, his hand on the phone behind the bar. "I feel like a fish in a fishbowl."

"Just make the call, Doyle," Agent Keane said.

Doyle waited, checked his watch, and waited another ten minutes. "OK, she should be in the air now," and he picked up the phone and dialed the number in Delaware.

"Good morning, O'Mara residence," said a crisp voice.

"Get me the Old Fruit," Doyle said, trying to sound tough.

"I don't know what you're talking about, sir," the voice said. "No fruit here. You might want to try the A and P in Dover."

"I've got his Mercedes and his daughter," Doyle said. "Just tell the man that."

A few minutes later, O'Mara came to the phone. "Doyle, you mother-fuck, I'll kill you!" he howled.

"So I heard from Meena," Doyle said.

"What's this about my daughter, you fucking punter?"

"Ask yourself this question." Doyle turned his back to the specta-tors at the bar and put a finger in his ear. "Where is she right now?"

The air-conditioning king drew a sharp breath. "What are you saying?"

"I'm saying I've got her here," Doyle said. "Your daughter's been kidnapped, you odious little shit! You want her back in one piece, you need to come out here right now and ask me nicely."

Silence on the other end. "You're bullshitting me, Gunslinger," O'Mara said, in a cold, calm tone, more ominous than any screaming.

"Hardly," Dole said. "You try and find her, then call me back."

A few minutes later the phone rang, and Doyle let it ring. He picked it up at last, to O'Mara screaming obscenities. Doyle waited, and the little man calmed down enough to speak. "Where is she?" he said, breathing heavily. "I can't find her, she's not answering her cell! She always answers her cell!"

"Like I told you, she's here," Doyle said. "Tied to my bed."

"Let me talk to her, cocksucking cunt!"

"She's a little indisposed at the moment," Doyle said.

"I'll kill you, Doyle!"

"Yeah, yeah," Doyle said. "I'll see you here, in person. You got exactly three hours before I start cutting on her. Don't be late, and come ready to deal."

O'Mara didn't say a word. Doyle could almost hear the man trembling with rage on the other end.

"Two hours or I feed her to the . . ." He paused, unable to think for a moment what to feed her to.

"Dogs," Maggie whispered.

"Sharks," whispered Constable Smoot.

". . . something," Doyle said. Then he hung up the phone.

18

At eleven a.m. exactly, two black armor-plated Lincoln Navigators pulled up along the Beach Road. The doors flew open and out sprang a dozen thugs, wielding various denominations of weaponry from shotguns to semi-automatics to Louisville Slugger baseball bats. The thugs quickly formed a skirmish line in advance of their diminutive commander and moved down the slope towards Doyle, standing alone and apparently calm at the skull mouth of the number-one hole.

Doyle picked out the homunculus, armed with a sawed-off; Feeney and Jesus were nowhere to be seen.

When the thugs reached the coquina path they broke formation and O'Mara jumped forward and caught Doyle with a forceful left hook. The punch had a kind of twist at the end and the engine of the little man's rage behind it and Doyle went sprawling to his back and O'Mara was on him, flailing away and screaming at the top of his lungs. "Where's Meena? Where's my daughter?"

Doyle took another blow to the chin and one beneath his left eye that brought forth a small explosion of stars before he was able to scramble up and take refuge behind the skull's newly painted jaw. "You'll want to calm yourself and listen to what I've got to say." He rubbed his eye.

"All I got to do is wave my little finger," O'Mara said, "and you're a dead man."

"And your daughter's toast," Doyle said.

"Where is she, villain?" The air-conditioning king clenched his little fists.

"She's safe for the moment," Doyle said. He took a breath and adopted a reasonable tone: "You're something of a sporting gentleman, are you not? So, listen, you're after Pirate's Island as another front for your poison-gas smuggling. You set up a Royal Blue stand and bring in your cans of freon cola from China. Great idea, really. That way they're out of the basement of your castle."

O'Mara's expression darkened, became — if that was possible — even more sinister.

"So here's my offer," Doyle continued, reasonably. "A contest of skill between Your Royal Highness and myself. If you win you get your daughter back and the place is yours, free of charge. I've got the deed at this moment in the cash register in the bar ready to go, except for the signatures. But if I win, you still get your daughter back, but you walk away, leave me in peace to live my life on my own property, darken my doorstep no more, got that?"

"Tell me about Meena first," O'Mara said, a faint note of fatherly concern entering his voice. "Did you hurt her?"

"Not yet," Doyle said, with all the grimness he could muster. "But my lieutenants are standing by."

O'Mara considered this information, then unexpectedly, a macabre grin cracked his lips. "You've got balls of brass, I'll give you that," he said.

"Thanks," Doyle said.

"I'm still going to kill you," O'Mara's grin grew broader, "this very day. Make no mistake about it."

"Listen, Your Majesty," Doyle said, "why go through all that trouble? You win, I walk away. It's very simple. Either way Meena comes back to your arms unscathed."

"So what's to stop me from killing you later on any day I please?"

Doyle shrugged. "Your word as a freon monarch."

"All right then. What's your game of skill — cards, dice?"

"Those are games of chance." Doyle shook his head.

"You *are* a fucking comedian," O'Mara said. "And now you're a gambler too."

"Not really," Doyle said.

"So listen to *my* proposition, gambler. I win, I get my daughter, take the deed and cut off your legs with an electric saw. Killing's too easy for you. I like the idea of you spending a lifetime in a wheelchair eating your heart out for the days when you were a big man striding around the world in seven-league boots. You win, I take the deed for nothing and you keep your legs — which is an honest-to-God bargain, considering the shit you pulled down there in Biloxi. You know my man Feeney was arrested for indecent exposure?"

"No kidding," Doyle said.

"That's right, cunt. Had a hell of a time getting him out of the clutches of those rednecks. So, what about my deal? Take two seconds to think about it."

Doyle took two seconds. Two seconds can seem like a long time when it comes out of what might possibly be the last hour of your life. The thick-needled pines shook their needles in a steady breeze blowing up off the beach. He glanced up and saw a brown pelican borne motionless on the thermals towards the ocean. These ungainly birds were once believed by the Oknontocokes to be the ghosts of their ancestors returned to earth from the spirit world. Doyle lifted his face into the breeze and thought he could hear the distant shouts of children playing in the surf.

19

The usual orange ball and Cold War-era rawhide-handled putter for Doyle; O'Mara, on account of his stature, took a child's club, a left-hander, barely used, among the last batch Buck had bought before he got sick and closed the course for repairs. O'Mara turned and waved the club at his incredulous thugs sprawled now against the armor-plating of the Navigator.

"I'll only be a minute," he called. "A fucking game of goofy golf."

Doyle accepted a five-stroke handicap because he'd grown up with the course and because it didn't matter anyway. O'Mara had only played once before — so he said — at Monopoly Land in Atlantic City. Doyle knew that course well, made to resemble a giant Monopoly board with large red hotel obstacles and little green houses squatting over the greens and multi-colored squares like property cards marking the path and the spry millionaire in the top hat done in plaster around every corner.

"Monopoly Land's a damned good course," Doyle said, offering his professional opinion. "Great concept, very challenging."

"It's all a load of bollocks to me," O'Mara said unpleasantly. "Let's get on with this charade."

The air-conditioning king lined up his ball at number-one hole, nerves steady as iron, and with a swift tick knocked the ball through the gap in the skull's teeth and right into the cup.

"I have a feeling you've played this game more than once," Doyle said, as the man retrieved his ball.

"Always trust your feelings." O'Mara grinned maliciously. "When I first came to this country, to New York City, forty years ago, I lived out at Coney Island in a crummy little rooming house right near all the boardwalk attractions."

"Shit," Doyle said.

"Them fucking rides were too expensive but for two bits you got a good hour at Neptune's Grotto Mini Golf in the company of big-titted mermaids and giant clams that opened and closed and blue waterfalls and crabs big as Buicks. Ah, the happy hours I spent there, dreaming about the promise of America and all the beautiful young boys I'd bugger when I was rich enough to buy them! Now, that was quite a course — not like this bargain-basement buccaneer sham you got going here."

"My uncle built Pirate Island with his own two hands," Doyle said quietly, "after the war."

"Screw your uncle," O'Mara said, and proceeded to make another ace on Port Royal and birdie the Palm Grove Desert Island. Doyle managed to birdie the skull and Port Royal, but he bogied the Palm Grove Desert Island and only made par on the crossed sabers and the treasure chest. At number-six hole, the Caribbean sugar mill, his ball bounced off the slaves as usual and he found himself trailing by five strokes, which, added to the five-stroke handicap, put him an impossible ten strokes behind.

"You better be thinking about how you want us to take off those legs," O'Mara said cheerily, as they crossed the feeder sluice for the lagoon on the footbridge recently patched and painted by Harold. "As I say, an electric saw would be the cleanest way, but a chainsaw I daresay might be quicker."

"Hell, why not forget the legs?" Doyle said. "I'll swill a six-pack of your freon cola and freeze to death."

O'Mara stopped short on the other side and gave him a cruel, squint-eyed look. Birds rustled from a nest hidden in the depths of the bamboo. "Don't think you're going to keep your legs just because you're a fucking comedian," he said. "I'm no soft-heart like my fool daughter. You're a good-looking bastard, I'll give you that, sort of remind me of — now, who's that old Hollywood actor?"

"Mitchum," Doyle said.

"Right. But I got no use for troublemaking Mitchum comedians in my line of work. Now shut your cockholster and let's get on with it."

Doyle struggled to keep his temper, struggled to stay cool. The sun shifted to the west and the hour after noon turned hot, locusts singing a high rattle from the trees. They played down through the plank and through Porto Bello, and Doyle cut the air-conditioning king's lead back to the five-stroke handicap. Sweat poured down Doyle's face in

rivulets; he shed Buck's World War Two coat and played in his pajamas, and sweat coated the black box taped to his back beneath the
striped top. O'Mara's forehead looked blistered and red.

"Tell me something," Doyle said, aiming his putter at the white sky,
"I know you're a gangster and I know it's a little strange asking a
gangster if he cares about the planet, but, hey, don't you ever worry
about what you're doing to the ozone?"

O'Mara snorted. "You've got to be kidding me," he said.

"Not at all," Doyle said. "You're not a stupid man, you must consider the consequences, at least occasionally. They banned fluorocarbons for a good reason, right? An international treaty."

"Don't believe everything you read in the papers, boyo," O'Mara
said darkly. "There are other theories, you know."

"Like what?"

"Like the theory that fluorocarbons, as you call them — more cor-
rectly sulfate aerosols — coat the clouds and make them shiny. And
shiny clouds deflect the heat and actually work against global warming. Did you know that now?"

Doyle admitted he didn't, but said it sounded far-fetched.

"Maybe," O'Mara agreed. "But we have theories put forth by one
group of asshole scientists and theories put forth by another group of
asshole scientists. No one really knows for sure. So which group of
asshole scientists are you going to believe?"

Doyle thought for a few seconds. "The asshole scientists whose theory lines your pockets," he said.

"Smart lad," O'Mara said.

At last they came across the rope bridge and stood beneath the
white plaster battlements of Maracaibo, wooden cannons guarding
the approach.

"What the fuck's this?" O'Mara said. "The gimcrack palace of the
Doyles?"

"Maracaibo," Doyle said. "My ancestor Finster Doyle sacked the
place with Morgan about three hundred years ago."

"Don't tell me you believe all this pirate bullshit," O'Mara chuckled.

"I do," Doyle said. "And so does your friend Roach Pompton.
Which is why I'm in the spot I'm in at this very moment."

"And why's that?" O'Mara said, suspicious.

"Treasure," Doyle said. "Buried treasure. But I don't suppose he mentioned that to you."

"You're just trying to save your legs," O'Mara said. "Telling stories like Scheherazade."

Doyle shrugged, and they mounted the stairs to the number-nine hole atop the battlements and stood in the sun looking out at the course. Doyle started to say something but interrupted himself with a groan and made a show of grabbing his stomach.

"Sorry, cramps, give me a minute." And he crouched down against the barrel of the cannon closest to the lever that operated the Trap-O-Matic.

The air-conditioning king watched, unmoved.

"I've had diarrhea all morning," Doyle said, in a pained voice. "Nerves, I guess."

"I'm not interested in the functioning of your bowels," O'Mara said. "Play or be damned."

"One more minute, please," Doyle said.

O'Mara sighed and leaned back against the parapet, now facing the open-mouthed plaster pirate at the fourteenth hole, plaster monkey perched as always upon his shoulder.

This seemed like the moment.

"You know, we had a hell of a time cleaning up all the blood," Doyle said.

"What are you talking about now, for fucksake?" O'Mara said.

"I'm talking about that goddamned possum," Doyle said. "Cut in half with a seasquab stuffed in its guts. My God, that thing stank. Whose idea was that, anyway?"

O'Mara grinned. "Me and Pompton came up with that one together," he said. "The lad thought one sufficiently gruesome gesture might set the stage for your eventual departure. And I said 'go ahead and try.' The dead fish was my personal touch."

"So, who cut the actual possum in half?" Doyle said, though he already knew the answer.

"I did," O'Mara said. "The fucking things are all over my property in Delaware, in the garbage, everywhere. One of the boys caught one in a trap and I took a nice electric saw and hacked it up just like I'm going to do to you. Should have heard that disgusting creature scream — sounded almost human."

"That's pretty gross," Doyle said, trying to keep his tone sufficiently casual. He chose his next words carefully: "So you might call it a conspiracy, a criminal conspiracy, if you will, to bisect an endangered animal. You know, there are laws against such an act in the United States, heavy penalties and fines."

"Fuck laws." O'Mara pushed himself off the parapet and took up his putter. "You Americans make me sick. Who cares about some fucking oversized white rat?"

At that moment, the wire on Doyle's back began to buzz loud as a telephone. One long buzz was followed by a pause, then another buzz and pause, then a third.

O'Mara went blotchy red. "What the fuck's that?" he said.

"Nothing," Doyle said, rising from the cannon. "Indigestion."

"Indigestion, my ass!" the air-conditioning king began, then the back door of the restaurant burst open and six men in Fish and Wildlife combat fatigues, armed with assault rifles, began a mad assault on Doyle's Pirate Island Goofy Golf.

"You set me up, you bitch!" O'Mara screamed. He gestured violently towards his thugs at the road and they went for their guns in confusion and the air was suddenly full of the sharp pop-pop of automatic-weapons fire and the shriek of flying projectiles, and an acrid cloud of tear gas blossomed over the course. O'Mara went fumbling for something behind his back and Doyle saw the nickel plating of a small 9mm pistol caught in the tail of the man's shirt. The 9mm came up, flashing in the sun.

Doyle lunged for the Trap-O-Matic lever and pulled with all his might. The green heaved and O'Mara went flying back. Doyle reached down and grabbed the string and caught the handle of the Police Colt and didn't think at all. The action came naturally to his hand, to the deep collusion of muscle and synapse honed by generations of Doyles whose hands had never tired of reaching for their guns. He wheeled around, thumbing the hammer as he turned. The explosion was loud as ever. The .45 slug hit O'Mara in the shoulder as he was in the act of firing and he dropped the 9mm with a cry and it discharged into his foot and he fell screaming, blood spurting out on to the Plastigrass.

For Doyle, there was no sickness this time, no qualms. Undismayed by the felled monarch's screams of pain, he dropped down behind the parapet and thumbed back the hammer again calm, and resolved, ready to meet the next threat.

20

Grand Opening, 15 June.

Balloons against the blemishless blue sky, buffeted by a thrilling ocean wind. Cars jammed bumper to bumper along the shoulder, halfway up the Beach Road towards town. The tourists stood patiently in the hot sun, an undulating line along the whitewashed wall past the course and into the shadow of the trees. Doyle smelled the happy rank-coconut perfume of sun-tan oil, saw the teenage girls tugging at their halter tops, heard the flip-flop of flip-flops on the dry road, the merciless screaming of kids for ice cream or just to scream, the exhausted squabble of suburban parents seeking relief from the nine-to-five grind of their lives in the suburbs of DC or Baltimore who had come to the beach only to find a grind of a different sort.

He realized now, and was comforted by the realization, that none of the things that mattered had changed, and he felt some long-gone afternoon of his youth return like a blessing. Here it was again: the happy clack of ball in cup, the sun like a burning hand on sunburned shoulders, the close briny ocean smell, the stylized, time-honored gestures of the game. All these things were eternal, they were America itself, the pursuit guaranteed by the Framers — in this case that small, ephemeral happiness of club, ball, tin cup, plaster pirate, plaster monkey, plaster hammerhead, and all the rest, under the sun, the beach near.

Doyle ambled through the crowd, his heart full, watching the tourists playing through Porto Bello and the giant squid, watching them bogie the Caribbean sugar mill and the galleon and thought of his uncle Buck, how the man had been serene and comfortable with all this, content with his little corner of the world and not in the wandering of it, happy behind his bar with the people outside playing goofy golf till long after dark, beneath the arc lights beneath the full moon, and he felt the little knot of scar tissue in his heart that had formed in Buck's absence. "This one's for you, old Buck, wherever you are," Doyle murmured, and for a moment he thought he heard an answering shudder, an echo coming out of the darkness of the trees, out of the scattered, unmarked tombs where fate has laid the tough, libidinous race of Doyles, out of the funereal shadows where they wait one and all for Judgement Day. But it was nothing, just a trick of sun and wind, and Doyle put the dead from his mind and pressed on to assist a young mother with two babies in a tandem Aprica coming down the shallow stairs by the pirate gallows where Finster dangled in effigy for his many crimes.

In his official role as smiling proprietor, Doyle knelt and patted the babies — one six months, one two years — and made the appropriate noises. "Cute kids," Doyle said, smiling.

"Thanks." The young mother smiled back. She was short and dark, tired-looking from the effort of having birthed two babies so close together, but with a sweet, mysterious wisdom held in the depths of her eyes.

"The future," Doyle said, smiling down at the babies again.

"Yes," the woman agreed. "The future." In her mouth the word still had the ring of hope.

A few minutes later, as Doyle was unclogging a ball from the ball chute beneath the pirate's grave, an old man approached and took off his sweat-stained golfing cap and wiped the sweat from his eyes with a white handkerchief.

"Glad to see you back on your feet," the old man said.

Doyle didn't think he'd been off his feet, but maybe he had. "Thanks," he said.

"I mean the course," the old man said. "I met my wife here, you know."

"No kidding," Doyle said, and he put his hands in his pockets, ready today to listen to any garrulous old duffer's stories from start to finish.

"That's right," the old man said. "This must have been, oh, 'fifty-one or 'fifty-two."

"Long time ago," Doyle said.

"Not so long ago," the old man said, looking around. "You know, it could be that day right now, all the people, all the kids, and my wife, beautiful in that sundress with the big flowers, coming down the path just there." He smiled wistfully at the memory. "You know, the place looks pretty much the same. Damned comforting, I'd say."

"I was just thinking that," Doyle said.

"Used to bring the kids too," the old man said. "All through the fifties and sixties. We played a good game here the day Americans landed on the moon. You remember that? Hard to believe anyone ever landed on the moon."

"Yes," Doyle said, "I remember," and called to mind the fuzzy images on Buck's old black-and-white rabbit-ear TV and Buck and one of his blondes whooping it up and dancing on the bar afterwards.

"Don't see them much any more," the old man said.

"Astronauts?" Doyle said.

"Them too, but I'm talking about the kids," the old man said. "They went away to college and got married and moved away. Got lives of their own now, just like everyone else."

"Yes," Doyle said, thinking of Pablo growing up without him in southern Spain.

"Here's what I think about the twentieth century," the old man said. "I mean, it's over now, right?"

"Right," Doyle said.

"Well, here's the epitaph in four words, here's what's carved on its gravestone — *Too Much Has Changed*. Know what I'm saying?"

"I do," Doyle said.

"But not this place."

"No," Doyle said. "We're the rock. The waves just wash over us."

"I'd like to shake your hand," the old man said, and he shook Doyle's hand. "I drove down from Cape May for this. Read about the grand opening in the paper, you know. Tradition is important," and the way he said the word with a slight trilling R had an old-fashioned elegance.

"Tradition," Doyle repeated, and he smiled.

21

They were on the bed in his uncle's room and Doyle was slightly drunk from three bourbon Old-fashioneds and his pants were off, his erection thumping between his legs, but he fumbled with the catch of Maggie's bra and his fingers trembled like a high-school kid after the prom.

"I can't get it," Doyle said.

"Here," Maggie said, impatient. She reached around in that backwards-elbow way women have and opened the clasp and her breasts spilled out into Doyle's hands. For a long moment, they sat there, looking into each other's eyes. Doyle felt awkward, embarrassed by his need, excited by hers.

"This had to happen," Maggie said, in a throaty whisper. "I been watching you watching me for six months now."

"What about Buck?" Doyle murmured, but Maggie put a hand over his mouth.

"Making love's no disrespect to the dead," she said, and lay back in the old-fashioned manner and put her hands on the underside of her thighs and held her legs open. Doyle followed her lead and dispensed with the preliminaries and when he entered her it was like a ship sinking to the soft mud of the bottom. He stayed hard inside her a long time and she felt solid beneath him, all meat and muscle, solid as a beach of wet, hard-packed sand. Maggie wouldn't let him change position and by thrusting up against him and wrapping her legs tightly around the small of his back she achieved her release and Doyle followed seconds later.

He lay on top of her for a while, his breath keeping time with hers, their skin stuck together with sweat. Then they disengaged, and he rolled off and lay beside her in the sheets. A pale moon hung over the forest and the ocean out the aluminum casement. Insects and frogs sang a lover's chorus from the marsh. Maggie squirmed down the mattress and brought her knees up to her chest and clasped her hands around them.

"What are you doing?" Doyle said. "Did I hurt you?"

"No," Maggie said, "but the way I figure it, you Doyles owe me one."

"You already got half the place," Doyle said, not understanding. "What more do you want?"

Maggie smiled at the ceiling. "Never mind," she said. Then: "What would you do if you had a hundred million dollars?"

"I don't," Doyle said.

"You might," Maggie said. "You know, Buck always told me the *Monstrance* was out there somewhere in the bay, wrecked against a mountain of oyster shells, all the silver in its hold in a big heap on the bottom."

"No more treasure," Doyle said. "Please."

"It's out there," Maggie persisted. "No one's found it and you got the map."

"Ha," Doyle said, unenthusiastically.

"So what would you do if you found it?"

"I'd retire," Doyle said.

"Then?"

"Then I'd get back into the restaurant business. I mean, I'd fix up the restaurant downstairs and reopen with good food, I mean really good food. I don't need to tell you we've got some beautiful seafood in these waters. All the locals do is breaded and fried. Breaded and fried! My God!" The gourmet in him, honed by Flor's sophisticated tastes and twenty years in Spain, was too offended for words.

"Nothing wrong with breaded and fried." Maggie sniffed. "But listen, I got some savings. We don't need a hundred million, we can start thinking about it tomorrow."

"How much do you have?" Doyle said, interested.

"Enough to get started," Maggie said.

"Why not?" Doyle said, and they lapsed into a companionable silence. Then he was ready again. He put his hands on her breasts and his lips to her ear but this time she pushed him away.

"Not now," she said. "We've got to wait forty-eight hours. Then we can do it again."

"But I'm ready now," he said pitifully, and Maggie laughed.

"You put a leash on that thing, mister," she said, and she sat up, pinched his arm playfully. "Hey, I've got another secret for you."

Doyle groaned.

"Try to move the bed," she said. "Go ahead."

"What?"

"Really. Try and move the bed. See what happens."

Doyle got out of bed and pushed against the bed frame, then he pushed harder and finally pushed with all his might. A low wooden creaking but no movement. He threw himself back on the mattress beside her, wearied by these fruitless isometrics.

"Some joke," he said. "The old man must have nailed the bed to the floor."

"Not exactly." Maggie smiled. "When Buck cleared the land he left the trunk of a single pine tree sticking out of the ground and built the whole place around that tree. It comes up through the utility closet behind the bar and through the walls. Then he whittled it down to look like a bed post and built the rest of the bed and here it is," she tapped the right post with her knuckle. "Buck's last little secret. Now it's yours."

Doyle reached up, and touched the bedpost and put his hand around the carved finial on top. He could almost feel the trunk extending down and the roots gripping in the darkness of the earth. And he lay down beside Maggie and pulled the sheets over their bare flesh, and they fell asleep to the soft music of the wind rattling the cattails in the marsh.

22

But this peaceful slumber was not to last for long: Doyle awoke in a mindless panic not two hours later, heart beating wildly, seized with a kind of blank terror. He sat up in bed and glanced down at Maggie, sleeping calmly there, and didn't recognize her for a confused instant. He felt himself choking, felt the breath being squeezed out, his lungs crushed by a pressure that was like drowning in cold water. He got out of bed and went down naked to the bar and fumbled for a beer but somehow instead found his hand on the phone. He dialed the international operator and gave her the number because he didn't trust his own fingers, they were trembling so, and the operator put the call through to Spain and he heard the thick beeping of the line in his old apartment, far away on the Iberian peninsula. He was certain no one would answer, but a moment later, there was a bright noontime voice on the other end.

"*Hola?*"

"Flor?"

A long moment of silence followed, in which Doyle could hear the vague echo of other conversations through the static of the line, other lovers perhaps, parted by distance and circumstance. "Please don't hang up," he managed. "I just want to talk to you for a minute."

Another long pause, which Doyle took for assent. A thousand questions raced through his mind but he grappled at the nearest one. "How's Pablo?"

"He's fine," Flor said, her voice flat. "He's with Mama and Papa at Ecija right now for a month."

"Ah, Ecija," Doyle said, remembering the old stucco mansion, a dusty, never-used bullring in the forecourt, a few acres of vineyard and the background of dry, rocky hills leading to mountains touched with snow. Stark but very beautiful.

"So, what do you want?" Flor said abruptly. Her voice was hard.

Doyle hesitated. "I want to see Pablo." Then he added, "And I want to see you."

"That's out of the question," Flor said.

"Which one," Doyle said.

"If you want to see Pablo, you go to Ecija and ask Papa," she said.

"I'm in America," Doyle said. "Wassateague. I've come home."

"Good. You belong there," Flor said. "You Americans are all so . . ." She paused, searching for the right word which she found in French "*louche.*" Meaning low-down bums.

"Thanks," Doyle said. "Are you seeing anyone?"

"None of your damn business," Flor said, and he could imagine her tossing her head in outrage, the long black strands gleaming in white light in the kitchen. "I won't even ask you such foolish question because I know the answer, *sí?*"

"Absolutely not," Doyle lied, without hesitation, without a second thought. "No one since I left Spain."

Flor gave a bitter little laugh. "You left Spain to live with a twenty-one-year-old French whore in Paris, remember? Now you say you don't sleep with her?"

"I meant besides Brigitte," Doyle backpedalled. "And that meant absolutely nothing. Didn't last longer than a month. I'll be completely honest, Flor, I left her because I couldn't stop thinking of you and that made everything no good. Then Uncle Buck died and I had to come on home to straighten things out."

"I'm sorry," Flor said, her voice softening a bit. "I know you loved him."

"But, really, there's been no one since Brigitte," Doyle insisted, "because —" he took a deep breath "— I love you. I really do. I think about you every day, you and Pablo." This, at least, was not a lie.

Another long pause and perhaps the faint sniffling sound of tears. "You dare say this to me?" Flor's voice full of emotion. "You love me, eh? Just me. No, you lie! You love all women and none of them, like Don Juan."

"No," Doyle said. "No, no, no, no. Just you."

There followed a strained silence, then the sound, in earnest now, of Flor's tears. "I stopped the divorce," she said at last.

"What?" Doyle gripped the phone so hard it hurt.

"I stopped the divorce," she repeated. "I didn't sign the last papers."

"Why?"

"I don't know."

Doyle waited for more, though he knew somehow that that's all he would get tonight, a small victory, so he spoke to fill the silence. "Listen to me, Flor," he said, "I came home and everything was different, changed, and I had some trouble for a while, some bad trouble, yes, but all that's over now. I've fixed up the golf course and we had the grand opening today and it even looks like there might be a little money eventually, and I'm home, I'm really home, after twenty years and I want Pablo to come just to see how beautiful it really is here, and maybe, very carefully, very slowly, you and me, we can start over again or at least we can try. What do you say? Come in the fall, in September, it's lovely here in the fall."

"I will never get married again," Flor said. She hadn't been listening to a word. "I am thinking about entering a convent, letting Papa and Mama raise Pablo and going to the nuns. I have already talked to the Holy Mother about this. It might be possible," she said, "but difficult for a married woman with a child. I am supposed to talk with the bishop next month but to him I must lie and say you raped me often against my will and the marriage was not a real marriage in the eyes of God, that you forced me to blaspheme against the Church and some other bad things."

"You're not serious?" Doyle said.

"Maybe," Flor said, sniffling.

"But they don't take married women, isn't that right?"

"Maybe not," Flor said. Then she said, "I must go now, I am tired. I do not sleep very well now."

"Can I call you again?" Doyle said, but she hung up and Doyle stood there naked, holding the receiver, alternating between hope and despair.

He had just talked to his wife for the first time in nearly a year. He sat down hard on the ice cooler, slightly stunned by this realization, metal frigid against his bare ass, and he thought of his wife and he thought of Pablo, of getting both of them here to Pirate Island. He would teach them both how to play goofy golf and how to eat crabs and how to catch the waves on a boogie board down at the beach, which was rough and turbulent, not at all like the tame Mediterranean at Málaga. And they would see how beautiful it was when the marshes bloomed with cardinal flowers, how beautiful it was with the great, shaggy, grey Atlantic heaving and rolling along the shore and the grassy dunes beyond the hook, and the forgotten coves, and the uninhabited little islands just bare scraps of sand hanging way out there and a kingfish mackerel leaping into the sun to take the lure off the *Chief Powhatan* in the deep water. Yes, Flor would take a good deal of convincing, a gentle, steady pressure, but he could do it, he could get them over here, if not this fall then the next, and everything would be all right.

These happy considerations in mind. Tim Doyle went to the linen closet on the landing, and wrapped his nakedness in a bedspread, and went out on to the porch and sat on the swing to watch the moon sink below the horizon and the stars fade from the heavens, without a single thought for the woman already gestating in his uncle's bed in his uncle's room upstairs. Then, with a warm feeling of debts paid and only good to come, he drifted off to sleep again, but as he drifted off there came a distant rumble and the sky shuddered with lightning in the west.

ENVOI

IN MAY OF 1846, one of the Doyles — it doesn't matter which of the many descendants of Finster — sold everything he had, gathered his family, and joined the great migration west. That summer, all summer long, full of dust, Indian raids, and rumors of war with Mexico, the wagons made a continuous line across the green-gold prairies from St. Louis and Cincinnati north along the Platte and through the passes to the Oregon Country.

The Doyles left Wassateague with eight children, four boys, four girls, aged fifteen to six months; it was the duty of the older children to mind the younger as their parents tended the oxen and gave their attention to the way ahead. The baby, a yellow-haired, blue-eyed boy named Benjamin, after the great doctor and patriot, spent the first half of the journey swaddled in a cast-off muslin shirt swaying in a basket woven from green rushes that had been gathered by the banks of the Chesapeake not far from the home they left behind. The basket was suspended from a kettle hook at the back of the wagon and left to sway with the uneven rumbling of the wheels over the rutted tracks — a perfect cradle with the clear blue summer sky above for a canopy.

Charlotte, the eldest, was specifically charged with looking after Benjamin, but somehow, in the blaze of prairie summer and the children running through the high grasses and splashing in the streams that ran alongside for miles, this charge was forgotten. The woven strips of green rushes that made the basket's handle had gone dry in the sun and thin from swaying to and fro and broke at last one afternoon somewhere in Blackfoot country and baby and basket fell without a sound to the soft muddy bed by the side of the trail. The Doyles' wagon was riding last in the train of twenty-five and today for some reason none of the scouts riding behind saw Benjamin fall. He was a quiet, contemplative infant who rarely cried and his absence was not noticed for some hours until after dark had fallen over the prairie.

When the loss was discovered the Doyles were frantic. Twenty-five wagons halted and the men assembled and fanned out back along the trail to search for the lost baby — though no one believed he would be found alive — as the women stayed with the wagons, muskets ready, on the lookout for Indians or wild beasts. Only Doyle's wife, a still-handsome, nervous woman named Eliza, accompanied the men on this certainly gruesome expedition along the trail lit now by burning brands, steeling herself to what she would find ahead: a pitiful carcass ripped apart by wolves, by the sharp talons of birds of prey or, worse — nothing, an absence, her baby simply gone, stolen by Indians to haunt her dreams to the end of her days.

Eliza herself had been a foundling. Left on the steps of a Catholic church in Baltimore and raised by stern, dour-faced nuns in a Catholic orphanage in that city, she had somehow grown into a willful, adventurous child and at fourteen ran away to become a bareback rider in a traveling circus whose menagerie, besides herself and the horse, comprised an aging one-eared elephant, a moth-eaten monkey, and half a flock of motley parrots who couldn't speak a word of English, though they possessed a sizeable vocabulary in a language nobody understood — some said Spanish, others Chinese.

Eliza was a woman of no religious faith, mostly because the poor, dour celibate sisters who raised her had known no other way than birch-rod beatings to discipline so many children — and she did not forgive easily and blamed God for the harshness of the nuns. But now, searching through this black prairie dark for what must surely be the bones of her last-born child, she racked her memory for the prayers they had taught her long ago that she had long since pushed from her mind, and remembering only a snatch of the prayer for Mary, she repeated the words under her breath over and over to whatever presence there might be in the darkness that was not man or woman or animal or earth or sky. Repeating the words over and over again, praying with all the fervor she could muster from her tired soul for the helpless babe she'd given unwittingly to the great continent they were crossing, like a sacrifice in the old books of the Bible.

The search party beat three hours back down the trail and found nothing. They were about to turn once again to the wagons when one of them saw a bundle in the shadows in the mud by the tall grass and let out a loud whoop that brought everyone running, guttering torches held high. Then they called Eliza from the back. She came through the men in silence and threw herself to her knees in the mud, sobbing for joy to find her baby alive there by the side of the trail where he had fallen, still wrapped in his calico swaddling in his basket of green rushes — hungry yet not making a sound, his blue eyes wide open, his round face tipped in wonder to the sky like black silk above, to the bright effusion of stars.